GUERNSEY MEMORIAL LIBRARY

A 0 00 04 0142780

W9-DBP-211

SEP 12 1997

Spaugh, Jean.

Something blue /

C. 1

24 ckarts			
11/2008			
3 copies			
32 = 11/7/14			
2 copies			

"If Jane Austen were alive and well and living in the American South today, *Something Blue* might well be the book she would have written. Jean Christopher Spaugh has Austen's clear prose, her subtlety, her quiet wit, and her keen-eyed attention to the details of daily living, but, unlike Austen, she knows that a real story doesn't end with a wedding but begins with one. . . . With *Something Blue*, Jean Christopher Spaugh joins the company of Lee Smith, Josephine Humphreys, and Jill McCorkle as an extraordinary chronicler of the lives of Southern women."

R. H. W. Dillard

JEAN CHRISTOPHER SPAUGH

Something
Blue

JOHN F. BLAIR, PUBLISHER
WINSTON-SALEM, NORTH CAROLINA

Copyright © 1997 by John F. Blair, Publisher
All rights reserved
Printed in the United States of America

*The paper in this book meets the guidelines
for permanence and durability of the Committee
on Production Guidelines for Book Longevity
of the Council on Library Resources.*

Design by Liza Langrall

Library of Congress Cataloging-in-Publication Data
    Spaugh, Jean.
        Something blue / Jean Christopher Spaugh.
          p.   cm.
        ISBN 0-89587-167-X (alk. paper)
        I. Title.
        PS3569.P3777S6   1997
        813'.54—dc21   96-48782

Second printing, 1997

To Jeannette and J.B. and Richard

■ ——— ■

CONTENTS

ACKNOWLEDGMENTS

I wish to thank the following people at
John F. Blair for their efforts on behalf of
Something Blue: Carolyn Sakowski,
Andrew Waters, Steve Kirk, Liza Langrall,
Anne Holcomb, Lisa Wagoner, Anne
Schultz, Sue Clark, and Heath Simpson.
They are a remarkably intelligent, profes-
sional, and caring group.

Something Blue

One

1

YESTERDAY MY TRAILER WAS TOWED AWAY. I went to watch.

"What are you going out there for, Judy?" said my mom. "The movers can handle it. You'll just be in the way."

"So what?" I said. "I'm paying them. I can be in the way if I want to."

I said this in my work voice, snippy and fast. My grandmother would have said "pert." "Don't be pert, missy," or admiringly, "You're a pert little thing this morning."

Different voices convey so much, don't you think? Like clothes.

My mom is beyond all that. She sits at her desk and stares straight through my words like she's standing at an open closet, looking. When she finds what she wants, she sighs and goes back to her typing. She is nervous about my uncertain future. I am nervous as well. Anticipation is terrible, like thinking you'll see a snake. Your fear is not of the snake itself, who is dry and inoffensive, looking for lunch, but of a dark hole and a bite. Not what is present, not the actual, but the horrible possible. Fearing abstract snakes, I pick up baby copperheads on my rake and carry them to the woods. Baby copperheads, death on a stick. They look like pencils with teeth.

"What the hell are you doing?" says my dad.

"Carrying off this snake."

"It should be killed, Judy."

But it never is.

I made a list: September 27—New girl. Payroll. Trailer.

The new girl is meant to free me from the lumberyard. I got her started on the payroll, drove to my place. At least it wasn't raining. Our driveway is practically impassable when it rains. It becomes a gully, returns to its roots, a narrow corridor of red mud sliding through scrub pines to the road.

The trailer was already disconnected from its moorings, anchored to the truck, wearing its tires. Even though we've not been gone so long, the yard has acquired a deserted look. The grass is shaggy. The wire around Reddie's old pen is sagging. For a long time nothing happened; the men seemed to be wasting time, clomping back and forth listening to their radio and tossing cigarette butts onto the ground.

"All set to go?" I said. "Need anything signed? Know where to make the delivery?"

I was still in my efficient mode.

"No problem, lady," they said, tolerant. The younger one called me ma'am, meaning no disrespect, his face shiny and blank. The older man grinned at me, flirted a little for politeness' sake, to atone: He's a baby, lady. Pay him no mind. You and I know you're only a kid yourself.

I trusted the older one because he looked like Crocodile Dundee. They glanced over at me occasionally as I wandered around the

4

clearing. I watered the marigolds by the shed, even though nobody lives there anymore. Flowers have a life. They can just bloom for themselves, useless and exultant like rich people, until frost. I walked down toward the pond to check on the Venus's-flytraps. Hamp planted them in a marshy place, and they are scruffy but not dead. The woods are dry, though. Leaves rattle like paper. It's second-growth stuff, mostly pines, not much undergrowth until below the dam. Seventy years ago, it was all a cotton field. The ground is ridged and furrowed with the last plow marks.

Finally I sat on a stump at the edge of the woods, tucked my skirt up, pressed my eyes against my knees, and rocked, fetal position, watching the spots in front of my eyes. If the trailer would just leave, I could get on with my life. Here's your house, lady. There goes your house, lady.

Not many people stay to see the very ends of things—a theater after a play, a funeral after the mourners leave. To me, that's the interesting part, the spaces between the performances, the moment when the gravediggers pull off the artificial grass, expose the mound of clumpy earth, their day's work, only their day's work, the machinery of death. Everything is so ordinary, really.

It's not a sad thing to see the trailer go. Nobody has died. My son Curtis is safe at school, not dead. He only dies in my imagination. Sometimes in my imagination, he drowns or gets hit by a car, and I see his little lifeless self, blond curls, fingers curled into palms, lying again on the asphalt or the bank beside the pond, and I get that falling-off lurch. But it's just pretend.

With my eyes closed and pressed against my palms, I can go to the top of the world, a dark night at the pole, stand and watch the future stretch out above and in front of me, thin glowing ribbons floating toward the stars, neon ribbons of choice and luck, fireworks blooming fluorescence of hope across the black sky. They are roads. You can travel them. Sometimes you can travel them all. They flare and

5

burn, you leap across, they shrivel quickly, shower sparks, have the half-life of a waking dream. But if you jump fast enough, you are halfway to a southbound nebula before your feet know there's nothing there, the sparks are dying, and you're going down. At that point, of course, you open your eyes.

■ —— ■

"We're leaving, ma'am." The young mover stood up against the light.

"I'll follow you out then."

There was absolutely no use for me to be there. Mom was right.

The young one climbed up in the truck cab, while the Dundee one stood in the yard, a semaphore. The truck cranked up with a roar and cleanly yanked the trailer right off its site, an enormous snail plowing a double trail in the dirt. The trailer seemed impossibly large off its moorings, lurching like a brontosaurus through the trees. The older man walked behind, his hand on the back of the trailer, patting, guiding. At the road he turned and waved, hopped up into the cab. I followed in my car. Out on the highway, the trailer seemed to shrink and sway. It rocked off, complete but still ridiculous, disappeared down the blacktop looking too insignificant ever to have been anyone's home.

Mom was still in the office when I got back to the lumberyard.

"So did you get your trailer off all right?" she said.

"I refuse to discuss it with you," I said. "You have no understanding. I'm calling Jimmy."

I did, too, long distance, and we talked for thirty minutes. Anything is better than doing the payroll.

"Aw right, Judy," Jimmy says, his voice twisting up at the end like he's taking notes. He says "bye-bye," too. I think that's sweet.

I never cared about Jimmy until my sister Tina Lee got engaged to him. I didn't dislike him; I just didn't understand him. I never both-

6

ered. Or maybe he wasn't the same person then, or as much of a person. He has a big Adam's apple and a square jaw, one of those big-boy faces that's all planes. Flat-eyed, and he swallows a lot. I thought of him as a cartoon, my sister's boyfriend. Dudley Do-Right. That was before we focused on each other. Jimmy, he's good at focusing. You think he's foolish and then wham! You fall into his face and lose yourself. That's exactly what Tina Lee did. She fell into Jimmy and she drowned.

■ —— ■

Tina Lee got her engagement ring on Valentine's Day. That's the sort of jokey thing Jimmy does, only he's not joking. They drove all the way up from Columbia to show off. Tina burst into the lumber-yard office jiggling her left hand like she'd burned it, stuck her fingers under my face and there it was, a little diamond, sparkling. She flickered it.

"Gosh," I said to Jimmy. He was lurking by the door. "Most men give chocolate."

He just smirked. They both had that half-proud, half-ashamed look of people who have discovered sex or fallen in love or had a baby. I remember wondering at the time if Tina was pregnant. They certainly looked guilty enough. Of course they were getting ready to break our parents' hearts, which would account for some nervousness. Mom and Dad had always looked on the romance between Jimmy and Tina Lee as a childhood disease.

We did a dance around the desk, a sister dance, hold and jump, squeal and hug. Her new pink-and-white ski jacket crinkled and quivered with the cold, and her hair lay pale and wispy across her cheek and muffler.

Dad came out of his cubicle, rubbing his face.

"Well, well! What's going on here?" Like a daddy on Christmas morning. He examined the diamond, too. "My goodness, this is

7

something, yes sir." He didn't say what. He smiled a big smile, shook Jimmy's hand, looked around the room.

"So! Congratulations. I think. What you got to say for yourself, bud?"

Behind his smile, my daddy's eyes were gray and noncommittal. Jimmy was a little taller, with a smaller smile.

"Not a lot to say, sir," said Jimmy. "Except I'm mighty lucky." He cleared his throat and sat on the edge of a table, wrapped one arm over the other arm, one leg over the other leg. Dad stood looking from him to Tina Lee, his eyes bright, head cocked to one side like he was watching birds eat.

"So where's Mom?" said Tina Lee.

The girl has always had nerve, I'll give her that, a kind of brazen gutsiness I thought was courage. Glowing. She shone like her diamond.

Mom came in from the store.

"Come over here, baby," she said. "Let me see that thing."

Tina went over to her. Mom bent over the ring, pushing her half-glasses up on her nose so she could see better, finally dropping Tina's hand, taking the glasses off, looking up at Tina, rubbing the back of her neck. She sighed. She is blonde, too, honey blonde, pale, with a nice, wide English face. She is the most beautiful one of us. We inherited only pieces of her—I got the forehead, Tina got the hair, nobody got the complexion.

"I don't know, Tina," Mom said. "I'm not sure about this, honey."

She felt Tina's forehead for fever. Tina's eyes went blank, like a cat being scratched. Mom slid her hand down the side of Tina's face, turning her jaw a little to catch the light. She touched the quarter-sized, chapped, pink circles on Tina's cheeks; her thumb brushed the corner of her mouth, which was bruised and bitten. She pushed back Tina's hair, tucked it behind her ear.

My own face tingled.

"You're planning a long engagement, right?" she said. She glanced over at Jimmy.

8

"Nope," said Tina Lee.

"We thought May, right after graduation," said Jimmy, recrossing his arms and legs onto the other side. He picked a piece of lint off his sleeve.

That was when I really saw Jimmy for the first time, really noticed him. He became human to me then, not a boy but a large, watchful man, bland and hard as a stone.

"Surely not May," said Mom. She came over to Dad, slipped her arm through his for support.

"Not May. Oh, we couldn't possibly do it by then. It's so hot in the summer. Wait until fall. Thanksgiving. Give yourselves some time." She patted Jimmy's arm to show it was nothing personal. "You know we think a lot of you, Jimmy."

He looked down at her and smiled his slow, sweet smile, turned his head aslant, listening.

"May, Mother," said Tina Lee. "Really."

Mom raised her eyebrows and exchanged a look with me and Dad that doubted Tina Lee's taste and intelligence. Tina ignored her. We all knew that this was merely the opening salvo in what would be a long, attritive battle. And we all knew who would win.

"I'll give you a thousand dollars to elope," said Dad.

"We just want a simple ceremony," said Tina. "Nothing elaborate like Hamp and Judy had."

"Two thousand," said Dad.

"Oh my God," said Mom, coming to grips. "Listen, Tina, I don't like this. But if you insist on right after graduation you'd better get over to the church right now and reserve your weekend before the Crowley girl gets it."

"Five thousand," said Dad. "And that's my final offer."

Jimmy looked interested, but Tina gave him a push.

The office looked dreary after they left, and our mother had a lot more to say about the wedding, her youngest daughter, her future son-in-law, the mess they were getting us all into, and her own Bob, who, she swore, had never learned to say no to the child and never would until his dying day. I finally went up front and relieved one of the clerks in the retail store just to get away from it.

Daddy was long gone by then. He had immediately remembered emergencies on the other side of town and disappeared. Which was fine with me; I knew he'd get an earful before the middle of May.

■ —— ■

Mom's objection to the marriage was personal.

"I have nothing against Jimmy personally," she said. "And the Hoopers are very nice people. Don't get me wrong."

"Then what's your problem, Mama?" I said.

"He's not right for her," she said. "Those people don't know how to act. She's throwing herself away."

Nobody cared much anymore. We had heard it all before.

Mom had been nattering on about boyfriends since we began to have them, and none of them were ever good enough to suit her. McAdamses founded the town. We were the Scots and the Irish, the first generations to run off the Cherokees and settle western South Carolina.

"Europeans seeking refuge from religious persecution," said my mom.

"And probably some scoundrels running from the law," said Dad.

"People who became landowners and political leaders."

"Farmers," said my dad. "Lumbermen and farmers."

"Exactly," said my mom. "Good, healthy stock."

She was not happy when Hamp and I started to get serious about each other.

"His father died an alcoholic, Judy. He's not stable."

"Great-uncle Bartow was an alcoholic, too, but the rest of us are doing okay. You can't hold it against Hamp that his dad had a problem."

10

"There are many things that I admire very much about Hamilton. And his mother is a lovely person. All the same. . ."

"What?"

"He seems immature. Too eager, somehow. Not enough thought to what marriage means. It's all happening too fast, Judy. Give it some time."

So now it was happening again. Tina and Jimmy had dated off and on since high school, and that relationship had bothered Mom as much as mine and Hamp's did. She had finally shut up about it, figuring Tina would meet some rich Sigma Nu while they were at the university and dump Jimmy. She hadn't. Five years she had spent in college, and all five of them she had been Jimmy's girl.

"Mr. and Mrs. Hooper will be your children's grandparents. Have you thought of that?" said Mom to Tina the next Saturday.

Tina was home for the weekend. We were at Mom's kitchen table eating salad.

"Come home and start planning," Mom had told Tina. What she meant was, Come home and give me a chance to teach you the error of your ways.

"I think the Hoopers are wonderful," Tina said.

Tina sat in her T-shirt and fidgeted, refused to eat dressing on her salad, went on about how natural the Hoopers acted and how darling the little sister was, and how she was sure we would all be friends, and why didn't Mom invite them over to dinner.

Mom stabbed a carrot.

"I would be happy to have the Hoopers over," she said. "But it's customary, you know, for the groom's family to call first after the engagement."

"The Hoopers are not very social people, Mother," said Tina Lee. "Maybe we could just have them over for a picnic or something."

"We could," said Mom. "And eventually we will. But I wouldn't dream of insulting Lucy Hooper by denying her the opportunity to invite first."

11

"Oh," said Tina Lee. "Why stand on ceremony?"

Mom sat looking at Tina while she played with her fork. Tina flicked a piece of lettuce at me.

"I don't see why we have to be so sticky about it all," Tina said, rolling an olive up and down the edge of her finger. "I'm sure you'll really like the Hoopers when you get to know them."

"I already do know them," said Mom. "Don't play with your food. I went to high school with Jimmy's daddy."

"And don't you like him? Isn't he the sweetest thing?"

"I like him fine," said Mom.

"And don't you like Mrs. Hooper? Did you know she makes all her own bread? And she used to be a missionary. Isn't that noble?"

Mom took off her glasses. "Don't mistake me on this, Tina Lee," she said. She set aside her salad bowl, leaned forward, spoke slowly. "Hear what I have to say. Lucy Hooper is not happy about this engagement anymore than I am. This is something you and Jimmy cooked up. We parents will all get through it as best we can. You must allow me and Lucy Hooper to find our own way through this, and do things in their proper time."

Tina flushed. "Mrs. Hooper likes me," she said.

"Like has nothing to do with it, darling. I like Jimmy. I've got nothing against Jimmy."

She glanced over at me, daring me to mention all the things she had against Jimmy. I shrugged and smiled.

She continued. "But people have dreams for their children. Hopes and dreams."

"And the children have hopes and dreams of their own," said Tina Lee. She rolled a Ritz cracker across the table toward me. It spun out of control at the edge of the place mat, and I picked it up and ate it.

"And what are your dreams?" said Mom. "To marry Jimmy Hooper and then what?"

"We haven't decided," said Tina, sliding her eyes around to me. "Exactly. Yet."

Another lie.

"I'll tell you what," said Mom. "I'll tell you exactly what. To marry Jimmy Hooper, and yet somehow be all the things you talked about being, and do all the things you talked about doing—the job, the travel, the courses you were going to take—to marry Jimmy Hooper and to have all that too, somehow—that's what's in your mind, your bridal mind, mixed up with the wedding dress and the honeymoon. And it's not going to happen, Tina Lee. Marriage is not a convenience. It's for life. Till death do you part. You're going to have to consider Jimmy Hooper and his wants, needs, and desires. And I can tell you, the boy has plenty. And if you think yours will take precedence, you'd better think again, daughter. Because there I have the advantage of you. I know the Hoopers. They are God's own mill, and they grind slowly but exceedingly fine."

Mom is a Methodist preacher's daughter and lapses into theology when heated. She was wasting her breath. We all knew it. I guess it relieved her feelings, though, to get it said.

"We just want to be together," Tina said in a small voice. "Jimmy wants whatever I want. He does. And I want the best for him."

"You have love on the brain, Tina. Are you absolutely determined to do this now? Couldn't you and Jimmy just—"

"Just what, mother?"

"Sleep together or something? Shack up for awhile? Get it out of your systems."

"People don't say 'shack up' anymore, Mom," I said.

"Get what out of our systems, mother? Jimmy and I *love* each other. We want to be together forever. Now. Now and forever."

"World without end, amen," I said.

They both looked at me.

"Sorry," I said.

13

"You're supposed to help me out here, Judy," said Tina Lee. She pointed at me, turned to Mom. "*She's* happy. She got married when she was my age. She and Hamp are delirious together."

I ignored the sarcasm.

"Look," I said. "I'm not in this. I don't care what you do. Jimmy's great, so marry him or not, your choice, now or later. It's all the same to me. Whenever."

"I choose now. Okay?" She shook our mother's arm.

"Okay," said Mom, like she used to say okay to us as children, hands spread in defeat. Meaning, I absolve myself. May it rest on your head.

"Mom, I really want this. This. It's me."

Mom closed her eyes, shook her head slightly at the words. Tina watched her face, fishing for the lemon in her iced tea.

"Want to go shopping now?" She caught the lemon and stuck it in her mouth to eat the pulp, leaving the bright yellow triangle of rind stuck up against her lips like a cork. She looked like a baby, sucking.

I began to clear the table.

"Or would you rather just stay home and send your charge cards?" she mumbled through the lemon.

Our mother smiled, stood up, scraped back her chair.

"Just let me put on a skirt," she said and left the room.

"Well phooey," said Tina Lee. She removed the rind, now bare, from her mouth and got up to help me load the dishwasher.

"I was hoping for an afternoon alone with all Mom's cards."

"Mom may be stressed out," I said, "but she's not insane."

"Is she going to lighten up, you reckon?" Tina sat on the counter, swinging her feet. "Or are we going to do this the hard way?"

"Too soon to tell," I said. "You know she was the same way when Hamp and I got married, and now she thinks of him as a son. She'll come around. You'd better just shut up and let Mom do her etiquette thing. It soothes and comforts her."

That was an old expression from our childhood, "soothes and comforts." It came from a cough syrup bottle, and meant to us menthol and a blanket on the couch.

"It's all so stupid, who cares?"

"Excuse me? Is this the same Tina Lee who made her very own sister fill out a wedding planner that God could have used as a rough draft for the twentieth century?"

"I just want to get on with my life. Did I tell you we're going to law school?"

"About a hundred times."

"We'll stay in McAdamsville and work for a year to save money. Jimmy wants a career where he can help people. Isn't that noble?"

"Really. Was his mom honestly a missionary?"

"She had a tropical disease and everything. They have family devotions. It's so sweet."

"And will she teach you to make bread?" I said.

"Gosh, I hope not," said Tina. She was cross legged on the counter, rummaging through the cabinet. "Though I plan to cook, of course. Did I show you those china brochures I got? Ninety dollars a plate, can you imagine?" She found the peanut butter, screwed off the top, dipped in her finger and coated it, handed me the jar. I did the same.

"Honestly," said Mom from the doorway. I held out the jar.

She came over and took a little, off the rim.

■ —— ■

So we began to prepare for the wedding of Tina Lee. We shopped. We shopped all over South Carolina, and we went to Atlanta and shopped there. We shopped outlets, malls, boutiques, and catalogs. We studied magazines, Miss Manners, and the pamphlets from jewelry stores on how to have a perfect wedding. Tina Lee wanted a simple family thing, but she also wanted four hundred guests, the perfect dress, flowers, food, honeymoon, trousseau. We spent months looking for the right stuff.

My husband Hamp bore it as well as he could, which is to say, hardly at all. Hamp gets along great with my mom, and he loves my daddy better than he loves me, but he does not do well with these happy family occasions. He suffers abundantly, rolling his eyes every few minutes in case you forget how much he's enduring for you, teases, pitches small fits, studies the checkbook with a worried frown.

He is always at his worst when trying to educate me.

"How could clothes possibly be such a big deal?" he says. "How can you travel two hundred miles for a pair of shoes?"

"Easy. The same way you travel two hundred miles to a gun show. And we like to see everything, to get the best bargains and the best buys."

"So you travel over three states to save fifty dollars on one thing, and next week you'll spend five hundred on something else."

He says this with an air of happy reason, like a puppy offering up a ball. Don't I see his point? Isn't that foolish of me? When I smile and shrug, he shakes his head, smiling too. I found his manner irresistible, ignored his fits and adored his teasing; it proved he loved me. I did what I pleased about the money. To me, teasing was the grit, the irritant, the sand-sunburn of the marriage beach.

We worked like dogs all spring. Dad and Hamp were busy with a housing development they had bought in on; Mom and I had, in addition to the wedding, the lumberyard to run. We would all meet for lunch at the office to catch up on business, talking and eating a bucket of chicken or something. I would get the skinless chicken, make a salad. Dad would ostentatiously eat two lettuce leaves, hide the rest under his chicken bones.

"Jennifer says reorder Exeter lighting this week. She says those 229s are going real fast," I would say.

Jennifer runs the store.

16

"I bet it's Ed," Hamp would say. "Ed loves those Exeter fixtures."

"How's his credit?" That would be Dad.

"Fine," Mom would say. "He's paid off all that lumber, remember?"
They would look at each other a minute, reading each other's
thoughts. They seldom use mere words anymore.

"Fine," Dad would say. "Order 'em then. Okay, Judy?"

I would make a note. I did the ordering. Mom did the bills. Hamp
ran the yard. Dad kibitzed. We wove in and out of each other's day
like dancers, bow and smile, sweat and turn.

Our lunch table was a beat-up brown desk at the back of the warehouse, surrounded by chairs, flanked by an old refrigerator and a
microwave. It is my spiritual home. I grew up at that table, did my
homework there, counted inventory, played my Walkman, learned how
to keep books. How to run a lumberyard. How to be married.

After the day's business came the day's plans.

"So what are you ladies doing this afternoon?" Dad said politely
every day, wiping his lips, folding his napkin.

"Going to Demaro," Mom said. "Tina's silver has come in, and
Judy has a fitting on her dress. And Baby—," this to me, "remember,
we have to find you some decent shoes."

"You know what gets me?" said Hamp, waving a chicken leg. "Is
the ritualistic nature of this thing. Ya'll did the same thing when we
got married. Look for the shoes. Look for the dress. Like some kind
of—," he shook his head, bit off another piece of chicken, "like some
mating dance or something."

Hamp watches a lot of *National Geographic* specials.

"Well, that's exactly what it is," Mom said. "It is a mating ritual.
Christian."

"Late twentieth century," I added, in case anybody had forgotten.

"Yeah," said Dad. "The ritual of Tina spending money. I'm real
familiar with it. It's because this is her last chance, marrying a boy
still in school."

17

"There's this tribe in Africa," said Hamp, "where the men do the dressing up, in feathers and so on. The women hang out and watch them, and then pick their favorite."

"I'da picked you," I said. "You'd look great in feathers."

"I still don't know how they expect to live," said Mom.

"They wear this paint," said Hamp. "They make it up themselves, and each family has its own designs. When they get it all on, they look real—"

"Beautiful?" I teased.

"Strange. But probably no stranger than I'm gonna look in my new tuxedo and my patent-leather pumps." Hamp threw down his bone and winked at me. His face, normally an excellent, intelligent, outdoor face, split open in a pink, cracker grin that shows too much gum—his good-old-boy grin. With his greasy fingers he smoothed down his hair, which is fair and feathery and gets all on end when he works outdoors.

"Jimmy says he's been saving money," said Dad. "Where are the mashed potatoes, Judy?"

"I didn't get any, Dad." Dad sighed, brushed crumbs from his shirt front.

"Leave your hair alone," I told Hamp. "You would spend the rest of your life in blue jeans if I let you, ordering your clothes from catalogs."

"There's nothing wrong with catalogs," said Hamp. "Is there, Bob?"

"Leave me out of this," said Dad.

"I ordered this shirt," said Hamp. "Now look at it. Would you say it lacked style?" He pulled at the front of his shirt, a plaid, flannel, torn-up thing he wears around the sawmill. I went around behind him and hugged, worked on his hair myself.

"I would say it lacked everything," I said. He reached around the chair and pinched me. I hit him, and he hit me back.

"Children!" said Mom. "It's a very nice shirt, Hamilton."

18

She got up, wiped off the table. "So you're going over that paper-work for me this afternoon, Bob?"

Dad grimaced.

"Don't forget to pick up Curtis from nursery school," I said to Hamp, sitting on his lap.

"Sure thing," said Hamp.

"He'll get squeaky-voice if you're late."

"I won't be late."

"And don't forget the haircut. You could use one yourself. Don't let them cut off all his curls."

"I can handle it."

"Last time they cut his hair too short."

"Go shopping, Judy," said Hamp. He dumped me off his lap, stood up. "Help your sister out. Get her married. Do the female bonding thing. I will stay home and do the male bonding thing."

"Will you now," said Dad.

"I can handle it," Hamp said. "You think I won't go into the barber shop and tell Lloyd to leave the boy some curls for mama? I do that all the time. And didn't I buy Curtis the anatomically correct doll with the wienie that looks like an eraser?"

"Didn't know they made those," said Dad.

"Damndest thing you ever saw," said Hamp. "I read all those maga-zines in the pediatrician's office. I know how to act. I do. Bought my boy the anatomical doll, by God. Don't want him growing up with any wrong ideas."

"I been meaning to talk to you about your ideas," said Dad.

"You're a perfect father," I said and kissed him.

"The way you bait these women," said Dad. "Gonna get you in trouble one of these days."

"They're going to do a show on you," I said. "Hamp the Perfect."

"Shows a tendency to self-destruct," said Dad.

"Where are you guys going to eat supper?" I said. "Because we

19

won't be back till late."

"No sweat," said Hamp. "Curtis and I will probably just grab a salad and some yogurt somewhere. Maybe Bob will join us and make it a real party. Won't you, Bob?"

"I can't wait," said Dad.

"No cholesterol, Bob," said Mom.

"What good boys," I said. "We'll bring you a surprise from the big city."

"I can't wait," said Dad.

■ —— ■

Of course Hamp went right ahead and let the barber cut Curtis's hair too short, which we all knew he would, and the three of them went to the steak place out on the edge of town and got the large T-bones, rare, with extra bread and sour cream on their potatoes. Then they stopped by the video store and rented *Terminator*, not even bothering to cover Curtis's eyes for the part where Terminator gets burned up, so that the child spent the next week climbing into bed with us, thus blowing our March opportunity to make another one just like him, only female.

"I hope you're satisfied," I told Hamp.

"On the contrary," he said.

Mom was somewhat testy also.

"I hate those colors," she'd say, shopping. "That material is so cheap. Don't they make anything decent anymore? Look at this. I'm not wearing sequins. You can just hang that back up."

She lit into Dad and Hamp occasionally, too.

"Is this menopause?" Hamp said to me on the way home one day. Mom had chewed him out about something at the yard. "What is this? Can't you do anything?"

"What are you complaining about?" I said. "I am with her all day. Of course I can't do anything."

20

"Was she this bad when you and I got married?"

"Worse."

"Is it inherited?"

"Very funny."

"You think I'm kidding. I'm not kidding. Your mama has the world's biggest corncob—"

"Hush."

"What?" said Curtis from the back seat, supposed to be asleep.

"The world's what? Grandma?"

"Nothing," we said.

The whole spring, it was like Mom was marking time, listening for something. Waiting. She got on Tina's nerves as well. Tina wanted enthusiasm. She wanted Mom to come over to her side, to think her marriage to Jimmy was a good idea, to sit beside her on the bed and help plot, like she used to do when we were kids. Mom wouldn't give her that. She maintained a quiet, reasonable distance, as you would from a loved one with a contagious disease.

Tina started calling her "Mother."

"Of course you may do whatever you like, Mother," Tina said. "Wear whatever you like. Invite whoever you like."

"Oh, I will," said Mother with a smile. "You can count on that, Tina Lee."

They had a little contest in their spare time, to see who could be the most forgiving.

Mostly, Tina maintained that maddening, superior calm that people adopt when they're getting their way. Jimmy had it, too. They wrapped themselves in it like monks.

Mom had the most trouble with Jimmy's family.

"Jimmy's great-grandmother dips snuff. Did you know that?" she said. "In the house. Do people dip snuff in the house? Do they need cans to spit in, or is that tobacco?"

"You sound like a snob, Edna," said Dad.

21

"I'm not a snob."

"I know it. But you sound like one. Let it go."

"I can't," she said. "I'm trying, but I can't."

■ —— ■

Then we went to the Hoopers for dinner. Mrs. Hooper apparently did muster the strength to cope with us because she called and invited us all to dinner the day after we talked about it, but the dinner was postponed twice before we got around to it. The families had met informally, warily, on a couple of Sunday afternoons, the mothers hugging with just their shoulders, the men leaning up against the hood of the car or hunched over a television ball game. Finally one Saturday, the dinner was on, for all of us, at the Hoopers.

We went the long way, a two-car procession into McAdamsville, around the bypass and out a narrow black road to the Hoopers. There are a dozen such roads spinning off in all directions from McAdamsville, like a clock face. McAdamsville is the hub, the county seat. We live west of town, at nine o'clock; the Hoopers are east, at four. Another day we would have cut across country, jumping from village to village through seven and six, swinging by five on an old logging road. But this was a formal occasion. Dad took the Pontiac. We wore good clothes.

I watched my parents' silhouettes through their car window. They sat up straight, Tina in the middle of the back like a child being driven to school. My mother occasionally gestured, turned to Dad or looked out the window, animated, pointing to something along the road. Travel excites her.

It was like Grandmother Caroline's funeral procession—my mother in the front car, the funeral car, inappropriately cheerful because she's going somewhere—"Oh, look, Bob, there's a cardinal!"— Tina Lee

22

and I red-eyed in the jump seat, aware of ourselves as mourners, our mother as frivolous.

Of course Mom was right. Her attitude was the one Grandmother would have applauded. The old lady's last ride should be a sightseeing trip. Grandmother Caroline had been the motivation for a thousand Sunday drives.

"Oh, let's go over toward Dacusville," she'd say. "Let's go over toward the mountains."

My mother was just as bad. They were like pencils on a string, describing pointless parabolas all over upper South Carolina, abetted by my father.

Absolutely anywhere was better than staying at home.

Grandmother Caroline was Mom's mother, the minister's widow, flat-backed and fair-haired into her eighties, shrinking but refusing to bend. She lived in an old Victorian cottage off Main Street in McAdamsville and walked about a mile every morning until her last heart attack. She had inexplicable and, to Tina Lee and me, maddening zeal. Other grandmothers were soft and weak, gave doll tea parties, wore purple dresses and floppy underwear. Our grandmother gave bird and mineral books, and wore denim skirts and walking shoes. She sat in the back car seat with us, held onto the door handle and clicked her tongue, rubbing our arms and feeding us candies to keep us pliant like she did in church, so she and my mother could talk.

It suited me to pretend that my father was their captive, as I was, that he would have preferred staying home and watching television. It wasn't true. My father enjoyed those trips, enjoyed being a patient man, acting that part—the enduring husband, the gentle son-in-law. He liked arranging the trip.

He would consider the route, ponder, mention it offhand like a wrapped present laid on the seat. Sometimes he would make up his own trip.

"Thought we might go over toward Pickens today," he'd say. There would always be a reason—a flea market, or pretty leaves, or a garden, but it would not be mentioned until we got there. We would come upon it as though accidentally. Dad would act surprised at his own prowess. "Well, look at that, Edna!" He would wink.

Between them, my parents and Grandmother Caroline knew everything about where they were going. They knew the provenance of the land. They traveled not only along a road, but back in time as well, dragging Tina and me relentlessly along behind them through a history lesson. The genealogical trips were the worst. For those we needed bug spray. We bumped down logging tracks and along fences, across some farmer's field to a briar-covered graveyard.

"Here's where the old McQuestion place used to be, Edna," Grandmother Caroline would say. "The one they burned during the war"— 'they' being Sherman's troops, the war being the War Between the States. "Bob, see if you can make out that inscription."

Bob would cheerfully do so. My mother would write everything down. Tina and I would sit on a gravestone, sulk, and swat mosquitoes.

"Believe it says, 'Charity Blaney' here," he'd say, scratching a little with his penknife. "Died 1848, aged twenty-two years and three months, and Beloved Son Matthew aged two days. Rest in Jesus."

"Childbirth," my grandmother would say dreamily, nodding. "A fatal effort sometimes. The Blaneys were Quakers. These woods were full of Quakers before the war. McQuestions bought much of their land. Lot of good it did 'em." She waved at a row of fieldstones. "Diphtheria. Scarlet fever. War. There's not a McQuestion left in this county now."

I was in high school before I realized that my grandmother, born in 1906, had not personally experienced the Civil War.

In the springtime we'd go to the river. Grandmother would point a wrinkled finger into the woods.

"Here is where Major Bryant surprised the British Colonel Sullivan's troops one morning, a week before the Battle of Cowpens. There was a skirmish. Do you girls know who won?"

"No ma'am," we'd say, rolling our eyes, burying our heads in comic books. And we didn't care, either.

"Major Bryant. Eleven killed on their side. None on ours." She sniffed with satisfaction. "Do you know what year?"

"No ma'am."

"1780. The American Revolution. What are they teaching you in school these days?" Grandmother would say. "You just ride along the tops of things, your nose buried in a book. Get out of the car and go see it."

She'd open the car door and sit with her feet on the ground, fanning while we waded and looked for artifacts.

"Your mother found a bullet here when she was a little girl," she would say.

"Where is it then?" I would say. "More likely a rock. How many bullets could there be left, with people finding them ever since 1780?" I had gotten that remark from my dad.

"Be polite when you speak to your grandmother," Mom would say. "Pay attention when she speaks to you."

"Now Edna," Grandmother would say, squeezing us, "they're only children."

Then it would be my mother's turn to roll her eyes.

Back at her house after the drive, Grandmother would give us a soft drink and a slice of pound cake, and we'd sit on the porch swing and balance the drink between our knees while the grown-ups talked. We'd break the cake off in bits and roll it into balls before eating it, to make it last longer. Grandmother Caroline made the best pound cake in the world.

■ —— ■

On the way to the Hoopers, we passed a filling station, an open space carved out of the pine woods stretching for miles on both sides of the road. Here were some farms, a few fields still etched in the wilderness.

"This is Pumpkintown, Curtis," I said. "They used to grow pumpkins here when I was a little girl. We would ride out here with my Grandmother Caroline and buy one every Halloween."

"I want one," he said.

"Those are soybeans," I said. "No more pumpkins in Pumpkintown." I sang it. "No more pumpkins in Pumpkintown, No more pumpkins for you, No more—"

We turned off the highway onto a dirt road.

"Now listen, Curtis," I said, turning around to look at him.

He blinked back at me from his booster seat. Curtis has strawberry-blonde hair. Other mothers run their fingers through it and say, "Where'd he get those curls?" and "Where'd he get those eyelashes? It's a sin for a boy to have eyelashes that long." He is almost five and has a sprinkling of freckles across his nose.

"Mommy needs you on your best behavior tonight, okay? This is a special time for Aunt Tina. It's important for you to mind Mommy. Can you do that?"

He nodded. Curtis usually behaves in a car.

We pulled into the Hoopers' driveway, drove up to an old, frame farmhouse surrounded by sedate, white outbuildings. The yard grass was so short it looked painted, and daffodils bloomed in bunches around the porch. It was six o'clock. The sun wouldn't go down for another hour.

"Well," said Hamp, "here goes nothing."

The Hoopers met us in the yard. They came out, with ceremony, to lead us in.

■ —— ■

It was still March, when green's so new it's almost yellow. Mom

26

and Lucy Hooper met valiantly, as kings do after a battle, taking each other's hand, crossing the bright, soft grass together to the kitchen door. They bent together, seeking common ground. They had brought all they had, the best of themselves, the most important, urgent, quiet quality they possessed to this hour and day—Mom's grace, her broad forehead and her wide, deep eyes, and Lucy Hooper's grave narrow shoulders and her thin-lipped pride. They would negotiate pain.

Their retinue hung back, the dads watching their wives out of the sides of their eyes, murmuring and shaking hands all around like honorary pallbearers—tanned, well fed, stubby fingered, my red-headed daddy with his hooded eyes and subtle mouth, James Hooper with a flatter face, more peaceable and bland.

Jimmy and Tina Lee took Curtis off to see some lambs. Associating with Jimmy and Tina was not worth the trouble, so I went on into the house.

"How may we help you?" said Mom in the kitchen. "Lucy, that pie looks delicious. Call me Edna, please. Bob, have you ever seen such a roast?"

The younger sister, Sally, stood at the counter, fishing pickles out of a jar and arranging them on a plate, studying us, licking her fingers. She is thin and quiet like her mama, with the big teeth and eyes of twelve, bony wrists, bony face, and brown, scraped-back hair.

"I'm sorry we have to eat in the kitchen like this," said Lucy Hooper. "Two tables. It's a shame. When Granny Glendinning had her first stroke we moved her into the dining room and took the big table apart."

"It's fine this way, mother," said her husband. He began cutting the roast.

"Oh heavens," said Mom. "Goodness. We always eat in the kitchen. Don't we, Judy? Or in front of the television. I know we shouldn't. And such lovely silver! That's Old Rose, isn't it? Isn't there anything we can do to help?"

When it was time to eat, Hamp and I grabbed the card table,

wedging Curtis into the chair next to the wall, and I waved Sally over to join us.

"Oh no," said Lucy.

"This is perfect," said Hamp. "Right, buddy?" He patted Curtis. "Really. Really." He grinned, showed all his front teeth, held up his hands.

"Well . . ." said Lucy Hooper.

Everyone else sat at the kitchen table. Lucy leaned over her chair while James said the blessing, personalized for the occasion.

". . . these thy servants, and the bringing together these families of Tina and Jimmy, and may they . . ."

Lucy Hooper served the meal. She did not sit down except experimentally, as though to test the weight of her chair. Mostly she handed food around, big ironstone platters and little glass bowls of food, smiling a half-moon smile, picking out choice bits of roast and potatoes for us all, resting her hand briefly on our shoulders.

She had given Curtis a tiny knife and fork and a big-bowled spoon.

"Look, Mama, my size!" he said. "Can I take them home?"

"No, honey. Mrs. Hooper has to keep those for her grandchildren to use."

"Speaking of grandchildren," said my daddy.

"Bob," said my mom.

"Well, James and I have to get this sorted out," said Daddy. "As interested parties. Who gets to buy the pony, who gets to take 'em fishing—"

"I want a pony!" said Curtis.

Lucy Hooper whispered in Curtis's ear, squeezed his hand. He began to eat.

"Kids today," said James. "I'll believe in grandchildren when I see 'em."

"All in good time," said Mom.

"No rush," said Lucy Hooper.

"We aren't having children for awhile," said Jimmy, propping up his knife. "We've decided to wait."

"Man proposes," muttered Hamp. He rubbed my leg with the side of his foot.

"That's exactly right, Hamilton," said Mom. "And God disposes. Babies come when they come."

"Amen to that," said Lucy Hooper.

"You young people," said James, shaking his head.

We proceeded majestically through the meal. There were roast beef and lamb, not referred to by name at our table—"Have some of this pink meat, Curtis." "What is it?" "Meat. Try it"—several cooked vegetables, raw vegetables, congealed salad, homemade rolls, bowls of relish, pickles, applesauce, jelly, preserved fruit.

"Simply delicious."

"—must give me the recipe—"

"—either one of you cook, Jim Boy?"

Our table lurched and quivered throughout the meal. We anchored it with our feet, cut meat carefully, elbows in, watched out for glasses.

"Don't get up, Lucy. You've barely started. Let me," said Mom.

"I'll just get the rolls."

Lucy made more forays from the stove with dishes of corn and beans, pouncing on plates that had a bare spot.

"Why, Tina Lee, you've hardly eaten a thing, honey."

"It's delicious, really. Two helpings of everything."

Tina buried her face behind her hair, pushed her fork through her rice as though it were a plow.

"Coffee?" said Lucy Hooper. "Who wants ice cream on their apple pie?"

"Mother," said her husband. "I'll do the pie. You eat."

"He's right, Lucy," said Mom. "You've hardly touched this wonderful dinner. James and I—won't we, James? We can manage fine."

After dessert the women did the dishes.

"Oh no," said Lucy. "We'll take care of those later."

"Nonsense. We insist, don't we, Judy? Tina Lee?"

Then we took a tour of the house.

The Hoopers live chiefly in the kitchen and den, a tiny room tacked onto the back of the house. The old dining room, Granny Glendinning's final home at home, contained the hospital bed, the cot, the stainless steel and plastic paraphernalia of the terminally old. Granny herself had recently gone on to the nursing home, where she lay incognizant, transparent, and mostly mute, her fingers endlessly quibbling with the covers and her gown. We continued the tour.

The rest of the Hoopers' downstairs was a maze of cold, well-tended rooms filled with the furniture and memorabilia of dead Hoopers. It was all perfectly preserved. The parlor had Victorian couches and chairs with the original, green plush upholstery, and an enormous pump organ covered with knobs and carved wood and furbelows.

"All this furniture has been in my husband's family," said Lucy Hooper.

"You've done a remarkable job," said Mom.

Stern Hoopers looked down at us from oval frames.

We climbed the stairs.

"What a lovely bedspread, Lucy. What a lovely patchwork quilt."

In Jimmy's room, all the furniture was red maple, and Tina's picture, taken the night she was crowned Miss McAdamsville, was on his desk.

"Here is where Jimmy studies when he's home," Tina said, touching his blotter.

Mom flinched. Lucy caught her look and smiled.

"I told Jimmy he might want this furniture when you get married," she said. "Maybe for a second bedroom, until you can afford something you like better. It was his dad's when he was a boy."

"The bed is so sweet," said Tina, touching the footboard.

The mothers looked at each other and sighed. Sally and I slipped out and went to her room.

"I know Tina Lee's acting pretty dippy right now," I said, "but I swear she's normally pretty decent."

"I know," said Sally. "She's not so bad. Jimmy's horrible. Horrible! He doesn't even hear us anymore. I will never fall in love."

"I don't blame you."

We sat on her bed and looked at horse pictures. My favorites were in *A Boy's King Arthur*, full-page horses on glossy paper, patient and celestial. She liked *Misty* best.

Sally's room was that comforting dreamscape little girls need, slant roofed, tucked under a dormer at one end of the hallway. Everything was squared off—the comforter folded neatly at the bottom of the bed, the bedspread even, the pillows plumped. The bedside table held a pink plastic clock with a cat face, a lamp with a ruffled lampshade, and a diary, locked. Horse statues were everywhere.

Curtis appeared in the doorway.

"I wanna see that organ down there."

"Come over here." I pulled him onto my lap. "Look at this, Curtis. This is King Arthur getting the sword from the Lady of the Lake."

The lady's arm rose sharply out of the water, a lovely Edwardian arm. King Arthur and his friends gazed impassively at it from their boat.

"Come on. I wanna go," said Curtis, squirming.

Sally turned the page.

"Look!" I said. "Here's—"

"I wanna goooooo!" said Curtis. His voice came from behind his nose, a high, petulant keen.

"All right! Go." I set him down on the floor.

"Maaahhhm," he said. "Maahhm. Mahm. Mom."

"Curtis," I said. "Go away."

"Maaahhhm."

31

"What is it? What do you want?" I began to whine myself.

"I wanna go! I wanna go down there and see the organ."

"Well you can't, Curtis," I said. "It's old. Nobody plays it anymore."

He stared at me, and I stared at him. Lucy Hooper appeared in the door.

"Come on," she said. "You can play the organ, and then we'll go out and ride the pony." She held out her hand.

■ —— ■

Curtis sat in Lucy's lap while she pumped and he played.

"Hit that key," she said. "Now this one." She pulled out various stops, and the thing roared and moaned and bellowed. She helped him play "Mary Had a Little Lamb" by pointing out the proper keys.

"Show him 'Twinkle,' Mother," said Sally.

"Next time," Lucy said. "We have to ride the pony in a hurry before it gets dark. Go out and saddle him, darling, and we'll be along." She put her face down next to Curtis's. "Will you come back to see me?" He nodded. "You can play the organ any time. Okay? And bring your mama." She set him down. "Go on out and find Sally in the barn," she said, and he ran out.

"Thank you," I said.

She began pushing in the stops. "Jimmy used to love this tacky old organ," she said. "He played it every day, sitting in here singing hymns and banging away by the hour. Said he wanted to be a preacher." She closed the lid, brushed her hand across the top. "Don't suppose I could foist it off on Tina, do you?"

"You could try," I said. "The bloom of first love and all. You never know."

"Nah," she said, getting up. "I'll just keep it. It would be too cruel."

■ —— ■

The dads and Hamp were all wedged into the den, staring at the

32

empty television screen like they were waiting for a vision. Mr. Hooper had the recliner; Dad and Hamp shared the couch, their feet wedged under the coffee table. They looked like the three bears.

"Hamp, want to go out and watch Curtis ride the pony?" I said.

"Believe I'll have a look at that myself," said Dad. "Want to come out with us, James?"

They all struggled to their feet.

Everything in the room was dust free. I went over to the television set, which was topped with a doily and pictures of Jimmy and Sally in grammar school. The glass in the frames gleamed, smelled of vinegar. There was Jimmy as a child, dark and solemn, earnest and thin. He had been a scrawny boy, his Adam's apple sticking out above his shirt. His sister had been scrawny, too. But they were appealing somehow. There was one small photograph of a young woman wearing a straw hat and standing in front of a palm tree, holding a little boy by the hand—Mrs. Hooper as a missionary. I hadn't realized Jimmy had gone along. He looked happy there in the hot sun, shading his eyes, squinting into the light.

The sun outside was gone now; a chilly ground mist hovered in the paddock beside the barn. Sally had the pony by the halter, leading him and Curtis around. Curtis lifted one of his hands briefly from the saddle horn to wave at me.

"Go for it, kid," I said, joining the others at the fence.

"That's my boy!" shouted Hamp. "He's scared shitless, look at his face," he said to me.

"He's a brave boy!" Mom waved to him. "Hush, Hamilton."

"You look like a real cowboy," said Lucy Hooper as they came back around. "And to think this is only your first time! Hold him, Sally."

"Sally is such a sweet girl," said Mom.

"We've enjoyed her," said Lucy. "Though she's not as . . . trusting as Jimmy was. Not as open."

"Girls," said Mom.

"What about girls?" I said. "Girls are plenty trusting."

"You wait," said Mom. "That's right, darling! Hold on, sweetheart!"

Lucy and Mom leaned on their arms on the top fence railing and talked horses and farming. Mom, who has never lived on a farm in her life, has absorbed an impressive amount of information and lore from visits to various relatives. "Once when I was chased by a bull," she'll say, or "When the hen flew up in my face"—like she had a bull or a hen, which she never did. But she did have a horse, somehow, and she could really ride. She still could, I guess, if she would.

"I am fascinated by the fact that you were a missionary," I said to Lucy. "I saw your picture in the den."

"It was a wonderful time," she said.

"And you were where?"

"Nicaragua." She said it the way I imagine the Nicaraguans say it, rolling the *r*, giving a lilt to the syllables. "I miss it. James and Sally and I are going back there for a visit next fall." Her face lit up as she spoke.

"You know," said Mom, "my father had a friend in Nicaragua. What was his name now? I hadn't thought of it for years. Anthony Carver."

"Tony!" said Lucy. "He was our very dear friend. He's in Columbia now, you know. In the Methodist Home. James and I go by to see him every time we're down that way."

"Well do you really!" said Mom. "Imagine that! Bob, did you know Lucy knew one of my dad's good friends in Nicaragua?"

"He was the greatest help to us," Lucy said. "It broke our hearts to have to leave him and come home."

"Why did you?" I said.

"Oh, James's father died, and there wasn't anybody to look after the farm. And then his mother got sick. And there was Granny Glendinning, James's grandmother. And I had some sort of nasty fever." She laughed. "We just all sort of collapsed at once."

34

"Mom was really sick," said Jimmy.

"I did okay," Lucy said.

Jimmy spoke a few words in Spanish, laughing, and Lucy answered him, pushing back her hair, looking suddenly younger, prettier. She explained.

"Jimmy says he doesn't think I'll be back from Bluefields. Of course he's wrong."

He spoke again in Spanish.

"Well, you should come along yourself and find out," Lucy said. "Speak English. You're very rude." She turned to Mom. "Before Jimmy and Tina decided to get married, Jimmy was coming with us to the dedication of the new hospital." She patted his arm. "Now I guess he'll have to find his own way back."

"I'll take Tina along," said Jimmy.

"Sounds wonderful," said Tina brightly.

"There's no mall in Bluefields, Tina," Jimmy said.

"I'm tough," said Tina.

■ —— ■

The pony was still circling the enclosure in a depressed shuffle, with Sally leading him and Curtis frozen to his back.

"Bout time to go in, bud," I shouted.

"Jimmy, run out there and get him off," said Lucy. "And put up the pony. Lazy Eeyore."

Jimmy was walking across the paddock when Curtis started batting the air with his hands.

"Don't swat him!" shouted Jimmy.

Then Curtis screamed. Eeyore stiffened and snorted, bucked out his back legs and came down in a bouncing sideways prance. Jimmy caught Curtis before he hit the ground, grabbed the reins from Sally. A handful of something flung itself up out of the ground, thickening the air around Eeyore and the children.

Lucy ran for Sally and I ran for Curtis, who were both standing in one place jumping up and down and screaming, batting uselessly at the yellow jackets that bumped into them. We scooped them up and ran for the house, leaving Jimmy to manage the unhappy Eeyore as best he could. In the kitchen I plopped Curtis down on the drainboard and began peeling off his clothes. He was still screaming.

"Hush! You're fine. Hush! Look at you, you smell just like a pony."

There were no bites under his clothes, no hidden yellow jackets. Lucy handed me a bee-sting pen, and I dotted it on the three or four welts that were rising on his arm and face.

"Hardly stung at all, see?"

Curtis's face was smeared with dust and tear tracks, and the sting under his eye made him look raffish, like a boxer. His screams subsided to snuffles, then he stuck his thumb into his mouth, which shut him up completely. I glanced around at Sally, who was half undressed and making a face at a spoonful of Benedryl her mother was holding in front of her mouth.

"Free colas to all those taking Benedryl," said Lucy. "Down the hatch, babe. There's a girl."

"I'll get the colas," said Mom. "How about some ice in a nice cold washcloth for those stings? Would you like that, Sally?"

■ —— ■

In a few minutes we had everybody fixed up. Curtis sat on the counter with his feet in the sink, swigging cola and telling his dad about the yellow jackets as he held ice under his eye.

"Millions of them," he said.

"I hope they're all dead," said Sally.

"Dad's out there spraying them now," said Jimmy.

Tina was studying the stings on Jimmy's arm. Sally was sitting on her mother's lap, holding ice on her neck.

"Look at you," Lucy said, rubbing her daughter's back.

"You're big as I am. My babies are growing up."

"Poor Eeyore," said Sally. "I hope he's all right."

"Eeyore's fine," said Hamp.

"Eeyore hasn't moved that fast since we got him," said Jimmy. "He's all worn out from the excitement."

"Probably sleep all night," said Hamp.

"Dream about large lady ponies," said Jimmy.

"Boys," said Lucy.

■ —— ■

After all the men except Jimmy left for the den, Lucy fixed a pot of coffee.

"Well!" said Mom with satisfaction. "What an adventure. I'm going to have to get some of this bee-sting stuff, Lucy. It takes the pain right out."

"Just take that one, Edna, I insist. I have several, and they are hard to find."

Curtis, now in my lap, was snuffling and nodding off. His head rolled against my chest, and I wrapped him in my sweater and rocked. It was black outside; the night poured in across the screen porch, edging the door beside me, held back by the bright lights of the kitchen. Outside the crickets rasped, and a dove began to call.

"I declare it's so peaceful here," said Mom, glancing out the door. "This is the most peaceful I've felt in weeks."

Lucy came over with the coffee and sat down.

"The strain of this wedding," she said. "I told Jimmy, anything I can do to help. To take some of it off you."

"Oh." Mom flapped her hands. "Well, there's nothing, really."

"The rehearsal dinner, James and I insist."

"Well—," said Mom.

Tina raised her head. She had been lolling on Jimmy's chest over by the refrigerator. "I suggested we use the country club, Mom."

37

"Whatever you want," said Lucy. "We are not members."

"We are," said Mom.

"Do you need us anymore?" said Tina Lee, swinging Jimmy's hand.

Lucy and Mom looked at each other.

"No," said Mom.

Jimmy was nuzzling Tina's neck as they left the room.

"That pair!" said Mom.

"Children!" said Lucy Hooper. "More coffee? Judy? That Jimmy just—" She shrugged. "I can't do a thing with him."

"Not Jimmy," said Mom. "Tina Lee."

"Jimmy used to have sense," said Lucy, emptying the coffee pot. "Edna, when I was his age—"

"But when we came along, Lucy—," said Mom.

"Not even a job!" Lucy got up and got a plate of cookies, set them on the table. "Not even graduated yet. No sense of responsibility. No sense—"

"—at all. No sense at all. Neither one of them. I honestly don't know what's going to happen to them, Lucy. I honestly do not."

Lucy Hooper nodded, and they sat there together stirring their coffee, bobbing their heads like cows.

Two

2

I DON'T KNOW. Hiring Melissa to do the payroll has got to be a good idea. I keep telling myself that. Mom and Charley insisted. Charley's my cousin and mentor, and he's right at least as often as I am about things. Probably more. My confidence isn't what it used to be.

"You've got to free up some time for yourself," he says. "You've got to cut yourself some slack."

"So how come I'm not free? I have spent more time with Melissa in the last two or three days than I have with Curtis."

"Give it time," says Charley.

So I do. He's right. I stomp on my impatience. Next week will be better. In another month, by the end of October, it'll be fine.

■ —— ■

Jimmy called this morning to say he got the heater fixed in the trailer. The problem was only a bad connection after all. He sounded excited. He's already met his neighbors at the trailer park—four Asian medical students and a lady who sits by her stoop in a folding chair and smokes. I asked him if Tina had been out there yet. He said no. He said she was busy with her classes.

Later Tina called to fuss at me some more for sending Jimmy the trailer. What did I mean, she said. I said I didn't mean anything. The trailer was standing empty, and if Jimmy could use it and save himself some money while he was in school, I was glad for him to do so.

"You like this, don't you?" she said. "It's revenge or something."

"If I were into revenge," I said, "I could do much better than that."

There was a small silence.

"Have you talked to him?" she said. "Did he sound all right? Wonder if he needs any more dishes."

Now I sit at my desk eating vanilla yogurt, wondering, staring at the wall. The inside of the lumberyard office is just one big room, utilitarian, with desks in the back half of the store. I have been staring at the wall for years. There's a calendar there from the insurance company with their name written all over it. It occurs to me, scraping out the last spoonful from the yogurt carton, that we need a window; then we could watch the seasons change as we work. I get up, find a piece of chalk, and draw a window on the wall—a big window, not a picture window but a series of panels. I go outside to check the view, then on to the warehouse to see if we have frames in stock that will serve. We do. I come back, adjust the markings on the wallboard, and begin to cut.

■ —— ■

Last spring Tina Lee and her wedding functioned as a sort of firework. It fizzed around my feet. It was dazzling, buzzed, caused me to jump and turn. Then it began to work deeper, like a powder burn. It set me free from my routine. I began to float, and think.

I had renounced thought when Curtis was a baby. Sitting in the rocking chair with him at two o'clock one morning, watching his little lips work against my breast, I said good-bye to my brain. There was simply no room for it in my body. No time for it, no need. Instead of thinking I read long trashy novels about people screwing their way through the French Revolution, the American Revolution, World War II. I retained a certain low cunning which I used to obtain naps and sandwiches. And at work, of course, I worked. When I walked into the lumberyard office, my brain clicked on and functioned rather well, within a limited range. But I hadn't thought beyond, say, supper, or a new dress for myself, in nearly five years until Tina started planning her wedding. And I was better off. For one thing my brain was rusty and didn't function well. For another, I discovered that instead of not thinking thoughts, I had merely been packing them into a sort of storage closet in my brain, and when I opened the door that spring to get a few thoughts out to use during Tina's wedding, the whole pile of them fell down on top of my head. I walked around all spring going, "What? What?"

"Judy, have you seen the bill of lading for the concrete mix?"
"What?"

"Judy, Curtis and I are going to tee-ball practice now."
"What?"

"Judy! Phone! Judy! Door! Judy! Man here to see you!"
"Huh?"

It's a good thing Curtis was so crazy about hiding Easter eggs. Curtis found out about Easter eggs at nursery school. He knew about them before, but I had managed to convey the impression on previous Easters that hiding them was something whole families did for one afternoon a year. In nursery school he learned that other children hid eggs for weeks before Easter, that other mothers hid eggs for their

41

children, that eggs could be hidden before breakfast and in the rain. I don't know what I pay those nursery people for. The child barely knows his letters.

However, the Easter eggs really saved me because they gave me a good excuse to sit outside and do nothing. I made this big deal about how important it was for a working mother to spend time with her kid, and I skipped out of work and hid Easter eggs instead. Curtis and I would zoom home, shove open the front door, rush for the electric skillet and the television set. I'd brown some chicken and throw on some rice, while Curtis sucked his thumb and watched *Sesame Street*. Then we'd let Reddie out and walk down to the pond. It's only a couple of hundred yards from the trailer, along a rutted dirt road through pine trees. Then the road widens into a clearing, which consists of a marshy creek at one corner, and the concrete slab we poured for our house at the other. Reddie and Curtis would be there before me, would have circled the pond, checked out the little rowboat, frightened off lurking squirrels, rabbits, deer. Reddie is a young golden retriever who believes Curtis is her puppy.

We used plastic eggs, and we had a certain routine. I always hid the eggs on one side of the clearing while Curtis and Reddie played on the other. Then I held Reddie while Curtis looked. Since I always hid the eggs in the same places, and Curtis always peeked, he was a pretty good finder. But lacking patience, he always missed a few. They would be for Reddie, quivering beside me, sticking out the tip of her pink tongue, jerking her head down in silent urging as she watched Curtis dash around the pond.

"Ollie ollie oxin free!" Curtis would shout, running and swinging his basket. "Ollie ollie oxin free!"

I'd let Reddie go. She'd race over and bounce in front of Curtis, then make a big show of pointing out the eggs he'd missed—sniff the hollow log where a big frog lived, the little bridge over the marsh, a

42

daffodil clump beside my fishing bench, the stiff grass near the boat. Dash and sniff, freeze and point, like a picture of a dog. If Curtis did not obey her and come up immediately when she pointed, she called him with one stiff bark. And when he got to her, she'd look at him out of the sides of her eyes, look from the egg to Curtis, Curtis to the egg, imploringly, until he got it. Then she'd lick his hand.

It was a great routine.

At first I tried accomplishing something between hiding sessions, but I soon gave it up. Watching a child is like playing baseball; you spend a lot of your time standing around squinting into the sun, but when you move, you gotta move fast. And you can't do it right and cross-stitch, too. So I crouched on the slab like a catcher, waiting for mistakes.

Hamp and I thought we were being so smart when we bought that pond. The natural life, we thought—fishing every afternoon, a little rowboat, long evenings listening to the crickets chirp. We completely forgot about drowning, water moccasins, and fish hooks in the toes. When we imagined children, we sort of skipped over the early years and went straight to the eights and nines. What did we know? We were in an ecstasy of reproduction. We figured there would be a few diapers, a carriage, and then voila!—campouts and baseball.

Just goes to show you how ignorant an adult can be. People really have no idea. I had no idea.

"Just wait until you have children yourself," said my mom, darkly. "Then you'll understand."

So now I understand.

"Be careful," I say to Curtis. "Didn't you see that ditch? Don't you look where you are going? Never stick your hand in a hollow log. Don't go up to strange people like that. How many times do I have to tell you?"

Curtis closes his eyes against the sound of my words, beating time with his arm or foot until he can wiggle away.

He is capable of trying absolutely anything. If it occurs to him, he will do it.

"Curtis," I can say, "don't play in the creek in your good clothes."

"Yes ma'am," he will say.

Then he will go out, strip naked, and play in the creek under the impression that he is doing exactly the right thing. He has broken his arm and fallen twice into water over his head. He will cross a street without looking in either direction if he sees something he wants on the other side. So I tend to hover. At first it's boring, like being tamped down, having to be still and vigilant at the same time. A sentinel. Then you get into it. You wait for the sun to warm your back, scratch in the dirt with a stick, poke pine needles into ant hills. You become a lizard. You sit and wait for something to buzz by across the hot air, all unsuspecting, and then snap! You grab it.

■ —— ■

By Easter, Mom had calmed down. She and Lucy Hooper now chatted on the phone, called each other "Dear." It was a temporary alliance, but one based on real trust.

Mom had the wedding organized and kept her notes and files on a card table in her den. She and I spent hours at that table while Hamp and Dad watched the Braves play baseball on the television across the room.

"I don't know," Mom said once. We were addressing invitations. "I guess Tina and Jimmy really do mean to go through with this. They seem to suit each other. God knows what will happen to them."

"Now Edna," said Dad tentatively. He kept one eye on the television screen.

"No, Bob, I really wonder," she said. She leaned forward, tapping her pen against her palm. "You're the hard-headed one, Judy." She looked at me accusingly. "Tina Lee was always—she knew what she wanted, but her judgment was mature. She has always been willing to plan and wait for what she wants."

"I can plan," I said.

"You *can*," said Mom. "You are able, but you do not. That's all right. You'll learn."

"When?" I said. "Will I get an appointment book and everything?"

"Oh, don't be silly," Mom said. "You're creative, impulsive. Though actually you could use an appointment book. You'll rein in. Like your father."

I looked over at my father.

"Jesus Christ!" he said, slapping his chair arm. "Did you see that? Is the man blind? Look at that replay."

"He certainly looks reined in," I said. "I had an appointment book, but I lost it."

Mom ignored me.

"Tina Lee is a planner," Mom continued. "Organized. Single-minded. And Jimmy is so—"

"Focused."

"Exactly."

"You might say, narrow."

"Oh, he's all right," said Dad. There was a commercial on. "Says he's going to law school. Good to have a lawyer in the family. Right, Hamp?"

"Get all our wills free," said Hamp.

"Very funny," I said.

"He apparently loves her very much," Mom nodded. "And Jimmy is a strong, capable boy."

She looked at me wide-eyed, with a little shrug.

"Sure enough," I said.

"Well, I guess the best thing I can do—," she gathered up a handful of addressed envelopes and handed them to me to stuff, "is shut up about it."

"I think that's best," said Dad. "Considering."

"I know you do," said Mom.

The Braves were up, and Dad barely took his eyes off the television set. He spoke with a kind of impatient sigh, like, thank God she's not going to talk longer. If Hamp had done that, I'd have gotten up and left the room, muttering and slamming at least one door on my way down the hall. But Mom didn't seem to care. She just looked at the wall a minute, picked up her pen, and checked off another name.

"If anybody can make it work, I believe Jimmy can," she said to me.

"Yes ma'am," I said.

Easter weekend Tina came home alone. Jimmy stayed at school. We were all relieved to have her back among us again, really among us, not filtered through Jimmy. She sat in the den and read an early childhood development textbook, made another chart of the bridesmaids, little circles with X's through them, and squares for the pulpit and the communion table.

"How about if you stand a little closer to Helen?" she said. "Or would that unbalance that whole side?"

"I don't know why you asked Helen to be in your wedding in the first place," I said. "It's not like you're still close or anything."

"She has been my friend since I was in kindergarten. We used to plan our weddings together in chemistry class. And we go to the same college, and we're still friendly even though—," she shrugged. "I don't know. I just wanted to."

"She has never liked me."

"That's not true."

"Yes it is, and you know it. In elementary school she didn't like me. I think she was always jealous that I was your sister and she wasn't. But I admire your loyalty. That's one thing about you, Tina Lee."

"Then will you stand closer to her at the communion rail?"

"Have you read this chapter yet?" I said. "It says here that four-year-olds are supposed to know their letters. It says some of them can read."

"Curtis is very bright, Judy."

"He can't read. Maybe he's dyslexic."

"Will you look at this chart?"

"Have you seen any dyslexic children in your school?"

Tina was practice teaching.

"Yes. Curtis is not dyslexic, Judy. He does not have any learning problem, or any problem at all except a paranoid mother. Will you pay attention to this chart?"

■ —— ■

Saturday morning Tina and Hamp took Curtis out for breakfast, and I cleaned house. I was actually grateful. You live a certain way with a child, crayon marks, yogurt stains, old mail and odd socks, and after awhile you get used to it. You adjust. Then a visitor like your sister comes to the door, with her manicure, and her creamy blouse and creamy skin, and a little silver cross lying on its chain in the hollow between her collar bones.

"Oh," she says. "Please don't pick up. I don't mind. I'll just sit right here."

And you have to look at your house as she is looking at it, and even though you know she really doesn't mind, you feel bad. The plastic cereal bowls perched on a bed of yesterday's newspapers look suddenly tawdry, and you notice the dust on the window sills. As you clean, you feel better. The house will always be clean after this, you think. After this, it will simply be a matter of keeping it straight.

I was still cleaning when they got home.

"So quit that and come shopping," said Tina. "I need company."

"Okay," I said and left the vacuum in the hall.

"You need some new lipstick," Tina said. "You need some new shoes. No, we are not going to buy little-boy clothes. You need some new silver earrings. Try this. No, this."

She studied me critically, put me through my paces. It bothered

47

her that I had grown soft and dull witted, didn't keep up with the styles. She prodded me as one would poke a snail, to make me get up and go on. Go on through my life and get it right.

For my part, I was smug. Tina too would gain five pounds and worry about it, obsess over dyslexia and tetanus shots, break her fingernails refinishing a chest of drawers. And so what?

But that wasn't all of it. An undercurrent of uncertainty that had not been there before I married and had a child ran through my days. Now I had to take others into account. It wasn't just my house, my life.

"Family life is messy, Tina Lee," I told her. "Messier than you think."

"How do you mean?"

We were rummaging through the sale racks in a department store.

"All the other people you live with have their own ideas," I said. "You have to compromise and forgive, live with decisions and situations you don't really like because—"

"Because why?"

"I forget. Because you're married. You're part of a family. Like the trailer. I think it's time we moved, I really do, but—"

"So move. Insist on moving. You know Hamp will go along, if you just put your foot down."

"It's not that simple." I held up a shirt I had found. "How do you like this?"

"How do *you* like it?" she said. "It is that simple, Judy. Suit yourself. Live for yourself. You can't *not* be yourself just because you're married. I see you doing that. I see you wimping around, deferring to Hamp about this and that when I know you ain't made that way, girl. You are bossy as hell. And it scares me. Mom says she doesn't understand what's gotten into you. That time your car was broken and you bummed rides from people for two months before you got it fixed because Hamp told you to wait. *Because* he told you to."

"It was a joint decision. We were saving money."

48

She just looked at me.

"All right," I said. "I was wrong about that. But that's what I'm saying, Tina. There's lots to be wrong about. I've screwed up lots of times. Given too much, given too little. What do you do, insist on your way all the time? Half the time? When I compromise, you and Mom have a fit. You think I'm a wimp. When Hamp compromises, his mother and all his friends probably think the same thing."

Tina took the blouse out of my hand and hung it back on the rack.

"The point being, when has Hamp *ever* compromised?" she said. Women swirled around us in the aisle of the department store.

"Give me time," I said finally. "I just can't think of any occasion right now."

"Look," Tina said. "I'm just saying, live for yourself a little. Don't give over so much. Suit yourself. Your old self. My sister. I know you're in there somewhere." She pointed to the mirror on the wall in front of us. I looked at myself.

"Oh, *that* self," I said. "That self wouldn't even be in this tacky place looking at the sale rack. That self would be over at the underwear shop, buying some of that useless and expensive lace stuff."

"Then let's go," she said.

Tina worked hard to keep me straight, to make me keep my act together, prodding, questioning, and tallying as we went. I never minded. She worked even harder on her own act. I did not even dream then how much of an act it was.

We all went to church and sat together on Sunday morning— heavy, exultant Easter—church full, sanctuary full of flowers and the smell of flowers, hats, perfume, everyone muttering, praying, folding back the bulletin, the congregation standing and sitting with a rustle and a rushing heavy sigh, like a breath of God.

Another Lent done. Easter bunny come. The family together again. I sat there and actually felt it to be important. Remember this, remember this, I said. Let us pray. For those of us who . . . Look: the light through the windows, wine-dark rug, smooth black seat against the back of your knees, Hamp's knuckles resting on his thigh, the small, round bone of Tina's wrist, Bob and Edna congenial on the other side, Mom barely breathing, eyes barely closed, Dad leaning forward like the preacher, forearms on knees. Praying for what? His lips moved. The fullness thereof, amen, amen.

Then we went to my parents' for Sunday dinner. My parents live in a big, white, rambling ranch house built in the sixties. They have about twenty-five acres, mostly woods, and a huge yard studded with oak trees, azaleas, flower beds, and a garden, fenced off to keep the deer out. It is Easter egg heaven.

We lined up in the sun. Dad took videos. Hamp took snapshots.

"Over here, Curtis, beside the azaleas."

"—get the other lens—"

"Come on, Edna! We're waiting!"

"—like you're picking up an egg, son. Just—"

"—the year it snowed? Remember?"

"Edna!"

"—and the time Mom dressed us both in those dippy pinafores?"

"Don't pick your nose, son."

"Edna! Goddamn it, Judy, go tell your mother—"

■ —— ■

We ate in the dining room. We used the best white tablecloth, the best napkins, and the high company china that has to be washed by hand. In the center of the table sat the collection of miniature rabbits in paper grass that always decorated the Easter table, and the real boiled eggs, nestled in little straw baskets.

It was Tina's last holiday at home. We would never do this again. The china bunnies would be back, but the real family would change, shift. Jimmy would be a new permutation; there would be more children. Tina and I would not be the children here anymore. Things were tilting, sliding around.

Curtis said the blessing, slowly and with accents.

". . . and we *thank* him for our *food*. A - *men*."

"Very well done, darling!"

"So sweet."

The food began its way around the table, clatter and scraping of spoons.

"Well, Curtis!" said my dad, helping himself to ham. "You say the Easter Bunny did pretty good by you this year."

"All right." Curtis twisted his knife. He was trying to make it stand on its blade.

"I see you got that nice stuffed bunny there, and what else?"

The bunny sat on a chair beside him, wearing a hat and blue jacket. Curtis picked it up and hugged it.

"Teresa says there is no Easter bunny," he said, rubbing its head with his fingers, tweaking its nose. "She says it's your parents."

"Shoot," said my dad. "You think your mom could afford a nice bunny like that?"

"Yes," said Curtis. "She has lots of money."

"Have some broccoli, Curtis," I said. "You can use your fingers."

Curtis put down the rabbit to pick up his broccoli.

"Teresa says real bunnies can't carry baskets," he said.

"Who is this Teresa person?" said Hamp, helping himself to scalloped potatoes. "And how did she get to be such an authority anyway?"

"In Sunday School," said Curtis.

"Well, she doesn't know anything," said Hamp. "Your mother may buy you something or not, I don't know. But I can tell you that the Easter Bunny is real, because when I was a little boy, I saw him."

We all looked at him. He buttered his roll.

"You did not," said Curtis.

"Oh yes," said Hamp. "I certainly did." He ate a piece of ham,

51

chewed thoughtfully. "Wonderful ham, Miss Edna," he said.

"Well?" said Tina, sitting beside him. "What did he look like?"

"Who?" said Hamp.

Tina punched him.

"The Easter Bunny," she said.

"Was he big?" said Curtis. "Did he have a blue coat? Teresa said rabbits don't wear clothes."

"Generally they don't," said Hamp. "This one did. I saw him on Easter morning when I was five. I woke up early, just like you always do, and I ran out to the kitchen pantry to see what he'd left me—"

"The pantry!"

"Because that's where he left my basket. In the pantry."

"Oh."

"And my mother, Nana Marie, was standing at the sink, and she saw me, and she whispered, 'Oh, Hamp! Go back to bed! It's early, and the Easter bunny isn't through delivering baskets.' And she sort of cut her eyes around, you know, and gestured at the pantry, like he was still in there. Like at that very moment the Easter bunny was in my house."

"I'da caught him!" said Curtis. "I'da rushed in and closed the door on him, like Nana Marie did the mouse!"

"Oh no," said Hamp. "No no no. Not the Easter Bunny. If he even thinks you see him, he might never come back."

Curtis hugged his bunny.

"So I went back to bed," said Hamp. "I tiptoed. And I got in the bed and closed my eyes and waited. And when I was sure he was gone, I got back up again."

"How long did you stay in bed?" said Tina Lee.

"Seemed like an hour. Looking back on it, I'd say, a minute-and-a-half. And then I got up again, tiptoed back out through the living room, the dining room, slowly, slowly, listening, listening, until I got to the kitchen door. And just as I got there, I heard a sort of rustle and a scramble and a little thump, and I looked up and there he was, going out the back screen door. I saw his flank and his tail, and just a piece of a blue coat. The screen door slammed, and I went into the pantry and got my basket. It had purple paper around it, and a chocolate egg."

Hamp took a mouthful of potatoes.

"Wow," said Curtis.

"What color was the Easter bunny?" said Tina Lee.

"White," said Hamp. "What do you think?"

"And he was big," said Curtis.

"Oh yes," said Hamp.

"That Teresa!" said Curtis. "Old dumb."

"You tell her your daddy said," I said. "Here, let me cut your meat."

I was doing that, and Mom had begun asking Tina something about the wedding when I heard a chair scrape.

"I don't know!" Tina said. "I don't know if I even want to get married. I don't even know that." She looked around. Her face was pinched, pale. She began pulling the white center out of her roll. "The whole thing is just feeling kinda weird, is all."

"Well, then," said Mom, "you're tired."

"I mean I love Jimmy, I really do." Tina threw bits of roll at Hamp.

"Glad to hear it," said Hamp. "Why are you throwing food at me?"

"Because I feel like it," said Tina. Her voice broke; her eyes filled with tears. She pressed her palms to her face, got up and left the room.

"What did I say?" said Hamp.

"What did you *do*?" I said.

Hamp stared at me.

"Not a goddamned thing," he said flatly.

"Did I hear Tina say she wasn't getting married?" said Dad.

"She said she didn't know," I said.

53

"Excuse me," said Mom. "Will you get the cake, Judy?" And she went out, too.

"Did I miss something?" said Dad.

"Can I have cake now?" said Curtis.

■ —— ■

Every week my cousin Elizabeth calls me from Atlanta.

"How long has Jimmy had possession of the trailer?" she says.

"Let's see," I say. "Since September. It's been a couple of weeks now. But I told him he can have it as long as he likes."

"Are you giving it to him?" she says. "Or is it a loan?"

The phone crackles. In my mind I see Elizabeth in her office, leaning on her desk, listening for my reply.

"I guess a loan. I'll probably sell it eventually."

"You have title, then," she says. "You might just mention to your insurance person, and your tax person—"

I write it down on my calendar. "Insurance. Taxes. Trailer." The page is already full of tense little messages.

"To tell you the truth," I say, "I'm cutting this window, and the plastic cover over the hole worked loose, and there's this dirt all over my desk. I feel like I'm working in the Dust Bowl. A slight exaggeration. Metaphorical effect. But you get the picture. I'm afraid it's going to be Halloween before I get it fixed. Plus it's getting chilly in here now. About the trailer, I hadn't really thought about it."

"Well, honey," says Elizabeth in her lawyer voice, "I'd think about it."

"I know," I say. "I need to do that."

I put an exclamation mark after "Trailer."

"So is my godson sleeping through the night yet?" I say.

"Oh hell no," she says.

We talk about babies for awhile. After she hangs up, I call the tax people. I almost always listen to Elizabeth. She almost always listens to me. A line stretches between us, stronger than the phone. As children we could almost read each other's minds. We guessed each other's hands at cards. We loved cards, Parcheesi, and duets on the piano, but we could only play inside when it rained. Otherwise it was, "Go on outside, girls, and get some fresh air. Can't stay cooped up in the house all afternoon."

■ —— ■

Elizabeth came over on Easter, after Tina said she wasn't getting married. She drove up after Sunday dinner with her mother, Aunt Bessie, in the Cadillac, Bessie barely visible behind the wheel. It was essentially the same as all their other Sunday visits for twenty-five years, the same as when we were children, the top layer of a thick sediment of time spent together. Seeing them was like wading into a river, part the pull of flowing water, part holding rock, the heaviness of mud.

"Whew!" Bessie would always say, stretching out her neck. "Hot!" or "Too cold for me!" Then, "How you doing, Judy honey? You girls get those apples out the back for me, please." Or peaches, or clothes.

I went out to meet them, to tell them about Tina's latest thoughts on her wedding. Bessie gave me a fluttering hug.

This time it was rose cuttings.

"Get those rose cuttings out the back for me, please, I brought your daddy some from the old Suiter place. Mind now, don't scratch yourself. Just lay 'em right down on the step there." She picked some lint off my arm. "And I wouldn't worry too much about Tina Lee, honey. You know she's always going on about something. I told Sister, I b'lieve she's a little hysterical."

Bessie is Mom's sister, a rounded, whitened version, like a biscuit, a flour sack, without pores. She is finely milled. Elizabeth looks like that, too—wispy, brown-blonde hair, an open, happy face, sturdy body with no particular grace until she smiles. Easter, she was very pregnant. She heaved herself out of the car.

"Oh God," Elizabeth said. She let herself down on the back steps. "I feel like an atomic bomb."

Aunt Bessie studied her daughter's belly.

"I think you're retaining water." She turned to me, bobbing. "I told her. 'Biddy,' I said, 'you better get yourself on back to Atlanta and stay there, because you're going to get no peace until this baby comes now'."

"It's not due for another month, mother."

"Honey, babies can't count. And I had four, and I can tell you this one's ripe." Bessie went on up the steps and into the house. I sat down beside Elizabeth.

"Ripe!" she said. "Did you get that? Like a melon." She thumped herself. "So is Tina serious or what?"

"Who can tell?" I said. "Your mom's right. 'Hysterical' is the word. She sat at the dining room table and threw bread crumbs at my husband. 'I don't know if I want to get married,' she said. 'I love Jimmy,' she said. And Hamp said, 'Why are you throwing bread crumbs at me?' and she said, 'Because I want to'."

"Wonder if she still has a thing for Hamp," Elizabeth said. "When was that? That was in high school, wasn't it?"

"The summer before her senior year. She went to Columbia for a leadership training thing. Enrichment. Hamp was one of the counselors. That was how we met, through Tina."

"She was ticked about that at the time, as I recollect."

"She didn't speak to me for about a month. 'Hello, Tina.' Slam! 'I'm home, Tina.' Slam! She had a crush on him. That's all. That Christmas she got secretly pinned to Jimmy and has lived her life around him ever since. I mean, she dated him all through high school anyway. But every once in a while, she feels like reminding us all that she and Hamp have a special relationship. It's like he owes her. And when she's upset, she calls him up. Not me. He's her counselor. Not me. About certain things. Sometimes I think it's re-

56

ally sweet. Sometimes it pisses me off. Mostly I don't care one way or the other."

Elizabeth opened a cloth bag and pulled out a small white quilt top and a needle. Rows of appliquéd blue sailors alternated with yellow sailboats. She was on the last sailor. Her hands flowed around the little blue man, tacking him down, smoothing him out. She made it look easy.

"Well, Hamp has certainly settled down, that's for sure," she said. "Remember that girl? What was her name? Gina. Hamp took her to that dance at my school and I saw him, and I called you."

"And I came up there the next weekend to spy on her. God, that was embarrassing."

"And we used to call people, trying to find out things about her and Hamp."

"And I was so miserable I thought I'd die. And finally I told Hamp about it, and he said she was just a blind date for a cousin of his, and he couldn't stand her."

The thread lay pliant in Elizabeth's boxy hands, needle pushing just to the edge of one calloused finger, then diving into the little man again.

"I've always wondered about that," she said. "Not, of course, that it matters anymore."

"No," I said. "Not that it does."

I watched her sew for awhile.

"So tell me," I said. "How are you really? Really."

Sometimes Elizabeth and I meet only in the present; sometimes we break through the crust. Now her eyes shifted, turned. She looked at me, but her thoughts traveled down to that dark future child resting beneath her breasts. I could see him in her eyes, turning, turning in his warm, wet sac. Hello baby.

■ —— ■

Peter, Elizabeth's husband, was not along. He, like the other men in Elizabeth's family, her father and brothers, often skipped ordinary family visits and worked or napped before the Sunday drive back to Atlanta. When Peter did come, he and Hamp talked as people do who are obliged to get along, jovially and with no pleasure. When Peter didn't come, Elizabeth and I talked about ourselves. Hamp could talk, too. He does wear well, and he's known us long and long.

"Got your pillow packed?" he said to Elizabeth. "Doing your breathing?"

He hissed at her in a Lamaze pant, and she joined him, puffing out her cheeks and panting, then leaning back and laughing at herself.

"You got to get it right, Miss Lizbet," he said. "Can't have none of that foolishness in the birthin' room."

We told birthing stories.

"Nobody would listen to me," I said. "I kept saying things like, 'Hey guys, something is happening here,' and they all patted my arm and said no, two centimeters and three centimeters, and don't eat that ice, and stuff like that, and going back out in the hall. Finally I said, 'Hamp, the baby is coming now. If you don't want to deliver it yourself, you'd better get somebody in here.' So he did. He got the nurse, the resident, and a man who was mopping the floor. And the baby came."

"Curtis was born in about fifteen minutes," said Hamp. "And Judy got him settled in his blankets and then sat up and cussed out everybody in the whole damn hospital. I mean she had little pitiful student nurses running away in tears."

"Tell me I don't know I'm having a baby," I said. "You weren't any better. You lifted that resident clean up off the floor. His feet were just pumping."

"He was a jerk."

"It was his first baby, too."

"He was still a jerk."

"This is all so reassuring," said Elizabeth.

"Oh, it's great," said Hamp. "It changes your life."

"Does Lamaze do any good at all?" Elizabeth said. "Peter bought a stopwatch. But I think he's nervous."

"Nothing I have ever done has meant more to me," said Hamp.

Like Mom and Dad, we had a routine, a Gracie and George routine. I read in a magazine that George Burns once said he couldn't stand it after Gracie died, it just drove him crazy lying hour after hour awake in his bed, looking over at the bed she'd slept in, until finally one night he got up and moved over to her bed and slept there. And then he slept better.

■ —— ■

"I've got Tina's present in the car," said Elizabeth. "You reckon she wants it?"

"I don't know," I said.

"Sure she wants it," said Hamp.

"Do you know something we don't?" I said. "You've been talking to her."

"Look," said Hamp. "Have you ever known Tina Lee not to want to marry Jimmy?"

"There was Eddie Beck," said Elizabeth. "In ninth grade. And of course you."

"But after that it was always Jimmy," I said.

"Exactly," said Hamp. "And she's been planning her wedding ever since. She wants this. And what Miss Tina wants—"

We joined in the chorus. "Miss Tina gets."

"Then like I told you," said Hamp. "No sweat."

"Sounds like Princess Pet," said Elizabeth.

■ —— ■

That was a game the three of us played as children: Princess Pet. I

59

invented it, and I made Tina the princess. When Tina was a baby, she was like a doll, tiny and blonde, and she'd sit and stare at me like she was memorizing my face. I adored her. I brushed her hair, took her for walks, taught her to spit and find roly-polies and play dress-up. She trusted me. She'd put her little hand in mine and look up at me and smile. I named her Princess Pet, wrapped her in Mom's old peignoir, and threw apple blossoms in her path. She was regal, too, a tiny regal girl. I paid obeisance. "Here comes Princess Pet! All bow down to Princess Pet!"

The trouble was, Tina never got tired of playing Princess Pet. The cute two-year-old toddling across the grass became the imperious four-year-old, the demanding six-year-old. And for the longest time, the game had to be played a certain way. When Elizabeth came over and we wanted to climb trees or play cowboys or cards, there would be Tina. "Mama said you had to take me, too. Mama said! I'll tell Mama!" There she was, in the center of our time together, plumped right down and fussing. Oh, it was agonizing having a sister, sharing your life, your time, your friend.

■ ——— ■

Elizabeth and Hamp and I were in the garage getting down some things for Elizabeth. The garage has no cars in it; it is used for odds and ends. The stuff we wanted was stored, along with other possessions, on planking laid across the crossbeams that made a loft. Hamp climbed the ladder.

"What the—" Mutter, mutter.

"What's the matter, Hamp?"

"Somebody has put boxes all over the goddamn floor up here, and I can't—"

"Gosh," I said. "Wonder who could have done that."

There was the sound of shoved and falling boxes. Hamp appeared above us, straddling the rafters, reading a box. "Baby clothes."

60

"That's them."

He disappeared. "There are maybe a dozen marked 'Baby'."

"Hand us the dustiest ones first."

Elizabeth and I pulled chairs out into the driveway to catch the sun.

"Oh, here's that backpack thing. Do you have one of those yet? And cloth diapers. You must take those. Not that you'll use them, but they make nice dust cloths."

When Tina came out, she looked fine. She had on her new-teacher jumper and her bright pink shoes, and her bright pink smile.

"I'm so glad to see you!" she said to Elizabeth. "And how's Atlanta? How's Peter?" She used her beauty-queen voice.

"Tina," I said, "are you still getting married, because if you are, Elizabeth has an enormous present for you in her mama's back seat, and if you aren't, we are dying to be on your side and think bad things about Jimmy."

"Of course I'm getting married," said Tina.

"Of course she's getting married," said Elizabeth to me. "What's your problem, Judy?"

"Gosh," I said. "I have no idea."

Hamp went back up the ladder to get the crib. Tina followed him. "I'll help," she said.

"Stay down there," he said. "I'll hand it down to you."

"No," she said. "I'll help."

Elizabeth still sat in the sun. I stood in the door, watching the easy way Hamp balanced, walking the beams.

"Careful!" I said.

He smiled. "Come get this, Judy, will you?" He handed down a crib side. Tina walked out behind him, carrying another side. She stood over the open section of the loft and rested the crib on a beam. Hamp reached for it. As he did, it rocked and threw them both off balance. Tina fell forward through the open rafters, taking the crib with her. Hamp caught her. He reached down and grabbed her arm

61

as it went by and held her, dangling, while the crib clattered to the concrete floor below. Tina hung absurdly by one arm, straight down like a broken doll, yelling. Hamp's fingers were white and strained against her skin. I put my hands up and grabbed her legs, braced myself, took her weight as he lowered her into my arms. Hamp swung himself down.

"Jesus!" We all leaned on each other in relief.

The garage filled up with people.

"I've never seen anything like that," said Elizabeth. "He caught her in midair, like a circus act. Guys, you ought to go on the road."

"Oh, your poor hand!" I said.

Hamp's fingers were raw and splintery where he had grabbed a beam; we all gathered and stared.

"Poor baby," I said, hugging him.

"Poor Hamps," said Tina, hugging him.

Curtis squeezed between us to get part of the hug.

"Everything's fine," we all said. "We are fine."

"Easter eggs," said Curtis. "It's time. You said."

■ —— ■

The sun was warm in the side yard, the grass still soft and bright. I hid most of the eggs in clumps of daffodils, or against the roots of trees, the same spots where I found them as a child. The daffodil leaves were spongy, resilient, and cold, the azalea bushes bowed down with blossoms. I stood and watched Curtis picking up eggs, watched my family sitting on the steps across the yard, my folks, Hamp with his hand bandaged, Elizabeth and her mom. Tina sat in the center, unwrapped her present—outer paper, box top, tissue paper. She held it up. China. Cheers, applause. Hugs. Dispersal. Dad and the sisters gathered up the rose cuttings, went off to plant them, their words floating like blown dandelions across the grass.

"—like I told Fred, with nobody living there, poor old Mrs. Suiter dead, and that trifling grandson, and her lovely arbor—"

"—sin and a shame—"

"—just heel them in today—"

■ —— ■

Later we gathered at the swing set under the big oak tree in the back yard.

"So are you ready for a wedding?" Elizabeth asked Tina.

"Yes and no." Tina was swinging, her dress blowing out under her knees. She swung past us, back and forth, stretching her feet up, then doubling them under her and pumping back.

Elizabeth and I looked at each other. Elizabeth sat in a swing beside Tina; Hamp and I were draped on the slide. Curtis dashed back and forth across the yard hiding Easter eggs.

"We were talking about your old boyfriend Eddie Beck," said Elizabeth. "Whatever happened to him anyway?"

"He grew up," said Tina. "He got bony wrists and little curly hairs on his legs, and he joined the army last year right out of Carolina."

Tina walked herself to a stop.

"I really am going to marry Jimmy," she said. "Stop treating me like some kind of weird person. A person can cry. It's allowed. It's going to be a great wedding."

"A gaggle of bridesmaids," said Hamp. "A mess of presents, a truckload of champagne, and enough shrimp to choke a school of dolphins."

"I'm only going to do this once," said Tina. "I mean to get it right."

"I'm sure it will all be lovely," said Elizabeth.

Tina backed herself up until the swing was taut and propped herself there.

"Sometimes I just feel like pouting," she said. "I know you guys never do, but I do." She lifted her foot and started swinging again, but not as high as before. "How long does it take to *feel* married?"

"A week maybe?" said Elizabeth.

"A month," said Hamp.

"A year," I said.

"Maybe never," said Elizabeth. "Depending on what you mean."

Curtis ran toward us, waving his arms.

"Ollie ollie oxin free!" he shouted.

Tina left the swing, ran across the yard to Curtis, feinting and dancing. They began to chase each other.

"Ollie ollie oxin free!" they yelled, like a chant.

■ —— ■

After Elizabeth and her mother left, I stood at the garden fence and watched Hamp plow for awhile. He sat on the tractor in his good clothes, Curtis in his lap, wrapped in the monotonous roar of the machine, etching the measured rows, leaving a rich foam of turned-up earth in his wake. At the end of the row, Hamp jerked the wheel around, and they roared impassively back. I left them and walked out toward the apple trees at the edge of the lawn. The ground was too cold for sandals, too cold for spring. At dusk a chill hovered, swirling around my feet. The apple trees were in bloom, drifting white.

I climbed a tree and sat, the damp bark biting into the backs of my thighs. Tina was in the swing again, winding herself up in her rope and twirling, balancing on one foot, her bright pink leather toe turning, making a little intent circle in the dust beneath the swing.

Three

3

I WAS GIVING THE BRIDESMAIDS' LUNCHEON. I said I'd do it. I insisted.

"Are you sure?" said Tina. "Really? Really?"

"I'm sure," I said. "How many sisters do I have?"

Even as I said it, I had that heavy, committed feeling, that lead weight in the gut. Something in me sighed, scrabbled to get away. I nailed myself down.

"No problem," I said. "I'll have it at the country club."

Then the luncheon sat on the landscape of my days, a white canvas lump as big as a mountain. "Wait," I said to it, "not yet," because I knew that once I started up that mountain there'd be no coming down for awhile. Secretly I began to reconnoiter, to think about invitations and a color scheme, and one day I found myself already climbing, stone and roses. So I called my cousin Charley who manages the country club.

The country club is a rustic looking stone place built in the thirties, with a big dance floor and bar that overlook the pool and the golf course. It's a WPA project, no big deal but nice. It has the scruffy look and feel of a club where the members don't want to impress anybody; they just want to play golf and give their kids a place to swim. Charley is in and out, and weekends and summers a couple of high school kids run a canteen.

The day Charley and I met over there to plan the luncheon, it was raining, a retrograde day, spring going backward. I stood in the main room and fussed, walking around, feet clacking on the wooden floor, staring out at the rain. Nothing fit my luncheon vision, which had been allowed to flourish these many weeks unchecked by a dose of reality. My vision was part bride magazine, part *Architectural Digest*. The club is entirely American Legion. The whole pool side is mostly glass, so there was a lot of rain to look at, flowing in sheets across the eighteenth green and down the fairway.

Charley was tap dancing, muttering a tune, moving back and forth between the main room and the bar, whose floor had a different tone. For emphasis on the downbeat, he rattled the accordion wall which, when closed, separated the two.

"Da da, da pop a dow! Da da, da pop a dow!"

"I won't do it," I said. "I need a different place."

Charley danced backward into the bar, flopped onto a bar stool, and stared at me, waiting, his eyebrows lifted like black ink tents at the top of his face. Charley has straight dark hair and a thin, round-eyed, high-boned face. He looks like a pale Indian. He cocks his head to listen, opens his eyes wide, purses his lips, chatters. He has a big mouth, like me. We have the same lips. He is my cousin and, with Elizabeth, my oldest friend.

"This whole place needs redecorating," I said, fingering the back of a stool. The stools were upholstered in green plastic. So were the chairs at the tables that overlooked the pool. The room smelled of chlorine and beer.

"So what else is new?" said Charley. "You're on the board. Appropriate some money, and we'll fix it up."

"You know the golf course comes next, Charley. You set that all up yourself, remember?"

"So whatta ya gonna do, Scarlett?" Charley said. "We could fix you up something outdoors. A marquee, like." He drew one in the air.

"On the eighteenth green?"

"In the side yard, stupido. Where I'm gonna put the croquet court."

I stared out at the empty patch of grass. It didn't look very promising.

"Oh, shoot," I said. "I don't know. Same old same old. You know what, Charley? We need to finish one of those back rooms."

Charley laid his head down on the bar.

"Come on," I said. "Let's go look at them."

The back half of the club has a kitchen and bathrooms, an office, and a jumble of half-finished and unfinished spaces used mostly for storage. Every year or two, somebody gets the idea of putting that space to use. The board talks about it, appoints a committee to study the idea. They meet with Charley and talk, measure, figure. Then the pool house gets termites, or the dishwasher collapses, and the money goes to fix that up instead.

We opened the door next to Charley's office and waded in, through floats, rope, broken chairs, and stacks of tables on flats. The interior walls had never been hung; the stone walls were dry and cool, dark like a cellar.

"This is perfect," I said.

Charley picked up a stick and began to rap it against the wall.

I could see the way it should be, the stone, a small amount of wood, white walls, directed light. It should almost grow up out of the ground.

67

"Frank Lloyd Wright," I said. "This is perfect Frank Lloyd Wright."

"I hate it when you get ideas," said Charley.

"Is it wired?"

He pointed, and we looked up at the ceiling fixture, a bare bulb hanging from a drop cord.

"Oh. Is it up to code?"

"Surely you jest." Charley headed back to the door, leaned against the jamb, drumming on his leg with the stick.

"Elimination of the insignificant," I said. "That's what Frank Lloyd Wright wanted. Secret potentiality. Rough structure."

"I'll give you rough," said Charley, tapping on a string of floats.

"Did you notice the hardwood floors? Really, they could get by with buffing."

Charley stopped playing the floats and stared at me.

"You're really going to do this, aren't you?" he said.

"I'll donate the material. Three or four hundred, that's all we'll need."

"Three or four hundred won't begin to cover it, as you know," Charley said. "Have you talked to your daddy about this?"

"How could I? I just this minute thought of it."

"Well, would you do me a big, big favor?" said Charley. "Tell him it was your idea. Tell him I was reluctant, okay? And if you mention it to Hamp, don't even bring me into the conversation at all. Don't say, 'Charley said,' or 'Charley thought it would be a good idea if . . .' Tell him I wasn't here. Okay?"

"Where's your sense of adventure, Charley?" I said.

The family in general has low tolerance for my brainstorms. But Dad thought fixing up the room was a good idea. He said he'd give the materials.

"Clubs could lunch in there," he said. "Might generate some members. Just don't involve me in it, okay? I've got enough to do."

"Have the luncheon in the main room, Judy," Mom said. "Don't put yourself through all that now."

68

But I was determined. I nagged some of the other members into doing some work for free. Barnie Thompson said he'd do the rewiring, and the Cutter twins put in some ducts. And Hamp and I hired Mr. Amos to finish the room. Mr. Amos and I began spending a lot of time together.

"This wall needs to be left plain, Mr. Amos. Bare rock. And the other three wallboarded."

By now the room was empty, Charley and I having spent one whole day carting everything out. Mr. Amos, short and all in white, walked up to the stone and laid his hands on it, leaning.

"Sticks out," he said. He looked at his hands.

"I guess it needs cleaning," I said.

"Needs more than cleaning," he said.

"And we have to figure something about the lights," I said.

Mr. Amos raised his face hopefully to the ceiling.

"Recessed," I said. "Along the tops of the walls."

He blinked, scratched his cheek.

"You paying for this, are you?" he said. "Plus, me'n my brother doing some finishing out over in Demaro, nights. I got a lady promised on her kitchen. She and her family eating outa cartons three weeks now." Mr. Amos sketched a little box with his hands and sighed.

"Maybe not recessed. Maybe mounted flush, a foot from the top, with something angled over them."

"Glass mounts."

"Something long, I was thinking stained wood. An unbroken line, along three walls."

He took out his tape and measured, figured, pressing the keys of a tiny calculator and staring at the results.

"What do you think?" I said.

"Track lights'd be 'bout as cheap," he said.

"Jesus."

69

Mr. Amos shrugged, slipped the calculator and tape into his pocket, folded his fat, peeling fingers into a church steeple.

He was covered all over in a fine, wallboard silt.

"I guess we just better do a regular thing, then," I said. "It's a shame."

I felt Frank Lloyd Wright turning from me in grief.

"Thing to do," said Mr. Amos, inhaling, tapping the steeple fingers against his nose. He walked over to the stone wall. "Mount your lightin' these two walls here. Stone and wallboard. Give you what you looking for. Not all messed up."

"You're right," I said. "But how would you mount it on the rock?"

"Oh," said Mr. Amos. "It'll be a booger." He patted the rock and smiled.

■ —— ■

It was a booger, too. We had to chip away some bits of rock to get the supports for the lights flush.

To save money I did a lot of the work myself. I cleaned the rock, sealed it, buffed the floor. I spent an hour or two over there every morning. Mom loved that.

"What have I done now?" I said.

"You know very well." She started her neck exercises, rolling her head around in a circle. "You've gotten this room in your head, and come hell or high water, you're going to have it, and it's going to be perfect. This architect business. I'm all for it. Go back to school and *be* Frank Lloyd Wright. I just wish you'd waited until after Tina's wedding. And with all the May billing to be done."

"I'm doing the room for Tina's luncheon," I said.

"No," she said. "You are doing the room for yourself. You are no longer thinking in terms of Tina's luncheon."

She began rotating her arms forward.

"I read in a magazine you can dislocate your shoulder doing that," I said.

70

■ —— ■

My friend Diane got excited; she helped me. "What a clever girl you are!" she said. "What an excellent idea!" She talked me through it, painted with me, took my lighting worries seriously. The night before the luncheon, she went over to the club and helped me paint trim, sitting on the floor in shorts and a halter top, long brown legs bent up at impossible angles, jiggling a paintbrush into corners to get them white. Diane has a milky complexion and thick, coarse, black hair that she wears fastened back with silver clips. She runs her hand through her hair, and it looks better than it did before.

"I'm starving," she says. "Let's order a pizza."

Diane is always either starving or stuffed.

"Two salads, two diet drinks, and a large vegetarian pizza. And a . . . what do you have for dessert? . . . one cheesecake and one brownie delight."

"Hamp and Charley are coming."

"And another large pizza."

The first time I saw Diane was at Charley's Christmas party. Charley is famous for the perfection of his parties, especially his Christmas party, for which all the females like to buy a new dress. Diane wore jeans, boots, and a suede cowboy jacket, leaned against the wall, tossed back her hair, talked fast in a western drawl. Made fun of the way we talked.

"You all," she said. "You *all*," drawing it out and smiling. "Come over here, you *all*."

She sang scraps of songs, fiddled with the radio, played with her earrings, rings. She kissed people. She had come east to help out a sick aunt who has a horse farm on Salem Ridge. She had been in McAdamsville a year, teaching riding, teaching school.

"She's just passing through," I told Charley. "Don't get attached."

Charley was already attached. I argued with him.

"She's from New Mexico. Why would anybody from Santa Fe want to live in South Carolina? Get real, Charley."

I did not realize until I met Diane that I considered my town not good enough for some people. But she seemed to like it here.

"Let's go to that farm auction Saturday morning, you *all*," she'd say. "Pick up some of those lovely South Carolina country pieces. Look at this feedbox!" She'd rub off dried chicken droppings. "My God, in California this thing would be five hundred dollars."

She bought feedboxes and old chairs and took them home to her aunt's, got Charley to help her fix them up. Charley collected English antiques. He had bought an old wreck of a house off Main Street and was fixing it up with tea tables and so on. Every time he went somewhere for the weekend, he came back with another horse print or a bit of silver. And Diane came back with a peeling board to make into a coffee table.

She teased Hamp and Charley, and they loved it.

"You guys work all the damn time!" she said. "Let's go to the movies. Let's go out to lunch."

■ —— ■

That night at the country club, she sang them a cowboy song while they worked. We all took turns at the buffer, eating and buffing.

"Could you work on that area in the corner just a little longer?" I said.

"This reminds me of high school," said Charley, "when you were chairman of the senior prom, and it went to your head."

"You were the one who insisted on having a wall of roses, Charley," I said.

"Jesus H. Christ," said Hamp. "Not that Eisenhower High shit again."

"I like it," said Diane.

"It's not bad for the first four or five years," said Hamp. "Then it starts to get old."

72

■ —— ■

"What a good idea this was," said Diane later. She pulled the cheese off a piece of pizza and threw down the crust. "It looks perfect. What else is there to do tonight, besides the rugs?"

We had persuaded Charley to loan us a couple of his small oriental rugs.

"Nothing. Go home. Have a good horse show tomorrow."

"Save me some chicken salad."

Diane was convinced that we served chicken salad at every meal.

"Thank you," I said. "You are all wonderful. I feel bad, you giving up an evening like this."

"No problem," she said. "We enjoyed it. What are friends for? Right, guys?"

For a minute Hamp and Charley looked as if they agreed with her.

"See you at the wedding," said Diane.

■ —— ■

I took the rollers and pans to the kitchen, put them in one of the big metal sinks, and turned on the water. The light in there was really bad; I could hardly see, and the pans clanged and battered together in the sink as I sprayed them clean. I left everything on the drainboard to drip for a minute and walked out the door that led into the main room. I had no premonition of what I would see out there. I was wandering, killing time. There was a vacuum whining in the back room, Charley was cleaning up.

The main room was dark; moonlight fell in through the windows facing the pool, and it lay in streaks across the floor. I walked out into the streaks, using them as stepping stones, thinking of how many dances and parties I'd been to in that room. I had grown up there, formed a vision of life there, indoor dress-up winter life—stiff, crinkly, scratchy dresses and scrubbed-up boys—and summer life, too—

loud music, the bass beating an insistent thump that vibrated bones, and rich, heavy, chlorinated, open-mouthed adolescent, golf-course kisses.

When I was a little girl, I used to watch my parents dance in that room. My mother had a black net dress, long, with a full skirt that swished when she walked, and dangly pearl earrings. She had danced there with Dad and all their friends. They had drunk gin-tonics. That was adulthood to me, to dance on a wooden floor and drink gin-tonics. By the time I was eighteen, nobody drank gin-tonics anymore. I had tried one once anyway. It was bitter. Mom still had the dress.

That night I could almost see my child self on the other side of the windows, looking in, standing among the cold metal tables that stood on the concrete patio, watching my parents dance. Part of me was still out there, the child watching and the girl kissing in the dark. The pool shimmered and sloshed gently, bobbing the floats.

There was a breeze. It fluttered the flag on the eighteenth green. The golf course was patchy, pale. I turned to leave and caught, out of the corner of my eye, movement at the corner of the building. Two people stood in deep shadows that stretched from the building toward the side parking lot. They were just outlines, I could barely see them, but I thought, that must be Hamp and Diane. As I watched, the man put his arms around the woman and kissed her. It was not a brotherly kiss. Her arms were wrapped around his neck like he had just rescued her from drowning. Finally they quit kissing and held each other. Then they stood apart. The man stepped back, touching the woman's face in a gesture of farewell that I knew so well it made me gasp with pain. She turned and disappeared into the darkness towards the parking lot. Hamp stood there with his hands in his pockets and his back to the building, watching her go.

I went back to the painted room. Charley turned off the vacuum, started twisting the cord around the handle. "Looks great, doesn't it? Of course we'll have the tables in here tomorrow. You look beat."

"I am."

"Hamp carried the drop cloths out. He said he'd meet you at the truck." Charley swung the vacuum up and edged past me out of the room. "Go home, Judy. See you tomorrow."

I walked back to the kitchen, picked up the paint rollers and pans, and carried them out to the truck. I threw them into the back. Hamp was sitting in the cab, his face in a shadow.

"I'll follow you home," he said.

I nodded. We didn't have to pick up Curtis. He was spending the night with Mom.

"See you in a minute then," I said.

My voice sounded sort of fake to me, but Hamp apparently didn't notice. He started the truck. I got in my car and started home, the truck's headlights bouncing off my mirror as I rolled down the black-top of the country club drive, turned out onto the highway. The dash lights gleamed; my feet disappeared into inky blackness at the bottom of the car. I felt lonely and absurd. But I was acting normally, doing a normal thing. I hadn't said anything to Charley. I hadn't said anything to Hamp. And I would not say anything to him when we got home.

We passed through the straight flat stretch of bottom land outside town. Pastures floated in the dark, outlined in black streams, black trees. It looked so peaceful I felt like I could just sail off the road and float out into the middle of the grass. I rolled down the window, turned on the radio. The wind felt good. We rode past my parents' house. It sat up on the hill away from the road, windows gleaming through the trees. I tried to pick out Curtis's room. He would be asleep by now, but his light would still be on. He was afraid of the dark.

About a mile-and-a-half beyond my parents', we turned down the dirt road to our trailer. In the yard, I turned off the car and sat there. I didn't know what to do next. The dog was barking and throwing herself against the fence. Hamp got out of the truck, slamming the door with a loud, solid smack.

"Hush, Reddie! Hush, girl."

He walked up under the arc light beside the dog pen, talking to his dog—"Come on, Reddie, come on, girl, supper time"—and filling a bowl out of a fifty-pound sack in the shed beside the pen, scratching the can through the dog food, pouring it into the bowl. "Good girl, Reddie! Sit! SSSSSit!" He set the bowl down on the concrete with a thin clang.

He looked just the same. He stood there in his old knit shirt and painted-splattered pants watching his dog eat, hawk face thrown into relief by the light, our woods dark behind him.

He had touched her face with his fingers, just like he touches mine.

I got out of the car.

■ —— ■

The air conditioner was roaring in the trailer. I dropped my purse in the chair beside the door. Hamp came in behind me.

"Well," he said, and sniffed. He has a way of sniffing that drives me crazy. "I'm beat. Want a beer?" He walked into the kitchen, which is actually a corner of the living room, and opened the refrigerator door.

I couldn't think of what to do next. In my mind, I saw myself walking up to him, grabbing his shirt and shaking him, pushing him away. I saw myself running down the hall, locking the door, and trying to climb out the bedroom window before he broke it down. I saw him kissing Diane. It must have been Diane. Her shadowy outline, arms around Hamp's neck, swam before my vision indistinctly, metamorphosing. Sometimes Diane. Sometimes, unthinkably, my sister Tina Lee.

"You drink too much," I said. "That's the fifth or sixth beer you've had tonight."

He popped the top of a can and took a swallow, wiping his upper lip with his finger.

76

"Are you counting?" he said, and belched. "It was free, remember? Charley bought it to grease my wheels a little." He came around the end of the counter, flopped down on the couch, picked up the TV remote, and switched on the set.

"And did he?"

"Did he what?" He was watching the end of the Braves game.

"Grease your wheels?"

"I reckon." He glanced up, smiled. "You got your room, didn't you?"

"And what did you get?"

"A bellyful of this wedding," he said. "I'll be glad when it's over." I was standing beside him, and he reached up and patted my thigh. "Sit down," he said. "Come sit on the couch with me."

"I'm dirty," I said. "Maybe later."

I went down the hall, balancing one hand on either wall. The brown wood-grained wallboard in our trailer is so thin you can feel it give, vibrate under your hand. You can feel the air behind it. Our bedroom is on the left. I was afraid to lock the door. The bed was unmade, sheets still rumpled from that morning. Hamp makes the bed when he thinks about it, edging his way around the bottom corners, bent over, the room too small. We can barely get around in the bedroom. The bed fills it up. We laughed about that when we bought it, a king-sized bed.

I stepped up onto the bed, walked across it, sinking down with every step, and stepped off into the bathroom, locked myself in. I turned on the shower, began to shake, pulled off my clothes and threw them on the floor, got in and covered my face with the washcloth, shaking, laying my head up against the shower wall, hiding in the roaring water.

Once I took a cruise around the Mediterranean. The ship was wonderful—everything tidy and self-contained, all the edges rounded, smooth—even the handles fit in little grooves. The trailer had been like that when it was new—fascinating and compact. A box. A land boat. An adult tree house. Gradually it became too small. Its furniture was cheap, cheaply made. Things didn't really fit together all that well. The whole place felt hollow and insecure, and the bathroom sank slightly when anyone stepped into the shower. You could feel it rock. Nevertheless, it pleased me. It was precarious. And the water was fierce and hot.

"We want a special nozzle in the master bath."

Instead of a shower, the cruise-ship bathroom had a spray nozzle sticking out of the wall over the sink. Above the nozzle was a metal ring with a shower curtain suspended from it. To take a shower you were supposed to pull the curtain around you like a giant cloak and turn on the nozzle. It didn't work. The water spewed out in a fine, stinking, ineffectual spray, landing everywhere, soaking everything in the room, towels, robe, toothbrushes, mirror, finally dripping onto the floor and sloshing out a drain beside the toilet.

"We want enough hot water."

"Thirty gallons?" said the man.

"Fifty." The corner of Hamp's mouth had twitched.

We had sometimes made love in the shower in his apartment at school, Hamp backed up against the wall and me astraddle him, ankles locked around his hips. The hot water never lasted as long as we did. We finished on the bathroom floor, or hall, or bed, laughing and shaking with lust and cold. In the trailer, hot water poured down over us like a blessing.

Of course we didn't make love in the shower any more.

My heart hurt. It actually hurt. I bent over, sank down in the tub and held onto the rim, drowning.

"I wish I had a sister like you," Diane had said. "Nobody ever gave me a lunch."

When I covered my face, closed my eyes, they were right behind my eyes instead of purple spots. They flickered, jerked across my thoughts. Her leg slid up against his leg. His shoulder tensed, holding.

I noticed I was humming. "Oh, kiss me once, and kiss me twice,

78

and kiss me once again; it's been a long, long time."

I stood up. After awhile I bathed, thinking, My body isn't so bad. There was a little pouch from being pregnant under the tracks left by my waistband. It would not go away. But it wasn't bad. My nipples were too dark, large, wet. I had freckles on my arms.

I got out of the shower. I still didn't know what to do next. It did not seem possible to stay there any longer. But I did not know how to leave. Hamp was like a wall to me now, a wall between me and the light. And yet he was the light. I'll just gather some things together, I thought. Gather myself.

The bathroom was a mess. I hadn't put anything away for days. All my makeup was scattered across the front of the sink. I pretended I was in the *Titanic*. Abandon ship. I picked up my favorite lipstick, comb, and eye shadow and wiped them off, carried them out of the bathroom and laid them on the bed. Then I got two fresh towels, wrapped up in one and spread the other one out. I put my lipstick, comb, and eye shadow on it. I opened drawers and got out my best underpants, my new bra, my favorite sachet. My passport and birth certificate. My scarf from New Orleans. I bunched it all up in the towel, folding the towel in three and then triangles like a flag.

I found my blue nightgown with the spaghetti straps and put it on. Then I noticed Curtis's drawings that I had tacked up on the wall above the bed. I wanted them, too.

"What are you doing?" Hamp was standing in the door.

I stepped down off the bed, drawings in my hand.

"Taking down these pictures."

"At 11:30?"

I smiled, shrugged. We were sinking, weren't we? I felt generous.

I took the pictures and the towel full of stuff into the living room, laid them beside my purse. Went back for the dress and shoes I would need for the luncheon. Hamp was undressing, getting ready to take his shower.

"I'll be along," I said. "I want to pick up the kitchen."

He looked at me from under one arm, taking off his socks, shaking his head, balling up the socks and throwing them toward the dirty clothes hamper.

"Are you all right?" he said.

"I'm tired," I said. "I don't feel good."

From the kitchen, I heard him in the shower, heard his yelp when the hot water went abruptly cold. Heard him coming out, opening the drawer to get his underwear.

"You used all the hot water!" he shouted. "You used all the hot water!" He came on down the hall, stood dripping in the hall, holding his towel. "Judy. There is no hot water!"

I burst into tears.

"Oh, for Christ's sake," said Hamp. "Jesus. It's no big deal."
He tried to put his arm around me, but I backed into a cabinet and swished him away.

"What is the matter with you?" he said.

"Nothing," I said. "I don't feel good."

"Come to bed, honey," he said.

But I didn't. I went into Curtis's bathroom and blew my nose, locked the door softly so he wouldn't hear the lock, stared at myself in the mirror until I heard him get in the bed.

"Judy?" he said. "Come to bed."

"I'll be there in a minute," I said. "I'll take some aspirin."
The bed springs creaked.

A few minutes later he called again. "Judy?"

I went out and stood in the dark beside the bed.

"My head aches," I said. "I'm going to sit up for awhile."

I bent over and touched his back, brushed my lips against his shoulder.

"Goodnight, Hamp," I said.

He put his hand on mine. "Goodnight, baby," he said.

80

I felt like I was saying goodbye. I will just leave now, I thought. I will just leave now and drive away and never come back, never see him again, never see any of them again. That way, I can survive. But I did not leave. I tiptoed out into the living room and sat on the couch, wrapped in an old blanket Curtis had left there. After awhile I lay down, closed my eyes, and thought about lifeboats, how you paddled them and where they went.

Four

4

I SLEPT ON THE COUCH, AND I DIDN'T SLEEP WELL. I kept falling off things in my dreams, bumping awake with a heavy jump, heart racing. I thought I would leave when it got light. I would just drive west. I had credit cards and my own money. I would take Curtis, we would see the country. When we were a thousand miles away, I would call Hamp and say, "Now you can have your girlfriend." Then Curtis and I would find a new life, rent an apartment maybe on a beach or near some mountains. But toward morning I began also to plan my luncheon.

At six o'clock, I got up, put on shorts and a shirt from the pile on the washer, picked up all my stuff from the chair, and went outside the trailer into the early light. The dog was awake too. She nosed her bowl around to make it clatter. She would shove it and then look at me, shove and look, turning her head sideways. Come on, Judy.

"How can you eat at a time like this?" I whispered to her. "I am having this tremendous emotional crisis."

She glanced up apologetically.

"Never mind," I said.

I fed her, scrabbling my hand through the feed because I was afraid of the noise of the cup, rolling the pellets out through my fingers into the bowl. Reddie gobbled the food out of my hand as fast as I got it down to her, slobbering and leaving trails of spit between all my fingers, her pink tongue eager and warm. I patted her, laid my face against her head, held her tag so it wouldn't clang against the bowl.

I love to smell dogs on a chilly morning, watch their noses twitch, feel them snuffle and lick the goose bumps off my calves. Finally I got ahead of Reddie's mouth, filled up her bowl, wiped my hands on a patch of grass. Reddie looked up at me as I let myself out of her pen, her head turned sideways, legs splayed to play. I shushed her and got in the car. At the highway I looked west, to the right. I could be in Memphis or New Orleans by bedtime. My mind sailed ahead of me on down the road, floating, crossing the mountains, crossing the Mississippi, on to Texas, Oregon, Montana. Canada. I could just step out and off, into the abyss of the North American continent, like Lewis and Clark. They were my spiritual ancestors. I had read their adventures as a child thinking, I could do that. And I knew that I could. I had the feel for it. But if I left now, people might think I was dead. They might call the police, try to trace my car. I could imagine Curtis and me being arrested, locked up while somebody came for us. It might get on the news—"Local Woman Disappears," with a picture of a worried Hamp, my tearful mother hurrying into the trailer, slamming the door. Tacky.

I would go Monday. If I went Monday, Tina would be safely married and I wouldn't spoil her wedding. And I could figure something out about my parents and Hamp. I turned left toward my parents' house, passed the convenience store, railroad crossing, mountain of sawdust that marked an earlier McAdams' sawmill. I pulled into my folks' driveway and parked in the back. The dew was already drying on the grass. It was going to be in the high eighties by noon.

The back porch was stacked with stuff for the reception the next evening—card tables full of linens, a pile of coolers, and vases and stuff for the flowers on the potting table. Opening the kitchen door, I thought, maybe Mom could help me out, help me deal with this. Did Dad ever fool around? Surely not. He looked angelic enough, sitting at the kitchen table, reading the paper and eating a piece of toast with jelly, his face still slick from shaving. Curtis was sitting beside him in his boat pajamas that he keeps at grandma's.

"There's my sweet baby boy!" I said, and Curtis jumped down from the table and climbed me.

"I slept with Granddaddy," he said, and gave me a jelly kiss. I looked across the table at Dad, who nodded.

"He kicks like a damn mule," he said, refolding his paper. "And he snores."

"Do not."

"Do too. You snored all night. I didn't get a wink of sleep."

"*You* snored!" Curtis yelled, giggling. "Youdy doody snored." He waggled his finger. "You do." Then he buried his face in my neck to end the conversation. I sat down, hugging him. He still smelled sweet, and his hair was soft and curly against my cheek.

My dad picked up Curtis's uneaten toast and spread a knifeful of jelly on it, precisely to the edges just like he used to do for Tina and me, laid it on the bunny plate and pushed it over to him.

"Eat up, sport," he said. "Cup of coffee, Judy?" He carried his own cup over to the counter.

"Please."

I watched him as he set out a fresh cup, got out milk and a spoon for me. He didn't look like a man who had ever kissed anyone except my mother. He lived life precisely, cleanly. He smelled wonderful, like lumber fresh from the sawmill, and was so clean he rustled, like a starched shirt. And yet—he was a good-looking fellow, and only fifty something. Who would ever know, if a daddy got a little on the side? Especially a careful, fond daddy. When I first heard about sex, I was appalled to learn that my parents not only did it but apparently enjoyed it, that it might even be a regular thing with them. Now here was another thing: a daddy could fool around. A mama, too, for that matter.

Curtis began kicking the back of the chair. I turned him around and held him, squirming, on my lap.

"I appreciate your baby-sitting," I said, as Dad set my cup down in front of me. "We got the country club finished. It looks pretty good."

"Glad to hear it. You look tired. Glad to get this wedding over with." He tucked his paper under his arm and drained his coffee. "You need any help this morning with your lunch?"

"I don't think so. Charley will be there."

My father set his cup in the sink.

"Good. Then I'm going to work. Tell your mama she can get me at the lumberyard if she needs anything. Is Hamp coming in to work today?"

"I guess. He was asleep when I left."

My dad patted us both on the head and left, his mind already turning toward the business. I just sat. Curtis was calmly eating toast, licking his fingers. Mom's cat, a bushy white matron, finished the breakfast she had been eating by the sink and came over for a rub, jumped into Mom's chair and curled up for a nap.

The refrigerator gurgled. I was nearly asleep myself. My parents' house is a warm, safe place, sturdy and tight. The kitchen is white, a fifties kitchen. Last year my mother got out all her old fiesta wear and her plastic salt shakers that she and Dad had when they first got

85

married. She says if you live long enough, everything comes back into style.

Enough space in a house, enough light, a white cat on a blue cushion and a yellow sugar bowl—a person could never betray that. Could he?

He could, of course. A person could do any damn thing he pleased.

"Want to watch cartoons, Curtis?"

"Yeah!"

We went into the den and turned on the set. Curtis settled onto the floor a foot from the screen and stuck his thumb in his mouth. I went into the living room.

Tina's presents were there, stacked up like plunder among the chintz sofas. Tina's stationary box, full of thank-you letters, was there, too. I went over and riffled through them to see who she'd written lately. "Dear Aunt Louise, Jimmy and I really appreciate your . . ." Tina's handwriting, a round, careful script, has not changed since she was in eighth grade. Her china and crystal were stacked on a table against the wall, appliances still in the boxes rowed up on the floor. A Cuisinart. A bread maker. Sets of knives. Sets of salad bowls. Silver toast racks and those little silver dishes nobody ever uses. Two toaster ovens. All the promise of a fruitful domestic life right there before her, and she, unlike me, would get herself a house to put it all in. Not that she would use any of it. Tina Lee is no cook. But she would make it look good, which was more than I had done. Most of my wedding presents were still in my old bedroom under my bed. I pulled one out occasionally and carried it over to the trailer. The appliances were going out of style.

I went back into the den. The living room is Mom's: chintz and a piano, novels in bright jackets on white shelves. The den is Dad's: brown leather chairs with chips in the leather, an ugly, comfortable couch, brown bookcases with brown books. Dad's guns are in a rack in the den, too. The rack is locked. He never hunts anymore.

"I'm thinking of redoing this room," Mom says. But she doesn't. She and Dad have their lines drawn. At the lumberyard she refers to him by his last name. "Mr. McAdams isn't in right now. May I have him call you?" He invites her out to lunch. "Edna, will you join me for a bite at T.J.'s today?" And she looks up, considering, listening to the air for five seconds before she answers. "Yes, I believe I will, thank you." She never says no.

I wrapped up in an afghan and lay down on the couch. I did not know what to do. In one of my trashy novels, there would be drama here—a renunciation of some kind, decisions, revenge. Murder. The path in my mind that I walked every day already looked fake, like a bad drawing, flat and unreal. My new life was the stuff of melodrama. My parents were going to love it.

I imagined Dad standing on the back porch in his hunting clothes, checking his gun, snapping it shut with a deadly little click. Once my father shot a rabid fox in the back yard. Mom saw it out the kitchen window and called him, and he ran out through the sun porch, popping shells into his shotgun, jerked the back door open and shot it, just like that. I screamed, and he turned and gave me a long, considering stare, his face sharp and dark.

Dad was in Korea, but he won't say if he killed anybody. He tells funny stories, and a few sad ones, and keeps his war paraphernalia locked up in a chest in his closet. He got medals but doesn't show them to anybody. Now, instead of hunting, he walks in the woods.

I used to think I would like hunting until I did it. I begged to go, shot into a covey of quail, and actually killed one. A dog brought it to me, dropped it in my hand, and I was sick at the way it lay there with its heavy, cupped feathers and its head flopping over to one side. That night at supper, a dozen quail came in on a platter, all brown and crisp, looking like doll's chickens with their little legs up in the air. It was terrible. I sat and stirred up my rice and gravy, drinking tea and swallowing. After that I shot clay pigeons.

Of course my father would not shoot a person anyway. We are not violent people.

■ ——— ■

The afghan was wooly against my nose. I pulled it up over my head, closed my eyes. My dad would be a joke as a Victorian father. If I had a problem, he would tell me to work it out. And he certainly would not want to know all about it. Hamp was Dad's son now. Figure it out, he'd say. For God's sake, Judy, handle it. I went to sleep.

Ten minutes later Curtis started patting my cheek.

"Mom. Mom. Come on, Mom. Are you asleep?"

"Of course not," I said. "Whatever gave you that idea?"

We went outside to cut roses for the luncheon.

"You play on the swing set, baby. I'll just be a minute."

"I wanna help."

"Give me a break, Curtis. Just go on over and play on the swing set for five minutes. Please. And Mommy will be through."

His chin buckled, and he stood there barefoot in his pajamas and cried.

"I wanna *help*."

What's going to happen to him? I thought. How will I ever tell him if I can't fix it with his daddy?

"All right, darling," I said.

I had to carry him.

The rose beds are dotted over the back yard like enormous graves cut into the grass, topped with spikey canes. The sun was heating up the ground; the top layer of dirt lay in powdery balls. Underneath, the ground was still loamy. There were hundreds of buds and some open and blown roses. Dad had been preparing the hybrid teas to peak this week. I took the open blooms. I wanted a passionate bouquet, velvety and heavy, petals dripping onto the tablecloth. The rose canes rocked against the tension of my hand as I sliced through the stems, shuddered and sprang as I let them go, the blossom heads nodding in my hand like little dead birds. The bucket filled up with them, bristling green, stiff tough stems, obstinate mean things and their blooms.

Some birds were singing like crazy. It was all peculiarly noticeable and bright. The air tilted and swam.

"Be careful," I said to Curtis. "Cut right here. Mind the thorns."

Mom was up when we got back to the house, drinking her coffee. My mom looks old in the mornings. Her blood pressure medicine has given her vague new ways. By nine or ten, she is her brisk self again, hair combed, makeup in place, giving orders. But when she sits there in her robe, too pale without her lipstick, she's fragile. I become afraid.

"So," she says, stirring her coffee. Every morning she stirs her coffee for about five minutes.

"Grandma! Make me some oatmeal!"

"Fix the baby some oatmeal, Judy."

"Instant or real?"

"Real!" said Curtis, dragging a stool to the stove. He likes to stir the pot. "Real with butter and sugar and milk. Don't stir it. And I pour."

I started the oatmeal.

"Is the club clean?" said my mom. "Did you notice the main room?"

"Looked fine to me." Actually, I hadn't noticed. "So is it all going to work out all right?" I said.

Mom took off her glasses and rubbed her nose.

"We haven't forgotten anything," she said. "Though like I told Bessie, those flowers for the church—"

"I mean their lives," I said. "Our lives. How do we know everything will be all right?"

"Don't be ridiculous, Judy," she said, glancing up at me. "Of course we don't know." She closed her eyes.

"Then why bother?" I said.

"Well what else are you going to do with your life?" she snapped. "Bothering is what it's all about, for God's sake."

"Sometimes it seems like too much trouble."

"That's because you need a vacation. I told you after Christmas, take a few days off. Looking after an active child, working all the time, and that room of yours, and this eternal wedding . . ."

The oatmeal looked so good I had a bowl myself. I felt like I was saying goodbye to Mom, and to my old life.

"Go wake your sister. Those girls'll be driving up soon."

"The girls who are coming to the bridesmaids' luncheon are all probably still in bed, Mama."

"Some of them will be here soon, I tell you," she said. "Get Tina up."

Mom has never been bothered by a fear of nagging.

"Sure thing," I said. I fixed Tina a bowl of oatmeal.

She was already awake, looking bridal in her French Provincial bed, her ruffle-edged sheets and her lace nightgown. Curtis jumped onto the bed, and I gave her the oatmeal. Tina doesn't drink coffee or tea, or anything much except water.

"Hi, guys," she said. "Don't shake the bed."

She ate a few bites, set the bowl aside, sat gathering her hair up in a ponytail and running her fingers through it, studying the ends. Her hair is smooth, fine, slick.

"So," she said. "Are we ready or what?"

"I am," I said. "Except for my dress."

"And your hair and makeup. And your nails."

"I'm not getting married, Tina Lee. You are. And Mom said to tell you to get up now before your friends get here."

Tina sank slightly lower in the bed.

"I just love Mom when she gets excited, don't you?" she said. She studied her fingernails. "Do you think this polish will look good to-night with that blue dress, or should I change it this afternoon?"

"It'll look great," I said.

"You don't care," she said. "You don't even wear nail polish."

"This is true," I said. "Mothers don't have time for all that bride stuff. Do we, Curtis?"

Curtis had gotten down and was rooting in Tina's closet for his train.

"With us mothers, it's all lift that barge, tote that bale, get a little drunk and you—"

"You mothers are full of it," said Tina, getting up. "You never painted your nails when you were a bride either. I had to tie you to the bedpost to paint them on your wedding day."

"And I spent my whole honeymoon peeling them. They nearly drove me nuts."

"Poor baby," she said from the bathroom. "Come in here."

I walked to the bathroom door. Tina was leaning over the sink examining her face in the mirror.

"Look at this." She pointed to her forehead. "Could this possibly be a pimple?"

Her eyes looked back at me from the mirror, blue and unblinking.

"I don't see anything. Put some stuff on it."

"I will. That would be just my luck. A pimply-faced bride."

She began dabbing creams onto her face. Tina Lee spends probably two hours a day on her face and hair. She mixes her own creams, lives on vegetables and wheat germ. To her, a pimple is like a heart attack.

"Sit down," she said, pointing to the toilet, and starting to spoon something green and gritty onto my cheeks.

"Will this make me happy?" I said. "Will I still be able to play the violin?"

"Don't talk," she said. "It has to set."

She started brushing her teeth.

"Your trouble is," she said, spitting, "you don't care."

I didn't say anything. Tina grinned at me, stepped out of her night-gown, turned on the shower.

"So what's the secret of a happy marriage?" she said, testing the water. "Just so I'll know."

I touched my face. I could feel the green stuff stiffening across my nose.

"Don't look out any windows," I said.

"What?" Tina stood there naked and stared at me.

"Last night I looked out a window and saw Hamp really kissing this girl. For a minute I thought it was you."

Tina wrapped herself in a towel. I touched my face. The cheek hollows were still damp and sticky.

"Me!" she said.

"In fact I can still see it, in my mind, and it was definitely you. But then it sort of changes and becomes Diane."

"How odd," she said. "So how much had you had to drink?"

"Nothing."

"Well," she said. "It was definitely not me. I was kissing with some-body else." She laughed, then sobered, leaned toward me, touched me on the knee. "So what did Hamp say about it?" She was paying whole, careful attention, something she does well.

"Oh, I didn't tell him," I said. "What could I say? I didn't want to talk about it. Suppose it was nothing?"

As I said it, it was becoming nothing. Trivial. I made the most devastating thing that had ever happened to me into an incident. I could feel its effect lessening as I spoke. Tina by listening, and I by speaking, turned a nightmare into a conversation. She took my hands, held them in her hands, looked sideways into my face, spoke intently.

"It doesn't matter what you saw," she said. "These things happen. It wasn't me. But so what if it was Diane? Hamp loves you very much."

"You should have been there," I said. "It was bad. They were all over each other."

"Hamp loves you," she said. "We all know he does. What's a kiss, for God's sake? Probably everybody does something like that occasionally. It's meaningless. You are married to him, you, not anybody else. He chose you. It really bothered me at the time—" she gave another little laugh—"but I was a kid with a big crush. Jimmy and I are . . . meant for each other. "

"Corny but true."

"Please ignore this, Judy."

"Easy to say."

"You have to. Promise."

"I'll see," I said.

"You must. Promise. Don't screw this up, Judy."

"All right," I said.

She hugged me.

"You're green," she said.

■ —— ■

An hour later Curtis and I were both dressed, and I had a version of a makeup and hair job, though not the one I would have done myself. Tina fixed me.

"Oh, shut up," she said. "Just sit still for a minute, for God's sake. You won't let anybody do a thing for you."

Then I put the bucket of roses and the silver bowls, two more silver bowls which my mother made me take, the place cards and platters, the guest list and some extra cloths, Curtis and Curtis's bag for swimming in the car. Mom and Tina walked me out of the yard, apparently figuring that I wouldn't be able to negotiate the driveway unless they helped.

"I will make you a hair appointment for tomorrow, darling," said my mother.

"Great," I said.

Every once in a while, they tried to fix me up, not that I am all that ugly to start with, but if it couldn't be done with soap and a hair dryer, I usually didn't bother doing it. It never meant that much to me. Maybe that was a mistake.

"You know Hamp loves you very much," Tina had said. That was comforting. I felt better, more hopeful. It seemed foolish after all to be that upset. The bundle of papers on the passenger seat that I had brought out of the trailer in a towel seemed ridiculous. Running away seemed ridiculous. Whatever was messed up could be fixed, maybe would even mend itself. I put the bundle under the seat. It was a relief to be normal, think of normal things.

■ —— ■

It is not easy to do a small-town wedding. Cities have clubs and dining rooms, caterers and florists and dress shops. McAdamsville has Wal-Mart and a national forest. The hunting is great here, and the fishing, and the living, and the soil grows roses as big as dessert plates. But the best restaurant is a fish house, and the nearest place to order china and invitations for a wedding is fifty miles away. The clubs are mostly racist. And if you want a nice room to have a luncheon, you have to build the damned thing yourself. Take in your own silver. Arrange your own food supply.

Charley was already at the country club. I set the places while he fixed the flowers, sitting at the end of a table with his clippers and roses and silver bowls spread out on a newspaper, snip-snipping and twisting, hardly looking as he worked. His fingers are long and thin, the fingernails nearly flat. The roses settled into their bowls like an audience during the overture, with a final wiggle, then attentive.

The place looked good when we finished it. It all worked, the white, the lights, the stones and silver and the roses and the linen napkins. All the cooks and lifeguards came to see and admired it tremendously. Another success for Judy. I was asleep on my feet.

"It's only eleven o'clock," I wailed. "If I had my suit, I could go swimming with Curtis."

I had arranged for one of the lifeguards to baby-sit him for the morning.

"And ruin your makeup. Right. Tina Lee would just love that. Come into the bar and have a cup of coffee, and I will regale you with stories of my dissolute past."

"Cream and lots of sugar. And you don't have a dissolute past, Charley. I was there."

"Fine. How about my dissolute present?"

We sat down at a little table up against the glass wall which overlooked the pool.

"Charley," I said. I laid my hand on his arm. "What about Diane? Do you love Diane?"

"How should I know?" He pulled his sleeve away, restlessly.

"Don't love her," I said. "She's not right for you."

"I didn't say a word," said Charley.

"You didn't have to. You look like you love her. You're considering it. That's the way it starts. You're a certain age, and you think you ought to get married. You want to belong to someone, have someone belong to you. And you fall in love and do it. You marry. But it doesn't make any difference. Do you know what I'm talking about?"

"No," said Charley.

"I mean, you're married, right? And you wake up one morning and you think, I'm still alone. I have somebody to sleep with—you look over and there the person is, and you are very glad because after all somebody to sleep with is a fine thing—but essentially there is nobody there. Your bodies touch. But most of the main stuff goes on inside your head, you live mostly inside your head, and that part never marries. You're still alone in there."

"Well," said Charley. "Maybe you are. I know what you mean."

"No you don't," I said. "You're thinking, She doesn't know what she's talking about. It will be different with me. And I tell you it won't. You think—but it won't. For a minute it is. And that's just as uncomfortable as too much sex. You think, God, I'm smothering. He's in every pore."

Charley nodded. He was waiting for me to change the subject.

"Just like now," I said. "Even people who are really close to you don't share things once they're grown. You are thinking, When will she finish? You don't believe me."

The cook hollered from the kitchen, and Charley walked over and brought back our coffee. He clattered the cups down on the table.

"No," he said. "I'm thinking, why are you talking like this? Can this be talked about? Some things are too sophomoric to say. Words cannot express, and so on, the essential loneliness of the human spirit. And so what?"

"Just don't propose to Diane any time in the next five minutes, okay?"

"Okay!" He was irritated.

"It's very boring, isn't it? Let's talk about something else."

I drank my coffee.

After a few minutes, Charley began to talk about Curtis, who was in the middle of his swimming lesson. We could see him out by the pool with the other kids.

I made a sort of leap in my mind over all the trouble I was having and landed down on the other side, out there in the sunshine with my son. He was standing in a line of children by the side of the pool, dripping. A little girl in a pink suit hopped beside him, one foot and then the other, and they looked at the swimming teacher, who was in the water catching them one by one.

"Come!" she said, patting the water as though it were a bed.

"We did that," I told Charley. "We stood on that very spot and jumped in together, just like that." I looked at him. "You used to believe me about things."

96

But it wasn't true. I used to tell him things that were almost true, or true in my heart, or true for my purposes. Once I called him and said I had a wreck and my car was torn up, and it wasn't. I had had a wreck at school on Friday afternoon, but the car was not damaged at all, except I had spilled a drink all over the seat and hurt my knee a little bit because I wasn't wearing a seat belt. I was just mad at him because it was the weekend and I was lonely, and I wanted him to drop everything and come over and pay me some attention. He was mad when he got there. I felt bad about it, and every time I thought about it since then, I felt bad.

"Is life just an accumulation of mistakes?" I said. "Do we just go through, screwing up and feeling bad about it forever, waking up in the middle of the night in a sweat, remembering stuff we did to people in grammar school?"

"I hope not," said Charley. "Because half the people in this town would not do business with me if they remembered how I treated them in grammar school. Or how they treated me."

"Remember when the Cutter twins tripped you and you fell down the locker-room stairs and broke your arm?"

"And you glued their lockers shut and told everybody they were queer for each other?"

"And their mother said we were monsters and she wouldn't invite us to their big summer party, and we made up with them so she wouldn't tell our parents, and then put water in all her liquor bottles?"

"Yeah, I remember," he said. "I remember I was the one who got in trouble, and you did not."

"Only that time. That was the only time, Charley."

Of course it wasn't.

Mrs. Cutter was our Sunday school teacher and the most feared mother in town. She was relentless and had a big mouth, and she had made Charley's life miserable until my daddy told Mr. Cutter to shut her up. And even then she gave Charley dirty looks in Sunday school for a year, and looked at him whenever we talked about stealing. She was the assistant teacher. Fortunately she didn't come every Sunday, or Charley might have turned out atheist.

"Well," I said, remembering Sunday school, "I apologize for every bad thing I ever did to you. Thank you for being my friend. Go ahead and love Diane. Because now I think of it, it doesn't seem to make much difference. I mean, I love Hamp, right?"

Charley closed his eyes.

Then Tina Lee and Mom got there, and everything started happening. I showed them my room. Tina put on the rose Charley had fixed her. We all said those floaty words people say when they're at the beginning of an event, drifting into the wind.

The room smelled of fresh paint, roses, and new-polished silver, and when the other women got there, their perfume and soap all mixed in together, heavy and sweet like a girls' dorm on Friday afternoon. I was happy, buoyed up by them all. We all seemed to be floating along together on a sea of scent and good will toward the wedding.

"Wine?" I said. "Here! Put your bag over here. You look wonderful, darling. You look grand."

The party was for Tina, but I felt that it was more for me.

"You've done such a good job on this, baby," said Aunt Patsy, gripping my arm.

Aunt Patsy is Charley's mom, a large, florid woman, a female version of my daddy, her hair curled so tightly to her scalp that her forehead looks burned. There were tears in her eyes, and she dabbed at her face as she talked.

"Such a good job," she kept saying to everyone. She meant not only the room, but us all, how we looked and how we had turned out. She meant love, that we loved and were beautiful, and that we had good manners. She has always cried for us, ever since her husband died when Charley and I were children.

"I'm just sentimental," she says, wiping her eyes.

98

"Oh, for heaven's sake, Patsy," says Aunt Bessie.

Jimmy's women blended fairly well with our women. You hardly could have told, looking at them, which aunt belonged to who. They all gripped their purses, darted their eyes around, pounced at each other. They chattered brightly, saying things like, "It's so lovely to see you again!" and, "How have you been?" even though most of them see each other every day or two. They squeezed each other like fruit, pinching and screwing their mouths around, testing out skin.

"My goodness," said Jimmy's mother. "I really should stay with Granny Glendinning."

Granny Glendinning sat in a wheelchair and wore a straw picture hat with a big blue rose.

"Oh no, Lucy," said one of her flat-cheeked cousins. "You go on ahead now. We'll look after Granny G."

The old lady was wheeled to the end of a table, where she sat looking very sour and picking at her silverware as though it were for sale.

"Have a glass of wine, Mrs. Glendinning," I said to her.

"Yes. Thank you very much." She plucked a glass from the tray with long, wrinkled fingers.

"I don't know if you ought to, Granny G.," said the cousin.

"Awk!" said the old lady, like a bird. The cousin retreated. Granny Glendinning made that sound periodically throughout the meal. It was like sitting in the room with a parrot. She didn't seem to care for anyone there but was enjoying herself as people do on airplanes, waiting impatiently for the food, the movie, the safe landing at the end of the trip.

Little Sally was there, crossing her legs at the ankles.

"Are you ready to be a bridesmaid?" I said. "Of course you are. What a thing to say. I have forgotten what people do at twelve."

"That's all right," she said. "Not very much, actually."

"Yes, it's coming back to me now. School, homework. Tap and music and church fellowship. Do you take music lessons?"

"Actually," she said, "I play the violin."

"I'm impressed. And of course you ride horses. I have a friend, Diane, who teaches horseback riding, and she's going to give Curtis some lessons. Perhaps you'd like to go out there with us sometime and ride."

There were now two Dianes—my friend and the other one. They shimmered indistinctly in my consciousness like the Trinity.

Tina's friends from college remained apart from the aunts, giggling and whispering like kids in church. Tina's roommates, Kate and Cheryl Ann, and her old friend Helen would be bridesmaids and were busy fulfilling the first duty of bridesmaids, by reminding the bride with jokes, punches, and whispers that a wedding is all just an elaborate and expensive way to get laid. The aunts, having no part in that, ignored them. To aunts, a wedding is a family thing, having to do with china and dynastic ritual.

"Wait till you see my dress on me," said Cheryl Ann. She has short black hair and buys boy's clothes. "It makes me look exactly like a piece of key lime pie."

"You're so tiny you're gorgeous in everything," said Helen, who has grown stout. "Don't try to tell me."

"You just wait till you see." Cheryl Ann spread out her arms and minced. "A green triangle."

"I am a head of lettuce," said Helen. She pointed at me. "All because she is tall and has red hair and tits."

I smiled and shrugged.

"There have got to be compensations for being the bride's sister," I said. "I have eight bridesmaid's dresses. 'I picked out something you can wear other places,' the brides always say. We all know that's bull. I wouldn't wear any of the getups people made me buy to mow the grass, pink polyester and garbage like that. And I'm getting kind of old for this gig, you know? So I thought I'd go out in style. You have to admit it's a nice dress."

"For a tall, thin person," said Helen.

"Oh come on, Helen," said Tina. "It looks great on you."

They began talking about breast enhancement.

The dress did look good on me. It was green and cream. I had picked it because it made me think of dancing, and I thought, I'll wear this to the club for Labor Day. The women make the men dress up for a dance on Labor Day weekend. Hamp hates it, but I make him take me anyway.

Kate was talking about the bust developer they had all ordered from the back of a magazine when they were freshmen. Kate has brown hair and is tall like me. She brought her hands together in front of her chest.

"Squeak, squeak," Kate said. "We all walked around for a month squeezing the thing. Squeak, squeak. Half the dorm did it. Up and down the hall, squeak, squeak. We all looked—" she cupped her hands in front of her breasts—"by spring break."

"So it worked?" said Sally.

"Don't get any ideas," said her mother. "I've never understood why you girls want to improve on what God gave you."

"Me either," said Aunt Bessie complacently, glancing down at her weighty bosom.

"Oh yes, it worked," said Kate. "After a fashion. The breasts can't be enlarged, of course. But you can strengthen the supporting muscles. It's just . . . foolish. Not exercise, but . . . enhancement. The whole business of—"

"Sex," I said. "And sex appeal. Horribly overrated."

My mother rolled her eyes, changed the subject.

"This chicken is delicious, Judy," she said. "You must give me the recipe."

I didn't know the recipe, as she well knew. I had just asked Aunt Patsy to tell her circle something good to fix. They cater luncheons.

"Tina," said our mom, raising her chin and eyebrows.

Tina presented the bridesmaids' presents—pearl earrings. I got a second present—a string of pearls.

"Wow. Thanks."

Tina leaned over and hugged me, holding her face hard against mine for a second, bone to bone.

"Thank *you*," she said.

I took the pearls out of the case and held them in my hand, let them flow through my fingers, smooth and cool. Tina nodded at me. I handed them to Aunt Patsy, who fastened them around my neck, her hands soft and whispery against my spine. I could feel her fingers trembling.

"There," she said.

She stood back and smiled at me, smiled around the room.

They all smiled, looking at Tina, at me, and each other, smoothing down their hair, pressing their hands lightly against their collarbones, adjusting their clothes. There was no irony here. No one was gnashing her teeth. We were all earnest, cheerful, and proud. We came together because one of us was getting married, came to celebrate and defend love and the possibilities of love with honest approval, young or old, shy or proud, our hair smooth or frizzled with middle-age permanents, some of our faces already etched with love and the terrible effects of love.

If things didn't work out, well, that was a shame. No one in this room had a guarantee, but they were prepared to help get each other off to a good beginning. They were all standing in the water, smiling, saying, "Come on in. Come on in now. I will hold you up. I will support you. Jump."

I proposed a toast.

"To Tina Lee," I said, "who is joining a great sorority of married women. Welcome." And I started to cry. Not great boohoos, but a break in the voice, and a choking up.

Everyone chalked it up to my being nervous.

102

"Say being married is lots of fun, Judy," said Kate, and patted me on the back.

Five

5

I WENT HOME AFTER THE LUNCHEON and picked a fight with Hamp about money. "I'm going to get more cash out of savings," I said.

"This wedding has already cost us a fortune," he said. "We decided to use our savings to finish the house, remember?"

"We never will finish that house," I said. "We just can't spare the time. It's only been, what? Five years now."

"I've been slightly busy."

"Doing what?" I succeeded in making him mad.

"My job, dammit. Our kid. All the extracurricular activities you think up for me to do."

"I think up? I think up hunting? Watching the Braves every day is my idea?"

"No. But most everything else we do is."

"I thought you liked our life," I said.

And so on. It was one of those change-of-direction fights.

"What the hell's the matter with you?" he said finally.

He spoke uneasily, his eyes wary. He chewed a cuticle. But I lacked the courage to say. He walked up and hugged me, lifted my arms to wrap them around his back.

"Come on," he said. "I'll start on the house again as soon as I can spare a man. Okay?"

"Okay," I said.

"And so what if we blow a couple of hundred more on the wedding? Get Tina married and out of town. Cheap at the price." He rubbed my hair. His shirt button pressed into my cheek.

I had the feeling, with my eyes closed, that we were swaying at the edge of nothingness, the edge of the world. Beyond us yawned a chasm. I chose to step back.

"I love you," he said.

"I love you, too," I said.

Later I sat on the bed beside Curtis, who was curled up like a cat on the pillow. Something in me had grown cold and thoughtful. Something was watching me try to work this out, and that something didn't care for Hamp at all. "Get out," it said. "Get out of this. Back away."

I argued with it, the something that didn't care.

"I have a commitment," I said. "This is my life. I have a child, and I do love my husband. I do. People don't back out of a relationship just because they are having a rough day. They work it out."

"So work it out," said the self that didn't care. "But I'll be packing, just in case. And don't get careless again."

I tried to think of how to go on with my life. There was now a gap there that words would not bridge. My thoughts did not yet stretch to that other shore. I was afraid of falling, and of what was on the other side. I tried to push myself, but something inside me turned in panic and clung, desperately, to the silence.

We went to the wedding rehearsal.

First Methodist Church in McAdamsville is gray stone and stands on a corner off Main Street, bounded by a cemetery and a parking lot. It has a cavernous, dark sanctuary and stained glass in high, arched windows, Episcopal wainscoting, and walls of cool milky plaster that you lean toward as you sit in church, wanting to put your cheek up against them. It's the sort of church designed to remind you what a mote you are, how insignificant. The carpet is wine colored, the cross is dull gold, the choir loft is murky. Charley and I used to sit up there for junior choir practice on Sunday nights. We sat on big chairs, our feet disappearing toward the floor, our thin voices cutting like knives into the stillness. God, we figured, was actually there listening, lurking behind the organ pipes or floating above the pews, a masculine Anglo-Jewish mist.

The wedding factions were aligning themselves when we got there—a pew of older women in the back, a scattering of bridesmaids around the communion rail, the young males in a clot nearby shoving, ducking, and jumping around, the females all elbows and wrists, murmuring and cutting their eyes around. The older men circled the minister. The groom's family floated apart, dark and resolute like sticks in a stream.

I could smell Hamp sweating behind me, hear his breath. He stood like a wall at my back, pained but resolute, his chest hot and hard in its Sunday suit. Now in the aisle of the First Methodist Church, we were a couple again. Hamp put his hands on my shoulders and squeezed them, rocked me back and forth. This is all right, his hands said. We can do this. Here we are together, getting it right. His palms pressed into my collar bones with a heavy reassurance, the warm pressure of a family man. Then he and Curtis walked down the aisle toward the groom's faction, while I sat down with Mama and the aunts.

"What a pretty family you make," said Bessie. She patted my knee.

My eyes followed Hamp down to the front of the church. I could still trace the outline of his hands against my bones. So this was love. Here it all was, alpha and omega, not train tracks lying parallel so long they seem to come together, but spinning planets colliding in the pitch dark night, showering sparks, shattering rock, lurching off into another orbit, bound toward more destruction. How love enlarges us. How it makes us grow. What a lightweight I was just day before yesterday, now to have such a heaviness in my bones. My heart lurched.

This fluttering struggle to get away, this cooling along the verge, the impatience I felt with my whole life and existence to date—this all was love. The movie was over, but I had gone home with the star. There he was, holding our son, his face quick against the dead of everything else. This was the beginning, the real beginning of love— not a wedding or a child or a fight, but a lurch, and heaviness in the bones.

"You've got chill bumps, dear," said Bessie.

Aunt Patsy sat beside her, both of them in flowered prints, their cheeks a powdery pink. Mom sat on the other side in her navy blue.

"Wear that blue one," Dad had said. "It makes your bottom look like a bag full of cats."

"It does not." Mom stood up straighter.

Dad held up his hands, cupped, palms up, lifting one and then the other, like hips walking.

"Sweet," he said, rolling his eyes, sucking in his breath.

"Honestly," said my mother.

I leaned over in the pew and asked Mom if she had on her girdle, and she said it again: "Honestly."

I laid my head on Bessie's shoulder. I felt great. I had survived a planetary collision. Boom! My head was bloody but unbowed. I would stay here, in the safe enclosure of the married women's arms, and lick my wounds, listen to them bitch and chat, relax and enjoy the wedding. They didn't take any of this rehearsal seriously. This was a sporting event to them, a snack, a little nibble of pre-marriage non-sense. The main course would not be served for years. Tina was over there with a wedding consultant thinking she was the star. Well, she was, but this was not the main event. The aunts and moms were here for her, watching as they'd watched her learn to walk, standing as they'd stood out in the lumberyard parking lot while she got that tricycle going, got the training wheels off that first little bike, took them all for a spin in the family station wagon the day she got her driver's license. They were the cheering squad, the Greek chorus of her life. Their own lives rattled on underneath, roaring like an underground train. And I could stand on the sidewalk listening, feeling the vibrations of their forcefulness shaking the concrete underneath my feet.

The aunts and my mother were discussing the wedding consultant. Once they decided to like Lucy Hooper, or at least to shelve her as being practically a member of the family and therefore an improper topic for dissection, the wedding consultant had become the focus of their mutual interest and alarm. Her name was Mrs. Hardacre, and she had driven all the way up from Columbia to direct the wedding. She had been part of a sort of package deal with the wedding dress: Buy this and you get a consultant. Mom and the aunts chose to view the whole business as very strange.

The whole ebb and flow of their conversations had a comfortable aloofness about it that was like a water bed. They were definite, had definite opinions, knew how to think and act about almost everything. If etiquette didn't tell them, God did. Working out the finer points, arguing all sides of the question would take them the rest of their lives, and be time well spent. It didn't matter so much what the topic was or what they decided about it, but that they were together figuring it all out. They were like a Protestant Talmud.

They were not predictable. The line they were taking about the wedding consultant sounded pretty conservative. Mom was not at all interested, she said, in experiments in wedding etiquette. So far as she was concerned, she said, the last word in what was correct had been written about a hundred years ago and never improved upon. Innovations like black bridesmaids' dresses and silk roses were nothing but trash. Scandalous, in her opinion. Of course, that was only her opinion. The other aunts would nod their approval. But they could just as easily be radical. "I think it's high time," one of them would say. "These outmoded ways," and so forth. "Think for yourselves, you girls today! Don't be such conformists!" And the others would nod their heads about that. You absolutely never knew what side they were coming down on, though I was beginning to have some glimmers.

So the out-of-town lady was useful as a conversation piece and shock absorber, should one be needed. Or, God forbid, a scapegoat, should one be needed.

"Nonsense," Aunt Patsy said. "I'm sure Mrs. Hardacre will do a better job than I've ever done. After all, I was never trained as a consultant." She emphasized the word *consultant*, making it sound absurd. "I'm a florist. I've helped out, when people needed me and were kind enough to ask my opinion. Like sweet Judy here." She patted my leg, folded a pleat across my skirt. I was a pet. "We had such a good time at your wedding, didn't we, darlin', and you were so sweet to ask me to help. But I really think . . .," she glanced at Mrs. Hardacre, marvelously efficient looking in a pink suit and clipboard, "I really think, Edna, that this will be best for Tina. Tina is so *particular*, you know."

"Oh my dear," said Mom, lowering her face, looking out of the tops of her eyes. "How well I know."

"It's been too much on you, Edna," said Aunt Bessie, shaking. "I told Fred the other day, 'It'll be a miracle if Edna gets through this thing with her health'."

Other people's health was one of Aunt Bessie's main conversational themes—how they were ruining it, what they could do about it, and where they could go for a second opinion. She was the family shaman.

To forestall her, Mom put her finger to her lips and glanced toward the pulpit.

"I need the wedding party down front, please," said the wedding consultant. She clapped her hands. "Bridesmaids! Maid of Honor!"

I got up and walked down the aisle. The bridesmaids had been positioned in a semicircle in front of the pulpit, but Helen broke ranks and hurried up to me, squeezed me up against her chest.

"Judy! You look marvelous! Little Tina's getting married! Can you stand it?" She gave me an extra little squeeze.

"Not really."

"I know. I'm manic. I know I am. Aren't I manic?"

"A little." A dark, solid-looking man walked up to her and smiled.

Helen introduced us. Nick Stephanopolis was from Philadelphia, almost a doctor, with hard black eyes and a benign smile.

"He's doing his residency now. He looks the part, doesn't he?" Helen eyed him like an artist.

"Perfectly."

"That's absurd," said Nick.

Helen had an arm around each of us, and we stood together and chattered, too close, breathing each other's breath.

"Oh no it isn't," she said. "Doesn't this man look like a doctor?" she said to the other bridesmaids.

"Of course," they all said, gathering around.

"And doesn't Tina over there look like a bride?"

Tina stood in deep consultation with the wedding director.

"All you have to do to look like a bride is get married and be female," said a groomsman.

"Wrong!" said Helen. "There's an aura. Doctors inspire confidence; brides inspire—"

"Fear," Hamp said.

110

Everyone laughed. Nick Stephanopolis and Helen and I began to flirt, to nod and tease and smile outrageously at one another and with the others. Soon we had drawn a crowd, all of us leaning back in our shoes and forward on our toes, smiling and sparkling and showing all our teeth. Nick had very white teeth. His accent was just different enough to make him exotic, and when he smiled at Helen, I thought, well, she deserves him.

People always have a good time around Helen. She just has that gift. When I told her so once she said, "It's not a gift. It's hard work." And I began to notice how hard she was working. She was right. It isn't a gift at all. And now she had met a man who appreciated her Botticelli self, her full breasts, pink cheeks, amplitude. And her hard work.

I was a little jealous.

"Attention, please!" said Mrs. Hardacre.

"Ah!" muttered Helen. "The general speaks."

"Nick's adorable," whispered Kate to Helen. "Where'd you get him?"

"We're just friends."

"Right."

"Places, girls!" said Mrs. Hardacre.

We all scattered. I went around the communion rail and stood on my mark. We all assumed the helpful and tentative stance proper to a wedding rehearsal. Hamp winked at me. Mrs. Hardacre rapped her pencil against her clipboard, and we began.

Tina stood mostly in the aisle beside Mrs. Hardacre, to whom I took an immediate and profound dislike.

"Sit over there, little boy," she said to Curtis. "Ladies, please do not slouch." And so on.

It was a very long practice.

The groomsmen began to sweat and mutter and play basketball with an imaginary hoop. The bridesmaids began to step out of their shoes and stand beside them between trips. We all began to feel resentful of old Mrs. Hardacre and to make mean bits of conversation about her behind her back. It was tedious, interminable. We stood and walked to shreds of Mendelssohn and scraps of Vivaldi, halted while Mrs. Hardacre and Mrs. Brown, the organist, conferred, then we marched again, slower, faster, here and there. Mrs. Hardacre and Mr. Carruthers, the minister, jockeyed politely for control of the actual ceremony. Mr. Carruthers won. He is thin and mild but doesn't take any sass. Then I got a break. Curtis began to make an ass of himself, and I took him out.

■ ——— ■

The air still felt thick and hot, but the sun was low, and the iron fence around the graveyard cast long, wavery shadows across the tombstones. Curtis ran up and down the rows of graves, touching each tombstone like a base runner as he passed. I walked down the center path to the gate at the far side of the churchyard. Across the street along the railroad tracks, the wild poppies were in bloom.

When I was a kid, there were thousands of poppies. They covered the whole hill on either side of the tracks, growing wild in the tall grass. I used to stand and look at the poppies and think about how much fun it would be to go among them. One day I reached up to the top of the gate, fingered the smooth iron latch, squeezed it, and swung back the gate.

"Come on, Charley," I said. It was after Sunday School. "Let's go pick some of those poppies."

We crossed the street and went into the grass toward the poppies. Up close it was rougher going, rougher ground than we had figured, full of briers and hot, shifting gravel and empty liquor bottles. It smelled. The poppy stems were tough and wiry, the air close and hot. Nevertheless, we enjoyed it. We pretended it was Flanders Field. We would make bunches, we decided, and sell them after church. People would buy them to put on graves. Then we would give the money to the church. Since we were skipping church to pick the poppies, it seemed a logical plan.

Back then I was afraid of the railroad tracks. Charley was not; he walked up and down right beside them and seemed to be getting the most poppies. So I joined him, finally, beside the rails, scrambling up the last few feet, looking uneasily up and down the track.

Then the front door opened on a little shack of a house across the tracks from where we were standing, and a woman came out on her porch. She started screeching at us.

"You kids get off those tracks, you hear?" she yelled, swinging on the screen. "Go on, now. Go on home."

Of course we did. She was an adult. We held hands and eased each other down the embankment, clutching our poppies, muttering under our breath: What business was it of hers what we did, and who did she think she was anyway?

She fanned us off, stood in the shadow of her porch post, clinging to the bannister, watching us go. She did not move until she saw us safely inside the graveyard fence and the gate closed. Then she sat on the porch and rocked, her fly swatter swishing, watching us as we sat on some grave curbing and bunched up our poppies, twisting long strands of wire grass around the stems to keep them together.

■ ——— ■

"Whatcha doin'?" said Curtis.

He climbed up on the fence beside me.

"Thinking about those poppies over there."

"Wish I could go over there."

"You want to?" I said.

I opened the gate.

The grass verge was not as high as it had seemed to me as a child. The poppy stems were not as tough. The whole scene had shrunk. The old woman's house was shut up tight. It looked empty. I told

113

Curtis about the old woman while we were picking poppies and warned him not to go over there alone. After a few minutes, he started pulling me back the other way.

"What's the matter with you?" I said. "I'm not going to let anything hurt you. Come on."

But he had grown afraid. So we went back to the churchyard. Curtis found a stick to rake against the fence railings, and I put my poppies on Charley's daddy's grave.

After a few minutes my daddy came out to join us.

"Are they still rehearsing in there?" I said.

"Yep." He rubbed his face with his hands and shook his head like a dog, as though to clear it.

It was practically dark. Curtis came running over for a hug and then zoomed off again, careening from monument to monument in his favorite game, fighter plane, dropping pebble bombs on all the graves, screeching.

"Neeaowww-phowh. Neeaowww-phoow. Airplane to general. Come in, general."

"Active, ain't he?" said my dad, lighting a cigar. He insists that he doesn't inhale.

"I want to apologize," I said, "for all those tantrums and fits I had as a child, for all those meals, parties, and conversations you missed while walking me around outdoors to calm me down."

"Apology accepted," Dad said. "That's the beauty of a grandchild. Revenge."

He brushed some dirt off his parents' double headstone, squatted and pulled grass, idly, from around the base of the monument.

"I really enjoy watching you chase Curtis. It gives me satisfaction. Yes, ma'am."

"He's trouble."

"He's a fine fellow. He'll be all right." Dad squinted after him in the gloom.

114

"I hope nobody sees him taking rocks. The old ladies made a stink last summer about the kids playing out here on Sunday mornings."

"Screw 'em," he said. He stood up, brushing off his trousers, and walked over to Charley's father's grave. He poked at the poppies I'd laid there. "I gave the damn gravel, and those crappy little goldfish pebbles they insisted on laying in the outlined plots, too. You know that damn stuff runs forty-five dollars a ton?"

"We're obviously in the wrong business."

He nodded. My father believes that everyone except himself and the farmer takes too big a wholesale profit.

"You know," he said, "I still miss old Chubs." That was what everybody called Charley's dad.

"I can't remember anymore what he looked like. I remember him giving us hell about picking those poppies."

"He looked just like Charley," Dad said. He picked up a handful of pebbles and let them run through his fingers. "You reckon they're about ready to wrap it up in there?"

"No."

"Aw hell." He stood up, brushed off his pants. "I must be getting old. I can't take this much aggravation, all this rehearsing and hysterics and all. Tina Lee shoulda taken the money and eloped."

"You lie. You wanted her to have a big church wedding, just like you did with me. Only going to do it once, you said. Might as well do it right."

"I was an innocent then," he said with dignity. "Now I have smarts."

"You're a big faker."

"Mebbe so," he said. "But I know my rights."

"And what are they?"

"Bragging, bitching, and paying the bills."

"Mama does all the bitching these days."

"We go halvsies," he said. "I bitch to her, and she bitches to everybody else."

"That way you maintain your reputation for quiet dignity, and still get what you want."

"Correct."

He ground out his cigar and buried it with his toe under a dandelion.

"The weeds are taking over," he said. "We're going to have to get somebody out here to spray. You coming?"

I reached up and stuck a poppy in his buttonhole.

"So what do you think, Pop?" I said.

"About what?" he said.

"About anything. Life. Marriage."

"What difference does it make what I think?" he said. "Since when have you girls listened to anybody but your boyfriends? I'll tell you something," he said, turning back. "You think you got problems with that one?" He pointed to Curtis. "At least now he's short enough to wrestle to the ground. You can force him. You want him to take his medicine, you can pour it down his throat. When he's seventeen, darlin', that's when it's gonna hit the fan. Because all of your experience, and all of your love, and everything you know or could do for him, everything you've painfully learned about life—," he snapped his fingers in the air—"are nothing to him. Nothing. He knows it all. And you are going to have to stand there and watch him launch himself off every cliff he can find, waving and smiling at you all the way down. And then your understanding of the matter will be complete. Your education will be complete."

"I can't wait," I said.

"I can't either," he said, putting his arm across my shoulder. "And you know something? It doesn't make a whole lot of difference anyhow. I don't know why the hell I did half the things I did when I was a kid. Or even when you girls were little. Glands or ambition. And we've all turned out all right. I was so damn lucky, sometimes it scares me when I think about it. Especially with your mother. I could as easily have screwed up."

116

"Dad, you're so reassuring."

"Trust your instincts," he said. "That's what you gotta do. Hell, at twenty-one that's all you got. You sure as hell don't have any judgment. Just an instinct. You know what you want. You don't know why. You think you do, but you don't." He laughed again. "You guys don't know shit." Patted my back.

"I feel a lot better," I said. "I'm so glad we had this little talk."

"Cheer up, baby," he said. "It'll ease off when we get this wedding done. Get Tina Lee out of our hair."

■ —— ■

Inside, things had deteriorated. The wedding party was almost dead of boredom. Tina Lee was standing in the aisle, her back rigid, gesturing and murmuring to Mrs. Hardacre. Mrs. Hardacre was smiling and nodding her head. They made an ideal couple—two perfectionists against the world. The wedding party slouched behind the communion rail, sulking. The organist played and swayed, played and swayed, away in her own Mendelssohnian world.

"How's tricks?" I said.

Tina gave me her most pitying, lady-of-the-manor look.

"Where have you been?" she said. "We are still trying to get the recessional right."

"Outside baby-sitting, where do you think? Where do you reckon Helen got that purple dress? Is she in love with that Nick person?"

"Probably. Will you behave?" said Tina. Her eyes were dilating.

"Look," I said. "Give us a break, will you? Everyone is crazy to get out of here. The wedding will be beautiful. No sweat. Nobody is going to look at anybody but you anyway."

Mrs. Hardacre nodded agreement. "The placement of the wedding party is perfect. Really."

Mom came up. Mrs. Hardacre stared at her, fascinated, like a rabbit looks at a dog.

117

"Can't we wrap this thing up?" Mom said.

"The recessional's not right," said Tina Lee.

"People are getting hungry," said Mom, "and your father says he's leaving in thirty minutes."

Of course our father had said no such thing. He might have done it, but he would never have threatened it. That was just Mom's way of lighting a fire under Tina Lee.

"We have to do the recessional again, mother," said Tina.

"Then get down there and do it." Mom gritted her teeth and flapped her arms, as though she were shooing chickens. She pushed us toward the alter and began to throw her weight around. Everyone came to attention.

"I know you darlings are all starved," she said. "I promise you we'll have you out of here in ten minutes."

Mrs. Hardacre nodded as though it were her idea. In ten minutes the recessional was all accomplished, and Tina Lee was standing at the back of the church, rigid.

"Did that suit you, Mother?" she asked sweetly.

"It looked fine to me," said Mom. "How did it look to you, Mrs. Hardacre?"

Mrs. Hardacre sniffed. "Beautiful. Perfect. I just had a few announcements . . ."

We all flopped into the back pews and listened as Mrs. Hardacre admonished us not to get drunk, not to be late, not to forget anything.

It was dark, and the sanctuary shrugged us off into the gloom. All the aunts and onlookers were already gone. We were there by sufferance only. Mr. Carruthers turned out lights at the front; Mrs. Brown at the organ, the last bright light in the firmament, gathered her music, clicked off her lamp, and wrapped the choir loft in shadow. She just sat there, staring out at us, in the dark.

118

Six

6

THE CLUB WINDOWS GLOWED, LIGHT SPILLING OUT in wavery puddles across the grass. We bounced into the parking lot. Curtis had fallen silent in the back seat, his head on his chest. Hamp turned off the ignition and sat staring out the window. It was nine o'clock, and the sun was gone except for one hot pink smear above the tree line. Lightning bugs were rising across the golf course, spread out like a meadow below the club.

"Ready to go?" I said. "I'm starving. Aren't you?"

He looked at me.

"No. I really hate this."

"It's no big deal, Hamp. Come on. You'll enjoy it."

He sighed.

"So don't go in," I said. "Go home. I'll say you had a headache."

"Right," he said and got out of the car.

Curtis bolted awake. "Are we there?" He fumbled with his seat belt.

"Come on, sport." Hamp lifted him out of the car. "We got to go to the par-tee." He danced across the gravel, feet scrunching, Curtis swaying. "Goin' to the par-tee, you and me, goin' to the par-tee, yes sirree."

Charley met us at the door, wearing his professional party posture. He stood like he was getting ready to bow, tall and sucked-in, stiff in the upper arms, with a quirky smile. Now that *you* are here, said the smile, the night is complete.

"You've been forever!" he said, ushering us across the floor. "The kitchen ladies are on my case. So how was the rehearsal?"

"Endless," said Hamp. "Mindless and endless."

"These McAdams girls are something, aren't they? Here, you need a drink."

He poured us each a glass of wine.

"It's beautiful, Charley," I said.

He had set up the buffet and a scattering of tables and swathed them all in soft white cloth. The floor gleamed, and the flower arrangements were huge. The bar was closed off, but a promising throb echoed from the jukebox through the floorboards, rather as though the building were alive. Tina's friends swished around among the tables nibbling, sipping, and laughing. The older adults bunched and nodded, patting one another on the back.

"It is nice, isn't it?" said Charley. "Got to go. Diane's around here somewhere. Keep her company, will you?"

Hamp and I stood together and watched our son make the rounds of the hors d'oeuvres table gathering up chicken wings.

"Smile," I said to Hamp. "Get happy before you take me down with you."

He grinned his largest fake grin. "Here comes my mother. That should cheer you up."

120

"I like your mother."

"I don't."

"Hamp!"

He grinned again, this time for real. Bad-mouthing people improves his disposition.

Curtis noticed his other grandmother and ran up to her. "Nana Marie! Have a chicken wing!"

"No thank you, darling. And how are you, Judy? Hamp?"

Marie is tall and straight and wears her brown hair pulled back in a soft bun. She walks and talks just like a twelfth-grade English teacher, which is what she is—precise, immaculate, and kind.

"How's tricks, Ma?" said Hamp. "Still pouring it to those poor bastards at Demaro High?"

"With a will," said Marie. "And you?"

"Fine." He turned to me, friendlier. We are always the happy couple for his mother. "Listen, sweetheart, are you ready for me to take Curtis and the baby-sitter home yet?"

"I don't know. What do you think, honey?"

Hamp sighed, looked at his watch. "It's mighty late."

"Go on ahead if you think it's best," I said. "Whatever you like. I'll fix a plate for them in a minute."

We all parted, like butter wouldn't melt, to mingle and do our little duties. I carried Marie over and introduced her to all Jimmy's relatives, like the good little girl that I am. Then I found the baby-sitter, Heather. Heather is seventeen years old, a senior at McAdamsville High, and Curtis's swimming teacher. Her mother is a friend of mine from church, and her daddy is an enormous, somewhat irritable ex-Marine.

Back at the hors d'oeuvres table, Curtis was spearing toothpicks full of cheese and pineapple. He already had a little pile of chicken bones on his napkin. In a little while, he began on the raw vegetables. Heather and I joined him, scooping up globs of dip with our celery

121

sticks, bending over to eat so the stuff wouldn't plop onto our chests.

"Boy, this is great," said Heather. "What a neat party!" Her blonde French braid bounced. She was wearing her mother's best attempt at a young girl's clothing, a cotton sundress, but on Heather's body, it merely looked voluptuous.

The room began to achieve the pleasant, anticipatory buzz that accompanies a good time. I was just finishing my little gorge of vegetables when Mom came toward me looking grim.

"Where is your sister?" she muttered.

"I have no idea." I wiped Curtis's chin.

"Well, go pacify Lucy Hooper for me, will you?" she said. "Give me that." She took the napkin away from me and wiped my own chin with it.

"Don't lick it," I said.

"Don't lick what?" she said.

"Don't lick the napkin," I said. "When I was a little girl, you always used to lick the napkin before you wiped my face with it."

"Gross!" said Heather. "You know, I think my mom did the same thing. Yuck!"

"I never did," said Edna. "What a mess you both are. Go on."

"I don't want to. I have to fix a plate for Curtis."

"Get Lucy to help you." Mom turned her back to Heather, and whispered and gestured furiously at me. "Tina is not here. She and Jimmy are not here yet."

"So?" I said.

"So I don't know where they are," said Mom.

"Maybe they had a fight," said Heather, leaning around my mother. "Gosh. Maybe they've decided not to get married or something."

"I sincerely doubt that," said Mom, making faces at me.

"Of course they are probably just—"

"How exciting!" said Heather. "Or maybe they eloped. Can I tell my mom?"

122

"No!" we said together.

"You stay here with Curtis and make sure he doesn't eat the table-cloth," I said to Heather. "I'll go get you guys some supper. Okay?"

I finally found Lucy in the hall by the back door, looking down the driveway for headlights. She had on high heels and her hair was sprayed. She looked all wrong, like she was wearing somebody else's clothes. Her face was tight.

"Where could they be? Jimmy knows better than this. I'm gonna wring his neck." She wrinkled up her mouth so that threads of lip-stick showed around the edges. Her hands went up to her hair, felt the spray and stopped.

"Do you have any idea where they could be?" she said.

"Maybe they eloped," I said. "Have a carrot stick."

She bit it contemplatively.

"You know, they could. That sounds about right. No," she said, pointing the carrot end at me. "Tina would never give up her wedding."

"Good point," I said. I noticed she didn't say, Jimmy would never give up his wedding, probably because we all knew that it wasn't Jimmy's wedding. Jimmy was just along, as it were, for the ride. "Maybe they had car trouble. Or they could be—"

"What?" She stared at me.

I shrugged.

"What do you really think?" she said.

"I really think that Tina is sitting in a car somewhere running off her mouth, and Jimmy is sitting there listening and looking at his watch, and when Tina runs down a little and stops for air, he'll bring her on to the party. And everything will be fine."

Lucy looked at me, ate the rest of the carrot. "You're right," she said.

We went to the kitchen to see about the food. Three women were tending it, friends of Lucy's from her church, and they jumped at her when she walked in.

123

"Honey, what you want us to do?" said the biggest lady. She was the most dressed up, her hair arranged and sprayed much like Lucy's, only very black.

"I don't know," said Lucy. "They're not here yet."

"Well where are they then?" said the lady in the pantsuit. She was younger, with a bun. "I've already cut the meat. If we'd've thought . . . well, you can see." She opened an oven and pulled out a foil-covered pan of roast beef slices, peeled back the foil. The roast was laid out in rows, floating in juice. Only a few of the slices were still pink. She ladled some of the juice over them, touched one piece delicately with her finger.

"See?" she said, flicking a ribbon of crust. "It's curling up." She pressed her lips together, smoothed the foil back down, shut the pan back into the oven.

On the stove were tubfuls of tiny spareribs glistening in their sauce, more foil-covered casseroles, pans of homemade rolls. The third lady, the thin one in an apron, stood at the other oven door punching holes in a large pan of broccoli casserole.

"It's all gon' dry up to nothin'," she said. "Mert, take out those vegetables, would you please? And check the ice."

The lady with the bun picked up a pile of more raw vegetables and their clotted dip and hurried out.

"Would you all mind if I fixed my baby and his baby-sitter a plate? They've got to get on home," I said.

"Of course not, honey. You go right ahead. Or let us. What does he like?"

Charley, who had been leaning over the sink washing glasses for more drinks, came up and slapped my hand away from the spareribs. He and Lucy had a consultation.

"What if they're not coming at all?" said the aproned lady. "What was that girl's name, Babs, called off her wedding that time?"

"Of course they're coming," said Lucy Hooper. Her eyes darted to mine. "Let's just go on and serve dinner. Don't you think?"

"Absolutely," I said.

"That would be best," said Babs. "I really think so."

I got everything ready and went to look for Hamp.

"I don't wanna go," said Curtis. "I wanna stay here."

We made a procession—me, Curtis, who held my skirt and sucked his thumb between sentences, and Heather.

I couldn't find Hamp. He wasn't anywhere. We stood by the buffet table making jokes about my sister.

"Isn't that just like them?" I said. "Honestly."

I used my best grimace, my rueful smile, my can-you-beat-that-sister-of-mine shrug. Curtis began to cry. My mother had a nerve jumping in her neck, a small pulsing cord. She touched it.

"Mom, no sweat," I said. "You know everything's fine."

I thought everything was fine. I did not worry that they had had a wreck or a fight, because Tina Lee is my sister and I know her. When Tina Lee needs time, she takes it. She takes it right then, right out of the middle of everybody else's time if necessary. That's just the way she is.

Finally I got mad, packed Heather and Curtis and the food into the car and drove them home myself, having one pleasant conversation with Heather while I drove and another one, not so pleasant, with Hamilton Duncan and Tina Lee McAdams in my head. By the time I got back to the club, Tina and Jimmy had arrived and everybody was eating.

"Hamp found them," said my mother. "They were at the nursing home taking flowers to Granny Glendinning." She looked like she had a headache. "Sit down, baby," she said, patting the chair beside her. "Eat."

"I think I'll find my husband," I said.

"Well, give him a kiss for me," she said. "He's a hero."

The tables inside had mostly the people my parents' age, so I wandered out onto the patio, where more tables had been set up beside the pool. It was dark, in spite of the candles on each table, but I found Hamp, sitting with Diane. Their plates were in front of them, but they weren't eating.

They were talking. Hamp was in his shirt sleeves, leaning toward Diane, one arm propped on the back of her chair, the other hand gesturing in the light of a candle. Diane laughed at something he said, twisting a dark tendril of hair that had fallen onto her neck. When they saw me, Diane looked up and grinned, waving her fingers. Hamp moved his arms down, rested his wrists on the table. His face settled from delight into resignation.

"Mom says you're a hero," I said. I bent to kiss him, but he didn't kiss back. I sat down.

"Did you take Curtis home?" he said politely.

"Yes, I did." I was polite, too. "I looked for you, but you weren't there."

"I looked for you, too."

Our politeness was implacable.

"So how was the horse show?" I turned to Diane.

"We got a first and two thirds," she said. "Not bad for our first year."

"Great!" I said. "Nice suit."

It was a plain blue suit with a little silk camisole. Her tied-back hair made her face look thin, smudged with shadows at her temples and cheeks, the hollows of her throat. Another time I would have mentioned that I hated her cheekbones, and she would have said that she hated my breasts. She would have done that funny twist to her mouth that makes one of her appealing faces, and I would have stuck my tongue out at her. But none of that seemed appropriate at the moment.

We chatted, and I told some rehearsal stories. Hamp mostly kept quiet. I watched his face but read nothing new there. I wanted to ask

126

him why he was delighted with Diane and bored with me. I wanted to ask him why he let it show. But I did not.

It had struck me all of a sudden, like a blow to the gut, that Hamp was just going to be that kind of husband. He just was, and there was nothing I could do about it. He might be nice to his wife privately, but in public he would act bored. He would be the man who, at parties, got a little drunk and looked down women's dresses. And he would always get away with it because one of the stupid women, one of the young ones or one of the lonely ones, would always be a little in love with him.

I had watched it happen before, watched women love him while he loved me, and I had not minded. He was, after all, so easy to love. I was prepared to forgive the lonely and the stupid women who trespassed into my marriage. I was generous. After all, he made such fun of them going home in the car. Or he spoke of them with pity.

"Helen's a nice person," he'd say. "She can't help it if she dances like an anteater. No, she really is a nice person."

Now I was the nice person, the bland, stifling wife. Now for the first time, I saw myself down a corridor of years, sitting and watching Hamp snow other women. Because he worked at it: I had recently figured that out. He put out signals. He worked to convince other women how brave and good he was, how he was doing his best, how cute he was, and what a shame it was they couldn't have him.

So I watched him, sitting there beside Diane, and I decided, he's not so much after all. They can have him. Let the next one have him. It made me sad, though, that it might be Diane. After awhile I excused myself, saying I had to get some supper. Actually, I didn't get any supper. I had lost my appetite. I sneaked outside and walked around on the golf course. Then I went into the bar. Tina and Jimmy and their friends were there, and after a while, they opened the door to the main room, and some people started dancing.

Jimmy danced with me, holding me carefully, like a boy in dancing school, and making awkward, brotherly conversation. And I sat for awhile with Helen and Nick, talking about school.

"So where's Hamilton?" said Helen.

I shrugged. "Is it important? I can get him. He's just outside. Helen, you know Hamp hates to dance."

"Nick loves to, and he's good."

"Don't rub it in."

So Nick and I danced. He wanted to know all about Curtis. They had had a conversation, it seemed, about rocks, rockets, swimming.

"He is very charming," said Nick.

"Like his daddy."

"No. Like his mother."

Nick isn't like Jimmy, who grows on you. Nick hits you all at once. We talked about Greece. He had been there some as a kid, visiting relatives. I had been once, with Mom on a cruise.

"I went to a nightclub in Athens," I said.

"How did you like it?"

"It was very shiny, like aluminum foil. Strange dark men asked me to dance with them. Only they spoke a foreign tongue."

"Greek."

"Probably. 'Apen Zanadu?' they said. 'Holpe Maria?' And I had to keep shaking my head and laughing. Because I didn't understand a word that they said."

"Probably just as well," laughed Nick.

■ —— ■

But finally I began to wish for Hamp, not that night's version, but the earlier one, the one who had loved me and enjoyed my company. Sometimes being married is the loneliest thing of all.

Hamp came into the bar after awhile with Charley and Diane and tossed down a few drinks to show his dissatisfaction with the world. People began looking over at me like they did when Curtis acted up.

128

I ignored the looks. I would have to deal with Hamp, I knew that, but I put it off. I was not, after all, Cinderella. And it was fun sitting in the light, talking, remembering Greece and how much I had liked it, liked traveling.

I felt almost that I was back there again, wandering the brown Greek hills, sailing between the islands. I did not want to step outside that interlude, that stateroom, which was bright and barely leaking, into a corridor slanting toward the deep.

Then Helen passed out.

"I'm not feeling so good," she said. She began to slide toward the floor.

Nick caught her. He propped her up against his hip and took her pulse, looking doctorish. Then he began to tap her wrists. "Helen? Helen? Time to go home now. Helen?"

"Let me help," I said.

We half-walked, half-carried her into the hall.

"Helen, dearest," Nick said, staggering. "Helen. See if you can walk. I will take you home."

Helen did rally. She pulled herself up suddenly, put her hand over her mouth, and lurched rapidly into the ladies room, from whence disagreeable retching sounds immediately emerged.

Nick and I looked at each other.

"I guess I'd better go in there," I said.

"I guess you'd better."

"Does she do this often?"

He nodded, closing his eyes.

Eventually we wrestled Helen out to her car, tucked her in, closed the door.

"I'll follow you," I said. "Do you know the way?"

"Not really. I'll follow you."

■ —— ■

129

On the way to Helen's, I decided that someone else could as easily have done this little chore as me. Then I decided that someone else's problems were a cinch. I should be taking my own drunk home, but how pleasant to be escorting someone else's.

Helen talked all the way into her house.

"This is so nice of you, I am so sorry, God I feel like hell."

At the door Nick propped her up against the wall and reached for her purse. She held it away from him. He jerked it out of her hand, opened it, and took something out which he held in his hand. She grabbed at it, but he held it behind his back.

"You shit!" she hissed. "That's mine! Give it back!"

He slipped his hand into his pocket. The door opened and Helen's mother stood in the hall in her curlers and bathrobe.

"What's going on?" she said.

"Goodnight, Helen," said Nick.

"Nothing, Mother, go back inside."

"I'll call you tomorrow, Helen," said Nick.

"Nice to see you again, Mrs. Cook!" I backed off the porch, waving, turned and ran out to my car. Nick was right behind me. He opened the passenger door and swung into the seat. We watched Helen's mother lead her into the house.

"What was that all about?" I said, starting the car.

"Nothing. Don't worry about it."

We were halfway back to the club when he spoke again.

"Helen has been very nice to me," he said.

"Helen can be a very nice person," I said. I turned a corner.

"But she has a problem," he said. "I am trying to help her with it."

"Oh, and how are you trying to do that?" I said.

We pulled up in front of the club, and I turned off the engine and turned to him.

"Probably all the wrong things," he said.

"Then why are you trying?"

He just sat there in the dark, looking at me.

"Do you think you can fix everybody?" I said. "Everybody? Every little thing? Because I'm way ahead of you, and I'm here to tell you that you will waste your life trying."

"Helen is a friend of mine," he said. "And her problem is not such a little one. Plus, it's fixable."

"What makes you so sure you've got the right answers?"

"I'm not," he said. He flicked his wrist to make his watch slide down. "In fact I was just thinking what an idiot I am for interfering. If your friends are determined to kill themselves, maybe you should just let them. Is that right?"

He fished in his pocket, drew out two pill bottles, and pressed them into my palm.

"You decide," he said. "I'm tired of playing God." And he got out of the car.

I scrambled after him.

"I do not want this." I following him to the door. "I don't want this. Take it back."

He turned around and looked at me, his face in the yellow light.

"Take it back," I said again. I held the bottles out.

He took them from my fingers, opened one and turned it upside down. A thin thread of white powder poured out, caught a slight breeze, and spread out into nothingness through the air. He scattered the gravel with his foot and slipped the other bottle, which rattled with pills, back into his pocket. The crickets were chirping, and down across the golf course a few lightning bugs still rose, flashing, from the grass. We went inside.

■ —— ■

The grownups had all gone home, and the party had achieved a drowsy wind-down. Tina and Jimmy waved us over to their table.

"You guys still getting married?" I said.

131

They held up their entwined hands.

Hamp was asleep, his head on a table. His yellow curls were flopped over onto one side, and there was a trail of spit on his chin. I wiped it off. With Charley and Diane's help, I roused him and got him to my car.

Down on the underside of my mind, I could hear the terrible suck and cracking in the engine room as the sea poured in. But what could I do? I felt that at the last minute I could jump free, kick off my shoes and swim free. I felt like I could do anything.

"Sure you don't want me to follow you home?" said Charley.

"No. Thanks, really. We'll be fine." I even waved good-bye.

I drove home. When I pulled up in the yard, Reddie set up a howl, so I fed and watered her and petted her for a minute, standing there in the pen in my good dress watching Hamp's head on the car seat to see if it moved. The crickets were chirping like crazy, and the car lights, which I had left on, cut a haphazard path of light across a patch of yard and off into the woods.

I went into the trailer. Heather was asleep on the sofa. I went back into the bedroom, packed a bag with stuff I'd need the next morning, and put it in the truck. I wrapped Curtis in his blanket and carried him out, too. Then I woke up Heather. On the way out, she saw Hamp sleeping in the car and gave a squeal.

"There's a person over there!" she said.

"Hamp had a little too much to drink," I said. "He's resting."

"Are you just going to leave him there?" she said.

I went back into my bedroom to get another blanket. Curtis had left his drawing pad and markers on the bed, and on an impulse I wrote Hamp a note in big black letters: "I saw you the other night in the parking lot at the club." I propped the pad against the pillow. I took the blanket outside and laid it over Hamp, easing the car door shut so the mosquitoes wouldn't get him. He didn't stir.

After taking Heather home, I drove over to my parents' to spend the night. The back door was open, and through it I could see people moving around in the light. There was the sound of laughter, and a scraping of chairs. I gathered the limp, heavy-headed Curtis and walked up the steps. Mom was in the kitchen with Tina Lee and Jimmy, drinking a glass of milk.

"Darling! I thought you'd be home in bed." Mom had taken off her dress already and put on her robe. She looked like she did when we used to drink milk together at night when Tina and I were in elementary school.

"I think I'll spend the night here with Curtis, if you don't mind, Mom," I said.

I was trying to pick up Curtis's blanket, which trailed behind. Jimmy took him and carried him out. My mother looked down at her hands.

"Did you get Hamp home all right?"

"Fine," I said. I got a glass of milk. "He'll be all right in the morning. Good party, Tina."

Curtis was sleeping in my old room in my double bed, and when I joined him, he snuggled up beside me. I cupped his head in my hand.

When I was a little girl, Mom would sit at her dresser—she had one of those dressing tables with the three-part mirror—and brush her hair, put on her makeup, and I would sit on the bench beside her and watch. Once a photographer was coming to take our picture in the living room. It was for Tina's christening, because Tina had on the long white dress. So I was sitting with Mom on the bench looking into the mirror, twitching and making faces at myself. And I noticed that I could see myself over and over, reflected in my reflection by the three mirrors. There were me's within me's, back and back into the dresser. And I noticed that I had red hair, and I thought it was beautiful. A smocked dress and red hair, and a gap-toothed smile. I saw myself for the first time, really saw myself. Here I am, I thought, sitting at the dresser. And the remarkable thing was, Mom saw me, too.

"Look at you," she said.

She picked up a brush and brushed my hair, and when she finished

133

she leaned over and put her cheek next to mine, and looked at us in the mirror.

"Don't ever forget," she said. "You are beautiful, and you can do absolutely anything."

And I could see fifty Moms all squeezing me, looking back at me with a big lipstick smile.

$\mathcal{S}$*even*

7

THE NEXT DAY I LAID LOW. I retreated to the center of my life and hunkered down just outside the cave entrance like a lion at home, watched and waited, hoping to be ignored. Since it was Tina's wedding day, I figured I had a better than even chance. First I hid in bed, my old bed in my old room at home, and watched the sun slide across the floor. When the sunbeam reached my bookshelf, I got up and got a book and hid in that for a while. *Freckles*—it's an impossibly romantic book about a one-handed orphan who guards timber in a swamp. He is noble, honorable, and pure, and I am crazy about him. I read bits to Curtis when he woke up.

"'Something big, black, and heavy came crashing through the swamp near him, and with a yell of utter panic Freckles broke and ran—how far he did not know; but at last he gained some sort of mastery over himself and retraced his steps. His jaws set like steel and the sweat dried up on his body. When he reached the place from which he had started to run, he turned and with measured step made his way back to the line.'"

Curtis stuck his face in my neck and nuzzled.

"What was it?"

"What was what?"

"The big black heavy thing."

"It doesn't say. Freckles never knew what it was. He was just afraid of it, and he ran, and then he decided to be brave and it went away."

"Oh. I'm hungry."

"Me too. But we have to be quiet, okay?"

We dressed and went into the kitchen. I carried *Freckles* along. We found corn flakes and had a bowl each, with bananas. I plugged in the coffee.

"'He was compelled to plunge knee deep into the black swamp-muck,'" I read. "'There seemed to be a great owl hooting from every hollow tree.'"

"Can I have some orange juice?" said Curtis.

"Sure," I said, reading while I poured.

"Look," said Curtis. "There comes Daddy."

"'Nature can be trusted to work her miracle in the heart of any man . . .' ."

"He's at the door, Mama."

"I know, I know. '. . . the only thing that relieved his utter loneliness was the companionship of the birds and beasts. . .' ."

I opened the door.

"'Freckles turned to them for friendship.' What do you want?" Hamp stood on the stoop and waved at his son.

"Hi, bonk-bonk."

"Hi, bonk-bonky too!" said Curtis. "What'cha doin'?" He ran up and jumped out the door into his father's arms.

136

"Came to see you. Came to see your mom. Apologize. Grovel and eat worms and see if I can make up for being a jerk."

"Whadya do?" said Curtis. "Are you really a jerk?"

"Sometimes. The biggest. You think she'll let me in?"

Curtis turned to me.

"Sure," he said.

"That's not fair," I said. "Unfair."

I put my finger in the book and closed it. Hamp put Curtis down.

"Go on and finish your cereal, sport," he said.

Then he looked up at me.

"I am so sorry," he said. "I would not have had you . . ."

He spread his hands. "But I want you to know one thing. I do love you. There'll never be anybody else. And if I could take back . . . I'd give anything. I am crazy about you."

He quit talking and dropped his eyes.

"Well," he said. "So what do you want me to do now?"

I shifted the screen door to the other hand.

"It's not up to me," I said. "You blew it. I didn't."

"Well, I guess I'll go to work then." He turned away, turned back. "Are you coming home?"

I shrugged.

"I really messed up, huh?" he said, over his shoulder.

I could hear Dad behind me in the kitchen.

"Judy?" he said. He walked up beside me. "What you standing there lettin' in flies for?" he said.

"Mornin', Bob," said Hamp. "Just passing through."

"Well come on in and have a cup of coffee," said Dad. "I want to talk to you about that shipment supposed to come in yesterday and didn't."

"Can't right now," said Hamp. "Judy's mad at me. Won't let me in."

Dad looked at me.

"Oh for Christ's sake," I said. "Come on in. Have a cup of coffee.

137

But don't think I'm happy with you, because I'm not."

He stepped into the kitchen, and he and my daddy exchanged a look. Dad went over to the coffee.

"Yep," Dad said, "that demon rum's a terrible thing, ain't it?" He set three mugs out on the counter, reached for the milk. "Makes a man do terrible things. I remember once in Korea, friend of mine got drunk on leave, woke up next morning with 'Darla' tattooed on his chest. Big letters." He outlined letters on his shirt front. "Oh, he was sick. He had to get skin grafts to get the thing off. Painful. And expensive."

He poured the coffee, brought us cups, and sat down with his own.

"Why did he bother?" said Hamp. "If it was on his chest."

"Because his wife's name was Betty Lou," said Dad, sipping.

Hamp choked on his coffee, and Curtis and I slapped his back for him.

"So," said Dad to Hamp, "if that stuff comes in I want you to call Beatty . . ."

I reopened *Freckles*, sat there a few minutes and listened to them talk. Dad would not be going to the yard today. He would stay at the house and supervise the setup of the outdoor part of the reception. Hamp listened, nodded, wrote a couple of things down. He had shaved and showered. He kept flexing his fingers like they hurt, and he didn't look at me.

"Anybody want toast?" I said. "Eggs? Bacon?"

Hamp just wanted toast.

By the time I had fed everyone Mom came in, so I fed her too. She looked tired.

"Well," she said. "Glad to see you up and around this morning, Hamp."

That meant, You asshole. Why did you get drunk at my daughter's party?

138

"Yes ma'am," said Hamp.

"Hangover?" said Mom.

"Yes ma'am," said Hamp.

"What is it they say, Bob, about the hair of the dog? I never understood that."

"It means another drink will cure a hangover."

"I thought, something like that. Will it?"

"Sometimes."

"Well, Hamp, we have some Irish whiskey. Don't we, Bob? You could try that in your coffee."

That meant, I am a liberal person and I forgive you, but don't let it happen again.

"No ma'am," said Hamp. He held up his hands. "No thank you. Thank you just the same. But no."

Satisfied, Mom nodded.

"My great-great-grandfather once got so drunk he rode his horse up the stairs of the church steeple, and it took a block and tackle to get him down. The horse, not the man."

This was one of my parents' favorite routines.

"Because horses—" said Dad.

"Can't back down stairs."

"And there was no place for him to turn around in the belfry."

"They had to lift off the steeple," said Mom. She always said that part with a little lilt of surprise.

She and Dad smiled at each other.

Tina wandered in wearing her nightgown and scrunched herself up in her chair with her knees drawn up to her chest.

"So what's happening?" she said.

"It's your wedding day," I said. "Rejoice, dear heart."

She buried her face in her knees.

"The caterer is coming at nine," said Mom. "To deliver some things. Charley said he would be over this morning to do flowers. And Bessie

139

is bringing Lee straight on here from the airport for lunch. You'll be here, won't you, Judy?"

"Sure," I said.

Lee is Mom and Bessie's New York sister.

"Are you saying you want me to get my clothes on?" said Tina Lee. "What about the happy family breakfast I'm supposed to have my last morning as a single person?"

"Tina Lee, you haven't eaten breakfast with the family since second grade."

"It's the thought that counts," said Tina Lee. "Is there any cranberry juice?"

I walked Hamp out to the truck. When he got there, he opened the driver door, leaned against the top of it.

"Listen," he said. "Let's go off somewhere tomorrow for a few days. Maybe alone. Or we could take Curtis. Drive down to the beach. Or Florida."

"You can't do that," I said. "You can't act like a jerk, a pure, stupid, pie-faced asshole and then say, 'Oh, sorry, let's go to Florida.' I feel awful. I feel worse than I've ever felt in my life before. I feel like my whole life is some kind of idiot's delight. How could you do that to me?"

"Look at me," he said. "Listen to me." He turned my face toward his. "I am crazy about you. You got that? It kills me to think I've hurt you like this, you understand? If I could change it or make it go away, I'd give anything. But I can't. I'm going to have to live with it. We are. And we are going to have to deal with it somehow, too. Because I can't let anything convince you that I don't love you. You have to keep listening, and give me another chance to prove how much you mean to me. Promise me at least that much. Promise me you'll let me try to make it up to you."

He stared at me until I nodded.

"Thank you," he said, and was silent. After a minute he said, "I've got to go call my mother."

140

"That should be fun for you."

"Oh, God." He looked up at the sky and sort of flexed his jaw a little. "She just . . . it's the drinking. I'll make it all right. She knows I don't . . . it's just because of Dad, is all. She just . . . well, she has a right."

Hamp's father drank himself to death. He died in the V.A. hospital of liver disease when Hamp was twelve. Hamp looked out toward the edge of the yard, took a deep breath and smiled. He was trying to blink away tears.

"So," he said. "I messed up, huh?" He brushed his hand against the bottom of his eye. "Well! So will you think about it? I mean going somewhere later on. When you can stand the sight of me. So we can . . ." He was breathing like he'd been running, and he put his hand on my shoulder, awkwardly, squeezing. "I . . . Okay? When you don't hate me so much."

"I don't hate you," I said. "I just don't want to be married to a man who hits on other women."

"It didn't mean anything."

"It does to me. It's sick. Get help, for God's sake. And we need to talk, or something."

"So I'll get help," he said. "And I'll talk. You want me to talk? What do you want to know?"

"I want to know why you kissed Diane."

He stared at me.

"Are you in love with her? What's going on?"

"Diane?" he said. "No, I'm not in love with her. I'm not in love with anybody but you."

He pulled me to him and hugged me, and I felt a shuddering sigh go through him, like we were making love.

"You don't know," he said, "how much I love you. And how scared I am. I'd die if I ever lost you." He started kissing my hair and neck. "Don't you know that, girl? Come on. Come with me now. Get in the truck. We'll go somewhere and talk."

"Will you tell me the truth about you and Diane?"

"I'll tell you anything," he said.

I pushed him away so that I could study his face. He looked back at me.

"I want you," he said. "More than I've ever wanted anything in my life. Right now, and forever." He bent over and kissed me, held me hard against him. "Let's go," he said, into my ear.

"We have things to do."

"I have some things I'd like to do to you," he said. "You are driving me crazy, girl. Get in the truck."

I got in the truck.

He was back in a minute, got in without a word, and started down the driveway. I put my hand between his legs.

"What did you tell them?" I said.

"That we'd be back in a while."

I unzipped his blue jeans.

"Hope they're not in a hurry," I said.

"Me too," he said.

■ —— ■

The phone rang about lunchtime and woke me up. Otherwise I guess I would have slept all day.

"Where are you?" said Tina. "Lee is here. Shall we wait lunch?"

"Start without me," I said. "I'm just taking a shower."

I certainly couldn't go over there without one. I smelled like Hamp. I got up and went into the living room looking for him. He'd left a note.

"Call me at the yard," it said.

I got a diet coke and went back to bed, balancing the phone on my stomach while I dialed.

"Hello, beautiful," Hamp said. "How do you feel?"

"I feel great. I can't walk, of course. And I have, like, carpet burn on my back. But other than that . . ."

"Where are you now?"

"In bed."

"Figures. I straightened the living room. Sorry about the lamp."

"We'll get another one," I said. "I never liked it anyway."

It had broken somehow when we first got home.

"I've got Curtis," he said. "Why don't you go back to sleep? Rest up for your vacation tomorrow."

But I couldn't. I had a lunch. In the shower my hands shook, and I thought, I don't know anymore where he leaves off and I begin.

■ —— ■

After lunch I hid in the den and read *Freckles* until Mom and her sisters rousted me out.

"Sitting here with her nose in a book!"

"She hasn't changed a bit," said Lee. "Come talk to me while I press my dress. I want to see how you've been getting along."

She put her arm around my waist and squeezed.

Mom and Bessie escorted us back to the kitchen. I understood that they had all been talking about me, and that this was to be a sort of inquisition.

Lee is the youngest sister, but she looks older than Mom. Her skin is wrinkled from years of tanning. She is the elegant one, thin and alien, expensive smelling in her suits and bracelets. She always brought the aura of the city with her, and when we were children, we would visit her every summer with Mom, and she would take us to museums and plays.

As I grew older, I realized Lee and I didn't like each other. There wasn't anything I could do about it, or anything Lee could do about it either. So I pretended I didn't know.

The kitchen was incredibly clean and bare. All the usual homey touches like the sugar bowl and fresh tomatoes from the garden that

143

usually sat on the counter had been ruthlessly swept away.

"Let me do that," I said as Lee laid her dress on the ironing board. Ironing is my one household talent.

"So how's married life, Judy?" said Lee, watching me from the table.

"Great," I said.

"You look marvelous," she said.

"Thank you."

"And what are your plans after you get Tina Lee married ?" she said.

"To live happily ever after," I said.

There was a small silence, while I laid my wet finger on the iron to test it, and began to press the dress.

"Hamp's mother said last night that you were going back to school," said Mom from the sink. She was cutting lemons.

"Did she really?"

"Well, I must say I think it's a marvelous idea," said Lee. "Personally. Not that it's any of my business."

"I was thinking about it," I said. "I've gotten really interested in design. Architecture. I thought maybe, a course or two, one day a week."

"I'm so glad," said Mom. She walked over from the sink and put her arm around me, just the elbow part because she was holding a knife.

"That room she did at the club, Lee . . . I'll take you over there. She has talent. You need to do this, Judy."

"I may," I said.

"I'll baby-sit," said Mom.

I held up Lee's dress.

"Got anything else you want ironed?" I said.

"Get that tablecloth from the dining room, darling, if you would."

"—deserves a better—"

"—hate to see—"

They quit talking when I came back in.

"Hamp's mother also mentioned that she thought you might be pregnant," said Bessie.

I spread out the tablecloth. "I'm not pregnant," I said. "Hamp's mother ought to mind her own business."

"She was very concerned, Judy," said Mom.

"Marie is always very concerned, Mom," I said. "Concern is her calling. Her hobby. You know how some people play bridge or go to circle meetings? Marie worries."

"Marie is a careful person," said Mom. "Hamp frightened her very much last night. That whole business was uncalled for."

"And he apologized, Mother. He screwed up, okay? He's sorry."

I eased the tablecloth along the ironing board. This was the tricky part, to get the short edge pressed without wrinkling the other.

"His mom decides every six months that he's going straight to hell. She thinks he's like the bad seed or something, just because his father was an alcoholic."

"Those things do run in families," said Lee.

"They do not," I said. "Drinking is not genetic."

"A tendency to alcoholism—"

"Is not genetic. The children of alcoholics are least likely of any group to become alcoholics themselves."

"That is not what I have read."

"You're reading the wrong thing."

"I certainly do not think that Hamilton is an alcoholic, Judy," said Mom. "And I am sure neither Bessie nor Lee does either."

She raised her eyebrows at them.

"Of course not," said Bessie.

"He has been a very good husband and father, and a good son-in-law," said Mom.

"Of course he has," said Bessie.

Which meant, We'll see.

I finished the tablecloth, carried it to the dining room table, and went outside. I walked around the yard, looking at the canopies and the funeral home chairs grouped among them.

My people were now divided into two camps. There was an open split, as there had been at the time of my marriage, between my old family and my new one. It did not matter that I loved my old family. If they made me choose, I'd choose Hamp. And it didn't matter to me that I'd been afraid of him myself only the night before. Since then my life had realigned. What mattered was Hamp. My thoughts and feelings flowed toward him like water.

He loved me, wanted me. He was sorry he'd hurt me. He wanted to try to make it up to me. He was my family now, my future family, the father of my child, perhaps future children.

As I was standing out in the yard, he rode up with Curtis, as though I had called him up by wishing.

"You through?" he said.

"I'll follow you. Let me get my purse."

"Hamp's here," I said in the kitchen. "Bye."

■ —— ■

We went home and watched a Braves game on television. I knew that everything was not all right. I thought it would be, though. We did love each other. Love would stretch, I thought, cover every gap, every mortal dread and failing if it was big enough. And ours was big enough.

Hamp had grown. I had begun to think of him as ordinary, an ordinary man. I had begun to consider him dispassionately. But I had never seen him suffer before. I had never seen him stricken at the thought of losing me. It broke my heart. At the same time, it caused a fierce possessive joy to well up in me that was more important than anything that had ever happened to me. This, I felt, was real life.

So I sat beside him on the couch and tried with all my heart to

146

belong to him. I memorized his face again, touched his hand with my fingers. When it was time to dress for the wedding, I combed Curtis's hair one curl at a time, wrapping each strand around my fingers, sprayed it, held him still by the shoulders while he looked in the mirror. He smiled and patted his head, decided to like his looks. He put on his suit with the terrible short pants, white knee socks, little black shoes. To pass the time, he made faces.

"Guess who I am." He stiffened, began to kick his way across the room.

"Hai! Aighh! Ho!"

"A ninja turtle."

"No."

"I don't know then."

"Batman. Don't you know anything, Mom?"

"Apparently not," I said.

I was still in my underwear, trying to pack what we'd need at the church.

"This is how I'm gonna walk down the aisle." Curtis reeled and staggered, grabbed his chest and fell onto the bed.

"Don't mess up your hair," I said. "Go watch television. Your show is on, and there's a root beer in the refrigerator."

Hamp came out of the shower wrapped in a towel and sat on the bed while I dried his hair, turning his head from side to side, leaning him against my chest. His hair is darker than Curtis's, more wavy than curly.

"What time do you want to leave tomorrow?" he said.

"Late."

"Okay by me," he said. He wrapped his arm around my hips. "Where do you want to go?"

"Oh," I said, "Some place good."

He began to kiss my breasts, pinching them with his lips.

"Does this feel good? Disney World? Hilton Head? Kiawah? What a nice bra. Look, it slips right down."

"It's strapless."

"Um."

I turned off the dryer.

"Hamp, we have to be there in forty minutes."

"Forty minutes is a long time. Just stand here for a minute and relax."

"Hamp, I'm not relaxed."

"You will be," he said. "Just let me . . . don't you like this? Doesn't this make you feel really good?"

"We'll be late."

"No we won't. This will just take a minute. Shall I stop? Tell me you want me to stop and I will."

"No."

"Do you want me to continue? Like this?"

"Yes."

"Then hold still and we'll get this done."

He pulled down my pants and locked the door.

■ —— ■

Thirty minutes later I was doing my makeup and Hamp was sitting on the bed putting on his rented shoes.

"It's a big job, being ring bearer," he said to Curtis. "A lot of responsibility. Aunt Tina's counting on you to do a good job. Just like she's counting on me and Mom."

"Can I wear a weapon?" said Curtis. "A gun? Yesterday they wore a gun. I wore guns yesterday. I did."

"No guns. People don't wear weapons in church, Curtis. It isn't polite."

"I won't shoot anybody. Please, Daddy. Promise. Please!"

"Just in the car. Not in the church. Promise."

"Promise."

Curtis ran out to get a gun.

"So!" said Hamp, standing behind me in the mirror. "You ready to go?"

"Go on out to the car with Curtis," I said. "I'm coming."

"You look great," he said.

I grabbed my makeup and brush, stepped into a skirt. I did not look great. I did not look calm and radiant, the way bridesmaids look in magazines, or even well groomed. On the other hand, I was very relaxed.

Eight

8

Do you ever—when things don't seem to be working out, when a marriage isn't working out or a life isn't working out—do you ever regret the money you spent on it? I do that with my wedding dress. It's in a big box in Mom's attic, what the cleaners called "preserved." That is, the box is sealed, and you can see the dress folded up inside like it has a body in it. It must be stuffed with tissue paper. Every time I go up to the attic now I notice it and wish I had my thousand dollars back. Not that I'm sorry I married Hamp. I just wish I had my thousand dollars back. A thousand dollars for a dress! My God.

Priorities change.

I tried to say something like that to Tina when she was buying her own dress, but it didn't work out. Some things, you just have to find out for yourself. Besides, maybe in Tina's case it doesn't matter. Tina is one of those people who don't have regrets. When she says, "I am so sorry," she doesn't mean remorse, she means inconvenience.

Anyway, you would have thought, with Tina and Jimmy's marriage such a nebulous, uncertain affair even before the proofs got back from the wedding pictures, that she would have held off on ordering the album, or ordered just a few prints, or something. But no. With an Egyptian-like reverence for the corporeal, she ordered page after page of herself and Jimmy and the rest of us, smiling in prim marital rows or grinning in glossy informal abandon, and she bought a huge white album to put them in, as though she could already imagine herself showing us all off to some grandchildren.

Her instincts were good. The marriage may be up for grabs, but we all love the album. Sally looks at it all the time. After supper she goes into the den and pulls it off the coffee table onto her lap—it weighs nearly as much as she does—and studies it, a little girl bending over a big white album, poring over the pictures, one finger against her glasses to hold them on her nose. She touches the pictures. She turns each page carefully, and the plastic crackles, and she studies the next page. Curtis crawls up on the couch beside her with his blanket and looks, too. Sally points out salient features on each page.

"Here you are in the hall before the wedding, Curtis," she says, "and here you are in the vestibule, and there everybody is, remember, after the ceremony? When we all had to go back inside? And the reception. Remember the champagne glasses?"

Sally and Curtis both saved champagne glasses from the reception. They clutter up the top shelf of Mom's cabinet, but whenever Mom tries to throw them away, Curtis and Sally reappropriate them and spend the rest of the day drinking ginger ale from them, carrying them daintily by the stems and grinning, Curtis smacking his lips, Sally sipping.

"And here I am, dancing with Jimmy," says Sally, triumphantly. It is one of her favorite pictures.

"Dancing is for doo-doo heads," says Curtis. "Only doo-doo heads dance."

"That's not true. You danced. There. See? There you are, dancing with your mama."

"I never did."

Sally stabs at a page with her finger.

"There you are, Curtis, right there in the picture."

Curtis looks away, over toward me.

"They had square dancing in the gym today," he says. "They tried to get me to do it, but I wouldn't. Lewis said he wouldn't either, it was for doo-doo heads, but then this big fourth-grade girl made him."

"Did a big fourth-grade girl make you?" I say.

He shakes his head. Sally turns another page.

I'll never know about the dancing, whether Curtis would square-dance that day or not, whether there's a fourth-grade girl for Curtis. Whether he calls people doo-doo heads routinely or only in the bosom of his family. I listen silently to the crumbs he is willing to throw me, knowing I'm lucky he trusts me this much, knowing there's a lot about Curtis I'll never know, now that he is in kindergarten. I depend on his reports, edited for humor and their power to stun. Sally edits for neatness. What she tells me is designed to say, I am fine. Everything's fine. You don't have to involve yourself with my life at all.

I am Sally's guardian, empowered to sign her report cards and take her to the doctor in her parents' absence, but her essential self remains beyond my ken. I do not know Sally. Both children lead, to a remarkable degree, unknowable lives.

They come in from school to the lumberyard, setting their books down, picking up the threads of their lumberyard life without a ripple. They have a desk and do homework. They play with the computer and the calculators, and are building something secret out of scrap lumber in the woods. I take them to scouts, to violin. I take them riding. Sally sits beside me in the car and stares out the window on her way home, her small knobby hands fiddling with the radio, ink-stained fingers curled against the palm. Curtis's hands are marker colored. He draws circles on himself, parabolas and squares. "Boys!" says Sally, in explanation. She seems happy, but who can know? She cries when she gets a letter from Nicaragua. She hides behind the letter and we pretend not to notice, and after awhile she sniffs and reads parts of it aloud.

"Mom met a little boy today whose legs were covered with sores, and the doctor gave him some medicine to make it better. She says Daddy says the bricks down there are all crumbly. He says they are using . . . i-n-f-e-r-i-o-r . . ."

"Inferior."

". . . inferior material to rebuild the hospital."

This brings an angry mumble from Dad which I don't bother to interpret.

"Move over," I say, to Sally on the couch.

She is looking at the album again. She and Curtis make room, and I look at the pictures, too. They are beautiful. Tina was truly a beautiful bride.

We play a game—"What is your favorite picture on this page?" We all know each other's favorite picture by now. Curtis always hesitates over his choice, as though he were just now making up his mind. If Sally or I point to it first, saying, "This is your favorite, remember?" he gets mad.

Curtis's choices always include himself or his father. Sally picks the romantic ones, the ones that show Jimmy and Tina simpering, or Tina in her veil before the wedding.

"Don't you like that one?" says Sally. In it, I am helping Tina with her veil. Tina looks like a soft-focus angel descending from tulle heaven. Even I look okay.

"It's all right," I say.

We are all right in the album, frozen there in plastic, floating around the Ladies' Parlor before the ceremony, all the girls in long dresses with their laughter and their thin young arms, the aunts and grand-mothers leaning together, and the little girls who watch with intent expectancy, absorbing the rows of ruffles, the stiff sway of the skirts, the way the bride looks up, whispers to her groom, her lips brushing his ear, his fingers squeezing her arm. You can almost hear their clothes rustle. It's important, the rustling dresses and the white fingers press-ing into arms. It makes chills in your palms.

Mostly people in the pictures just bob along like corks. They are Curtis's ducks in the bathtub, nod and bounce, bump and smile. We watch them, through the album. They slide up against first one and then another, brushing lightly or with a rude push, but only in pass-ing, never holding on. There's just that little contact, that little thrill of touch. But occasionally the camera has found something else. Love or loneliness or some other true emotion seems to have washed over some of the faces, and they are caught by it. They are recorded that way, and they seem to look out at us with overwhelming poignancy. We trace them through the wedding book like buoys.

So the heavy oak doors to the Ladies' Parlor open, and the doors to the Roy P. Miller Men's Bible Class open, and men in tuxedos spill out and jostle with women in taffeta, and Mr. Carruthers stands at the end of the drafty hall and raises his hand and says, "Let us pray." And we all bow our heads, Mr. Carruthers in his robes more episco-pal than he has been, the rest of us more hushed. We file up the linoleum stairs.

Here are Mom and Lucy Hooper standing together, outlined in the open doorway of the sanctuary. Mom is thin and elegant, her hair short and smooth, her back straight. Lucy is holding her pocketbook in solemn dumpiness. Mom is twitching, Lucy is relaxed. And there Mrs. Hardacre stands beside the door waiting for the rest of us, guid-ing us through, her hand in Kate's back as we stand at the top of the aisle. Mr. Carruthers and Jimmy stand at the bottom, nodding us along. Come on in, jump, come on down, through, along. Come on. Then the beginning is almost complete. The music swells. Mom is standing up, everybody else is standing up, and Tina and Dad are walking down the aisle, Tina glowing and white, and Dad crisp, respectable, grave. "Who gives this woman? Her mother and I, Do you James Pike, Do you Tina Lee, What God has, let no man . . ." Then it is all over, we are all hurrying out, triumphant, to a great flurry of Vivaldi, like we are rushing to catch a plane instead of out onto the front church lawn to wait for more pictures.

Outside, Curtis explodes into a rash of circles, Sally throws all her rose petals on her brother, Jimmy chases her down the sidewalk, and Tina stands briefly still and alone, touching her veil like a real princess on the bright green grass.

■ —— ■

Sally, of course, is much too old to play with Curtis as an equal. She is more my age. But she obliges him, occasionally rolling her eyes in boredom, occasionally forgetting herself and getting into the game.

"Let's play ninja," says Curtis.

"Let's play wedding," says Sally.

She and Curtis sit on the floor of the den, dressing their plastic dolls. They march the tall dolls through a form of ceremony; the short dolls are guests. They rush the church part to get to the reception, at which time they will eat the food they've gathered from the kitchen.

"I do!" says Sally, sliding her doll up a makeshift aisle.

"I do!" says Curtis. "Dum, dum, da dum dum dum dum, da da da dum ta da dum dum."

Then they mash all the dolls together, face to face, twisting them through the air as they sway and sing. That's the party. Then Sally props them up against the hearth in pairs, locking their plastic arms together, and she and Curtis eat up all the food.

"Pick up the dolls," I say before they go to bed.

Sally always does. I have to make Curtis, arguing with him over every doll.

"I didn't get that one out. I didn't play with that one."

"Give me a break, Curtis," I say, knowing he never will.

After they have gone to bed, I go to the doll house and smooth all the dolls' hair, laying them properly down in their places, grouping by sex and size. My father watches, with a little smile.

"I can't help it," I say. "I can't stand to have the Battlestar Maiden sleeping with a ninja transformer dump truck."

My father shakes his head, goes back to the ball game. He watches a lot of television now. So, for that matter, do I.

"We're just like Uncle Tommy," I say. "I am living Uncle Tommy's life."

Tommy is on my mind. I have just been looking at his picture in the album.

"Don't be silly," says Mom. She is doing needlepoint.

"Look at this," I say. "The TV guide even falls open to the right night. Next I'll be having conversations with fingerling trout."

Uncle Tommy runs a fish hatchery.

"You could do a lot worse than turn out like Uncle Tommy," says Mom.

Dad and I turn to stare at her.

"I mean," she says, prodding the needlepoint canvas, "he makes a good living. He loves his work. He is a devoted family man."

"His wife left him, Mother."

"We don't know that."

"She was suffering from terminal boredom. Uncle Tommy is the world's most boring man. And he has worn the same suit for twenty years."

156

"She was no great catch herself," says Mom. "Remember, Bob, that terrible dog she used to have?"

"Skippy," says Dad.

Mom nods. "Skippy. Nasty little thing. Not the slightest bit trained. No discipline whatsoever. And it slept in the bed with them. It's no wonder they didn't have any children."

"Sounds like a great life," I say. "The perfect couple."

"Stop playing with the curtain," says Mom. "Sit down, for heaven's sake. You're just a nervous wreck, Judy." She pinches her needle through the canvas, looks at the underside to make sure the thread isn't tangled. "You need a hobby. Something to relax you."

"Fingerling trout?" I say.

"Why don't you try needlepoint?" she says.

For some reason Dad finds that hysterically funny.

"I think I'll go out for a little while," I say. "If you don't mind."

Their eyes flicker.

"For a drive."

"Well, be careful, Judy."

"I will, Mother."

I can hear them arguing as I get my jacket.

"—can't see why she—"

"—doesn't want to—"

I let myself out quietly, so as not to wake the children.

■ —— ■

Tina's reception was everything she wanted it to be. The sun shone, and the whole back yard was full of happy people sipping champagne and eating marinated shrimp. Half the silver platters in McAdamsville had been pressed into service, and they were all loaded with little goodies: sandwiches, cakes, nuts, mints, and bites of things in pastry shells. I spent some time with Uncle Tommy, thin and absent-minded in his suit. Happy. I make fun of him, but he's really adorable.

"So how've you been?" I say to him. "How's the hatchery?" And he tells me, in great detail and at exquisite length.

"Just between you and me," he says, from behind his hand, as though there were spies everywhere.

And I was there in the dining room when Granny Glendinning made her famous remarks about some of the guests.

"Look!" she said. "Nigras, Lucy!"

"Behave yourself," said Lucy. "Or I'll take you back to the nursing home."

And I was there to see Helen get sick again. I held my arm around her waist and helped her into the house, into my bedroom, onto my bed. I brought a wet washcloth for her forehead. I sat with her on the edge of my bed and patted her hand while her breathing slowed, returned to normal. She smelled like sweat, and the skin on her face glistened. Droplets condensed on her upper lip. I told her she was killing herself.

She put her hand to her chest, pressing down.

"I've lost twenty pounds. And I feel great. Another twenty-five and I'll be there," she said. "I just made a mistake not eating a little something." She blew her nose.

"Cocaine is not a diet pill," I said.

"Don't lecture me, please. I have heard the lecture, whatever it is. Okay?"

She raised her head and looked at me.

"Should I get you a sandwich or something?"

"No. Thanks. Maybe a glass of milk."

I returned in a minute with the milk. She sat up and sipped it. I sat beside her on the bed.

"I really don't know what I'm doing here, you know?" she said. "We haven't been close for years, Tina and I. Though it was sweet of her to ask me to be in her wedding, don't you think?"

"She said you used to plan your weddings together in chemistry class."

158

Helen smiled.

"I hope it works out between her and Jimmy. I truly do. Tina deserves some happiness."

"Don't we all," I said. "What about you? How about you and Nick?"

I was just making conversation, thinking I needed to get back to the party.

"Nick's a good friend. He's helping me. I'm getting it all together, and I'm getting out of here. And I'm going to have a decent life if it kills me." She looked at her washcloth, refolded it, held it to her face, and lay down again.

"Well," I said. "I guess I'd better get going."

"Wait. Stay a minute." Helen grabbed my arm, peeked out from under the washcloth. "I want to ask you something."

"What?"

"Were you pregnant when you married Hamp?"

I stared at her. She raised her head and stared back, nearsightedly, catching the washcloth as it fell across her nose. She began to wind it between her fingers.

"I know it's none of my business," Helen continued, "and I shouldn't be asking. Curtis was born early, I know, a bare eight months after the wedding. But it's not like it was a rushed wedding or anything. And it really doesn't matter, does it? I mean, people get married because they love each other, right? And it was obvious that Hamp loved you."

"Helen, I really need to be getting back to the party."

"Judy, bear with me." She put her hand on my arm again. "This is hard." She sat straight up, put her feet on the floor, laid the washcloth carefully in the ashtray beside the bed.

"I've just always wondered, because I thought it might explain, you know, about Tina and Hamp. But then I thought it shouldn't matter. And then I thought you surely must know about it and not care, and then I thought you didn't know and that I ought to tell you. But

159

now I'm thinking . . . God, this is so hard!"

"Helen, what are you talking about?" I said.

"I'm thinking, you ought to know, Judy. I'm putting myself in your place. Ignorance is not bliss. That's what I used to say, but it's just because I didn't put myself in your place. I talked it over with Nick, and he said to mind my own business, not to tell you anything. But men stick together so, you know? I mean they protect each other. Don't they, Nick?"

I turned around. Nick stood in the door.

"What are you trying to say, Helen?" I said. "What ought I to know?"

"About Tina and Hamp," she said.

"What about Tina and Hamp?" I said.

"See, Nick? I told you she didn't know," said Helen. Nick came silently into the room. Helen continued.

"Tina told me it was over, but she's said that before and it wasn't over then. Besides, a person who will do that kind of thing one time is often the kind of person who will do it over and over again, you know, and that's not right. If a man has one girlfriend, where's it gonna end, you know?" She leaned forward, her hands no longer nervous but folded simply in her lap. "Judy, I'm sorry to be the one to tell you this, but Tina and Hamp been having an affair off and on for years."

■ —— ■

So Tina had thought of everything when she planned her wedding. All the lists, books, file boxes, all the months of planning and the thousands of dollars had paid off. The yard was full of well-wishers; the living room was full of wedding presents. Tina's bedroom, when I went in there to watch her changing her clothes, was in the final stages of disarray. Her bag was packed. She had only forgotten one thing.

"I'm glad Kate caught the bouquet, aren't you?" she said, unzipping her dress.

"I didn't see that." I stood by the window. "I was with Helen. She got sick."

Tina pushed the stiff material from her shoulders and down off her hips, stepped out of the circle of wedding gown on the floor, gathered it up, laid it across the bed. She walked to the dresser and began fiddling with her earrings. I watched her small, neat back, the curve of her spine above her slip. She turned back toward me, picked up her going-away dress and stepped into it, her breasts showing above the lace of her strapless bra as she bent over. I thought of Hamp.

"What's the matter with you?" she said. "You look terrible."

"Why did you sleep with my husband?" I said.

"What?" She glanced up, stepped into her shoes.

"Why did you have an affair with Hamp?"

All the color drained out of her face.

"I don't know what you mean," she said.

"Helen told me just now. She said it was like a long-term thing. Going on for years."

"Helen is heavily into cocaine, did you know?"

"I do now."

"I almost told her she . . . but I decided that would be unfair. To write her off, you know?" Tina sat on the edge of the bed, looking out the window, clasping and unclasping her bracelet with a little snap. "Looks like I made a mistake."

I just looked at her.

"What did she tell you?" Tina said.

She looked up at me, and there was no fear in her face, no joy, no sadness, just nothing.

"What difference does it make?" I said. "You have ruined my life."

She wouldn't look at me. She snapped her bracelet until the clasp broke, and she took it off and held it, twisting it in her hands. Then she looked up.

161

"Did she tell you I loved him?"

I just stared at her.

"Did she? I loved Hamp before you even met him. I introduced you. I watched the two of you love and marry, and I watched you have a child. I would have given anything, anything in this world, to be you. But I wasn't. And I finally realized I had to make a life for myself, and get on with it. So . . ." she gave a little laugh, "so I married Jimmy. So now I'm out of your hair, right?"

She stood up, dropped the bracelet in her suitcase and shut the lid, looked up, smiled a little.

"Right?"

"You have ruined my life," I said. "You have ruined my life. You have ruined my life."

"I have not."

"The funny thing was," I said. I had to stop and take a breath. "The really funny thing was, I already knew. 'Tina and Hamp have been screwing for years,' Helen said. I wasn't even surprised. How could a person know a thing like that and not know it at the same time? Why wasn't I more surprised? Why did I hear it like . . . of course. Like a confirmation."

"I don't know," she said. There were footsteps in the hall. Tina picked up her purse. "I've got to go."

"Tina!" said our mom's voice. "Tina? Come on."

"I don't believe this," I said.

Tina walked up to me and touched me on the arm. "Hamp always loved you. It was always you. I hated you for that. But it was true."

I jerked my arm away. "He touched you!" I said. "I can't stand this! Just like I wasn't even there! Just like I didn't even exist!"

"You were always there. He always loved you. It was awful."

"Tina!" Mom was standing in the door.

"How could you?" I said.

"He was mine first," she said.

162

■ —— ■

It was dark outside when Tina left on her honeymoon, and the strings of lights Daddy had rigged in the yard and on the porch were glowing, casting the people moving among them in the half-light of a summer party. The photographer took his final pictures of Tina and Jimmy as they came out the back door dodging bird seed, laughing, running for the car, and the half-light plus the photographer's flashes gave the final wedding pictures a sort of tabloid look—figures too bright, background too dark. Jimmy and Tina looked like old-time movie stars caught coming out of a night club or off an ocean liner— too close up, all white teeth and surprised hair. Nobody liked those prints but me. I thought they were perfectly appropriate.

Nine

9

I LEFT HAMP THE DAY AFTER TINA'S WEDDING.

"Where are you going?" Hamp said. "When will you be back?"

"I don't know," I said.

"Don't do this, Judy," he said. "You are not in the best shape. Let me drive you to the beach like we planned. Get away and talk this out."

"I don't want to talk. I can hardly stand to be on the same planet with you, much less in the same car."

I was trying to pack a few things. I picked up my hairbrush and looked at it, and it had Hamp's hair and my hair and Curtis's hair all tangled up together in the bristles, and I sat down on the bed and held it up.

"Look," I said. "Look at this."

I waved the brush at him, like he would understand, and began to cry. He came over and sat down beside me and put his arm around me.

"I am so sorry," he said.

"Don't touch me," I said.

He took his hand away.

"Let me ask you," I said. "In what way are you sorry? How does it work with you? Are you sorry you've been screwing my sister, or sorry I found out about it?"

"Both."

"How can the words 'I'm sorry' cover that kind of thing?" I said. "I'm sorry is what you say when you bump into somebody or spill a cup of coffee or break a dish. You slept with my sister." I began pulling hairs out of the brush. "Well, was it a thrill or what? How did you manage it, Hamp? I mean the logistics of the thing. Did you ever do it on this very bed?"

"No," he said.

"No what?"

"No, we didn't. No, it wasn't fun. No, you do not need to hear any more of this right now."

"What I need or do not need is no longer any of your damned business," I said. "I am sure of that."

"Please don't do this," he said. "I love you. It kills me that I've hurt you like this. Please give me a chance to make it up to you."

Naturally I did not see how that would be possible. I could only see that I had two choices: leave or go crazy.

"What am I going to tell your family, for Chrissake?"

"You have such an inventive mind," I said. "I'm sure you'll think of something."

Curtis was quiet as I put our suitcases into the car.

"Where are we going?" he said.

"Remember? We were going on a little vacation after the wedding."

165

"I want Daddy to go." He ran to Hamp and wrapped his arms around Hamp's knees.

"Daddy can't go this time," I said. "Maybe another time you and Daddy can go."

Hamp picked him up and hugged him, looking at me over Curtis's shoulder. I thought Hamp might just walk back into the house with Curtis in his arms and shut the door. But he didn't. He walked Curtis to the car, put him in the front seat, buckled him in.

"You have a great time, okay, sport?" he said. "Take care of your mama for me."

"Why can't you go?"

"I've got some work to do." Hamp shook Curtis's arm. "You'll be fine, buddy. Bring me something, all right? Huh?"

Hamp ducked his head up under Curtis's bent forehead and gave him a quick kiss, ruffled his hair, stepped back. I got in the car. Hamp came around and put his hand on my door.

"Where are you going?"

"We haven't decided yet." I started the car.

"Call me tonight. Promise."

"Let go of the door, please."

"Promise."

"Don't pressure me. This is not a vacation, Hamp. I'm furious. I'm angrier than I've ever been in my life. I'm not going on some little rest cure, to call up my husband every night and tell him I'm fine."

He raised his hands to show helplessness.

"I'll see," I said.

"Please, Judy. So I'll know you're both all right."

"Every concession counts, right?" I said.

"I'm not trying to win concessions. I just want to know if you're all right every night. He's my kid too, you know."

"Wish you'd thought about that earlier."

"I do too," he said.

166

I looked at him. He looked down at the ground.

"I'll call you," I said. "And let you know where we are."

As I drove out of the yard, I looked in the rearview mirror and saw Hamp, standing and staring after the car.

"Want to sing songs?" I said to Curtis.

We drove to Demaro, singing "Zip-Ah-Dee-Doo-Dah" and "She'll Be Coming Round the Mountain." Between verses Curtis whined.

"Well, you pick a song then."

"I don't want to sing any more," he said. "Where are we going? I want to go to Disney World. Why can't we? You promised."

"Oh come on now," I said. "We'll have fun. It'll be fun. You'll enjoy yourself. Want some breakfast?"

"No."

"I do." I pulled into Sparky's Drive-In and ordered a hamburger.

"A hamburger for breakfast?"

"Sure. This is vacation. Sure you won't have anything?"

He ordered a hamburger, too, and onion rings. We ate in the car. The onion rings were delicious.

■ —— ■

Demaro sits in the foothills of the Appalachians, part farm town and part mill hill, a red-brick, oak-tree, convenience-store sprawl that was wham-bamming its way up and down the interstate with careless southern abandon until the textile mills began to close. So did half the stores in town. The malls emptied. Corner lots grew up in weeds. Finally the good old boys and girls began to reel in some new out-of-state companies looking for a tax break, cheap labor, and a river to dump their sewage, and Demaro was back in business, adding a wing to the local hospital, ripping up parking meters to promote down-town. Demaro has three colleges and a speedway, and all the radio stations play country music. It's a great town.

Kids come from fifty miles around on Friday nights to eat at Sparky's and lean against their cars and look one another over—tough boys with slick hair and thick necks and football jackets, clusters of small-mouth white girls and big-eyed black girls flashing gold class rings that dwarf their fingers—kids from Demaro High, McAdamsville High, Windy Gap, and Granitetown, kids who want nothing more than to find something, they don't know what, at Sparky's.

I was once one of them. Charley was, too.

Now I sat in the parking lot with my son, sipping a cola that would fill a gas tank, thinking the kids who dress up and come here on Friday nights should just forget the love and stick with the onion rings.

Across the street from the drive-in was a bunch of new apartments. "Model Open!" the sign said. "New! Today! 1-2-3 Bedrooms Available!"

"Do you know," I said. "That's where your friend what's-his-name lives, Helen's friend. Nick. Wonder what those apartments rent for."

"One o'clock, two o'clock, three o'clock rock," we sang.

We pulled out onto the highway going west, toward the interstate. As we crossed Demaro, I felt like I was stepping off into the wilderness.

"Want to go to the mountains, Curtis?" I said.

"I want to go to Disney World," he said. "I'm hungry. I have to go wee-wee."

"We can't go to Disney World this trip," I said. "It's too far. You just ate. Why didn't you wee-wee at the drive-in?"

We pulled off at a gas station at the northwest corner of Demaro right before the interstate. The mountains loomed on the horizon in a purplish haze. Curtis tried to get out, too.

"Stay in the car while I get gas," I said.

While I was pumping the gas, he got out anyway.

"Did I say stay in the car?" I said.

"Why? I have to pee-pee. I want a drink. I'm hungry."

A car whizzed by us, pulling into the next lane.

"Come over here and stand still."

"I want some crackers."

I grabbed a handful of his shirt.

"Stand still. That passing car could have killed you. Stand by me until I finish getting gas. Come here. Don't put your hand down in the trash can. Curtis!"

"I want to hold the gas."

"No."

"Daddy lets me."

"Daddy isn't here." The metallic smell of trucks and gas mixed with the deep cool smell of the mountains. "You see that greasy spot on the cement over there?" I said. "That used to be a little boy. Only he didn't mind his mother and a tanker squashed him flat."

He looked up at me, over at the spot. I swung the pump nozzle back into its slot and walked Curtis into the station, keeping my hand on his shoulder as we walked. He jerked reflexively, like an animal, when he saw the rows of candy.

"Bathroom first, Curtis."

"I don't have to go."

I steered him toward the women's rest room.

"I don't want to use the girl's," he said.

"You have to. Daddy is not here. I can't go into the men's room with you. Come on." I held the door open.

"No."

We were standing in the dark anteroom outside the bathroom doors. I let the women's room door swing shut.

"Are we going to spend the day here?" I said, looking at the tile, the soiled wall. "Is this my life, here by this water fountain? I have a future, Curtis. I would like to get on with it, please."

Curtis stared at me, jaw stuck out, eyes narrow.

"You have two choices," I said. "You come into this bathroom and go, and we will get a nice snack and be on our way. Or we can stand here forever. It's all the same to me. I am miserable anyway. I don't mind this. I'm an adult. We adults are trained to be patient and spend our time in obscure and stupid places. You, on the other hand, are a child and may not want to live your whole summer in front of this bathroom door. Think about it."

He started to walk away, and I grabbed his arm. It felt thin and pitiful, the shirt wrinkled under my grasp.

"Think about it, Curtis," I said.

He yanked his arm away, pushed past me into the women's bathroom. I stood outside his stall and waited.

"Wash your hands," I said when he came out.

He jerked on the faucet and fanned his hands briefly under the water, yanked at a towel from the dispenser. It wouldn't come out. He rattled it, kicked the wall, began to cry. When I picked him up, he fought me.

"Here, buddy, here," I said. I slapped the dispenser. "Mean old thing."

I set Curtis on the counter and handed him a towel, tied his shoes while he dried his hands.

"Are we going to have an adventure together or not?" I said.

"I don't want to have an adventure," he said. "I want to go home." His eyes were frightened and dull.

"I know," I said, picking him up off the counter. "You scared?"

He nodded.

"Let's go just a little farther," I said. "If it's a dippy place we'll come home. Deal?"

He nodded.

"I saw some cheese doodles out there. And I bet we can have lunch at McDonalds, if we can find one."

"Really?" he said. "Okay!"

■ —— ■

170

We pulled out onto the interstate and started up the first incline into the mountains. Curtis had his drink propped between his legs, his snacks spread out around him. I rolled down the window.

"Feel that mountain air, Curtis?" I said. "It's cooler already."

The highway cut a wide, sweet swath up the side of the slope, wrapping itself around ceremoniously and with flair—not a timid road, or a road that huddles and hugs curves. A bold road. Lewis and Clark would have loved it. In another half hour, we were over the top. I pulled off the road at an overlook.

Curtis, asleep in the front seat beside me, did not stir. His legs were covered with goose bumps and cheese-doodle crumbs. I leaned out the window and looked at the Smokies, rolling below us like a lumpy blue quilt, cold and alien.

I had gone as far as I belonged. From here on, I had to kick free and float, travel as a balloonist in a sort of soar—floating but not belonging, passing but not caring for the land. I would be a traveler only. I would not be bound.

We drove off the interstate at the next exit and into Windy Gap, past the little motels which lined either side of the road into town, small stucco or brick buildings right next to the highway, some refurbished and bearing signs saying "Weekly Rates. Vacancy." Some were dumps. We could stay in one of those, I thought. We could just check in and I could call home and say I'd be back tomorrow. One more day. Then I'd call again the next day, and the next. See how it went.

I pulled off the road into one that had a white and green sign, "The Hideaway." The buildings were bright white with green shutters, and the lines outlining the parking spaces were all bright white, too. A tiny pool sat out in the middle of a green yard, surrounded by cement and a fence. It looked promising. A seventyish man in a brown cardigan was sweeping the walk in front of the office. He followed Curtis and me inside, walked behind the counter.

171

SOMETHING BLUE

"May we hep you folks?" he said.

"We'd like a room," I said.

"Sure thing." He slid a registration card over the counter. I had to go outside to read my car tag number. When I got back, Curtis was pulling folders out of the wire rack beside the counter.

"Can we see this? Look, Mom!"

"How much is the room?" I said, handing the man the card.

"By the day or week?"

"Day."

He told me.

"Is that your best rate?"

He looked chagrined. "By the month is our best rate. Then by the week. Then by the day."

I felt my face grow hot. "I mean, is there a discount?"

"Ten percent for seniors. I'll show you the room."

We traipsed across the grass to one of the little houses, and the man scratched the key in the lock, shoved open the door. It was a perfect fifties room—knotty pine, a red maple dresser, two double beds with tufted spreads, and crook-neck lamps. The bathroom had black-and-white tile.

"It's perfect," I said. "We'll take it."

I felt like I could stay there forever. We found a McDonalds across town, went in and got more hamburgers.

"Look, Mom! They have little seats here!"

Curtis was beginning to enjoy himself. He raced to a tiny table. I squeezed in on the other side, onto a yellow plastic stool designed for someone three feet tall.

"I feel like Alice in Wonderland," I said.

The place was filling up with families on the way home from church, patient, suited men standing in line like brown maypoles while children twisted and jumped at their feet.

There was a rack of applications for employment next to the daily

172

newspapers, and I picked one up and began to fill it out while we ate. It took me the whole meal. When I got to the part that said, "Preferred Hours," I folded it and put it into my purse.

"Can I go out on the playground now?" said Curtis.

"Sure. I'll come with you."

We moved outside and I sat in a corner, huddled against the wind, reading *The Windy Gap Mountaineer* while Curtis ran up the wooden ramps and slid down the slides. We had worn shorts. I had forgotten it would be cooler.

The Mountaineer had a lot of white space and spoke eloquently of zoning and the upcoming rhododendron festival. There was a big picture of a wreck on the front page. Apparently nobody was hurt. The only Help Wanted ads were for baby-sitters, paper carriers, and convenience store clerks.

We could live here, I thought. We could just stay here. We could drive around this afternoon and check the place out, go spend the night at the Hideaway. Perhaps many nights. Perhaps I could find a job and put Curtis in school here. Change my name back to McAdams. Or we could keep on going, across the mountains to anywhere. Or we could go home.

I sat there while Curtis outlasted three groups of children who came, played, and left. He became king of the slides and boss of the pirate's nest, began to give tours. The grown-ups glanced at me with the casual superiority of the well churched.

Finally Curtis came up to me and said, "I'm cold. Can we go now?"

"I'll force myself," I said.

We went out to the car. I turned on the heater.

"What are we going to do now?" he said.

"Buy you some long pants."

"Then what? Go see the Indians?"

He picked up one of the folders he'd gotten from the motel office. "Cherokee Land."

"Why not?" I said.

There were signs at the next intersection for Cherokee Land, a rock shop ("South's Largest Selection"), and Appleby's Discount House ("Straight Ahead 3 Miles The Most For The Least Try Us"). Other delights were promised. We followed the signs.

Main Street Windy Gap is as charming as gray stone, red geraniums, and a ruthless tourist policy can make it. There are quaint lampposts and benches, shops called "Christmas Village" and "Ducks Galore." We passed a new stone building and a sign that said "Windy Gap Elementary School." There were flowers planted all around the sign.

"Nice looking school," I said. "Like to go there, maybe?"

"I'm going to where my friends go," said Curtis.

I was making him nervous.

"Oh, that's right," I said. "I had forgotten." I smiled at him like I had been teasing.

Appleby's Discount House is a large aluminum building in a valley of asphalt. Hundreds of parking places have been marked off; all were empty. A few cars huddled up next to the building. We joined them.

"Get me a toy," said Curtis.

Inside were many tables piled with stacks of stiff blue jeans, bins of knit shirts, belts, cheap dress shirts in crinkly cellophane. We found a pair of jeans in Curtis's size and took them to the checkout counter. The girl who rang us up was an anorexic fourteen-year-old wearing a tank top through which her nipples poked like raisins. I asked her anyway.

"Is it easy to get a job here in Windy Gap?"

"Sure," she said. "If you like working fast food."

"Happy Jack's always needs somebody," said her companion, another adolescent with a rash of angry pimples among his whiskers. "That Seven-Eleven down on the highway?" He tossed the blue jeans into a sack. "Man got shot there last week. D'you hear about that?

174

Right in the chest." He took aim with his arm and fired off two shots. "Pow! Pow!"

"Yuck!" said the girl. "Did he die?"

"Of course he died," said the boy. "My cousin's on the squad, he said he'd never seen the like of blood."

The boy took the receipt, dropped it into the sack, handed the sack across the counter.

"Have a nice day," said the girl.

Cherokee Land was all Curtis desired—tepees, people in head-dresses and velvet clothes, and shops with rubber tomahawks and feathered headbands that had been made in the Philippines. Curtis bought a headband and, for his daddy, a corncob pipe and a screw-driver with a removable handle.

"Perfect," I said. "He'll love it. Look at these coloring books, look, see, here's one about the Cherokee language, and one about how the Cherokees had to leave their homes and go on the Trail of Tears. See? Do you want these?"

"Sure. But not with my money."

"Will you color in them?"

"I don't like to color."

I got them anyway.

■ —— ■

We ate dinner at Mom's Good Cooking. There Curtis found a genu-ine rubber knife for himself and a plastic rain gauge for Hamp.

"What do you want to eat?" I said.

"Dumplings."

"You like fried chicken best."

"I like dumplings."

"You're just getting dumplings because Daddy gets them."

"I'm not."

So we got them.

"Eat."

"I'm not hungry." He stuck his fork through a dumpling and held it up, dripping. "It's gooey."

"It's a dumpling. It's supposed to be gooey. Don't drip it on the tablecloth."

"They're not gooey when Daddy gets them."

"You want some of my fried chicken?"

"Is it gooey?"

■ —— ■

We went back to the room. I got Curtis ready for bed, turned on the television set.

"I want to call Daddy," he said.

There was no phone in the room.

"Put your shoes on," I said.

There was a phone booth out at the other end of the parking lot. I counted my change, and we went out there, wedged ourselves into the booth, dialed the numbers. I handed the phone to Curtis.

"Daddy?" he said. "Hi. Fine. Fine. Fine. Okay." His voice grew smaller and smaller. He handed the phone to me.

"Hello?" I said.

"Hello, Judy?" The line crackled.

"Yes."

"So where are you?"

"In the mountains."

"Having a good time?"

"No."

"Why don't you come on home then?"

"I may."

"When?"

"Tomorrow."

176

"That'll be great," he said. "When can I expect you?"

"I don't know. I've got to go."

"Judy?"

"What?"

"I love you."

"Right," I said. "See you later."

I hung up the phone, and we walked back to the room, me looking behind me, quick glances to each side as we crossed the dark patches around the corners. The ice machine and a couple of drink boxes stood in a shed, haloed in light.

"Want a soda?" I still had a handful of change.

Curtis was trying to choose a drink, and I heard footsteps coming up behind me, a middle-aged man with an ice bucket.

"Excuse me," he said, digging into the ice.

"Hurry up," I said to Curtis.

He dropped the money and mashed a button. Nothing happened.

"Need any help?" said the man. "Let me see." He put down his ice and shook the machine, banged on the front of it with his hand. "What kinda drink you want, hon?" he said.

Curtis pointed to something and the man punched the button. The drink dropped.

"Need another one?" he said to me.

"No thank you. Thanks for your help."

I walked back toward our cabin. The man walked beside me.

"Nice night," he said.

"Yes," I said. "It is."

"You folks on vacation?"

"Just passing through," I said.

We had reached our door. I did not want to open it while he was standing there.

"Nice town. Windy Gap," he said.

"Yes, it is," I said. "Good night."

"Good night."

He moved on slowly toward the next cabin.

"Open the door, Mom."

"In a minute, Curtis."

"Open the door!" He started rattling the knob.

"Shut up!" I whispered. I put my fingers over his, tore them away from the knob.

"Mom! Open the door! Mom!"

I looked around, and the man was still moving away, looking back at us as though to see what was the matter. I jammed the key into the lock, swung it open, and jerked Curtis inside, slammed the door, turned all the locks, leaned against it.

"What'd you do that for?" said Curtis. "Whassa matter?"

"Nothing. Curtis, you don't stand around in motel parking lots talking to strangers."

"I didn't. You were talking to him."

"And you don't open your room door when a stranger is standing behind you. You wait until he goes away."

"Why?"

"Because. Drink your coke."

"He was a nice man," Curtis said.

"It's a matter of trust," I said. "You don't trust strangers."

"Why not?"

"I don't want to talk about it right now, Curtis, okay? Just drink your drink and go to bed, okay?"

I tucked him in, read him a story, kissed him goodnight, went into the bathroom to take a shower. When I opened my eyes from lathering my hair, Curtis was standing at the foot of the tub, peering through the curtain.

"Mom?"

"You're supposed to be in bed, Curtis."

"I'm scared."

He sat on the toilet seat until I got through bathing, and I led him out to his bed and tucked him in again.

"I'm right here, okay?"

I dried, dressed, towel-dried my hair under his watchful eye. When I went back into the bathroom, he followed me.

"Whatcha doin'?"

"Peeing. Do you mind?"

He shook his head.

"Would you give me a break?" I said. "I'm not going anywhere. I'll be right here. Please go to sleep."

"I'm scared," he said. "I want Daddy."

"Oh don't be ridiculous," I said and put him back to bed.

He was like glue all night. If I got up to change the channel on the television set, he opened his eyes and sat up. If I went into the bathroom or around the corner to brush my teeth or look at myself in the mirror, he crept in behind me. If I turned over in the bed, he watched. Finally I turned out the light and lay in the darkness, listening to cars ride up and down the road outside the motel. It was ten o'clock.

I woke up later because my heart was beating too fast. I lay there while it whirred in my chest, not wanting to turn on the light because of Curtis. The air in the room smelled cold and soft, alien, air-conditioned air.

The high sustaining tidal wave that had flung me from home had receded. It had thrown me down and gone. I was left clinging to the side of a lumpy bed, holding on for dear life, hands shaking, swallowing the metallic taste which rose like bile in my mouth.

This was not a great adventure after all. It was an act of mad folly, a running away from something which had to be faced. I couldn't be Lewis and Clark after all. I was more the man from Marrakesh. My destiny, like his, would meet me on the road.

I wanted more than anything simply to run away. To keep on going, to keep on moving away from a life that had become intolerable.

But I couldn't. No great moral courage was at work; I simply couldn't get any farther up the road. This motel room was the outer circumference of my day, my personal maximum, my ultimate stretch. What a joyless thought that was! How weak-kneed I'd become, how careless of protecting myself. How undaring. How scared.

And there was Hamp, on the other end of the phone, on the other end of my life, making it all seem normal, making it all seem okay. No problem. Let's talk about it. Come home and let's talk it out. And I knew what would happen; I'd say yes, okay, okay, that's all right, that's all right, too, reasonably, rationally, because after all the man did have a right to see his son, know what his son was doing. And after all the man did live in the house, did have clothes there, did work for the company. Was married to me. Was a nice man. And sooner or later, what I now thought was such a problem would just disappear. What I demanded, he would give. But what I forgot, he would take back. I would be playing that game I'd hated as a child, the one where you turn your back and count, and people slip up on you, and you whirl back around and try to catch them at it. To live with Hamp again would be to try to play that game and win it. And I had never won it in my life.

On the other hand, I had never played for keeps before. I was discovering that made all the difference.

Ten

10

NICK WAS IN FRONT OF HIS APARTMENT washing his old blue Ford when Curtis and I stopped by on our way home from the mountains.

"Nice knees," I shouted, pulling my car up beside his.

He was wearing cut-offs and a shredded T-shirt. He turned off the hose and walked to my window.

"I stopped by to see how Helen is," I said. "And to thank you." He had done me a very great favor.

"Any time," he said, bending down to look at us through the window. "Curtis, my friend, you are taking your mama for a little ride?"

"We are going home now," said Curtis.

"Would you like to help me wash my car? You can see I am only half finished." Nick turned and waved at it. "And I have to leave for work in a few minutes."

We got out of the car. Curtis picked up a sponge and began swathing the bumper with suds.

■ —— ■

Whenever I think of Nick, I still see him as he looked after Tina's wedding—in his tuxedo, sitting in the rose-chintz chair in my bedroom, talking with Helen, who was lying on the bed. In fact I am sure that I shall always see him like that, there, in that place and time, his coat open, one arm back against the chair, a dark shadow of beard already glossing his face.

"What am I going to do?" I had said. I spoke to Helen or to the room at large, but Nick had answered me. "What am I going to do now?"

"You are going to come over here and sit down," he'd said, rising. "And talk to me. We have much to say to each other. Come on." He patted the chair.

When I sat down, he sat on the stool in front of me and leaned forward, his jacket stretching across his back, looking at me until I looked at him.

"Now," he'd said, glancing toward the window. "What to do next. You need to stay in here with us for awhile and visit."

"But after that?" My mind skittered across to those dark places, after everyone had gone.

"It will work itself out," he said. "You don't need to worry about that now." He shrugged dismissively. "Now you are to sit with us and help me be Helen's nurse. This is a beautiful room, you know? So perfect. I was just looking at this collection of books. How nice to grow up here. Have you always lived in this house?"

And so he had led me back onto solid ground, away from the dark confusion in my mind.

"Do you still read these books?" he said. "This one. What's this about?"

"I just reread that one."

"Tell me about it. You must like it, then." He forced me to look at him, to be polite. He forced the conversation forward.

I knew I was being jollied along. I knew he was treating me like a child who'd gone too near the edge of a precipice, that he was talking to me to distract me because he didn't want me to go out into the yard and have a screaming fit in front of all Tina's guests. I knew his reasoning was social only. But I didn't care. I allowed myself to be led because I liked the way he smelled, the rustle of his shirt, the little catch of an accent and the way he said "books." "All these books," making an *O* with his mouth, holding up his palms.

I wanted to see him again, to hear what he had to say this time. And I wanted to be normal, to show him I was normal, that this was nothing, that I was coping, that Hamp and I would be fine. Therefore I smiled brightly and watched how I got out of the car. I remembered to keep my legs together, as I do when I'm trying to make a good impression. I read that in a book. When you want to get out of the car well, you swing both legs out and put your feet on the ground before you stand up, instead of just climbing out one long foot at a time, which is what I usually do.

So I got out well, stood there in the parking lot of the apartment having good posture while this man and my son were rinsing his car, which was faded from the sun.

"It needs wax," I said.

"It needs a new carburetor worse," Nick said, turning off the hose. "Let's go inside and get a soft drink, shall we? I have to leave for work in a minute or Curtis could swim in my pool."

"Could I? Could I?"

"Maybe another time," I said.

■ ——— ■

The apartments were arranged in a rectangle around the parking lot, rows of different colored doors, shiny brass porch lights that simulated coach lights and gracious living. Nick led us to his door, a blue one. We crossed the tiny stoop and went inside. His living room held only two lawn chairs facing a small television set on a wooden crate. A stationary bicycle and a rowing machine sat across the room.

"Excuse me," Nick said and disappeared upstairs.

Curtis climbed the bicycle.

"Be careful," I hissed. "Sit down. Don't break it."

"But I can't reach the pedals."

"Curtis!" I could hear Nick opening a dresser upstairs, walking across the floor. "Sit down!"

"Ouch!" Curtis began to wail. "You hit me! Ow! Ow!"

"Oh, for heaven's sake."

I could hear footsteps coming down the stairs. Nick came back in his street clothes.

"Mama won't let me ride the bike!" said Curtis. "She hit me!"

"Your feet won't touch the pedals, okay? You can't ride it."

Nick shook his head. "Don't you have any patience at all, boy?" He lifted Curtis off the bike, adjusted the seat, put him back on. "Now ride," he said. "Pedal hard, like that, and watch the needle jump. See?"

A furious clicking whirred up from the bike chain.

"See, Mom? See me? I told you I could do it!"

"Your mom knew you could do it. Moms are like that. Special people." Nick winked at me.

Curtis slowed down. His face was getting red, and the bike subsided to a routine click-click.

"Do you have a mom?" Curtis said.

"In Philadelphia. Your mom and I are going into the kitchen and fix a drink. Would you like a soda?"

"Are they the kind I like?"

"Probably not."

184

"Then I don't want one."

"Say 'No thank you,'" I said.

"No thank you!" shouted Curtis. "No thank you! No thank you!"

I followed Nick to the kitchen.

"I'm embarrassed," he said, sweeping aside dirty dishes. "Don't look."

"We barged right in," I said. "I apologize. The place looks great."

It did look pretty good. It didn't have that depressing, roachy, dirty-glass aura so common among the unwed. And the apartment itself was well designed, pleasant if cheap. All the kitchen cabinets were laminated pressboard, but they looked better than the ones in my trailer.

"I haven't bought furniture," he said. "Just a bed and what you see."

He handed me a diet soft drink, glanced at his watch.

"We mustn't keep you," I said. "I didn't mean to come in. I really just stopped by to say thanks. And to see what these places look like, in case I need an apartment sometime."

"So you think you may?" he said. "Please. Sit down."

The table was wooden, one of the finish-it-yourself kind, covered with two straw place mats and, in the middle, a tiny set of salt-and-pepper sailors and a metal napkin holder, empty. Nick brought napkins and laid one in front of me, pried open a tin and offered me a paper-covered pastry. It was delicious.

"My mother makes 'em."

"Your mother is a good woman. Old-fashioned, right? She makes dumplings as well as baklava?"

He pushed the tin aside.

"I don't want to talk about my mother or her baklava. I have something to say to you. What Helen did to you was unforgivable, Judy. I know she only meant to help, but that was no excuse."

"She told me the truth, which no one else in the world was willing to do. I am actually grateful to her, you know?"

"There are many versions of the truth. You did not deserve to hear that one, ever."

"Why not?"

"It was, I think, a little vindictive. Tina is married now. People make mistakes, you know?" He shrugged. "Sometimes the past is best forgotten. Nevertheless . . ." He paused, looked at me. "I am trying to get Helen into a treatment center. She's now somewhat . . . out of control." He pressed his drink can against his forehead.

"Do you think she'll go?"

"I don't think she'll have any choice." He drained his drink. "God, it's hot. So how about you? What are you going to do with yourself? You looked like the wrath of God the other day. I wasn't sure what you'd do."

"Thanks a lot."

"Oh, you look fairly decent now. So what's your plan?"

"I took a little trip to the mountains with Curtis. I meant to keep on going, but I didn't have the guts. So I came back."

"What are you going to do now?"

"I don't know. Look at apartments?"

"Are you serious about leaving Hamp, or are you just jerking him around?"

"I don't know."

"Where are you going?"

"I don't know. I drove all day yesterday and here I am back where I started from."

"Sometimes the greatest distance is in your mind."

I looked at Nick for a long time, trying to read his face. The bike chain whirred in the next room, whirred and stopped, clanked and slowed.

"I don't know what to do," I said finally.

"I don't know what to tell you," he replied.

I stood up, and so did he.

"You have to go," I said, "and so do I. I'm making you late for work. Thank you again for helping me through that the other day."

I held out my hand. He ignored it, put his arms on my shoulders.

"Listen, Judy. These things happen. Don't take it so hard, okay? If you want to go back, go. But if you don't want to, don't. Stay here if you like. Stay with your friends. But get out now, if you're serious about getting out. Because once you go back to Hamp, it'll be hard. Okay? Are you listening?"

I nodded, but I started to cry.

"You're going back to him, aren't you?" he said.

I nodded again. He hugged me, patted me on the back.

"However it turns out, you'll be fine, you know that, don't you? Don't you?"

I couldn't speak.

"Mom! Let's go home!" said Curtis, standing in the door.

ON THE WAY HOME, I DECIDED HOW TO ACT with Hamp. All I needed,
I felt, was a way to be, some format or pattern I could hang on to that
would get me through the day, so that if I forgot who I was or what I
wanted, I could use it as a sort of mnemonic to remind me. "Be nice."
"Be a bitch." Only I didn't want to be a bitch. Something more posi-
tive was what I had in mind, a persona closer to my true feelings,
which swung between rage, despair, and a kind of ecstasy.

I decided to go with the ecstasy. I would drive back to the trailer
and stay, at least for a while, because it was my home and Curtis's
home, and our stuff was there. To Hamp, I would be honest. Normal.
Aloof. There would be no tacky scenes, no tearful recriminations.
What was the use? We were no longer married, except in name. Hamp
was the father of my child, and I was therefore doomed to know him,

doomed to see and talk to him for the next dozen years. But emotionally, he was part of my past. I would sleep on the couch, keep my own counsel, fix my own lunch. Devote myself to my son. Be perfect. He would notice, and grow to regret his criminal treatment of me—too late, of course, because he would have lost me forever.

I honestly thought that would work.

■ —— ■

Hamp had taken the day off and cleaned up. The trailer was immaculate. There were flowers on the table, steaks and salad in the refrigerator. He had done the laundry and put up all the clothes. Since I was now perfect, I allowed myself the calm accepting smiles and nods of a visiting princess. Everything about him was so very nice—not too fawning, not too shamed or sad. He was hopeful, attentive. I sat on the couch with my hands folded and looked at him.

"What do you think?" he said.

"The house looks very nice," I said.

"I had some trouble with the flowers."

"They look nice."

He was nervous. I liked that.

"Judy, I know you said you didn't want to discuss it, but there's one thing I must tell you. You can kick me out or whatever, but you must know this." He cleared his throat. "There can never be anyone else for me but you." He held up his hand for silence. "I know I've blown it. You don't have to tell me that. It's the biggest regret of my life. I just wanted you to know. And the absolute worst thing is that I have hurt you. I know I don't deserve a second chance. But I'd love a chance just to make it up to you. Don't say anything. I'll go light the grill."

So we had a model evening in the pseudo-happy style, Hamp bathing Curtis, Hamp putting Curtis to bed, Hamp attendant, silent, watchful. When I spread out my sheet on the couch and got my pillow he said, "You don't have to do this. I won't bother you. I'll sleep out here."

"I will," I said. "You know the couch gives you a crick."

"Well, good night," he said and gave me a chaste kiss.

That lasted three nights. On the fourth night, I woke up with his hand in my pants. I was already wet and squirming in my sleep.

"Well, hello," he said, warm and heavy in my arms. "What have we here?"

He buried his head in my neck, pushed his thigh down between my legs, picked up my hand and pressed it to his shorts.

"Please," he murmured.

■ —— ■

Diane was disappointed. We discussed it later, riding horses on the dirt road behind her aunt's house.

"I was thinking you'd be moving in with me," she said. "And here you are shacked up with your husband again."

"Don't be mad."

"How can you be so forgiving?" she said. She turned in the saddle and looked at me, her hair whipping around her face under her hat. "How could you?"

"It's not about forgiveness," I said.

"Well what is it about then? What do you want?"

I didn't know.

I wanted my life back. I wanted my husband to love me, and to do it so completely and well that I could forget everything but the moment, forget all the thoughts that kept crowding into my everyday life when I wasn't with him.

You can't forgive something that doesn't happen to you, and adultery is love that doesn't happen to you. It happens to somebody else. For you, the unloved, it's a state of nonbeing, nonexistence. You are not yourself. If you get a chance to be yourself again, you take it, and you don't much care about anything or anybody else, or what they think or what they do, any more than you care about the rain once you are in out of it.

Tina and Jimmy came home from their honeymoon, came by the office to say hello.

"I heard you went to the mountains, Judy," she said. "I brought you some perfume."

"Thank you," I said.

She and Jimmy were both tanned and thin. You could see their pelvis bones through their blue jeans. They kept touching each other like they were surprised to be apart. I wondered how they made love. They must have looked like Tinkertoys.

"You know Lee's going back to New York on Monday," said Tina, "and we thought we'd have everybody over before she leaves. Can you come?"

"To your house?" said Hamp.

Tina didn't look at him. "Yes," she said, lifting her chin. "I hope you can all come, Judy."

"That would be nice," I said.

It was a shock seeing Tina again. She had shrunk, somehow. She looked too prim, and she was wearing her hair in an ugly French braid. It was too straight, too thin, the rows too fixed and flat.

"I remember the first time you ever had your hair done that way," I said. "It was on the cruise."

"What was that girl's name that used to fix it for me?"

"Miranda."

■ ——— ■

I make paper dolls for Curtis sometimes. I am good at paper cutting—can't draw, can't paint sweatshirts or smock dresses or anything useful, but I can cut out a profile of Abe Lincoln in his hat, a sailboat, or a string of tiny people in a twinkling. My elementary school career

191

was littered with strings of paper dolls. They were handy. I won Eva Belle Smith's friendship with them in third grade, thus ridding myself of the last-chosen-for-kickball stigma forever, since Eva, for an obscure reason, always chose a team. For my friends I would cut out rows of bears, boys, girls in long dresses, dogs sniffing each other's noses, goldfish, rings of sleeping cats. I gave them all away to be colored. My cousin Elizabeth was my manager, shrewdly acquiring for us hoards of Twinkies and Mary Janes, dozens of erasers. It was the only arty thing I did better than Elizabeth.

If the paper dolls were made on heavy enough paper, and if you bent their feet, it was possible to stand these people up, zigzagging them across your desk. Then if you put your head down next to them and squinted, they looked alive, a row of tiny elves or princesses joined at the fingers, dancing ad infinitum back toward the pencil slot.

That's what Tina, or anybody, is today, top doll in a long floppy string of them that opens out forever toward the past. You may only see the current version, but if you squint and drop your head a little, they are all there, all the Tinas she has ever been, connected.

"So how are you dealing with Tina?" says Diane. We stop at a stream, and the horses drink, blowing in the water, stretching out their necks. The saddle leather creaks.

"I'm not dealing with Tina," I say. "Let her deal with herself." I intend merely to keep a watchful eye, as for a snake.

"I don't understand your attitude at all," says Diane, laughing, shaking her head.

What she doesn't understand is that I don't have an attitude. I'm not even sure what an attitude is. I cling to Diane, her words, the saddle horn, Hamilton Duncan, not because I have any thoughts on the subject, not because I have an attitude, but to keep from falling down.

The water swirls muddy around the horses' legs. They have stirred up the stream. Upstream, the water ripples clear and smooth across the jumble of rocks that compose its bed. A salamander sits on a dry rock above the water, absorbing sun, his little neck wrinkled, pulse in his throat. The horses raise their heads and shake, we cross the stream and clonk up onto the blacktop, heading home. The horses trot, then canter, eager for the barn, and we let them even though it's blacktop, no car ever comes, Diane so relaxed she turns in the saddle to joke with me, me stiff, white-knuckled, and exultant. Ahead the woods give way to fenced meadows, and the sky is white.

■ —— ■

Miranda came on board the cruise ship late, running up the gang-plank with her boyfriend, laughing, waving tickets, edging by the men who waited to close the gate. She and the boy threw down their back-packs and leaned over the rail, looked out across the water with the rest of us gathered on the deck as we glided away from the dock, toward the Mediterranean islands pictured in our dreams.

They were Australians. They looked like a beer commercial, tawny and wild, and they had the same color hair, a faded sandy brown. He wore a leather hat. They talked so pretty you edged up toward them. She had a way of hiking up her shoulders and widening her eyes that made you want to dance or laugh out loud. We shared the same table for dinner, kept the same pace on day-trips, and swapped guidebooks and jokes about the ship. And Miranda braided Tina's hair. Tina was a sullen fifteen, pale and prim, and she sat at Miranda's feet and wor-shipped. Literally at Miranda's feet. One day on deck, Miranda patted the footrest of her deck chair so Tina would move up to it off the floor, and then braided her hair, picking up strands idly as she talked, weaving them into the loveliest braid.

"You haven't got an elastic or anything, have you?" she said, about to finger-comb it all out. Tina grabbed the bob-end of the hair and ran off with it. Every day after that, she got Miranda to braid her hair, coming up silently, holding out her brush.

193

The boyfriend called her "Tee-na." He whistled at her when she wore her bikini out to the decrepit ship's pool, brought her a chair, brought us all chairs. He was polite to our mother. He even helped us dicker with the local trinket sellers on the islands, sauntering up and giving the proceedings just the right amount of casual I-don't-care attitude. He actually said "G'day" and "mate." "Tee-na's my mate," he'd say, shaking her shoulder. Miranda always watched him with a little smile, holding onto her hat. Then she would stretch out her hand and he would take it, and they would stroll away.

They were perfect specimens. You meet people like that sometimes, and they make you gasp, they are so beautiful. They defy something, as love defies death. They are living art. Everybody knew it, not just me. They would walk through Rhodes and people turned to look at them in the street. Walking up Santorini—Miranda refused to ride a donkey, so we all walked too—I heard a woman say to her husband, "Look! There they are!" and point, as though they were movie stars.

Tina began to make a nuisance of herself about Miranda. She copied her. If Miranda bought a straw hat, Tina bought one, the same one, with the same ribbon. Miranda wore a lot of white, so Tina constructed white outfits for herself out of bits and pieces of mine and Mom's clothes, using up all our blouses, losing my favorite earrings.

"She's going through a phase," said Mom. "Let her be."

"I just don't want her to make a fool of herself," I said.

Actually, I didn't want her to make a fool of me.

But Miranda and the boyfriend dealt with it fine. They teased and ignored her, wrapping themselves in that special, inviolate peace lovers have that not even pesky adolescents can neutralize, and we parted friends when the boat docked, promising to write, to visit, to remember. Of course we never did.

The album of photos from the Greek trip is still in my parents' den. I flip through pages of white columns and dusty hills, Mom or Tina or me squinting in the foreground beside a lemonade stand. The

---

cruise pictures are at the end. There is Miranda at the pool, shading her face with her hand, the boy with his hat pulled down over his eyes, holding a beer in salute. In the next shot, there Miranda is again, this time with me. We have our arms around each other's shoulders, all elbows and knees, perched on a white wall under the endless Greek sky.

I touch all the faces with my finger, memorizing them again.

"See these people?" I tell Curtis. "See these stairs, going up that mountain? I walked up those. There's Grandma on a donkey."

There is a final picture of the three of us on the dock, the three girls, taken the morning we parted, one of those "one last shot" things. The wind is blowing our hair. We stand with our arms around each other, Tina in the middle, Miranda and I on each side, behind our bags. From this distance, it looks like we are all smiling and waving, and we all look the same.

■ —— ■

"This ought to be fun," I said to Hamp, as we were getting ready to go to Tina's.

"Right," said Hamp.

We had adopted a new, wry way of talking. Cynical. And we had a new way of looking at each other, Hamp shaking his head, with a new twist to his lip—admiringly, like he had just watched me win a race or something.

"You're something, you know that? Your mama's something, Curtis."

I was thinner, for one thing. I had worried off ten pounds and had acquired those lines at the corners of the eyes that are, at first, attractive. My mouth and eyes looked bigger because my face was thinner. And I was watchful.

Tina's house was in Pine Ridge, the town's newest housing development. It had straw in the yard and looked blank and shiny. Tina Lee and Jimmy were leasing the house from one of Dad's friends, and had barely moved in.

"Are you sure you want to do this?" said Hamp as we pulled up in the yard.

I was sure. Grace under pressure was one of my best bits. Besides, I didn't feel mad. I didn't feel much of anything.

Everybody else was already in the den perched on the edges of the new sofa or holding up the walls next to the kitchen. Tina's hair was still in that stupid braid, and she was nervous and kept wandering out of the den where we had uneasily gathered, to fetch things or to get more chips or another beer. Dad popped his knuckles. James Hooper picked his thumb.

"So how was Charleston?" I said.

Lee and Mom were wearing their Charleston clothes; they had been there for a few days visiting the cousins and had come home wrapped in tans and the printed cotton dresses that they always bought.

"How was Aunt Sophia? How is Emmie doing?"

"Fine, fine. It was unbearably hot. Oh! You wouldn't believe the heat!" They fanned themselves. "We were just soaked every day."

"You ought to move back home," Mom said to Lee. "This change has done you some good."

Lee shook her head. They had this conversation every summer. "I'd die down here."

"You'll die anyway," said Dad. "Might as well die happy."

"Your accent is already getting better," I said.

"Pick up some of that Gullah, you'll be all right," said Hamp, lapsing into it himself. "Get awn de plane tawkin' 'bout wantin' de mawnin' paiper an' all dat, dey wan' know whachu talkin' 'bout."

He grinned and everybody grinned back at him.

"Want to see the house?" said Tina. "Anyone?"

■ —— ■

It's just a regular little open-plan house, with a den, kitchen, and living room downstairs, and three bedrooms upstairs. The thing that

196

makes it cute is a nice, two-story entrance hall and open stairs floating up it, and the bedrooms opening out onto that space. I pointed to
the railings separating the upstairs floor from the twelve-foot drop.
"Look, Hamp, what a nightmare that would be if you had a baby."

"What do you mean?" said Tina, at the top of the stairs.

"She means the rails," said Lucy. "Children falling through."

"Too narrow," said Hamp. "More'n likely children dropping choo-
choo trains down on their daddies' heads."

"Well, I'm not going to have children in this house," said Tina.
"And I'd keep their toys up better than that if I did."

The rest of us nodded, smirking to one another.

Tina's bedroom furniture from home had been installed in the
master bedroom.

"This room doesn't do French Provincial any good at all, does it?"
I said to Mom.

"I don't know why you say that," snapped Tina. "I think it looks
fine."

"Of course it does, darling," said Mom, grimacing at me.

"It's just the wrong shape," I said.

Mom stepped on my foot.

"And the wrong color," I whispered.

"What's this thing for?" James's voice called from out of the bathroom. There was the sound of running water.

"I'll be glad to make you some curtains," said Lucy, looking at the
sheets over the windows.

"That'd be great," said Tina.

They talked about curtains for awhile.

"Oh, don't bother," said Jimmy. "We're only going to be here a
year, until I get money saved to go to law school."

"You can't use sheets at your window for a year, son," said his mother.

"Why not?" said Jimmy.

Sally picked up a bottle of perfume from the dresser and sprayed it at Jimmy. He leaped out of the way. She chased him.

"Please don't!" said Tina. She took the bottle out of Sally's hand with a teacher-smile. "A very good friend brought me that from Europe," she said, setting it back on the dresser.

"I'm sorry," said Sally. Her cheeks burned, and she walked to her mom and stood beside her.

"Oh, for heaven's sake, Tina," I said. "Give the child a break."

"Let's see the other rooms," said Mom brightly.

The other bedrooms were empty. We sniffed the closets and admired the view.

"Sally, this will be your room when you come to spend some time with us," said Tina in the end room.

"Yes ma'am," said Sally, sticking by her mom.

"That will be, goodness, just two months now! Got to get you some furniture in here, girl!" She squeezed Sally's arm.

We all went downstairs. The party dispersed, the men heading for the deck, the children for the TV set. I went into the living room with the other women to see the wedding presents. They were all stacked, still in their boxes, in a corner.

"I hope you're keeping up with your thank-you notes," said Mom. She and Lee bent over and began looking through the boxes.

"Look at that tacky salad set. After I gave their daughter a piece of her silver. Lucy, what are you finding over there?"

In the den Jimmy was at the television set, adjusting a piece of tin foil on the rabbit ears and wiggling the wires. Curtis and Sally complained.

"Move! We can't see! Fix it! It doesn't work. The picture's worse now! Jimmy!"

In the kitchen all the food everybody had brought was sitting on the counter.

"Well!" said Mom, rubbing her hands together. "This looks just wonderful, doesn't it?"

The stove still had its instruction book hanging from the oven door.

"Cook much, Tina?" I said, unwrapping it.

"Look," she said. She took the book out of my hand. "Are you through with the snide remarks now? Because I'd like to get on with lunch."

"I wasn't being snide," I said. "I was making a joke."

"Nobody's laughing," Tina said.

"Girls, girls!" Mom said. "Don't be silly. Now Tina, what may we help you do, darling?"

"Well," said Tina Lee, "I boiled the potatoes for salad. But I haven't made it yet."

She opened the refrigerator and got out a large bowl of congealing potatoes and a jar of mayonnaise.

"Let me," said Mom, taking the bowl. "Let's see. Where are the onions?"

"Oh, I don't have any," said Tina. "Jimmy doesn't like them."

"He's eaten them for twenty years at home," said Lucy. "It's his daddy that doesn't eat onions."

"Well then," said Mom. "Let's see. Help me out here, Lucy."

They bent their heads over the bowl of potatoes.

"Didn't I see some mustard in the refrigerator?" said Lucy. "That'll be just the thing."

In the refrigerator was a six-pack of yogurt, a bottle of wine, un-opened, a shelf full of diet colas, and a jar of mustard. I grabbed the mustard.

"Where are your spices, darling?" said Mom.

Tina opened a cabinet door. Lemon-pepper seasoning, salt, and pepper huddled with a box of diet sweetener.

"I haven't built up much of a collection yet," said Tina.

"I can see that," said Mom. "Never mind. It'll be fine."

Lucy Hooper and I looked at each other.

"Shall I make hamburger patties?" I said.

199

"No, I'll do that," said Tina.

"Shall I open this salad dressing then?" I said. Three new jars sat on the counter in front of me.

"No," said Tina.

I started taking the covers off the casseroles.

"Let's not do that yet," said Tina. "Okay?"

I went outside.

Dad was in a far corner of the yard kicking stones around and peering off into the next yard. Hamp and Jimmy were having a beer, and Mr. Hooper was tending the grill. I helped myself to a beer from the cooler and joined them.

"How you doing?" said Hamp.

I shook my head.

In a few minutes Dad came back and sat down on the edge of the deck.

"Gonna have to get another load of topsoil out here this fall, I reckon, Jimmy," he said. "The grass is mighty patchy. Help me remember and I'll send some out in time to top seed."

Jimmy took out a little notebook, flipped some pages.

"October be good, sir?"

"Yeah," said Dad. "Or November either. Depending on frost, you know." He stared at the notebook.

Jimmy wrote.

"What you got there, Jimmy?" said Hamp.

"A Finder-Keeper." Jimmy handed it to him. "See, it has a calendar, phone numbers, and a calculator. I ordered it through the bank."

"Interesting." Hamp handed it back.

"Lemme see that thing," said Dad.

"Jimmy has always written things down, ever since he was a little boy," said his dad. "Organized. Very organized."

"Dad!"

We all smiled and nodded.

"Well, you are, son. Nothing wrong in that."

"Good trait," said Dad. He was bent over the calculator. His large fingers hesitated over the tiny punch keys. He punched in a problem, squinted at the total.

"Can't see the damned thing. Must be getting old." He handed it back. "So James, how about the Braves this week?"

"They coulda beat the Dodgers. They never shoulda—"

"There's a game on now, I believe," said Hamp.

They all looked through the glass door into the den, where Sally and Curtis were sitting in front of the set.

"Wait," said Jimmy. "I'll get the portable from upstairs."

He came back with it in a few minutes, and they plugged it in and set it on the deck.

"Now we're cooking," said Dad. "Believe that fire's about ready, too, son."

I went back inside. Curtis and Sally were watching some old violent cop show on TV.

"Want to take a walk?" I said.

It was better out of the yard. The sky was baby blue, pale and dry, a June day. We went all over the whole neighborhood, up and down the narrow, black streets, scaring up dogs who rushed at us in spurious assertion and children, newly home from church, still in their good clothes, who paused in their front-yard play and stared at us as we passed. We kicked rocks. We stood at the end of a road that crumbled away to nothing, a smear of red dirt, dried tire tracks where people had backed up and turned around. We threw gravel at some cans somebody had already propped up and used for target practice. When we ran out of gravel, we began to throw dirt clods, aiming them against tree trunks, where they disintegrated with a satisfying smack and a shower of clay.

Nothing was working out. It was like the week after church retreat. Here I was, refreshed and forgiving, prepared to be generous, and nobody wanted generosity. I had come home, come back, made a huge leap of faith into the second half of my life, uncharted territory, forgiving ground, and nobody cared.

Tina wasn't sorry she'd slept with my husband. She was only sorry she'd gotten caught. Hamp, who at least had acted repentant a few days ago, was now viewing the whole thing as a huge joke. It wasn't a joke to me. I couldn't stand the way Hamp looked at Jimmy, with a sort of amused tolerance, Jimmy the bridegroom, the innocent, the dupe. Well, he was a dupe, and so was I. I was ashamed.

I stood and hurled dirt, listened to Curtis and Sally talk about baseball and what they could do.

"Look at me. Look. Watch me hit that stump."

I wasn't ashamed of staying with Hamp. I wanted to. If that meant I had no pride, so be it. I wasn't ashamed of forgiving him, or Tina. I hadn't forgiven them. I didn't even know what forgiveness was. I had quickly reached the point where I wasn't mad anymore, where I just wanted to forget the whole thing and get on with my life, and I figured that must be forgiveness. And yet a low, mean feeling ate at me sometimes. I started out okay, and something in Hamp's eyes or Tina's eyes told me it wasn't okay. There was a snicker there, a glimmer of wariness. I almost looked behind me to see who made them smirk.

They made me ashamed. They made my face hot, they made me doubt myself, they made me feel stupid and slow. I was different, and they were not. I had changed. They had not.

The sight of them, seeing them in each other's arms, had swept my whole life away, flooded my senses, washed out my brain. I saw with enormous clarity, as people must after disaster, what I now must do, how I must act, how my life had changed. I was transformed. Everything had been swept away, everything I had thought permanent, all my ideas about honor and love, but I had survived the crash, the flood, and had gotten up afterward with a kind of joy at my own survival, saying, "Okay! Okay! I know it now! I understand! Now let's get on with it," meaning, let's live transformed. But only I was transformed. I had left Tina and Hamp behind in their old selves, old habits, old ways. An abyss of experience separated us. Hamp and Tina were merely discovered. I was barely sane.

When we got back to the house, lunch was ready, spread out on the counter between the den and kitchen. Sally and Curtis and I fixed our plates, went out on the deck to join the others. Hamp was sitting between Tina and Lucy, and he rose with a hurried start to give me his chair.

"Come sit by me, darling," said Mom, patting the step.

I smiled at them all and sat on the floor with the kids.

During lunch I found that I was having trouble breathing. The air seemed too close. I excused myself, got up, and went upstairs to the bathroom. I splashed water on my face, looked at myself in the mirror. The person I saw, water dripping from her chin, seemed too large-pored and gagging to be myself. I had not realized how difficult the rest of my life would be. I had not foreseen, or wanted to foresee, the thousands of family parties, Christmas, holidays, the almost daily contact we'd all have. Now it stretched before me like a trip through cancer. I did not want it, not to deal with it, not to endure it. And how I hated them both, the awkwardness of Hamp's glances, the anger in Tina's eyes. When Tina came near me, my skin prickled with fear. I wanted her to die, not to prosper, not to live here in pleasure and self-satisfaction with our parents smiling at her, at her smug little self. I knew that I would have to get out. I went out into the hall to do that. I started down the stairs. Hamp and Tina were in the empty living room, talking.

"Do you think she—"

"Do you think I what?" I said, leaning over the railing.

They both turned to look up at me.

"Do you think I what?"

Hamp moved away from Tina. I think I would have been all right even then, if he hadn't moved away from her.

"Do I think you are doing all right," he said.

"I'm not," I said, coming down the stairs. "I am not. How could I? And how can you stand here now so carefully and talk about me behind my back?"

Hamp put his arm around me. "Honey," he said. "Let's go home."

Jimmy and my mom came through the kitchen. They were laughing.

"Jimbo!" said Hamp. "We got to go, good buddy. Nice party. Thanks for lunch." He moved toward the front door, pulling me along with him.

"Don't you want to see the proofs of the wedding pictures?" said Mom. "They're in the den. There's a real good one of Curtis."

"They need to go, Mom," said Tina, pushing me toward the door. "She can see them later."

"But I thought you said you were taking the pictures back to-morrow."

"Judy doesn't feel well."

Tina was actually pushing me out the door. I pushed back, threw off her arm and Hamp's arm.

"I need to get my purse, all right?" I said. "And my child. Or do you want him, too?"

I walked back across the hall toward the kitchen. Tina glanced around, horrified. She was wild to have me out of her house, out of her life. Gone. Invisible. I would always have that power over her, and over Hamp as well. I could see it in their eyes. I was still, still and eternally, the bitch-wife. The one to fear. The one to hide from, and sneak around behind.

"You can't have my son," I said deliberately. "You ruined my marriage. That was enough, don't you think?"

"Judy!" said Mom. She must have thought I was crazy.

"Well," I shrugged.

"Shut up!" said Tina.

"Why?" I said. "Why should I shut up? So Mom won't know you slept with my husband? Mom doesn't care. She'll get over it, just like I did. It's over, right? I mean, you aren't sleeping with him anymore, are you? Now that you've married Jimmy and all."

Tina screamed and came at me with her hands, like she was going to rake my face with her fingernails. I just stood there. Hamp was right behind her, and he grabbed her, then she turned and started screaming and hitting on him instead, sort of collapsing onto the floor as she did. I walked through the den and picked up my purse and my son.

"What the hell was that?" Jimmy's dad said. He and Lucy were half-standing, wedding pictures dribbling from their fingers.

"Tina is having a tantrum," I said and left.

Halfway home I noticed Curtis in the seat beside me, clinging to my sleeve.

"You need to fasten your seat belt, honey," I said.

"You need to fasten yours," he said.

Hamp came home some time later. He didn't say anything for awhile. He got a beer, sat down on the couch, and drank. His face was heavy, the muscles in his cheeks slack. He sniffed, looked at me.

"Well, babe," he said. "I gotta hand it to you. It was a great scene."

"I didn't plan it," I said. "It just happened."

"I can believe that," he said. "God, we never should have gone over there, you know? Why didn't you tell me you were going to lose it?"

"I didn't know it," I said.

"Well," he said. "It's done now." He stared into space for awhile.

"Was it bad?" I said.

"Tina went upstairs and locked herself in the bathroom," he said. "She says she wants to die."

"She would," I said. "She always wants to die when she doesn't get her way. She used to lock herself in the bathroom all the time at home. What did you do?"

"I left. I wasn't exactly what you'd call welcome."

I hadn't thought about that.

"I'm sorry," I said.

"No need to be," he said. "Not your fault." He drained his beer can and stood up, crushing the can between his hands. "Think I'll go for a walk. Want to come? Where's Curtis?"

"In his room. I'll get him."

So we went for a walk to the lake. We took Reddie, and she and Curtis went wading, looking for tadpoles. Then we threw sticks into the water, and Reddie swam for them, just her face showing out of the dark, glistening water, making a little rivulet out of each side of her mouth, trailing a V out behind her.

Twelve

12

MY NEW WINDOW IS FINISHED. It really was stupid that I couldn't get the damn thing in right. Mom bitched about it so much that I finally called in Mr. Amos a couple of weeks ago. He tut-tutted and looked at me out of the corners of his eyes, shook his head and sighed. He knows Hamp and I have had our troubles.

"What'd you mean to do here?" he said, fingering a corner of window that didn't plumb. He pulled out his level, and I hid my head. At last he lowered himself into the seat beside my desk and began to play, idly, with his tape measure, pulling it out, snapping it back.

"Tell me the worst," I said. "How bad is it?"

"Aw, it ain't too bad," he said. He smiled at me. "For a start."

"I thought I was almost finished. Maybe that was my trouble."

Mr. Amos began to clean his nails with a corner of the tape measure tab.

"You just impatient, s'all," he said. "My boy's like that, I got a kid same as you. Wants everything done yesterday. Can't understand." He put the tape measure down on my desk, pointed his finger into the wood in front of me. "Everything has a feel, you see what I'm saying? You got to keep on studying it, till you get the feel. Now you can pop in a window or it can be a booger, don't matter. What matters is, is it right, and is it worth your while. You see what I'm saying?"

■ —— ■

The view from the window makes it worth my while. Mom comes over and looks out, hugging herself, and we watch the line of saplings across the meadow lean and twist in the wind. There is one tree, an enormous oak that stands off to one side, famous for its leaves. I have watched it all my life, watched the calm climb of color down the leaves. It was one way I measured time as a child, the first cool, sweater week when a tinge of red would appear at the top, the deepening of the color and the flowing down, mingling of red and yellow overcoming green, until the whole tree was magnificent and aflame, and people pointed at it as they rode by in the car, then the slow lessening, the letting go of the leaves, the floating down, rustling and turning brown, piling up at the base for children to jump in after school. Now it's Sally and Curtis's tree. They have a playhouse under it. Today the top is faintly tinged with red.

"I'm going to have it put on the list," says Sally. "So it will be safe. My teacher says there's a list for special trees, and once a tree is on it, it can never be cut down."

"Really?" My father, the lumberman, is enchanted. He is interested lately in preservation. He and Sally send away for an application to preserve the tree.

208

"We own the tree, Dad," I point out. "Did you think we were planning on cutting it down?"

He shrugs. No, but anything is possible. And his eyes say so. He has looked at me like that since the day I informed on Tina.

Well Dad, dammit, I'm doing the best I can.

I know you are.

But it didn't make any difference. I did the best I could from that very moment forward, from the night I sat by the pond with Hamp and thought, Now we're even, Tina Lee. Now I can live again. From that second I did the best that I could. And it wasn't good enough. It didn't even come close.

I lost face with my family. I was now a woman with a problem, and a problem I apparently wasn't handling too well as far as they were concerned. And boy, were they concerned.

It took them twenty-four hours to get around to me, though. After we left Tina's, all the parents left, agitated but determined to mind their own business. Tina was busy in the bathroom swallowing bottles full of pills. By the time Jimmy figured out what was going on and busted the door down, she was in pretty bad shape. He carried her to the hospital. She had her stomach pumped out, and Jimmy had to talk to the police. The doctors kept her in the hospital overnight.

"Restrained," Mom said. "They tied her wrists to the bed. I'm calling now to see if we can get her released into a private clinic in Demaro this afternoon."

"Why doesn't she just go home?" I said.

"She'd love to," said Mom. "Unfortunately it's not that simple."

Mom had come by the office to make the calls. She unfolded a piece of paper, smoothed it out on her desk and studied it, picked up the phone.

"Hello, is this Woodland Center?" Tapping her pencil against the paper. "Dr. Williamson, please. Hello, is this . . . This is Mrs. McAdams calling for Dr. Williamson. I believe Dr. White has already . . . Yes,

I'll hold." Her voice was perfect, a perfect business voice. She looked up at me. "Is Hamp here?"

"He's out at the yard."

"Tell him, would you, Dad said to call the Bartows about that roofing." Her eyes traveled back to the phone. "Hello, yes?"

So they were still speaking to Hamp, anyway.

■ —— ■

Later that afternoon I went to the hospital to take Dad his glasses. He and Mom were going to drive Tina and Jimmy to Demaro, to Woodland Center. Dad was standing outside in the sun by the car, waiting, pacing, looking at his watch.

"We're going to hit there right at five o'clock," he said.

"How's Tina?" I said.

He merely shook his head.

Tina came out of the hospital in a wheelchair, flanked by Mom and Jimmy, pushed by a nurse, one of Mom's friends. We could hear her fussing across the walkway.

"—hospital rules," said the nurse, wheeling up to the car door.

"Well, I can certainly walk," said Tina. "I don't know why they have such a stupid rule."

"Because they just do," said the nurse. "Here we are now!" She put on the brake.

"Do you have my suitcase?" said Tina. "Did you get my book?"

She stood and turned in the narrow space between the wheelchair and the open car door, turned and looked at us, gathered around. Her face was scrubbed and pale, her hair disheveled, like the wrong person had combed it. But the thing you really noticed about her was her eyes. They shone like cat's eyes.

"I don't know why I have to do this," she said. "I feel terrible. My stomach hurts. Why can't I just go home?"

Her gaze locked on Jimmy, but he shook his head, smiling stu-

210

pidly, shrugging, bending as though to pick up her bag. Mom stepped up to Tina.

"Because," said Mom. "It's just the rules, that's all. You must go for a day or two for observation." She took Tina's arm, and the nurse took an arm, and they eased her into the car, patting her down, leaning in, tucking. "It's going to be fine, Tina. Dad and I had to pull strings to get you in Woodland so fast, you know. It's a very nice place. The best."

"Lovely," said the nurse. "I have a friend Gracie who works there. I want you to be sure and look for her now, you hear? Gracie. Tall woman, about my age—"

"I surely will," said Tina. "I think I'm going to throw up now."

The nurse held out a bag.

"Here, hon," she said.

Jimmy was standing with his back to the car, crying. I went over to him.

"I am so sorry," I said. "I am so sorry."

He put his arms around me and shook when I held him, like a little boy, choking on words I did not understand. We could hear Tina gagging by the car. Finally he stepped back, wiping his eyes. I gave him a tissue, and he blew his nose.

"Sorry!" He sniffed, swallowed, wiped. "Jeez. It gets to you, you know? Sorry." His eyes sheered off toward Tina, now quiet in the back of the car. "It's not your fault, you know. Don't think that. She just . . . I don't know. She felt bad about her folks knowing, I guess. About her and Hamp."

"She felt bad about you knowing," I said.

"Oh, I already knew," said Jimmy. "I never said anything. But maybe it's better this way. Out in the open. Can't hurt us anymore."

"I don't feel any better," I said. "I feel worse. Do you feel better?"

He closed his eyes. I reached up and smoothed down his hair.

"You look terrible," I said.

211

"I'm all right."

"When I found out about Hamp and Tina, I thought I would die. I never knew that just knowing something could hurt, really physically hurt."

"Here and here." Jimmy put his hand on his chest and on his head, rumpling his hair again.

I nodded. He looked again at the car.

"Just a couple more hours," I said. "She'll be safe. She's going to be fine, Jimmy."

He blinked and brushed at his face. "I know that. I know she will." He swallowed, flexed his jaw. "It's just that she says she doesn't want to go."

"I know."

"Like I ought to be able to do something. And I can't."

"I know. But she really will be okay." Of course I didn't know that. I just said it, and it sounded right. "Do you believe that?" I said. "I believe it."

He nodded.

"Now Jimmy," I said. "My next question is, will you be okay?"

He looked surprised. "Oh sure," he said. "I'm fine."

"Of course you are," said Mom, coming up, patting his shoulder. "Of course you are. I want you to sit in the front, Jimmy, and rest. I'll sit with Tina Lee."

We all walked toward the car. Tina Lee leaned forward in the back seat and spoke.

"Dad? I just want to go home, okay?" she said. "Please?"

Dad looked straight ahead. I went to his window and stood while the others arranged themselves in the car.

"Daddy?" said Tina, touching the back of his shoulder.

He stiffened briefly as though sustaining a punch, shook himself, wiped his hand across his cheek. His face was blank.

"Everybody ready back there?" he said cheerfully.

I stood in the parking lot and watched them drive away.

■ —— ■

For the next week, Jimmy appeared periodically at the yard or in my parents' kitchen, pale and cheerful, with reports on Tina's health.

"Let me get you something, Jimmy."

"No thank you, ma'am. I'm not hungry."

But Mom or Aunt Lee would fix him something anyway—a sandwich, or a piece of pie—and he would eat it, unconsciously, without looking at his plate, his eyes on them, telling what the doctors said.

"They said there's no guarantee she won't try it again," he said, amazed.

Mom shook her head. "Then they don't know Tina Lee very well at all, if you ask me. If she had thought for one minute what she'd be putting herself through . . ." She meant the stomach pump, the police, the public wonderment.

"The child was hysterical," said Lee. "All this must be very hard on you, Jimmy."

"What's hard on me," he said, "is waiting for her to come home."

"You are a saint from heaven," said Aunt Lee.

"They say it'll be another week or two," said Jimmy.

"We'll just have to be patient," said Mom, pursing her lips. "Have another piece of pie, Jimmy."

■ —— ■

I tried to read *Freckles* again, but I couldn't concentrate. Work was okay, except for people's questions—polite, whispered questions about Tina's health. "Is your sister feeling better?"

"Yes, yes, better all the time."

Once I heard Mom say to a friend, "I don't know. I'm not encouraged." I asked her what she meant. Of course Tina was fine, I said, had been, would be fine. Mom just looked at me.

213

"I'm not so sure."

"Don't be ridiculous," I said. "She took a few pills, Mom. She didn't even come close to dying. Not even close. Now she's in some expensive rest home getting her act together again and everybody's ballistic. What's the big deal?"

"And what if she'd died?" said Mom.

"She didn't die."

"But if she had."

"I'd feel terrible. But that doesn't alter the facts. And it doesn't erase anything."

"I can see that," said Mom. She tapped her pencil. "Don't you see that this isn't about you and Hamilton, or Jimmy, or the marriage— well maybe the marriage, a little—but don't you see? This is about Tina Lee."

"So what else is new?" I said. "Ever since I can remember, everything has always been about Tina Lee."

Mom laughed. "And honey, Tina Lee says exactly the same thing about you."

■ —— ■

Elizabeth had her baby in Atlanta. I wanted to go and volunteered to take the aunts for a visit. Bessie needed a driver, and Lee needed to get to the airport. She was way overdue in New York. And I needed to get out of town.

"I'll miss you," said Hamp. "Please don't go."

"I have to." I wanted to.

The old Hamp would have pitched at least a small fit. The new one was silent, considerate. I phoned Jimmy and told him I would not be going to see Tina Lee the next visiting day after all. And while I made sounds of grief and commiseration, my heart leaped up with joy. A reprieve!

■ —— ■

214

Bessie insisted we take her Cadillac. She and Uncle Fred always buy American, always something big with cushy seats and buttons for everything. Uncle Fred says he hates feeling cramped in a car. I guess if you drive a tractor all day, you grow accustomed to the wide-open spaces.

Anyway, when Hamp dropped me by Aunt Bessie's to begin the trip, he was looking passionate and morose, and he pulled me aside as Fred and Bessie were arranging and arguing about the car. He got my forearm in a vise-grip and dragged me over to the edge of a field.

"I really don't want you to do this," he said again.

"I know that," I said.

"I'll miss you," he said. He hugged me and gave me a real kiss.

"I'll bring you a present from Macy's."

"I don't do well without you." He pressed me against a fence post.

"Good," I said. "Glad to hear it. Hold that thought."

■ —— ■

We walked over to the car, where Lee looked us over speculatively. Uncle Fred and Aunt Bessie were having a fight, or what passes for a fight with them.

"It has to go in the car, Fred," Bessie said, her head vibrating.

"Where?" said Uncle Fred. "Just tell me where, hon, and I'll put it. Just show me a place."

He pointed to the giant red cooler and then to the interior of the car. The back seat was loaded with Tupperware. It looked like a Tupperware convention back there.

"What you got in there, Miss Bessie?" said Hamp. "Can we put some of that in the trunk, maybe?"

Bessie's vibrations increased. "Oh, no, no," she said. "No, we can't do that, Hamp. That is all food for Elizabeth. We just have to get the cooler in too, is all."

"I keep telling you—" said Uncle Fred.

"Could I possibly say just one—" said Lee.

"Just let me—" said Hamp.

"I don't mind—" said Aunt Bessie.

It wound up with the cooler and most of the Tupperware in the back seat with Lee, the cooler strapped in like a person, the Tupperware arranged artfully on the floor. Uncle Fred was sweating. "In case of a wreck," said Bessie, staring at the back seat floor. "I'm concerned about those eggs, Fred."

"If you have a wreck, Bessie, the eggs won't matter. Get in the car."

Bessie was riding in the front with me.

"We are not planning on having a wreck, Frederick. Don't borrow trouble."

Uncle Fred held the car door. "Get in, Elizabeth."

"I'll call you. Don't forget to take your medicine."

Uncle Fred pointed to the interior of the car.

"Don't rush me," said Bessie. She gave him a tart little peck on the cheek, and he patted her shoulder awkwardly.

"Give my love to Baby and the baby," said Uncle Fred. "And Peter, of course."

"You take care now, Fred." Bessie got into the car, patted Fred's arm through the window. "They'll be fine. You get the hay on in now, and take your medicine."

"Call me tonight!" said Hamp and Uncle Fred. "Let us know!"

They waved us out of the yard.

"Well!" said Bessie, as we turned out onto the highway. "Thank goodness. I can't wait to tell Baby what a fuss her daddy made over the car. He was always that particular, and I believe he's gotten worse with age."

The Cadillac had a button for everything. The dashboard gleamed and hummed; gauges quivered. It was like piloting a jet.

"Whew! Hot!" Bessie mashed some buttons, and with a roar cold air began streaming from the control panel.

216

"Gracious!" said Lee.

"I just hate half-ass air conditioning, don't you?" said Bessie, adjusting the vents. She turned around. "Now you tell me if you're getting enough air back there, y'hear?"

"I'm perfectly comfortable," said Lee.

"It's a relief, really, to be on the road," said Bessie. She opened the bag at her feet and got out her knitting, settled back with it. "Especially after all the trouble."

That's what they called it: The Trouble. Bessie and Lee were not averse to using the word "suicide"; they just couldn't agree on what it meant.

Bessie was past vice president of the county mental health association. Her approach was practical. What had Tina taken, she wanted to know, and how much exactly, and how much time had elapsed before she got to the hospital. Had she actually *said* she meant to kill herself?

No.

"She was simply hysterical," said Lee. "The child has such a vivid imagination. You can't possibly think she meant to do away with herself."

"It would be very foolish not to take her seriously," said Bessie. "Don't you think, Edna?"

Mom looked at them both over the tops of her glasses.

"I don't know," she said.

"It's just horrible," said Lee. "Horrible. What can she have meant?" She looked at me and shook her head.

I was silent. Silence, I had learned, was my best tactic. To say anything at all would be a mistake.

At the Georgia line we stopped at the welcome center. Bessie handed out pieces of fried chicken from one of the plastic boxes, it being nearly lunchtime. We sat at a concrete picnic table and ate, drinking colas and swatting yellow jackets.

217

"When Elizabeth and the boys were young," said Bessie, "Fred and I did this every summer. Traveled. New York, New England, out West—educational, you know. And for the first meal on the road, I always fried chicken. We would leave at five or six o'clock in the morning. And Fred hated to stop.

"'Just as soon as I see a good place,' he'd say. But of course he never would.

"Finally I'd say, 'Frederick, we must stop here, at this Esso.'

"'I hate Esso,' he'd say, 'and it looks dirty.'

"'Nevertheless,' I'd say.

"So we'd stop. And as often as not it would be dirty, but it didn't matter to the boys. And you know why he hated to stop so? Trucks he'd passed would go by us, and he'd have to pass them again.

"'What difference does it make?' I'd say.

"'If you drove, you'd understand,' he'd say.

"But it made him nervous for me to drive. He couldn't relax. 'Put on your lights,' he'd say. 'Watch that car behind you.' Nearly drove me crazy."

"Men are so bossy," said Lee. "I don't know how you married women stand 'em."

"They are, aren't they? But you can get around them," said Bessie. "And they come in handy sometimes. I don't know what I'd do without Fred." She smiled complacently, brushing crumbs.

"Well," I said. "Would you like to drive now, Bessie? We can switch back before we get into Atlanta."

"No," said Bessie. "If you don't mind. I'll just sit back and enjoy the ride."

■ —— ■

My heart lifted as we neared Atlanta. The traffic grew heavier, the interstate wider, the trucks thicker. Atlanta is a cheering place. It's the South, but tamed, paved over. It's a sort of triumph of commerce

218

over kudzu. Wide, important-looking roads zip here and there, over and under each other, and there are millions of cars with unsmiling drivers, just like cities everywhere. Yet it's still the South. People understand your accent, and the culture's right. The houses all look temporary and artificial, but who cares? They bulldoze history in Atlanta. They have about forty old houses in the whole town, and somebody's probably getting ready to turn them into insurance companies or something right now. Nothing matters but how much money you make. It's refreshing.

Elizabeth and Pete live in a suburban subdivision just like ten thousand others in Atlanta—new, with a sign at the entrance advertising how much the houses cost. "Exclusive!" says their sign. "Low 200s. Three left." When there are none left, the sign will come down, and no one will know how much the houses cost, except by judging the relative grandeur of the brick front entrances, the size of the flower beds. Two years ago the whole business was an overgrown pasture on the back side of a farm. Now it has a small lake, a swimming pool, and a clubhouse beside tennis courts.

Elizabeth's house looks just like a grown-up version of the houses she always drew in school, a two-story brick with trees, masses of azaleas, and a front lawn you could play croquet on. It also looks exactly like every other house in the subdivision, or near enough so that I could not have found it again without Aunt Bessie helping. We let ourselves in and unpacked the cooler and all the Tupperware. It was mostly food, of course—early vegetables from the garden, treats for Elizabeth in the hospital, and staples for us to eat during our stay.

I had to find a place for everything in the refrigerator.

The house was depressingly clean and beautiful. I wandered, waiting for the aunts to ready themselves for the trip to the hospital. The whole place looked like it had been ordered straight out of Rich's showroom, which it probably had, except the baby's room, Baby Patrick, who still lived in the hospital. His room was pure Elizabeth.

219

She had cross-stitched the pillow that sat in the rocking chair, knitted the blankets that were stacked beside the changing table, and hand-sewn the little quilt that adorned the crib. She had painted the bunnies and chickens that marched around the wall. It was perfect, a perfect baby's room. I wound the carousel music box and set it down. It turned, tinkling out "Waltz of the Flowers" as the pastel horses danced and reared in a delicate circle. Elizabeth, as usual, had gotten it right.

"Ready to go, honey?" said Bessie from the door.

■ —— ■

When we got to the hospital, I tried not to go up to Elizabeth's room. I let Lee and Bessie out at the entrance, told them to go ahead, but they were waiting for me when I walked back from the parking lot. We went up in the elevator. At the room door I hung back. Bessie pushed me on into the room.

"So how are you?" I said to everyone with a big smile. "And how's the baby?"

"And how's Tina Lee?" said Elizabeth. "We heard she was doing so much better! I know you're glad."

"She's fine," I said. "We are all sure she'll be her old self in no time."

"I'm sure she will," said Peter.

"Yeah," said Elizabeth. "Sassy as ever!"

And we smiled, nodded, rocked. My face ached.

"I feel fine, Mother, really," said Elizabeth, propped up in her bed. She did not look fine, in spite of the satin nightgown and the lacy robe. She was pasty, and her face was puffed. Her brown-blonde hair was carefully combed but limp against the pillow.

"It was an easy labor," she said, raising her hands and dropping them down again on the covers. She seemed ridiculously happy. She had a bright, smooth look, but too fragile. When she moved her hands,

220

her wrists came out of her gown and were bony, and there was a little bit of wrinkling about her neck when she turned her head a certain way that made me afraid.

"I am perfectly all right," she said. "Just a little tired, is all."

"It was a twenty-eight hour labor, Elizabeth," Peter said. He stood protectively at the head of the bed, having given up his chair to Aunt Bessie, who refused to sit in it. "It was not an easy labor. You came this close to having a Cesarean." He held up his fingers to demonstrate how close: an inch.

Peter was sweating, even though the whole hospital was chilly in the manner of hospitals everywhere, and his face was as flushed as his wife's was pale. He kept taking out a handkerchief and mopping his face with it, and running his hands through his thinning brown hair.

Bessie hovered against the mattress, her head vibrating at a great rate. Elizabeth threw Peter a smile, and he squeezed her shoulder.

"Are you warm enough?" said Bessie, straightening the covers. "They keep these places so cold."

"I'm fine." Elizabeth patted her mother's hand like her mother was the sick one and Elizabeth was comforting her. "Have you all seen baby Patrick yet? Peter, take them to see Patrick."

"Will you be all right?" Peter leaned over her, large and intimate.

"I'll be fine." She laughed and pushed his arm. "Go on."

It was a long way to the babies.

"I just don't understand it," said Aunt Bessie as we walked. "Why did they let the labor go so long?"

Peter shrugged. I walked beside him. He seemed to have grown somehow. His emotions had grown. I remembered him as a very quiet, contained man who just accompanied Elizabeth on family visits to humor her. Uninvolved. Now, suddenly, he was bigger than life, moist and breathy and male.

"Elizabeth's okay!" said Lee, taking her by the arm.

"So everyone keeps saying!" said Aunt Bessie. "In my experience women do not necessarily develop high blood pressure while they are having babies. I had four babies, and no high blood pressure. I think this is a more serious business than any of you seem to realize."

A couple of nurses turned to look at us in the hall. Bessie continued in a lower voice, almost muttering.

"Sounds like incompetence to me." She sniffed. "Where were the doctors? Why wasn't the thing managed more carefully?"

"Let's discuss it later," said Lee.

Peter's smile was becoming strained.

"You're mighty right we'll discuss it later," said Aunt Bessie.

Lee rolled her eyes at Peter behind Bessie's back, and he winked at her. Personally, I was inclined to agree with Aunt Bessie. All this reassurance was getting on my nerves. Bessie may be twitty, but she's nobody's fool.

We reached the nursery, and the infant Patrick was pointed out. He looked just like every other baby I've ever seen—tiny, flat eyed, and fuzzy headed. He cooperated with his relatives by waking up and waving his little arms wildly about as though saying hello.

"Look at that! He looks just like Elizabeth!" said Bessie and Lee. "Look at those ears. Nice and flat. And the fingers. An artist. Are you an artist, darling? Such a sweet baby."

"Does your mother say he looks just like you?" I asked Peter.

"Of course," he replied.

■ —— ■

We went back to the room.

"He is simply beautiful," said Bessie, consenting finally to sit down. "Nearly as beautiful as my own babies."

Lee stood behind her, pressing herself up against the locker that served as a closet.

"Come sit on the bed, Lee," said Elizabeth, patting the mattress.

222

"No. Really." Lee held up her arms as though to ward off the thought. "No. Please. I'd rather stand."

"Darling, would you please see if you can round us up a couple of chairs?"

"Not on my account," said Lee. "I'm absolutely fine."

Peter went anyway, looking like despair.

"Now what can we bring you to eat tomorrow, darling?" said Aunt Bessie. Her grandson had cheered her. "Fruit? A nice salad? This dreadful hospital food."

"We thought we might go shopping, too," I said. "We wondered if there was anything we could get you."

"Oh, would you?" said Elizabeth. And she gave us a gratifyingly long list.

Peter came back lugging two chairs. I took one and Lee perched on the very edge of the other one, as though by making herself barely comfortable she could atone for the bother.

"There was a lot I meant to get after the baby came," said Elizabeth, dictating. "And now they say I can't drive for awhile. I was going to make Peter go, but I know he'd rather turn that over to more . . . experienced hands." She patted his fingers and he gave her a pained smirk. "I know this is going to be trouble, Judy." She looked at me.

"On the contrary," I said. "My husband informs me that shopping is one of the things I do really well. Of course we will be delighted."

■ —— ■

The next afternoon Elizabeth waited until we were alone.

"Now tell me about Tina," she said.

So I did. I knew she must have gotten a version of the story from her parents, but I told her the whole thing again, leaving nothing out, not even the parts I felt bad about.

"I can't believe she and Hamp . . . doesn't that just make your skin crawl?" said Elizabeth. She was sitting up in bed, wearing a T-shirt

223

and scribbling addresses on thank-you notes as we talked. She licked a stamp and pressed it to an envelope, grimacing.

I shrugged. What could I say?

"So how's Tina doing now?" said Elizabeth. She pushed the bed table aside, folded her arms, listening.

"I don't really know." I was silent for a minute. "You remember that game we used to play in fourth grade with a jump rope, where one person holds the rope and twirls it in a circle, and everybody else stands in a circle just inside the periphery of the rope and tries to jump over it every time it goes around?"

"And if you miss, you're it."

"Yeah. And the closer in you stand, the higher the rope is, and the faster it comes around, and the more likely you are to get your feet tangled in the rope."

"So you stay out on the edges."

"Correct."

"But isn't it a bitch," said Elizabeth. "Here is Tina, still turning with the rope, and everybody else still jumping."

Later that day Bessie and I took Lee to the airport.

"You are marvelous, Judy," said the aunts. "Negotiating this traffic."

I am an expert at the Atlanta airport, I admit it, and also at escorting aunts. I am the official family airport driver. I do the accompaniment to the plane, too, and the pat-on-the-arm, we'll-wait-here-with-you thing. I make sure everyone has enough to read and do, and airsick pills and change for pay phones. Finally, I smile and wave—"Goodbye! Goodbye!"—my mind already turning to the long trip home, and to Hamp and Curtis waiting for me at the other end.

Lee had a lot of luggage, and her carry-on bag was full of lettuce, broccoli, and radishes. She had a lot of last minute worries and instructions. Bessie and I nodded, forgetting as she spoke the words what they were, forgetting everything but the pressure of her fingers on our arms, the look of her as she withdrew from our support, drew into herself, prepared for the journey.

Lee looks too small for airports now. She is too grateful for my help with her luggage. She makes my heart lurch, she and Bessie, looking oddly alike, patting each other and fussing. They have been so different to me always, and now they grow alike. Standing together by a row of chairs at the flight check-in desk, hugging, they merged, their brittle tan hair, rings, dry cheeks, and flutters.

■ ——— ■

Bessie and I had a good time shopping. Atlanta malls are huge and provide scope for the really lustful shopper from out of town. We got all the baby clothes on Elizabeth's list, and Bessie indulged in some of the absurd and fanciful things that only grandmothers give, like a silver spoon and a china cup and plate, and a slippery blue-satin quilt. I indulged too. I bought the little fellow some books, copies of the ones Curtis had loved. Then I got Elizabeth some trashy novels. Then I saw the lingerie store, and bought us both a new nightgown. And I got Curtis the sweetest castle night-light, blue china, to put on his dresser, and some books for his birthday. We could barely lug our stuff to the car.

"My God," said Peter, when we got back to the house.

"You should have seen the stuff we put back," I said. "This represents real restraint."

Bessie collapsed on the sofa with her packages.

"No it doesn't," she said. "I buy what I buy. The child can't go around in ugly clothes, eating off some old tacky plastic just because he lives in a town where you can't even get a decent baby pillow."

Bessie was miffed because the salesperson at one store had told her that they didn't sell baby pillows because they were dangerous.

"What does she think we're going to do with it, put it over his face?" muttered Bessie. "Baby pillows are for the mother to prop under the baby when she's feeding him, as any fool would know who ever had a baby. Of course this woman probably never had a baby, gets all her information from a magazine, and yet has the nerve to say to me—"

■ —— ■

"You'll have to come back soon for a weekend," said Peter that night.

I was leaving the next morning. Peter and I watched the eleven o'clock news in adult silence. Bessie was in her room, and Peter's smile was gone. He looked really tired.

"You won't need company for awhile," I said. "Except Bessie, of course."

She was staying on a few days to help out.

"You are not company," said Peter. "Elizabeth and I want you to know you'd be welcome here any time. If you need to get away. If you and Hamp . . . if things should not work out there, to your liking, come on down and spend some time with us."

"I think we'll be fine," I said.

"Not saying you won't," he said. "Just saying, if they shouldn't."

There was a knot in my stomach.

"I believe we're okay," I said.

Peter just looked at me, swirling his wine in his glass.

"Don't you think we're okay?"

"Not for me to say," he said.

"Spoken like a lawyer."

"Well," he said, "do you think you're okay?"

"Yeah. I truly do. But I get this dread feeling, you know? Sweaty palms and all. I keep having to take deep breaths."

"Why, do you reckon?" he said.

I shrugged. He poured us another glass of wine. We looked at the news for a minute, then Peter took off his glasses and began to play

226

with them, folding and refolding the earpieces, tapping them against the bridge of his nose.

"When Elizabeth went in the hospital, you know, I was cool," he said. "No sweat, I figured. After the second or third hour, I was a nervous wreck. After eight hours I was sick. Sick and shaking. I couldn't figure out what was wrong with me. I had read about sympathetic pain, and I thought, Jesus. But then I thought about it, and I figured it out. It was fear. I was just plain scared shitless, that she would die. I'm still scared." He laughed. "I was so scared I was violent. And I couldn't swallow. I kept leaving the room to swallow."

"Hamp threw up," I said.

He nodded, took a sip of wine.

"The thing I can't figure," he said. "Number one, it had nothing to do with the kid. I'm happy for him and all, and he's a cute little bastard, but . . . And also, when will this—," he clinched his fists—"this fight-or-flight thing go away? It's like I got some sort of shot of something in the delivery room. Elizabeth had a kid and I got—"

"Religion."

"Exactly." He leaned forward. "I can't help but feeling, on Hamp's side, that he loves you, Judy. But I can't help feeling . . ." He leaned back, stared into his glass.

"I know," I said. "That's why my stomach hurts."

"Well, if I can help. I got some Zantac."

"I'd love some."

He left the room, returned with a bottle from which he shook out several pills into my palm.

"Best thing in the world," he said. "For the family man. Or woman. When does that hole in the gut fill in, by the way?"

"You don't want to know," I said.

"That's what I figured," he said, shaking the bottle into his own palm.

■ —— ■

227

Going home the next morning, I didn't think much. I had turned against thought again. Beating in my head was the rhythm of home, and the desire for home. I thought of Peter and Elizabeth, the sweat on his face behind his smile, and the whiteness of her hand against the covers. I thought of Hamp and Tina, and it seemed to me that I had made peace with the thought of them together, like I would make peace with death or disease. It was bad, but I could stand it. It no longer mattered. It coexisted in my head with the full awareness that Hamp loved me, and that there was room in his heart for me only, forever and to the end. He was mine.

Holding two mutually contradictory ideas in your head at the same time is no small feat, even for a Christian. And any adult who can swallow the basic tenets of the Nicene Creed is no mean apologist. So I was used to figuring things out two ways, reasonably and on faith. Juggling God and evolution require a lifetime of compartmentalization. And on the whole, faith had worked better for me than reason. In my experience, reason was something men trotted out when they wanted you to do something you didn't want to do. "Be reasonable." Do it my way. So I did not have all that much trouble loving a different Hamp from the man who had somehow slept with my sister, any more than I had trouble reading my son stories about the dinosaurs interspersed with stories about Moses and Abraham. God is family. Evolution is those educational TV programs I make Curtis watch about the lions of Africa, and the smell of the science lab where I spent so many hateful Friday afternoons my sophomore year in college.

So I drove the Cadillac home changing the dial a lot, and whistling.

Thirteen

13

I MEANT TO APPLY MYSELF TO MAKING MY LIFE WORK. I tried to figure how a life does work; how, for instance, Elizabeth seemed to have all the parts of her life running along smoothly, while all the parts of mine were clotted, smogged, runny. If I tried harder, if I figured things out, if I were more lovable, less maddening—if, if, my thoughts ran in dark circles. I read magazines—"Thirty Days to a Better Marriage." Some of the advice worked, like smiling. Smile more, said the magazine, and your partner will respond. My partner did. I smiled, I was skinny, I did sit-ups, painted my toenails, wore a new bra. Laughed at myself. I was more amenable, while laughing. This is working, I told myself. Shut up and keep smiling. At the same time, I knew that all my effort was for nothing.

After a ship wrecks, if a person is thrown clear into the water, that person swims if she can, even in the middle of the ocean. If the waves are high and the land a thousand miles away and the ocean a mile deep—especially then, a person swims, grabs a board, climbs a lifeboat, maybe thinking what's the use, but still paddling, searching the horizon, hoping for rain, all the time knowing that nothing she can do will make any difference, it'll all be luck or happenstance or maybe God whether a boat or an island floats into view. But still, she swims, floats, paddles.

I rode horses. Curtis was still afraid of riding, and I felt like he needed to get over that fear. I decided to ask Sally to go along. The trouble was, I was afraid of the Hoopers.

I had not seen them since the afternoon Tina took all the pills. I was avoiding them.

"How are Jimmy's parents?" I asked Mom. "Do they hate Tina? How are they taking all this?"

"Of course they don't hate Tina. They are very concerned. How else would they be taking it?" Mom said.

"I thought they might think their son made a terrible mistake marrying Tina," I said.

"Perhaps he did," said Mom. "Perhaps he did make a terrible mistake." She stared off into space for a minute. "He loves her. If you love somebody . . .," she shrugged. "For better or worse, that's what it says, doesn't it?"

"I just feel people backing away. 'How is Tina?' people say to me. 'What can we do to help? What happened? How did it happen?' They are curious, that's all. There's a lot of talk. People are wondering if she will teach next year after all. Stuff like that."

My mother was silent. She sipped her coffee. Finally she set down her cup, looked up at me.

"Don't bother with gossip," she said. "Tell me, have you decided to stick with Hamp?"

"Yes and no," I said.

"Well, it's your business," she said. "I'll back you, whatever you decide. Right now I'm worried about you and concerned, as we all are, about Tina's health and the emotional strain on poor Jimmy."

I wasn't worried about me. And I was pretty sick of Tina's health and the emotional strain on poor Jimmy.

So Curtis and I drove over to the Hoopers to pick up Sally and take her riding.

"Won't you come in?" Lucy said, leaning into the car.

"We'd better get going," I smiled. "Curtis is eager to ride this morning."

Curtis struggled obligingly against his safety harness.

"Wave goodbye to Miss Lucy!" I said. "Goodbye, Miss Lucy! Goodbye!"

"Goodbye!" waved the children.

■ —— ■

Salem Ridge, where Diane lives, is up in the northern end of the county, miles from anywhere. We drove for thirty minutes, turned off the main road, which is itself just an old logging track that's been paved over, bumped down a red-dirt road for a while, then down a long dirt driveway past Diane's aunt's house and pastures of horses. Curtis and Sally quit singing "Ninety-nine bottles of pop on the wall" and began to bounce up and down.

The driveway ended in a large lot beside a barn.

Diane was in the ring riding, and she waved at us. A tiny girl sat in the saddle with her.

"Be through in a minute!" she said, brushing past on a large spotted horse. There was another child in the ring, on her own horse. We stood by the fence and watched.

"Trot him now, sweetie," Diane said. "Don't let him stop at the gate."

The little girl began to trot, jaggedly, and I remembered how it feels to trot before you get the hang of it—like riding a revolving door.

"Go with it," Diane said. "Stand on your heels, and meet him on the bounce. Don't fight it. That's it. You got it, girl! Keep going now."

It was a beautiful day. The ring and barn sit on the very top of a plateau, so that you could see for miles in every direction. It looked like a different part of the country from the one we lived in. Even the color of the dirt changed. The ridge was tan instead of red. You could almost see, to the north, the beginnings of mountains. They shimmered on the edge of sight, but disappeared into the horizon if you looked straight at them. Between us and the mountains, the land on all sides fell away in a series of green, bumpy pastures with secret little streams twisting through the middle of them. In the morning, the grass was still damp and luscious looking, but it wouldn't stay that way. It would be ninety by noon, and the tan soil, which now looked so rich and lovely, would become a choking dust.

Curtis stood on the bottom rung of the fence in front of me, suddenly small and quiet as we watched the two horses follow each other around the ring. The little girl riding with Diane looked half asleep, leaning forward into the crook of Diane's arm. Diane held her easily, held the reins with her other hand. It is an odd thing to see your friend at work, to see her doing something well and naturally, being professional. It's not that you don't think your friend can work, it's that you never realized before exactly what she does. It's a part of her you never even suspected. Though I had heard Diane talk about her horses and riding, it had never occurred to me that she would be so good at it.

Then the lesson was over. The two little girls dismounted, the littlest one giving Diane a hug first, and ran off across the meadow. When the horses came up to the gate, Curtis wrapped himself around my leg, astonished. They towered above him, their legs taller than Curtis's head, smelling of sweat, hair, and leather. They glistened and stamped, blew and swished their tails. Diane dismounted; Sally was immediately at the horses, patting and whispering. Curtis remained glued to my leg. Diane helped Sally onto the smaller horse and leaned over the fence.

"So Mister Curtis!"

Curtis turned to look at her. She held out her hand to him. He ignored it. Diane took off her cap and shook out her hair, which fell in a black cascade across her back, then twisted it up again and replaced the cap.

"I tell you what," Diane said, winking at me. "I'll get Sally started, then I'll get back on Buster, and you can ride with me like Julie does. Julie loves to ride with me. She comes with her sister all the time. Do you know Julie, the little girl who was here just now?"

"Yes, I know her," he said. "From school."

"Okay!" said Diane, as though that settled everything.

We watched her adjust Sally's stirrups, mount Buster. As she swung Buster's big brown head toward us, Curtis's grip on my leg tightened.

"Come on, bud," said Diane, reaching down for him.

I ignored the stiffness in his body, the fact that he was still clutching at my leg, and peeled him off me like a tight boot, handing him up to Diane. He reached out for me and began to cry. Diane settled him down in front of her.

"I tell you what," she said. "You want to ride with your mom?"

Curtis nodded, wiping his eyes, and I shook my head. Diane ignored me.

"Just let her get on her horse, and we'll sit right here and wait for her. Okay?"

Curtis nodded again.

"Go ahead, Judy," Diane waved. "Go ahead. The mare by the barn. You may need to adjust the stirrups."

I walked over to a sleepy-looking brown horse tied outside the barn and looked at it. The stirrups would have fit Curtis. By the time

233

I got them adjusted and got in the ring, Curtis and Diane were starting without me.

"Giddy-up?" Curtis said. "Go?"

"Well, look at that!" said Diane, as the horse moved out into a
walk. "You made old Buster move."

Sally and I got into line behind Buster.

"I want to ride with Mom," said Curtis.

"You're going to," said Diane. "Just as soon as she gets her bear-
ings. How you doing back there, Judy?"

"To tell you the truth," I said.

"What?" She turned around and grinned at me.

"Nothing. I am the happiest woman alive," I said.

After awhile Diane began to trot her horse, and like little stair
steps, Sally's horse and my horse began to trot, too. At first I held the
mare back, but then I thought, Oh what the hell, and let her go. She
had a nice trot, and I only grabbed the saddle horn two or three
times. I began to remember what I was doing.

"Looking good, Judy!" said Diane, prancing by, and she broke into
a canter.

We only cantered once around.

"Well, look at you guys!" said Diane, pulling up at the gate. "Sally,
you're a natural, honey. Judy, take Mister Curtis now while I show
Sally some things."

She handed him across to me. He clung like a monkey, and I settled
him into the saddle. He was hot, sticky beneath my palms, smelled
like a nickel.

"Having fun?" I said.

"Okay," he said, but remained stiff. For that matter, so did I.

When the lesson was over, we walked the horses into the shade of
the barn. Diane gave the kids a tour, showed them how to brush the
horses.

"Next time you can ride with your mom if you want to," she told

234

Curtis. "Or you can ride Sammy. He's out in the pasture today."

"I'll ride with Mom," said Curtis. "Who is Sammy?"

"Oh, he's my pony," said Diane. "He's got his own saddle. Sammy's a pet. Bring him an apple, and he'll be your friend for life. "

"Tomorrow," said Curtis.

"Day after, maybe," I said. "I have to work sometime. But we'll come again soon."

■ —— ■

I had to get out of the car at Lucy's to mop up spilled milk shake. It was in the french fries, a little, but we wiped them off. Curtis went in to wash up.

"Come in for a minute," said Lucy. "I'll give you a glass of tea."

"I really ought to be going." I looked around for Curtis.

"Come on. I need your advice about something I'm making for Tina Lee."

Well, I thought, here it comes. I followed Lucy into the house, through the clean, silent rooms, up the narrow stairs.

"So what is it?" I said.

"A sewing project."

We went into Jimmy's old bedroom. Tina's picture was still on the desk. A white froth of material lay billowing across the bed, a lovely foaming mass of puffs and gathers.

"These are Tina's Austrian shades," said Lucy, holding one up. "What do you think?"

She walked to the window with it, held it up to the light. The sun softened, shifted, settled into the folds of tulle. I remembered: Tina standing in her bedroom the day we went to her house for lunch, looking at her sheet-covered windows.

"What I really want," she'd said, scrabbling through a pile of papers, "is this."

She pulled out a magazine and opened it to a marked page. Mom

235

and Lucy gathered around, and they took the magazine over to the bed and sat down, engrossed. Lucy pointed with her little finger at some detail. Mom sat with her arm around Tina's back, rubbing. Tina's shoulder blade showed through her shirt. "Two minds with but a single thought," I murmured. "Getting those tacky temporary curtains down and their babies properly set up in the marital bedroom."

"Shut up," said Tina, smiling up at me. "I'm about to get my Austrian shades."

My mind shifted back to the present.

"Lucy, they're beautiful," I said. "What a nice person you are."

Lucy laid the curtain back down, patting the material. "I've just been at such a loss about Tina, not knowing what to do. Flowers and food. But I wanted something that said, Your life is going forward. She's been so nervous about the house, you know." I didn't know. I hadn't seen her.

"Then I wondered, what if she doesn't like them? I asked James, but you know James. He said they were fine. 'They look great, Lucy.'" She stuck out her lower lip, in imitation of her husband.

"She'll love them," I said. "Really. If she doesn't, she's crazy. Oops. Not crazy."

Lucy let out a sigh and smiled.

"Okay," she said. "I'm trusting your judgment on this, Judy."

We went back down the stairs.

■ —— ■

"How was riding?" asked Lucy. She set out glasses, added ice, tea, lemon.

"Sally's good. Curtis is still a little scared. He rode with me."

"So you rode?"

"Under protest. To tell you the truth, I don't like riding horses. I like the idea of horses and I like their smell and the way they look, but I don't like their bones. They also disobey. And it's a long way to

236

the ground. But I have this kid. I'll do anything to keep him from being scared. I spend half my life scaring him to keep him from jumping off buildings and half my life proving to him that it's okay, that he should try this, do this, overcome his fear. I mean, I don't want him to kill himself, but—"

Lucy handed me my tea.

"I wonder where Curtis is," I said. "We really must be going."

"It's hard, isn't it?" said Lucy. "Raising a child."

"It is that." I had heard it all before.

"I hope Tina and Jimmy change their minds and wait awhile. Now they're talking right away. But I don't think they need that extra strain, do you?"

"I have no idea," I said.

"Tina and Jimmy are at such a dangerous age."

"Yeah."

"Just out of college, at loose ends and all, putting all that pressure on themselves by getting married . . ."

I nodded.

"It's hard to know how this will affect them."

"Well, at least it's over," I said, glancing toward the door.

Lucy stared at me. "Oh no," she said, "it's only beginning."

"Why do you say that? Tina has done her spectacular-gesture thing. Jimmy loves her, all is forgiven, life will go on. Love and sympathy all around."

"She has paid an enormous price, you know," said Lucy. "For the love and sympathy."

"Right," I said.

"You haven't seen her, have you?"

"Not in Demaro, no." I set down my glass. "It's not that I don't care about Tina, Lucy. I do. And I'm scared for her. I think this time she really screwed up."

"Royally," said Lucy.

"But what am I supposed to do?"

"I don't know," she said.

"She'll be fine. She'll get her old life back. Tina's tough."

"Oh, I don't think she'll get her old life back," said Lucy. "At least I hope not. Her old life was intolerable to her. It's going to be hard. And long."

"Thanks a lot," I said. "I think I'll move to Alaska. Write me when it's over."

■ —— ■

That night I couldn't sleep. I had been having a lot of trouble sleeping. Finally, I got up and went into the bathroom, closed the door, and turned on the light. I looked at myself in the mirror, sat down on the bath mat. I thought about Curtis, about Tina Lee and Jimmy, about my life in a trailer in the woods. Then I started reading the sports page, which was the only thing to read in the bathroom. I read the box scores and memorized everybody's standing in the National League.

I had folded a towel to sit on and was resting my head on the side of the tub, just getting comfortable to work some on the American League, when Hamp came in.

"What's the matter?" he said.

"Nothing. I couldn't sleep." I patted the floor. "Would you care to join me?"

"No thank you." He turned to go back to bed.

"Hamp," I said. I followed him into the bedroom. "What if we bought a house?"

"Umm," he said.

"How would you feel about moving into town?"

"I'd hate it." He spoke from under his pillow.

"Seriously."

"Seriously, no," he said.

238

"Why not?" I said.

Hamp leaned up, looked at his watch, then at me. "Judy, it's two o'clock in the morning."

"What's the matter, you said. The matter is, I think Curtis needs to be in town. I need to be in town. We need to be normal, do a regular family thing."

"Can't it wait?"

"He'll be in school this fall."

"I mean the conversation."

"Oh sure," I said. "No problem." I got into the bed. "Good night."

In a few minutes he sighed, an infinitely weary sigh. "It's a dumb idea economically, you know. And you hate subdivisions, you said so."

"No, you hate subdivisions. So why do you build them?" I said.

"So I can make enough money not to have to live in one," he said. "Want to fool around?"

"No. I'm worried about this, Hamp."

"Worried about what, for God's sake?"

"Organizing the rest of my life."

"Let's work on a baby."

"That's it, Hamp. I don't want a baby until I get this all figured out, about the house and all. I feel like we're drifting."

"You're mad, right?"

"I want something real. I don't want to spend the rest of my life in a trailer."

"This is a test."

"No," I said.

I lied. If Hamp loved me, I thought, he would be willing to take this permanent step. We were still living in a trailer, I figured, because Hamp could not bring himself to make the commitment to live in an actual house with me. It was a test. But I was also scared for Curtis, scared that he would grow up weird.

239

Hamp and I talked about the move for days.

"Be reasonable, Judy," he said. "For Christ's sake. This is just some temporary harebrained idea of yours. Right? You don't want to move any more than I do."

"I do," I said. "I want it more than anything in the world."

I said that about midnight a couple of days later, and Hamp said, "All right. We'll move. All right, goddammit. Yes. Whatever you want."

He pulled the covers over his head.

I stared for a minute at the lump of him beside me under the covers. Let it go, something whispered to me. Let it go. Shut up. Lie down. Go to sleep.

But I didn't.

"When?" I said. "When are we going to move?"

Hamp pulled the covers down from round his face and looked at me. Then he got up, pulled on his pants, and opened the closet door.

"Tonight," he said. "We'll move tonight."

He pulled an armload of clothes off the rod and laid them on the bed, reached up for another load.

"Are you crazy?" I said. "We can't move tonight."

"Oh yes we can," he said, wrestling a huge wad of clothes out the bedroom door.

I followed him out to the truck and watched him dump the clothes in the back. He passed me on his way to get another load.

"Hamp, please," I said. I followed him back into the bedroom. "You're going to wake up Curtis."

"Well, we'll have to wake him eventually," he said. "We don't want to leave him here alone. Which house did you have in mind moving to?"

He threw a bunch of keys from the dresser onto the bed.

"Here. Pick one."

"No," I said.

"Well, what do you want?" he said. "Just tell me. Just tell me for Christ's sake what you want me to do."

"I want you to go to bed," I said.

"You mean we're not moving tonight?" he said.

"No."

"Then I can get some sleep for a change?"

"Yes."

"Great," he said, snatched up his pillow, and stalked into the living room.

I tiptoed after him.

"Hamp?"

He actually snarled at me, turning from the couch like a dog at bay.

"I just wondered if you were planning to leave your clothes out there all night," I said. "It's supposed to rain before morning."

I beat a hasty retreat to the bedroom, turned out the light, and dived under the covers.

The next morning Hamp's clothes were piled up against the bedroom door like a little cloth mountain, so I guess he did take them in sometime during the night.

■ —— ■

I was working at the lumberyard that week, but we didn't ride in together. On about the fourth day after that, Hamp got a call, and I couldn't find him. I paged him in the warehouse, the store, and looked for him outside. The call was not important, and I could have handled it myself. I was just mad he had gone off without telling me. I watched for him, and when he came back, I walked out to the truck and let him have it.

"When you leave," I said, "the least you can do is let the office staff know it, so we won't waste all morning trying to track you down."

"Next time I will," he said, slamming the truck door.

"Please do," I said.

He caught my arm as I turned to go back in the building.

"What the hell is going on with you now?" he said. "Are you still mad about the house business? Why are you doing this?"

"I'm afraid," I said. "You really don't want to move into a house with me, do you?"

"Not a house in McAdamsville."

"Not a house anywhere. Do you?"

"I don't know," he said.

The stone in my chest was dragging me down, down. I felt too heavy to move. I stood in the sun and watched my husband beating his palm rhythmically against the side of the truck.

"For twenty years I watched my father screw up," said Hamp. He laughed without joy. "And he screwed up royally, I can tell you, while my mother watched and kept book on him. He was probably so far down with her before I was even born, he figured it wasn't any use for him to try and climb out. So he kept on drinking, and she just kept on hurting, hurting and hating, until he died. And I watched. And you know what? She still hates him. You can smell it on her, the hate for him, like a kind of . . . And I swore, I swore —" he tore the papers in his hand, and they fluttered to the ground—"I swore I'd never wind up like that, Judy. And now I feel it . . . This thing with Tina, I—" His voice broke. He stopped and stared at me, wiped his eyes angrily with the back of his hand, then turned and walked on off to the sawmill.

When I got back into the office, Mom came in from the store. "What's the matter?" she said.

"I think I need to take the afternoon off," I said. "I don't feel so good."

I picked up my keys. Mom followed me to the door.

"What's wrong?"

"I'm fine," I said. "Forget it. I'll do the books tomorrow."

Around the bend from the lumberyard, I pulled the car over and had a good cry, leaning my head up against the steering wheel, watching the cars go by and trying to pretend I was waiting for someone. Then I got Curtis from Heather's house, where he had been staying, and took him home.

We made sandwiches and went for a walk down to the lake. Curtis took his pole.

"I'll catch fish and eat them for supper," he said.

There was not a chance that he would catch anything, but he likes to cast, and talk about fish and fish guts and eyeballs. And when he gets tired of fishing, there are minnows to catch and rocks to pile into little dams.

We let Reddie out, and she and Curtis bounced down the rutted dirt road and back up to meet me, down and up, like yo-yos. Hamp had recently mowed—I couldn't think when, he had been so busy—but Curtis and Reddie raced in circles around the perimeter of the clearing, jumped on and off the slab, dashed into the pine trees and reappeared on the far side of the pond near the dam. That's where we fish. I stood on the bank and watched them. We used to bring Curtis here as a toddler to ride his tricycle on the slab. We joked that we had the most expensive carport in town. Hamp and I used to walk down here all the time after work and on Saturdays. When I was pregnant with Curtis and meant to build a house here, we would bring chairs and cook out, just like we already lived here.

I walked on around to join Curtis, who had already managed to foul his line. When I got there, Reddie allowed herself a swim, then shook water all over us and flopped down to watch for rabbits. We were just eating our lunch and watching grasshoppers bounce in the sun, when I looked up and saw Hamp coming down the road from the trailer.

He's coming to say he's sorry, I thought. He loves me, and we will all live happily ever after. Isn't this a pretty sight, mother and son, and the light on the water.

But instead he rounded the curve of the pond with no wave or grin or any acknowledgement, stopped about ten feet away from me and said, "Judy, I'm afraid I have some bad news for you."

"What is it?" I said.

"It's your dad," he said. "They just took him to the hospital."

Fourteen

14

Mom was sitting in the emergency room waiting area in the hospital in Demaro. The waiting room is just a wide space inside the emergency room door, cluttered with green-and-brown plastic couches. Mom sat on the edge of one. She looked like somebody had taken hold of the skin on her face and given it a yank. She grabbed my arm and pulled me down on the seat beside her.

"I'm afraid it's a stroke," she said. "I know it's a stroke." She looked around as though she hoped someone would contradict her. "He said he felt sick. Went into the bathroom. I could hear him in there throwing up. Poor Bob, I thought, a virus, one of those twenty-four hour things. You know your dad is never sick. When he came out, he sat down in his chair, and I got up and went over to him, and he jerked, sort of, and fell out of the chair. I tried to catch him. I eased him down to the floor. I thought he was dead. His skin was grey, just like . . . but he was breathing."

"It could be other things," I said.

But we looked at each other in dread. Dad's father had had a stroke. Pop, we called him. He had survived it, and had lain for years in his bed at home, slobbering into his pillow until he died. We spent half our Sunday afternoons the whole time he was sick sitting beside his bed. I felt like I grew up in a corner of that old man's mind, sitting in the chinaberry tree outside his window eavesdropping on my parents trying to make conversation with him.

"It could be the flu. Or diabetes."

"If you had seen him," she said. "Oh, my God." She kept touching her face with her fingers as though to press it back onto her skull.

"I'll go get you a coke," I said.

When in doubt, eat. I brought back soft drinks and packs of crackers and ate them all myself to have something to do. The emergency room was very busy. People kept coming in. A woman ran in with her hand wrapped in a bloody towel, and some green-clad hospital people rushed up and led her through the swinging doors. Others, the ones who weren't bleeding, were directed to sit down in the room with us and wait. There were some sick children lolling in their parents' arms, and some old people who sat scrunched up, holding their elbows. Nobody looked worse than my mama.

"Go up there and see what's going on," she said.

She said that every few minutes. I would obediently walk to the counter at the far end of the hall and stand until I got a nurse's attention, ask the same question, receive the same answer, and go back and sit down. I did that for a couple of hours until the nurses would see me coming and answer me before I asked.

"We don't know a thing, miss. Just as soon as the doctor can, he'll be out with you."

"Jerry White is in there with him," Mom said. "I called his office, and he got here right after we did. What's keeping them?"

"I'm sorry I went home," I said.

"I had a time," she said. "Getting it all arranged. Your daddy lying there in the floor, Hamp not around . . . did you see Hamp?"

"Yes," I said. "He's getting someone to watch Curtis. He'll be along."

"I thought he would die before the ambulance got there. I kept thinking, should we use CPR? The girls from the front didn't know any more that I did. But he was breathing. There didn't seem to be anything wrong with his breathing."

"I'm sure you did the right things," I said.

The Reverend Carruthers came by, sat and patted Mom's shoulder, and her eyes grew bright with tears which never fell.

"Is there anybody you want me to call, Edna? Shall we get in touch with Jimmy, do you think? Or Tina?"

I had forgotten about Tina.

"I guess so," said Mom. "Better call Jimmy. Tina's supposed to come home tomorrow. Have Jimmy tell her doctor, and have the doctor tell Tina. Don't you think?"

Mr. Carruthers nodded and went to make the call. When he came back, Mom began to tell him the story of Dad's stroke. Her story had already achieved, with two or three tellings, a definite outline and phraseology. I noticed with chagrin that my absence from the office and Hamp's absence had assumed a role in the drama. When the stroke had happened, Mom had been alone. None of her children were there. That was significant. The story would reverberate through the years with those refrains: "And none of the children were there." "I was alone, of course, when it happened." "Since I was the only one with him at the time . . ."

Somehow, though, the thought was cheering: Dad's illness becoming just another family story.

■ —— ■

After awhile Dr. White came through the swinging doors and said that Dad was still alive. That he had had a stroke, a pretty bad one, and that it was too soon really to tell anything. But he was in his room in intensive care, and we could see him if we wanted to.

So we did. He was naked, more or less, hooked up to all kinds of machines, in a bare room walled round with glass. You could see the nurses in their central cubicle staring up occasionally through all those glass walls at their patients, blipping and beeping in their beds. Dad was still grey, but he looked at Mom and raised his fingers a little. Then he looked at me.

"Hi, Dad," I said. "That was not a nice thing you did there. You scared us. But it looks like you're going to be all right."

He closed his eyes briefly.

"You really are," I said. "Though you don't look so good now. Or feel so good. Dr. White says you're fine."

He blinked again.

"Bob," said Mom. "They won't let me stay with you. But I am right on the other side of that wall, and I'll be in for a few minutes every hour." She touched his face, bent over and kissed him on the cheek. "Old sweetheart," she said. "You'll feel better in the morning. I promise."

Of course I made a complete ass of myself by crying. I began to cry in the room, and by the time I got around the corner, my eyes were so blinded I couldn't see where I was walking and had to feel my way back to the waiting room.

That too became part of the story. "Judy took one look at him and just fell to pieces, bless her heart. She had to be practically carried from the room. One of the nurses had to give her smelling salts to calm her down. Thank God, Hamp got there about then."

■ —— ■

Mom did not leave the hospital at all that night. We moved up

248

into the intensive care waiting room. The couches there were flow-ered chintz grouped back to back around coffee tables, making a se-ries of roomlets. Mom picked an empty one and sat down, and people began to trickle in, Aunt Bessie and Uncle Fred—Aunt Bessie sitting close to Mom and holding her hands, Uncle Fred wiping his face with a folded handkerchief and saying, "Whew! Well, what happened, Edie? Was he sick or what?"

Patsy and Charley came. They smelled of flowers—Charley had been making deliveries from his mama's shop. Bits of fern clung to his rolled-up sleeves. He sat beside me, picked the bits off, and shred-ded them between his fingers.

Hamp came, and some friends from church. Someone brought sand-wiches, coffee. Every hour Mom and I went in for our minutes with Dad, watching his face, his eyes, his chest for signs of survival. After awhile I went back to McAdamsville to see my son.

Curtis had spent a nervous afternoon and evening with school friends, the first place Hamp could find to leave him. We drove on to my parents' house with him in the front seat asking a stream of questions.

"Where is Granddaddy? Will he die? What's a stroke? What's para-lyzed? Andy's granddaddy died. Andy watched when they buried him. Andy said it was weird."

"Your granddaddy is not going to die."

We pulled up in my parents' yard.

"Feed the cat," Mom had said. "Pack a bag for your dad."

In the twilight, the house looked dark, deserted.

"Turn on the light timer," Mom had said.

Indignant Fluffy followed me to the cat food, the dish, meowed impatiently while I fumbled with the spoon.

"You want milk, cat?" I said. "You better ask now."

Curtis wandered after me into my parents' room, sat on the bed and watched while I hunted for Dad's pajamas and a razor. Curtis found his favorite afghan, wrapped himself around and around in it like an enormous caterpillar making a cocoon, crawled up on Mom's bed, stuck his thumb in his mouth, and tuned out. I finished packing. I put in some things for Mom, too.

"Let's go into the den and wait for Dad," I said. "He's going to come by and pick you up and take you home, and I'm going back to the hospital and sit with Grandma."

"Why?"

"So she won't be lonely."

In the den, we curled up in Dad's chair, the recliner. I held the cocooned Curtis and read him a story from a fairy tale book.

"Is Granddaddy lonely?" he said.

"No. He said to tell you hello. He said to tell you not to worry, he's going to be fine."

Why did I keep saying that? I didn't believe it myself. I could smell Dad's lime aftershave, and his cigars. Maybe he will die, I thought, and his whole self will be lost to us forever. He would not want to be an invalid. Still, I wanted him alive. If he were sick, crippled, so be it. Any shreds of him would do, any bits to hold on to. I wondered if he had felt like that about his own dad, all those Sunday afternoons.

■ —— ■

Hamp came by to get Curtis, and he woke up fussing as we were putting him in the truck.

"It's going to be all right, son," said Hamp. "Your mom will be coming home."

Back at the hospital, only Aunt Bessie and Lucy remained with Mom.

"You go on home to your own family, Bessie," said Mom.

"If you're sure," said Bessie. "I declare, Edna. You don't deserve this. They say trouble comes in threes."

"Lord, I hope not," said Mom.

250

They patted arms.

"Call me," said Bessie, "if you need anything. You will call me, won't you?"

We all assured her we would.

"Now Edna," said Lucy, when Bessie was gone. "I want you to eat this soup."

She sat beside Mom and unscrewed the cap on a thermos.

"I made it special for you, and I want you to eat it now." She laid a napkin in Mom's lap and handed her the thermos top full of soup and a spoon. Mom ate. When she finished the soup, Lucy rinsed out the top and recapped it. She opened the second thermos, which contained iced tea.

"I put the lemon in already," she said. "The tea in this hospital isn't fit to drink."

When Lucy had Mom fixed to suit her—pillow and blanket ready on the couch—I walked her to the elevator.

"You get some rest yourself now, Judy," Lucy said. "Your mama's going to need you."

I went back into the waiting room and sat down on my couch facing Mom's couch. Lucy had brought a blanket for me, too. The room had emptied; only the hard-core relatives remained, squatters in a cold, shallow ditch outside the castle of pain. Like Curtis, I wrapped myself in my blanket.

At ten minutes to eleven, the intercom turned on with a soft little ding, and a voice told us that we could now visit, one at a time, our people. After the obligatory "You go first, no, go ahead," one representative from each cluster rose and walked obediently through the door.

I went first. Dad was sleeping, as he had been all night, still mostly naked, flat out on a flat, white bed surrounded by machines which gurgled and hummed. I touched the bed but did not touch him. Dad's always been a light sleeper, and I was afraid—of waking him, of

251

being seen by him, of not giving Mom enough time with him. I could see the other visitors from the waiting room standing in their glass rooms, too, by their people's beds. They all seemed to have more to say and do than I did. As I went out, I studied the central nursing station. It was filled with television screens showing pictures of the patients, and other screens showing wavy lines. Things hummed, blipped. A nurse sat looking at the screens. I wondered if she did that all night.

"How is he?" said Mom as we switched places.

"Asleep."

When she came back out from her minutes with Dad, she said, "You know, I think he looks a little better."

She said that every hour all night long. "His color is better," she'd say. "He's resting more comfortably now."

Once he was restless, and I got scared, but she said it was a good sign.

"He's coming back," she said.

She never doubted that he would make it, not after the first few hours in the emergency room. She seemed to feel that from that point on, he could be kept alive by her will, and his.

"Your daddy has a great will to live," she said. "When he went to Korea, I never doubted that he would come back. Not if he possibly could. Your daddy is a survivor."

She had me convinced until about five in the morning. I had dozed off and missed a visit, but a commotion woke me. There were only three groups left in the waiting room—us, a bunch of brothers and sisters of a heart attack victim, and a large group belonging to a man who'd been in an automobile accident. Apparently, the automobile accident wasn't doing so well. His mother, I guess, was listening to a man in a white coat, who put his hand on her shoulder. She shook him off and started wailing and rocking back and forth on her couch, and the others gathered around her.

"Oh," she said, "what'm I gonna do? What'm I gonna do without my Johnny?" She said it over and over, like a chant.

The doctor stood up, leaned over and spoke to the mother again.

"No!" she screamed. Everybody jumped. "You can't take his parts. He wouldn't like it. And he's breathing. He's still alive, I tell you."

The doctor backed away and started talking to one of the younger women. A couple of the others started crying. Finally two men helped the mother up and through the door in to Johnny, while the rest of them sat around and wiped their eyes. There was a big man about forty who laid his head down on his arms and shook in complete silence until I wanted to go over and touch him, but I didn't. After awhile the mother came out again, still wailing, and they carried her out to the elevator. The doctor went with them. The others began gathering their things.

"Don't forget Mama's pocketbook," one woman kept saying. "Do we go home now? What do we do now?"

After they left I looked at the other remaining group, and they looked at us. I was thinking, Johnny is tonight's offering to death. That means our people will live. But I was also thinking, if he can die so can Dad. We stared at each other, speculating.

"Want some coffee?" I said to Mom.

"Thank you. Yes, I would like a cup."

There was a machine in the corner by the window. The sky had lightened for dawn, and the lady at the desk had made a fresh pot of coffee which smelled like morning. She had also laid out some dough-nuts, apparently thinking that we all needed bucking up after poor Johnny.

■ —— ■

Tina Lee and Jimmy arrived midmorning, fresh and clean. Tina was big-eyed, without nerves, without edges, a smooth stone.

253

"So what happened?" she said, like a polite relative. "I'm so sorry, Mom. It must have been terrible for you."

Then she grew silent. She looked at her hands or, idly, around the room. Occasionally she smiled at Jimmy. Jimmy avoided my eyes. He seemed to know a lot about hospitals, and he began to run around and find things out.

"Dr. White's office says he'll see you this morning for sure," he said. "Bob's pressure is down and the swelling is not too bad, the nurses say. It looks okay for now." He was restless and kept touching Tina's hand.

"Is it good to be home?" I said.

"I haven't been home," she said, with a smile.

The intercom dinged, announced that we could now begin our procession in to Dad.

"Tina," I said, "Dad doesn't look exactly—"

"What?"

"He's still sort of out of it. He looks gray. He's a little paralyzed, and his face doesn't . . . match." I looked at Jimmy. "Maybe she doesn't want to see him," I said.

"Don't be silly, Judy," said Mom. "Of course she wants to see him. That's why she came to the hospital. Come on. We'll all go together."

"They won't let us, Mom," I said.

"Nonsense," said Mom, standing up.

She walked Tina across the waiting room. Jimmy and I followed, squeezed through the door behind them like we were getting into an elevator. A nurse glanced up, and Mom smiled at her, pointed at Tina. The nurse waved and went back to her screen-scanning.

When we got into Dad's cubicle, Mom pulled Tina to his bed.

"Bob?" she said. "Bob. Somebody here to see you, honey." She touched his face, and he opened his eyes. "Look who's here, sweetheart. Talk to him, Tina. He can understand every word you say." She moved around so that Tina was nearest the head of the bed.

Tina looked nervously back at Jimmy, who nodded.

"Dad?" she said.

His eyes traveled from Mom to Tina, focused on her face. The bones of his forehead stuck up like a rock from the mattress.

"I am so sorry, Dad." Tina bent closer, her hair falling down across her face, across his chest. "So sorry that this happened to you. The whole time I was in the hospital, I thought, I can't wait to get home, and have everything be like it was before, and last night Jimmy came and told me you had had a stroke, and I said, So it never will be like it was before, we have lost it and it was all my fault. But this morning I woke up, and the sun was coming through the window, you know, between the little slats, and I knew you were going to be all right. And I knew that I was, too. It'll just take time, you know? Time to heal." She laid her head lightly against his breastbone. "I can hear your heart," she said.

He touched her hair, looking up at us.

"Well," Tina said, "I'm home."

■ —— ■

Mom was holding on to some essential part of Dad that the rest of us couldn't see.

"That IV is making him uncomfortable," she said. "Have the nurse fix it." "He's trying to speak." "He wants you, Tina. Come and talk to him."

I thought it was creepy myself, but she seemed to know what she was doing.

Tina kept Jimmy busy at the hospital waiting on her. He brought ice and pills and commandeered a pillow for her. Then he sat holding and patting her hand while they whispered together in a corner.

I grew to like having Jimmy around. He wasn't much use except to entertain Tina—a full-time job to be sure—but he was sort of cheering. He tried to be suitably grave, but kept forgetting and getting cheerful again, like he was so happy to be alive and married to Tina that not even the evidence before him could convince him at age twenty-two that people got sick and died.

"I got a fellowship to law school," he said. "I can go this fall. Or I can go after Christmas, or next year."

"Well, what do you want to do?" I said.

He merely shrugged.

■ —— ■

Hamp's mother came, bringing food—muffins and fruit, all arranged in a little basket with a fruit knife and napkins. She sat beside Mom with her hands folded in her lap and listened, while Mom told her everything.

"It was so dreadful, Marie, to see him like that."

"Of course it must have been," said Marie. "Dreadful. And the worry. He's a strong man, Edna. Such an appreciation for life. And he's hung on so far. That's a very good sign."

"It is, isn't it? But he could die yet."

"Yes," said Marie. "He could."

"He's not out of the woods yet."

"No," said Marie. "He's not."

Mom nodded as though agreeing with herself, while Marie peeled her a peach, which she ate. Then Mom dozed a little, with Marie on guard beside her like an Irish setter, calmly watching while Jimmy and I ate half the muffins.

When I was in the hospital with Curtis, Marie brought me and Hamp a salad.

"Hospital salads are not nice," she said, laying plastic bowls on the table in front of us. She dished out some sliced oranges, grapefruit, and avocados on lettuce, and dressing drizzled from a little plastic cup. It was the most wonderful salad I've ever eaten.

Marie is one of those people who does the right thing.

■ —— ■

Dr. White came. Mom was awake by then, and had gone into the bathroom and washed her face. Dr. White is Dad's age, balding and pale, and was suited up for the office. He breathes in through his nose, a big breath, and holds it, then breathes out through his mouth in a sigh. It must drive his wife crazy.

"How is Bob?" Mom would say.

"Well, Edna—" Inhale. Hold. Exhale. Sigh. "It's hard to say."

It was certainly hard for him to say.

He said ultimately that they couldn't tell anything much yet, that you couldn't with strokes, but that Dad had made it through the night and that was something. That of course was what we had all been telling each other for sixteen hours, but hearing it from the lips of Dr. White made it official, and we all nodded as though he had said something new and profound.

■ —— ■

Four days after his stroke, Dad moved out of ICU into a regular private room. He got a gown, a top sheet, and a blanket, and the rest of us got a lesson in the intricacies of life in a hospital. The hospital became the heart of all our days. We had our favorite table in the cafeteria; we knew which drink machines held diet cokes and when the doctors would tell us anything. We knew the nurses—the cute redheaded one who leaned over the bed rail and talked to Dad with bright affection while he blushed and looked down her shirt; the large black woman with the cool, efficient touch who took his blood pressure in the afternoons; the night nurse whose hair bristled with escaping pins; the one with large, red, flapping hands and moist eyes, lipstick on askew. She called him "honey" and "sonny" and lulled him to sleep with soft patter and fluttery words.

Over the next couple of weeks, Hamp and I made friends again.

257

The stakes had changed. Dad's stroke had swallowed up all our other feelings along with Dad. We were all on the other side of the chasm now, the side of the waiters and the workers. All day Hamp and I worked. We were running the company, trying to find the threads of what Dad had been doing and weave them into our days before they got lost or tangled. After work we carried Curtis to Demaro with us, ate supper with Marie, and left Curtis with her while we went to the hospital. Mom was staying there, and sometimes she would eat with us too. Marie's was like a little haven for us. She would feed us in the den on TV trays, which would already be set up with mats and silver when we got there. Or we would eat in the kitchen, among the calico cats. All of the small appliances in Marie's kitchen are covered with cloth covers made to look like cats. Curtis loves them, especially the black cat with pink-thread whiskers that sits on the toaster.

"Where'd you get all these goddamned things, Mama?" said Hamp. "I feel like I'm sitting in a vet's office."

"Your great-aunt Ann made them," said Marie. "She gives me one every Christmas."

"Do you like 'em?"

"Sure," said Marie. She patted the yellow one surrounding her mixer. "They keep me company."

"If I'd known you were that lonely, I'd've bought you a dog."

"I don't want a dog."

"What you need is another husband, Mama." Hamp waved his fork at her. "Marry a rich one this time."

"No thank you," said Marie. "Have some more okra, Curtis."

"I'll marry you, Nana Marie," said Curtis, crunching okra.

"Thank you, darling," said Marie. "I got us a new movie to watch tonight."

"Oh wow!" Curtis started shoveling in applesauce.

"What is this?" said Hamp. "Remember when you wouldn't let me watch TV but an hour a day? Remember that, 'Come on in, Hamilton.

It's time for *Masterpiece Theatre*.'" He mimicked her, turning his head to one side and grinning.

"You turned out all right."

"Yeah, but now you're corrupting my son."

"With a VCR, I can fast-forward all the unsuitable parts."

"Like the kissing!" said Curtis. "And the parts where people get blown up."

"Unless Curtis hides the remote," I said, as Curtis edged out of the room.

I chased him to the den, grabbed the remote, which he was stuffing down between the sofa cushions, and brought it back into the kitchen.

"Have another deviled egg, Hamilton," Marie said. "Judy, help yourself to some more grapefruit salad."

We ate contentedly and let Marie wait on us.

I remembered there how I first loved Hamp. We used to go there when we were dating, watch TV, and make out on the couch in the den. Even now he is at home there; it is still his home. He stands at the open refrigerator, knowing where the leftover deviled eggs will be kept, and he keeps clothes in the closet in his old room. He and his mother will exchange a quick look or bit of news that is alien to me, and I remember with a sort of bump that he has a life of which I am only a part. It is an intriguing sensation, like the first time you fly.

Once after supper I helped Marie load the dishwasher, and Hamp and Curtis went off to the den to build with Hamp's old Lincoln logs. When I went in to get Hamp, he had fallen asleep on the floor, his head cradled in the crook of his arm, in front of a Lincoln-log home. Curtis was watching cartoons. I looked at the way Hamp's hair fell across his forehead in that silly little wave he's always plastering down, and I loved him. I went and got a pillow to put under his head, and when he woke up, I tried to get him to stay with his mother and let me go to the hospital alone. But he wouldn't.

259

"Have to go give your daddy a break from the Head Nurse," he said.

The Head Nurse was Hamp's new name for Tina. He said she had found a new calling in life—running the hospital. She spent all her time there, driving back and forth from McAdamsville to Demaro every day.

"Want some water, Dad?" one of us would say.

"Here, let me." Tina would take the cup, expertly fitting her hand behind Dad's pillow to hold his head at the correct angle.

Tina knew just how he liked his covers, just what he wanted for lunch, just how loud he liked the television set. The nurses rolled their eyes when they saw her coming.

"Mr. McAdams in room 337 needs another blanket. Could I just get one for him right now? Would you mind?"—"Mr. McAdams seemed so restless after his two o'clock medication. Could you possibly check the dosage with the doctor?"—"Are you working this weekend? Because my father really needs—"

She was just the sort of person you'd like to have on your side if you were a patient, and just the sort of person you'd hate if you were anybody else. Baiting her was Hamp's chief joy.

"Fired any doctors today, Tina?" he'd say. "Bust any ass?"

"That's my specialty," she'd say. "Lean over and I'll show you how."

And Dad would snort the little snort that had become his laugh. Mom and I would look at each other. Tina now saw herself as Florence Nightingale. She read up on strokes and told us at great length all the new and esoteric treatments we could get for Dad at Johns Hopkins or Duke.

"I'll talk to the doctors, Tina," said Mom.

"Well, if he had started this water therapy—"

"You aren't the world's foremost authority on Dad's case, Tina."

Actually, I agreed with her. I was for anything that would rouse him from the terrible lethargy and heaviness of his bed. It was just so satisfying to be on Mom's side for once. Tina and I chose Dad as our only topic of conversation.

"If we lived in Baltimore, or if Mom would let me take him to Baltimore—"

"People die in Baltimore, too. People die at Johns Hopkins."

"Dad is not going to die." She looked at me, closed her eyes in exasperation, tensed her jaw.

"Be reasonable, Tina," I said.

What a weird feeling, to be a conservative at twenty-six, to argue a side you do not even care about, to say, "Be reasonable," and feel smug when your own mind on the subject is like a Hieronymus Bosch picture.

"I appreciate all you both are doing," said Mom.

Mom has always been the soul of tact. Tina stayed exasperated.

"Judy, I don't think Dad needs any more juice right now," Tina would say.

"Is that written in stone?" I'd say. "Or can we maybe be a little bit more flexible about it?"

And I would give him the juice, and Tina would sigh a loud sigh.

"I'm just following the doctor's recommendations," she'd say, meaning none of the rest of us were.

"Give us a break, darlin'," Hamp would say. "Cut us a little slack, okay kid?" He would tweak Tina's cheek, smile his threatening smile, raise his eyebrows an eighth of an inch.

Tense times for the McAdamses.

"All that animal fat," said Tina, looking at Mom.

"All those cigars," said Mom, looking at Dad.

"Rotten luck," said Jimmy, looking at the wall.

"Genes." Hamp and I looked at each other. We were both eating more salads, watching each other's weight, looking for signs of decay.

Dad didn't get better.

"He's improving," Mom would say. "It's only a matter of time."

But it was not. After two weeks he still didn't speak. His right side was partially paralysed, and more often than not he slept. When you talked to him, he smiled, a very sweet smile, and then his eyes would drift away toward the window. He spent most of his time awake looking out the window. He started therapy. It didn't help.

Finally, Dr. White had the long talk with Mom. They arranged to transfer Dad to an intermediate-care facility in Columbia which specializes in intense therapy for stroke victims. Our long series of days between McAdamsville and Demaro was over. Mom would go to Columbia with Dad. She would stay there with him in a sort of dorm and help him with his therapy. She came home to pack.

"I feel like I'm sending you off to camp," I said, folding blouses.

We were sitting in her bedroom on her bed. The dresser with the three-way mirror had that forlorn look things get when they are not used. All Dad's pocket change and his watch and wallet that we had brought home from the hospital were piled on his bureau.

"You know," said Mom, picking up the watch, "I think I'll take this. Bob would enjoy having it back, I bet." She put it on her own arm.

"I wonder if I should go with you," I said.

"No," said Mom. She came back over to the bed, began filling up the suitcase. "You have your own family, Judy, and your own life to lead. You and Hamp have worn yourselves out running up and down the road for two weeks now. It's time for you to rest and regroup."

"Yes ma'am." I was relieved.

"And for God's sake discourage Tina if she gets any idea about coming herself. I can do without Tina's histrionics just now."

"Yes ma'am."

So we took them, Dad in the ambulance, looking lost under his blanket, Mom sitting beside him and holding his hand, Hamp in Mom's car so she'd have transportation, and me in our car, bringing up the rear.

I was thinking about Daddy, and how strong and determined he had been just a while ago, and how just like that he was out of it. I used to look at him in the hospital, sleeping, with his chest moving up and down in time to his breath. His heart was like a bird fluttering under his rib cage, its quivers written on a screen as a wavery line; his brain, another line. Asleep, he looked normal.

He must be in there somewhere.

Lately I have been looking in the mirror, watching myself grow older, thinking, Someday that's going to happen to you, too, Judy. Someday you too will be laid as low as Dad. Lower, because someday you'll be dead. Then I walk away from the mirror and feel younger. Gradually I young up. I figure my actual working self, not the one in the mirror, but the real one, the one behind my face, is about nineteen. A hopeful nineteen.

So I think of the young man who must be in Daddy, the strong boy who hurled baseballs, courted a girl, doodled in his Latin book. Is the boy asleep? Or is he alert, awake, lying with his eyes open, breathing in and out, gathering strength to rise up and be himself again?

When I talk to Tina I don't care what I say. I just blah, blah. When I talk to Mom or Hamp, I say whatever will flow along. When I talk to Dad, I say stupid things like, "Want some more applesauce, Dad?" But the girl in me who's nineteen speaks to the boy behind his eyes, all the time, a continual flow of will and words and hope and recognition. Hello, Bob. Get up.

Fifteen

15

HAMP AND I WORKED ALL THE TIME NOW. We did Dad's and Mom's work, as well as our own. Our old world had disappeared through a hospital door and would never come back again, and Hamp and I hung on to what we had left—each other and the business, and we weren't so sure about the business. Some of the people who had done business with my parents for their whole lives were scared now that the daughter was running things. "How's your daddy?" they'd say. "When's your daddy coming back?" "Your mom still in Columbia?"

It helped that Hamp had been running the yard for some time anyway. It helped that I did the bills. So when that skinflint old man Sanders announced up and down Main Street that he wouldn't do business with us anymore now that Daddy was gone, I was able to shake my head, laughing, and wonder aloud in a Chamber of Commerce meeting if that meant he'd finally be paying his bill. On the whole, people were very kind.

The worst thing was the ordering. Mom had done all that. I got so I called her every morning in Columbia, and she told me what to do. Sarah, our regular office clerk, a mousy brown woman who'd worked with Mom for years, came to work full-time, and we hired Heather to help us out, too. At first Heather was a glorified phone-answerer and baby-sitter—Curtis practically lived at the yard—but she had a real knack for bills of lading, and soon she was doing accounts, too.

The scary thing was the short-term notes we owed. Hamp and Daddy had borrowed enough on six-month notes to build some houses in Pine Ridge. Daddy called Pine Ridge his retirement policy. He figured to turn the houses over by fall and put the profit in some market fund, but when he had his stroke, most of the houses were barely started or half finished, and the work was still seriously behind schedule. We should have hired somebody to manage it for us. Hamp was against that. He wanted to do it all himself. He figured Dad would need the money, and I couldn't argue with that. Anyway, that's Hamp. He loves a challenge. He wants to be a hero, pull everything off alone, as though he were himself and Daddy and God Almighty, too. Even God took Sunday off, I told him. God could afford to, said Hamp; God wasn't paying eighteen percent.

So Hamp would stand out in the yard in front of the lumber shed, which is huge and forbidding—rows of boards as high as the sky, and the whine of the saw, blowing sawdust behind him—and he'd look confident, smiling, rubbing the back of his neck and scribbling on his clipboard. Then he'd walk into the office and sit down beside my desk, and his face would be covered with sweat, and he would wipe it and close his eyes and breathe through his mouth in a series of heavy sighs.

"Al says your daddy promised him a big raise this summer when his wife had her baby. Know anything about that?"

"No," I'd say, and we'd look at each other. I could smell his sweat. "Let's offer him three percent and dental insurance. I'm going to get it for us anyway."

"Dental insurance?" He opened one eye wide.

"Yeah. Not everyone has perfect teeth like you do, Hamp. Al's oldest daughter needs three thousand dollars worth of braces."

"God, is that what they normally cost?"

"If you're lucky and don't have to have much done."

"I shoulda been a dentist. I hope to God Curtis gets my teeth." He leaned back, looking at the ceiling. "Well, do it then, if you think it's right. Do you want to tell him, or shall I?"

"You do it. Send him in to sign the papers if that's what he wants to do."

Hamp slapped his hand down on my desk and hoisted himself up.

"Hell, I'd do it. I'll take a piece of that dental insurance action myself, I will. How about you, Heather? Sarah? That sound about right to you? Dental insurance?"

"Yessir," said Heather and Sarah.

"Jeez," Hamp would say, going out the door.

■ —— ■

The morning of the Fourth of July, I sat on the front stoop of the trailer with my coffee and waved at Hamp as he backed out of the yard. Reddie barked at me and hurled herself against the wire of her cage until I let her out, and she flopped down in the dirt at my feet and began to lick my toes.

"Silly dog."

She lifted her head for me to scratch it.

I had a whole day off and fireworks that night at the club. Hamp went to work as usual. He loved to work over holidays. Saturdays, Sundays, they were all the same to him.

I moved down a step, bouncing on my fanny, so that the sunbeam which fell across the step would rest squarely on my head. Today I wanted to be a lizard, to squat in the sun and turn my head slowly from side to side, stretching the tendons of my neck, blinking my eyes. The woods were dense in the heavy green of July, windless. A twig snapped, and Reddie raised her head, bounded up and off into the brush behind her pen with a crash. It would be a deer, we both knew, and she would never catch it. We knew that, too. Hamp disapproved of letting her run off in the mornings, but Reddie and I didn't tell Hamp everything.

What I ought to do was go inside and clean house, but I could not make myself. The trailer was dirty, neglected, forlorn. We had been merely sleeping in it, throwing clothes from the dryer onto the sofa and picking things out of the pile to wear, throwing food into the refrigerator and picking things out of it to eat. The whole place needed an overhaul. I thought of scrubbing the kitchen and bathroom floors, and dismissed the thought. Maybe later. Today was mine. I went inside and poured another cup of coffee. The dirty linoleum hung in the back of my mind, shadowy and irresolute, but I ignored it. Curtis was watching cartoons, still in his pajamas, his favorite plastic cereal bowl balanced carefully on his knee. Milk dribbled down his chin as he slurped. I cut off the TV.

"First we dress," I said. "Then we clean up our rooms for a few minutes. Then we go buy some barbecue to take to Granddad."

"Yeah!"

I threw dishes into the dishwasher, clothes into the washing machine, toys into the toybox, and junk under the bed. I had to lean against the closet door to close it thirty minutes later, it was so full of the crap I'd piled in there, but at least the place looked straight. Reddie was back in her spot in the dirt, hot and sleepy from her run, and we clattered down the steps, put her up, and jumped in the car.

In a few minutes we pulled off onto the dirt road that led to Mr. Brown's barbecue. Mr. Brown has a pit between his house and

267

the highway, and every holiday he roasts six or eight pigs. Sometimes he advertises with a cardboard sign stuck up on his mailbox, and sometimes he doesn't. There was no sign that day, and I was afraid that he would be all sold out. Mr. Brown is known to have the best barbecue in our end of the county. There was a discouraging number of trucks parked by the shed that covered the pit, but Mr. Brown, standing outside with some other customers, flapped up his hand when he saw me and grinned, which meant he had some left. Once I had been too late, and he had shaken his head at me all the way across the yard, sadly, like I had disappointed him by oversleeping.

"You got three pounds each of sliced, chopped, and hash?" I said, following him through the screen door, which slammed with a smack.

"Yes ma'am," said Mr. Brown. He went behind the table which served as a counter. His wife began to ladle chopped meat into round, white cardboard cartons, while Mr. Brown sliced meat onto paper plates.

"How's your daddy?"

"He's still in Columbia. In fact I'm on my way there now, to take him some barbecue."

"Oh, you are now," said Mr. Brown. "Well!" He walked over to the last pit, which apparently was still occupied because it was covered with a half-barrel top. He signaled to a boy—his son, I knew, from church—who lifted the top. Curtis gasped and ran over for a better look at the hog which lay there, smoking and beautiful. Mr. Brown picked up a bottle and squirted sauce all over the pig, watched it sizzle and soak in, then took his knife and stripped off some cracklings and several slices from the shoulder. The boy was waiting with a plate.

Mr. Brown wrapped the extra plate with a layer of plastic wrap, then with several squares of newspaper. He put the package into a paper sack and folded the top over, like a child's lunch. He patted the package tenderly.

"This is for your daddy." He reached under the counter and pulled out a mason jar full of a clear liquid. "And this is for your daddy," he said.

Mrs. Brown shook her head. "Mind you don't kill him, Ned," she said.

"This will make him feel better, Irene," Mr. Brown smiled.

"Or make him not mind so much that he doesn't," I said. "Thank you kindly, Mr. Brown, Mrs. Brown. And Mama and Daddy thank you, too."

I paid him, and he walked us out to the enormous black kettle which smoldered over a fire in the yard, where a lady I didn't know filled three cartons with hash.

"I put in two hot sauces and two regulars," said Mrs. Brown from the shed door. "Ned, see she gets it all packed up right in the car. And tea." She walked out, handed me another mason jar full of tea, with lemon slices floating in the top.

Curtis was kicking the edge of the fire with his toe and did not want to leave.

"Granddaddy!" I said. "Granddaddy's waiting. Come on!"

The car was hot.

"When you figuring on him coming home?" Mr. Brown asked, arranging the meat to suit him in the cardboard boxes I had brought along.

"Probably in a couple of weeks. Then he'll have to go somewhere for more therapy every few days for awhile."

"How far is he come back now?"

I shrugged. "He can talk a little," I said. "And he can move his legs. But whether he'll walk . . ." I shrugged again.

"Your daddy has a lot of gumption," said Mr. Brown. "And your mama too. I think a lot of both of them, you hear? You tell 'em I said so."

He slapped the top of the car, wiped his hands on his pants.

"You mind your mama now, fellow." He leaned in the window to where Curtis was sitting and handed him something, nodded and walked back to his shed.

Curtis's treat was bubble gum, several pieces of the good, sugary kind that come with the comics that I don't let him buy, and Curtis and I drove to the yard blowing bubbles and smelling the smell of hot pork all the way.

Hamp and Heather helped me unload our share of the pork so I wouldn't have to haul it all the way to Columbia. Then I grabbed the loaf of bread we keep in the office for lunches, and we had a barbecue sandwich, laced with the thin, fiery, yellow sauce that makes upper South Carolina barbecue distinct from any other in the world. We drank sodas, saving the tea for Dad. Curtis ate with his fingers, slice after slice of plain pork, and when he was full we had to wash him up to his elbows.

"Happy Fourth of July, folks," I said. "Heather, don't let Hamp keep you here all afternoon. Are you coming to the club for dinner?"

"Yes ma'am."

"Well, make him bring you early, you hear?"

"Drive carefully, Judy," said Hamp, walking us out. "And start home by four or you'll get caught in traffic."

Mom and Dad were expecting me, since I had called, but the barbecue was a surprise.

"Well, for heaven's sakes, Bob," said Mom. "Look at this." She began unwrapping cartons. "Your father really shouldn't have any sauce," she said, but she poured a little on anyway. She fed him, and I watched, and Curtis bounced on the bed. She fed him like he had just forgotten to pick up his food and she was being friendly, as a woman will feed an older child, casually, while chatting to him. She wiped the corners of his mouth after each bite.

The room is very nice. The whole place looks like a fancy rest home, with short little corridors and well-dressed nurses. Dad's room

270

has a love seat and coffee table, and room for his wheelchair next to it. Mom and Dad sit there together like they used to at home and watch TV, only Dad doesn't get up every five seconds to adjust the set or look out the window or answer the phone, and Mom doesn't get up every ten seconds to rearrange the magazines on the table or get somebody something to eat. They just sit there. Mom folds her hands in her lap like she's in church.

"Bob," said Mom, giving him sips of tea, "you must tell Judy what you did yesterday."

He looked at me, and his face twisted with effort.

"Uh wah," he said. "Uh *wah!*"

He stared at me, intent.

"Great, Dad," I said.

"He used a walker, of course." Mom paused to swallow. She was eating her own lunch. "But Shelley says he'll be using just canes in no time. Isn't that wonderful?"

"It is, Dad. It truly is," I said.

Shelley is Dad's therapist.

I told Dad some stuff about the business. He listened intently for awhile and then began to sag a little.

"Oh," I said. "I nearly forgot. Ned Brown sent you some moonshine."

I pulled the jar out of my purse.

"Can you have a little drop or two, or would it be bad for you, you reckon?"

"Be ah-ih," said Dad.

"Just a spoonful, Judy. Really."

Mom looked worried. I poured a dollop of the stuff into a glass and held it up to his lips. He took a bare swallow and choked.

"Don't give him any more, Judy," Mom said.

"Be ah-ih," Dad said, beckoning me back.

I gave him another sip, took a tiny sip myself. It tasted like liquid fire going down, but in a minute made everything about my throat and face feel warm and good.

"Nu Buh ma vu fi-nes coh lik ih—" He stopped, at a loss for words.

"Ned Brown makes the finest corn liquor in the state," I translated. "I know it, Dad. He sent that jar to you special, and said it would improve your diction."

My father laughed, silently, shaking, as though horribly tickled in church. He tried to wipe his face with his hand and poked himself in the eye. His hands floated helplessly in front of his chest. Mom got up and washed his face, and he sniffed and smiled.

"Now don't get overexcited, Bob," she said.

After awhile the nurse came in and said Dad had to take his nap. Mom and I took Curtis outside to a sort of courtyard where he could run around. After the artificial cold of the interior, the sun hit us like we'd opened an oven door. We sat on a bench in a shaded corner while Curtis dropped leaves into the fountain, which stood in the middle of a brick patio in the shimmering heat. We had the whole place to ourselves, being the only people stupid enough to brave the sun.

"Can I get you anything?" I asked. "Are you doing all right? Is Dad really getting any better?"

"Shelley says he has made some real progress," said Mom. "She says we must just be patient, and take it one day at a time."

"Will he walk, or talk, or feed himself? Is this it?"

She looked irritated. "He has come a long way, Judy," she said. "Half his brain is gone. Half. He could be a vegetable. By the grace of God, he's not. And soon he will be whole again."

"Mom," I said. "Do you always feed him?"

"He's learning to eat by himself," she said. "He has a special spoon, with rubber around the handle. Today I fed him, because for heaven's sake, you can't expect him to eat barbecue with a spoon."

"Of course not," I said. "Would you like to go out with me and Curtis for some ice cream?"

"Thank you, Judy, but I'd better not. When Bob takes a nap, I just sit and rest."

She looked older there, and unfamiliar. She had not been doing her own exercises, and her shoulders sagged. Mom, who has always had the posture of a soldier, looked like a patient herself. She was still wearing Daddy's watch.

"You look tired, Mom," I said. "Don't you want to come home for a day or two? Just for a change?"

"No. We're at an important stage right now," she said. "Shelley says the next two or three weeks will tell the tale."

Her eyes were already turning back, inadvertently, to the room we'd left. She needed to go back there and look at Dad again.

We said goodbye in the hall.

"Give Grandma a kiss," she said, bending over for Curtis. "And thank you, darling, for doing this. You really made our day."

Finally I got out of there and started home.

"He really is going to get much better," Mom had said.

I was sure he would.

He would be able to walk, after a fashion, and eat, after a fashion, and make himself understood to those of us who were around him enough to disentangle meaning from sound. But he would never be my daddy again. My daddy was nearly dead. Just tiny flashes of him remained, cruel, tiny flashes. And my mama would devote the rest of her life to keeping those flashes alive. I was jealous of Shelley, the therapist, who had opinions that mattered, and angry at my mother.

"Don't disturb your grandfather," she had said to Curtis. "Don't bother that, Curtis. Get him, Judy. Don't let him sit on the window like that."

Curtis sat beside me in the front seat and went to sleep. I wished I could join him.

■ —— ■

273

The pool was full of screaming children, and Curtis joined right in. Hamp was still at work. I put on my suit and staked out a reclining chair. Motherhood's profoundest compensation is the right to sit by a pool in the sun for hours on end and call it baby-sitting.

It was late afternoon and the air smelled of plastic and sweat and chlorine. I closed my eyes, almost dozing, to the pool sounds—screams, scraping of chairs, slapping of wet feet against concrete. Then the chair next to me scraped, and I jumped awake. Helen was sitting there looking at me.

"Judy!" she said, her eyes careful. "It's been a long time."

"Welcome home," I said. "You look great!"

Helen was home from the drug rehab clinic. She did look a lot better, thinner and rested. She asked after Tina and Dad, and I said they were fine, fine, how was Nick, and she said he was fine, too. Then Nick himself walked up and sat on the bottom half of Helen's chair, dripping. Water dribbled down his chest and legs into a puddle under the chair. Helen handed him a towel.

"Good to see you," he said, mopping. "Tell me about your dad."

Nick was doing his residency in the hospital where Dad had been. I hadn't seen much of him, but Mom had. I filled him in on the latest news about Dad's progress, answered his questions about the therapy and Mom's hopes. Helen took the towel from Nick, dried his back.

"Better get your clothes on," she said.

"Later," said Nick. "I'm going now and swim with Curtis."

Nick left, and Helen settled back in her chair. I closed my eyes.

"Judy," she said, "is it true that Tina tried to kill herself?"

"Why don't you ask her?" I said. "I don't feel comfortable talking to you about other people."

"I blame myself," she said. "I do. The whole time I was in the center I kept talking about it and talking about it, how could she, why would she, even if—Judy, there's just no reason for a person to take her own life, is there? I mean, is there?"

274

I opened my eyes. Helen raised her arm, examining the bracelets which jangled as she shook her wrist.

"I felt terrible about it," she continued. "I felt like it was partly my own fault. I mean it really wasn't, people bring about their own, I mean, I didn't actually do anything. Do you think it was partly my fault, Judy?"

"Give me a break," I said.

"I feel like I betrayed a friendship," she said. "I do. My therapist says friends are the most important thing in the world. Relationships. Don't you think?"

"Ummm," I said.

"Love," said Helen. "Love and trust. I tried to call Tina. I've left messages. Nick says to leave her alone. Isn't that typical? Men just have no comprehension of the depth of friendship that exists between us women. I mean the real depth. It surpasses, enfolds, don't you think? I just need to express some things, get back in touch with who I was, who I am, you know? Is Tina coming tonight?"

"I don't know," I said.

"Do you two get along?" she said.

"I simply must swim for a minute," I said. "Get the kinks out of my shoulder."

"Get Nick to give you a massage. Nick!" she shouted. "Fix Judy's shoulder!"

Nick was sitting with my son on the side of the pool. I joined them.

"Come on in, Mom!"

"In a minute. I have to get my toes used to the water. Go on without me. Show us that flutter kick."

Curtis threw himself off the side of the pool and plowed across the water. Helen knelt behind me.

"Where does it hurt, honey?" she said, her hands on my back.

"It's nothing," I said. "Please don't bother. Ouch!"

"There, see? Tight as a drum. Feel that tension, Nick?"

Nick's hand felt cool on my shoulder.

"She's just been under so much pressure, I told her, Nick, people just need to get in touch with themselves, get in touch with their pain, that's what they taught me at the center, it's just such—"

"Stop talking, Helen," Nick said.

Helen stopped. Nick rubbed my shoulder for a minute, and it did feel better.

"Thanks," I said, and jumped into the pool.

Later on Hamp showed up. He sat in his work clothes at the foot of my deck chair and held my foot, absently, patting it between his palms, watching Curtis swim. After awhile he and some men gathered around the barbecue, and I could smell hamburgers mixed in with the smells of suntan lotion, chlorine, grass, beer.

After supper the kids all lit sparklers, ran around the golf course screaming and singeing their fingers. The older kids began to set up bottle rockets beside the eighteenth green. Someone started the jukebox. The sun was going down.

"You have chill bumps." Nick sat beside me. He had changed his clothes.

"I'm too lazy to dress," I said. "Don't pick on me. I'm avoiding your girlfriend."

"Helen is not my girlfriend. She's my friend."

"She is a royal pain in the ass, especially now that she's reconditioned. God, I hope I never have a breakdown."

"You are the sanest person I know," he said.

"So how's the doctor business?"

"Hard."

"I want to do something hard."

"You are."

"I mean something mental. Study. I want to learn something. Something about tibias and fibulas and scapulas and scarpulas and stuff

276

like that. Don't laugh. Something musty and multisyllabic."

"Then I'm sure you will."

"I used to be smart," I said.

"You're still smart," he said. "Go put your clothes on. I want to talk to you."

"So talk."

"I can't concentrate with you lying there half naked."

"Oh thanks," I said. "That's the nicest thing anybody ever said to me."

In the dressing room, I looked at myself in the mirror, frizzy, half-dry hair, cut-offs and T-shirt, and thought, he likes me. The man must be desperate. Half naked indeed. Tina had arrived in one of her splendid white outfits; Helen had on some kind of transparent burnoose. Even Diane had on a crisp white shirt that looked like it had been ironed. I was definitely not the belle of the ball. In fact I didn't even feel like a girl. I felt neutral, a neuter, a mere nameless person who needed to have a little fun.

I made people dance with me. Diane and Charley and I danced with the children, made everyone do the electric slide. Even Tina danced, primly. Even Hamp danced. Heather and a couple of her friends were particularly good; they got Hamp and the stodgier male types moving, teasing, cajoling them along. Nick was good; I watched him. He danced like I remembered, holding the hands of little girls gravely in his own large hands, clapping and sweating as though he took dancing seriously, as of course he should. Once he danced with me. I flinched when he touched me, and we avoided each other's eyes. My face burned; we did not speak.

"Want something to drink?" he said when the music stopped.

"Please."

I followed him to the bar, and we got two soft drinks, walked outside. There were still a few kids in the pool.

"This has been fun," I said. "I need to find Curtis and go home."

"I need to talk to you first."

I looked at the ground.

"Judy," he said, "dammit, look at me."

"Why should I?" I said, but I did.

"I have stayed away," he said. "I have stayed out of your life. I avoided you in the hospital, and I don't even know how you are except what I hear from Jimmy. But I need to talk to you sometimes. Just talk. Okay?"

I nodded.

"I thought the first time I saw you that you were the most appealing woman I had ever seen. But you were married. I figured, my tough luck, right? I held your hand. I helped you go back to your part-time husband. But now I know something I didn't know before. Something I found out tonight."

"And what is that?"

"You want me too."

I looked around the patio; parents were getting their kids out of the pool.

"It doesn't make any difference," I said. "People do not have to humor their every urge. In spite of what you may have heard about my family."

"It makes a difference to me."

"Why?"

He smiled. "Because you owe me a lot of sleepless nights."

"Thanks bunches," I said.

■ —— ■

There is a ball suspended from the ceiling in the middle of the dance floor. It's covered with tiny little mirrors, and as it turns, it throws lights out all over the room. The lights bounce around and make the dancers look mysterious and special—better than just ordinary people. At least I've always thought so. I was standing in the door looking at it, waiting for Curtis to finish his last sparkler, and Charley wandered by and grabbed me for a last dance.

"Remember Miss Clarridge?" I said as we walked out onto the floor.

Miss Clarridge had run the ballroom dancing school our parents had made us attend in seventh grade.

Charley smiled. "*One* two three, *One* two three. Her breasts were straight across, like a shelf."

"And she wore chiffon. And the stern face."

"And the fanny that didn't jiggle. I wonder how she did that."

"A thirty-dollar girdle."

We danced for a minute in silence.

"So how are Helen and Nick getting along?" he said.

"Couldn't say. She says they're just friends."

"He's a nice guy."

"Ummm."

"Seems partial to you."

"The last in my long line of admirers."

We danced a minute more.

"And if I remember correctly," I said, "my very first admirer was yourself. Not counting Jimmy Bascomb in fifth grade. And the Fourth of July party when we were fifteen—"

"We sneaked out to the eleventh green and kissed, and vowed our eternal love."

"And we were going to run away together to California and live on love."

"Wonder if we could have done it."

"Nah," I said. "We woulda killed each other inside six months."

"Nevertheless," said Charley. "I have never quite forgiven your father for not letting us try. What did he call it? Not incest."

"Inbreeding. I think he was just afraid I'd get knocked up. Does it seem to you that love was simpler then, Charley?"

279

"Nope," said Charley. He held me away from him in Miss Clarridge's waltz position, and grinned. "Ready? *One* two three, *One* two three."

And we waltzed around the club, taking huge steps, just like we used to do in dancing school.

Sixteen

16

"DON'T YOU SEE?" I SAID. "I am ready to go ahead with this marriage. It doesn't matter to me that you are like a stone, that you talk only catch phrases and not real talk. I can live with that. I can live with a smiling, nodding, bright-eyed rock."

I said it to Hamp, to the mirror, to the dashboard. I said it to the tub, as I was scrubbing it on Saturday mornings.

I was especially good. I cleaned up the trailer, polished the furniture, washed the clothes. I picked up constantly. The house was always neat. Twice a day I wiped the water spots off the bathroom spigots. And Hamp began to question my every move.

He noticed what time I did things, how long they took me.

"I tried to call you."

"I must have been outside."

"When did you say you got home?"

Finally he came right out and said it. "Did you sleep with that Greek guy? I know you had a right. I just want to know. Does he matter to you?"

"This is so childish," I said. "No. I did not sleep with him. I am not. I will not."

"Then where were you that night you said you went to the mountains? Curtis told me you went to Nick's house. So you had a fling. I understand. Nick's a regular kind of guy. I'd like to break his neck for him, but I do understand how you might have been attracted to him."

After awhile I gave up explaining myself. What was the use? Hamp was determined in his own mind to even the score.

■ —— ■

Granny Glendinning died. At the funeral home she lay waifish in her coffin, a child in a grown-up bed, brittle fingers stilled. She had on lipstick and blush, and the same dress she had worn to Tina's wedding. I sat awhile with James and Lucy, visiting. Other friends wandered through, murmuring. Granny Glendinning was a saint, they said. It was a blessing, really. Asleep, asleep in Jesus.

"Is it a blessing?" I asked Lucy.

She shrugged. "Life is always good," said Lucy. "But when you're very old and bedridden, well, I think she was ready, I really do. Don't you, James?"

James stirred. "She just went down to nothing, there at the end. I could've lifted her up in one arm. Bird-boned, like. I told her, 'Granny, you got to put some meat on those bones,' and she'd just laugh and laugh."

He blinked.

■ —— ■

Mom came home for the funeral, and we went together to the white clapboard church. Tina was there with Jimmy on the front row. Mom and I sat toward the back, Mom pensive and alert, passing me a tissue when the choir sang Granny's favorite hymn. When the service was over, the family was led away first, self-conscious, with their eyes on the ground. We met up in the vestibule in a line of well-wishers.

"So sweet of you to come, Edna. And Judy. And how's Bob?"

■ —— ■

At the graveside, Mom and I stood decently to one side of the family, who sat under a tent staring at the mound of dirt in front of them. After the closing prayer, they filed out into the sunshine, and Mom tucked her bag under her arm and stood with her back to the open grave, chatting with Tina and Lucy.

Jimmy and Nick were standing together in another group.

"So how are you holding up?" I said to Jimmy.

"Fine," he nodded. "Great." Tears glistened in his eyes. He brushed them away.

"She was a fine old lady," I said. "Of course, I hardly knew her in her prime."

"She was a mess," said Jimmy, smiling. "I'm so glad I got to tell her before she died about my call from the Lord."

"Your call from the Lord?"

I felt Nick looking at me.

Jimmy continued. "I held her hand and said 'Granny' just like that— 'Granny?'—and she opened her eyes, and I said, 'Granny, I'm going to seminary. I've been called to serve the Lord.' And she squeezed my hand, and her face got the sweetest smile. She died about two days later."

"So what are your plans?" said Nick. "Going on to law school first or what?"

"Oh I don't think so," said Jimmy. "I'm going to Columbia tomorrow to get all that straightened out. Didn't Tina tell you, Judy?"

"No," answered Tina, coming up. She put her arm through his. "Nothing is certain yet, Jimmy. Seminary is not certain yet."

"It is to me," said Jimmy.

Some Hooper relatives gathered to speak to Jimmy, and I wandered away. Nick wandered after me. We stood among the tombstones at the edge of the crowd.

"Seminary?" I said. "Did you hear that? The Lord called him? I bet Tina is having an absolute fit. Did you know about this?"

"I heard just now."

"Is he crazy?" I said.

"Certainly not," said Nick. "The man's religious. He's always been religious. Now he's—"

"—more religious. I figured that out for myself."

"There is precedent," Nick said mildly. "His mother is, I believe, an ordained minister in the Church of Life. You look particularly good in blue, has anybody ever told you?"

"My mom, about a million times. In fact, she got me this dress."

"How've you been, Judy?"

"Okay." I took a deep breath. "I should tell you that Hamp has convinced himself that we . . . he thinks that when I left him, when Curtis and I went to the mountains, that I stayed with you."

"Does he really? Whatever gave him that idea?"

"Curtis told him."

"Oh." He looked thoughtful.

"And I think he sensed that . . . look, this is humiliating," I said. "I just thought you ought to know. He thinks we're lovers."

"How bad is it for you? Are you afraid of him?"

"Of course not. Hamp wouldn't hurt a fly. He's not mad or anything. It just evens things out for him, so to speak. If he can believe we —"

"And would it?" Nick said. "Even things out for you?"

"No," I said.

284

"Spoilsport." He smiled.

Am not, I thought. "People just need to stay straight with each other. I play for keeps. I know it's not that way for everybody, but it's that way for me. And I did not come to an old lady's funeral looking for trouble, or looking to get laid. Did not come to see you. If I'd thought you'd be here, I'd've stayed away."

"Sorry." He stepped back.

"Not because I don't like to look at you, because I do. I like your company and everything about you. But I don't need this, see? I gave out the wrong signals. I apologize. Not your fault. Please."

"I'm sorry."

"Don't be sorry," I said. "I adore you. Please don't be sorry." I put my fingers to my lips and pressed them into his chest, then turned away, walked to the nearest cluster of people and stood there, blinking. Lucy Hooper was talking about Nicaragua. She said she wasn't going.

"Oh Lucy, what a shame!" said Mom. "After all your plans."

I half-listened to them talk, watched Nick shake Jimmy's hand, walk across the grassy verge to his car, get in, and drive away.

"—so much trouble along the border—"

"—just can't ask Jimmy and Tina to—"

"Why don't I keep Sally?" I said.

They stared at me.

"Well, I'm a good mother," I said. "You needn't look at me like that. And Sally likes me, and I like Sally, and she and Curtis get along great. It might be better for her to stay with someone like me, who has another kid. We could go riding."

"Judy, that's very kind," said Lucy. "But I couldn't possibly ask—"

"She's got a point, Lucy. I think you ought to give Judy's suggestion some thought."

"Well I will," said Lucy. "I truly will."

I hung around the gravediggers with Sally and watched the vault lowered, the dirt piled on, the plastic grass. Then I rode home with Mom.

"I certainly can't picture Tina as a preacher's wife," I said.

"You may not have to," said Mom. She glanced at me as we pulled into her driveway. "Your marriage isn't in any better shape than Tina's is." She pulled up in front of the back door, stopped the car. "You girls today, I declare."

"What?" I said. "I'm doing all right."

"No you're not," she said. "You're doing the best you can, darling, I don't doubt that. But it is not a good situation. You know it."

"What else can I do?" I said.

"I can't answer that one for you," she said. "Try harder? Give up?" She picked up her purse, paused with her hand on the door handle.

"Your father and I just want you to know that we're behind you. Whatever you decide. Hamp is, has been good to us. Not a lot of sons-in-law would be happy in the family business, and now with Jimmy giving up law school, Lord, I don't know. And there's Curtis. But this business of Hamp and Tina Lee . . ." She shook her head. "I don't know what got into that child. What could she have been thinking?"

Mom shook her head. She didn't expect an answer.

I answered her anyway. "She was thinking that Hamp was really hers, because she loved him first."

"That's pure hogwash," said Mom. "The silliest thing I ever heard. How she could justify in her own mind such a stupid, selfish . . . And Hamp! With a child! His wife's sister! Just plain trashy is what it is. I just hope his mother never finds out. It'd kill her. It just astounds me, you young people today. Honestly." She opened the car door. "Well, you know what they say."

"All's fair in love and war? The world is going to hell in a handcart?"

"No," she said. "The way of transgressors is hard."

"What a comfort," I said. "I have to put up with a hard way too?

286

All this and heaven too?"

Mom, standing by the car, sighed in exasperation. "Honey, what I'm trying to tell you is, you don't *have* to put up with anything. Don't you get that yet? Hasn't it crossed your feeble brain yet? How many lives do you and Tina Lee think you're going to get?"

"One apiece? I'm guessing."

"That's right. One on this earth. Unless you're Hindu. My father had great respect for the Hindus. The point is, men need direction. You can't let them walk all over you. Give them an inch and they'll take—"

"—a mile?"

"—advantage. Give them an inch and they'll take advantage. Do you understand what I'm saying?"

"No." I got out of the car.

"You need to lay down the law," she said. "In no uncertain terms. And if he can't abide by it, you need to be prepared to deal with that."

"How?" A cavern yawned before me.

"Kick him out," she said. "While you still have a chance at a decent life."

"I'll consider it," I said.

■ —— ■

The fig tree was in a far corner of the yard, covered with green figs and a few ripe ones, and a few yellow jackets. I picked the ripe figs carefully, checking each one before I touched it. I had always picked the figs alone. Tina never would come. She was afraid of the yellow jackets that floated among the fruit, ate out its heart. I was not afraid. To me it was a fair fight, a war, me against them. Here, I had been an aborigine, made bamboo blowguns, stalked the dog. I had sat so still my skin tingled, built secret smoke fires under the fig branches until I set one of them on fire, cut off my hair as an offering to the sun god, scratched hieroglyphic messages in the dirt. I scratched one now, staring up into the sun, wiped out the message and went on into the house.

That evening I put on my new nightgown, went into the living room where Hamp was watching a Braves game and leaned over the sofa. I kissed the back of his neck, rubbed his shoulders.

"Ummmm," he said.

"Feel better? Your muscles are really tight," I said. "Come on to bed and I'll rub your back for you."

"I'll be along," he said. "Atlanta's tied in the eighth."

"Okay, give me a kiss."

I went into the bathroom, checked my legs to make sure I had shaved them well, brushed my hair again, polished the spigots, went to bed. Arranged myself with one arm and a foot on Hamp's side and waited. I heard the evening news came on, then the weather; then the channel changed to a sports program. Halfway through the sports program, I got back on my side of the bed and went to sleep. If Hamp ever came to bed, I did not notice.

■ —— ■

"Let's get a baby-sitter," I said a few days later, "and go to the movies or something."

"Can't tonight."

"When then?"

Hamp looked pained.

"I just can't tell you, Judy," he said. "We're just so busy right now. You know how it is without your dad."

"I know how it is without my husband, too," I said.

I walked out to the front and asked Heather if she could baby-sit for us on Friday night. She said she'd be happy to.

■ —— ■

Curtis and I left work early on Friday, and I took a long shower, fixed my hair, laid out my new dress, opened my new makeup and all the little bottles and tubes that had come with it. Hamp had been in a rotten mood all week. He had to get away for awhile, I figured, relax, quit thinking about Dad and the business. He had been under a strain. We would go to Vecchio's, his favorite restaurant, have a nice relaxing evening.

When I was dressed, I walked through the trailer, checking every room to make sure everything was perfect—Curtis's teddy bear sitting on his pillow, Hamp's shoes side by side in the closet. Curtis and I sat down to read a book. When Hamp was half an hour late, I called the yard and got no answer. He was probably on his way. When he was an hour late, I called Heather's house. Hamp had picked Heather up some time ago, her mother said. Why, was anything the matter? No, I said, no problem, they were probably still at the pizza place getting Heather and Curtis's supper. The pizza place was notoriously slow. We laughed about that.

When they were an hour-and-a-half late, I called the pizza place. Hamp had just left. They pulled up in the yard fifteen minutes later.

"Where in the world have you been?" I said. "I was getting ready to call the hospital and see if there'd been any wrecks."

"I know that," said Hamp. He slammed the pizza down on the counter, reached for plates. "Heather's father came looking for us at the pizza place. He said you'd called."

Heather had been crying.

"Ouch," I said. "I hope I didn't alarm your whole family, Heather."

"Daddy wanted to know where we'd been," she said.

I looked at Hamp, who was pouring cola into glasses.

"Where had you been?" I asked.

His eyes were narrow, his face set.

"I was out on Pine Ridge doing my job," he said. "I had to run by there on the way home to see if Ted had left the lumber. The crew needs it first thing Monday. I thought it would save time if I picked up Heather first, since it's on the way. And Ted was out there, and he wanted me to look at some things. And I stayed too long."

Curtis was halfway through his first slice of pizza. Hamp sat down beside him, ruffled his hair.

"Well, don't worry about it," I said.

"It was all my fault," said Heather. "Really, Mrs. Duncan. I was asking Ted all these questions about building, and he and Hamp started explaining it all to me, and, and—" She looked from me to Hamp, and her hands flew up in the air—"and that's it!" She smiled brightly.

"Oh, I see," I said.

And I did see. I was now good at noticing when Hamp was attracted to someone else. And so what? It could happen to anybody, as I knew only too well.

On the way to Vecchio's, I cleaned bits of paper out of the passenger-side storage compartment.

"I don't know if we'll be able to eat at Vecchio's or not," I said. "We've missed our reservations."

My fingers were sticky from a piece of gum.

"That neanderthal thinks I was messing with his daughter, Judy. You should have seen him. He came into that place like an outraged—"

"—father. Which is what he is. I'm sure he was worried."

"The girl works for me, Judy. Plus she's a child, practically. What kind of person does he think I am?"

"I'll talk to Heather's mother. I'm sure it'll be all right," I said. "You just have to remember, Hamp, Heather is seventeen. You are twenty-six."

"Jeez, do you think I don't know that? Do you think I'm not aware?"

"I'm sure you are."

"I did the best that I could, all right?"

"I'm sure you did."

"I'm always careful. Always."

"I'm not arguing."

"God, what an idiot. How could she be his daughter?"

We had a long wait in Vecchio's bar. Hamp drank and I talked. After awhile, we looked at television. There was a Braves game on. I looked around the bar at the other customers. They all seemed to be having a better time than we were. A large group of well-dressed couples clustered in one corner. Each time a newcomer joined them, the noise level rose so that the rest of us looked up to see what was going on.

"Look," I said to Hamp. "Do you want to forget the whole thing and go home?"

"I want a table," Hamp said. "I want to eat."

"Do you want to try somewhere else?"

He got up and went out to talk to the hostess. While he was gone, the large group was summoned. They gathered up their drinks and went out. Hamp came back.

"She said it'd be just a few more minutes," he said, sitting back down. "God, I hate this."

It was much quieter in the bar now. A man sitting across from us glanced up at Hamp's words.

"You could pretend to like it," I said. "Instead of telling the whole world how much you hate going out with me."

"I don't hate going out with you."

"You could smile occasionally and nod, and look me in the eye. Just for old times' sake."

"It's not you, Judy."

"You could fake it."

He wiped his face with his hands like my dad used to do.

"Do you really want me to?" he said.

"Yes."

The man who had been looking at us put some money on the bar and left.

291

"Sometimes I feel numb," said Hamp. "Do you know how that feels? Like there's a fake me smiling for me, being my face, and behind that I am numb."

I was silent.

"I feel like I'm suffocating," he said. He looked at me.

"So suffocate," I said. "Grow numb. You think if you hurt enough, you'll get some kind of free pass? I am not holding you, Hamp. Look." I held out my hands. "Look at these. Are they suffocating you? Is there a pillow over your face?"

He shook his head.

"But you won't say it, will you?" I said. "That's what I really don't like about you. You're a coward."

He was silent.

"All right," I said. "I'll say it. You think you love Heather. Don't you?"

He finished his drink.

"I don't know," he said.

"Wrong. Not a good answer. Incorrect."

"I know," he said.

"Do you honestly think I can stand this any longer? Are you going to make me do everything myself?"

"I never meant to hurt you," he said.

"Well you did hurt me. So get used to it. What did you think? That I wouldn't care? That I would say, oh, no problem, you're having a crisis, you're in love again but not with me, with a seventeen-year-old child, so go work it out, I'll wait?"

"I never meant to hurt you," he said.

"You are so full of it, Hamp," I said. "The only thing good about you is your son."

"I know that," he said.

The hostess waved at us.

"Table for Duncan!" she said.

292

Seventeen

17

WE HAD ALWAYS CANNED VEGETABLES from my parents' garden. This year we figured on letting that go. The garden was overgrown and unwatered, a jungle of bent-over vines and scraggly runners. But there were still a million tomatoes, a million cucumbers.

"Just let it go," said Mom. "It doesn't matter. Just pick a few tomatoes and put them in the refrigerator for me, please. You know how your father loves tomatoes."

I meant to let it go. Every day or two I stopped by, pulled off the good stuff, threw huge, watery cucumbers and blackish tomatoes on the compost heap. One day I carried the usual load into Mom's kitchen, spread it out on the counter, went back for more, spread it out, too. Suddenly I didn't want it all to be wasted. I wanted it saved, it was all so beautiful in the morning light, the creamy yellow squash, the silly, bumpy little cucumbers and the big dull ones, the slippery red tomatoes. I couldn't let it all spoil, go into the refrigerator and turn ordinary. I couldn't let anything else in my life go bad. So I started washing, put on a pot of water, found the jars, found the canner, found the recipes.

I needed more canning lids, but I didn't go after them. If I leave, I thought, I will stand in the grocery store in front of the canning supplies and realize what a stupid idea this is, and how foolish I am, and I will go on to work and everything will be lost. I must stay here, inching my way through. Perhaps I would go later, when it was too late to quit.

I heard the back door open.

"Judy? Is that you?" It was Tina. "God, it's hot." She threw her purse down, pushed her sunglasses back onto her hair. "Look at this stuff! You planning on starting a roadside stand? Judy's Vegetables? Oh, you're canning! I came to let Mr. Amos in."

"What for?"

"He's doing some work on the house. Mom called me last night."

"Oh."

She got a diet cola out of the refrigerator, started leafing through Mom and Dad's mail, which accumulated on the kitchen table between Mom's trips home.

"What kind of work?" I said. "Why didn't she call me?"

"Why should she? I can come out here and sit as well as you can. I'm not entirely useless, you know. I wonder if I should open this note from Aunt Lee." She studied a small envelope.

"What's Mr. Amos going to do here?"

"Measure to put metal bars in the bathroom. Maybe see about a new shower thing for Dad. Mom says there's a neat one in the nursing home with a seat in it."

"I could have measured for her. She didn't have to bother you and Mr. Amos."

294

Tina shrugged. "No bother to me," she said. "I got no responsibilities besides my weekly appointment with the head doctor. God knows we wouldn't want me to forget that."

"What's it like? Going to a psychiatrist." I was at the stove, blanching tomatoes.

"It's not bad, actually. He's pretty nice. And I see a woman sometimes too. His associate. They're okay."

She laid aside the letter from Lee, held another envelope up to the light.

"What do you talk about?" I said. "I mean, not to break any confidences. But how does it work? Do you talk, or do they? Do they ask questions?"

"Dr. Wells says, 'So what have you been doing?' and I tell him. Dr. Artinger says, 'So what are your plans?' and I tell her. It's pretty boring, actually. But I don't mind it."

"And what do you say?" I said. "About your plans? What are your plans?"

"Like I say, I don't have any. My principal, who was so happy to have me aboard last May, now says he wonders if I'll be well enough."

"Which means—"

"He thinks I'm nuts. He doesn't want me in the classroom." She lined up the salt and pepper shakers, wiping them shiny with her fingers.

"What does that mean?" I said.

I was burning my fingers on the hot tomatoes, rolling them around a plate, poking them with a knife to make the skins come off.

"I don't know," she said. "Dad says I should go back to school. Dr. Wells said . . . I told him Jimmy might be a missionary to Nicaragua someday . . . he said maybe I could be a teacher in Nicaragua, and just not tell anybody down there I was ever nuts."

"But you don't speak Spanish," I said.

"Well I do a little," she said. "Unos, dos, tres. Besides, I'm not going to Nicaragua, so it doesn't matter."

"You could come to work at the yard," I heard myself saying.

"I could," she said. "But I probably won't."

"Why not?"

"Daddy doesn't want me to." She got up and walked over to the stove. "So what can I do?" she said. "Peel tomatoes? That looks like fun."

"It isn't."

I decided to go get some lids while Tina finished the tomatoes and watched the stove. I got a flea collar for the cat, too, and a loaf of bread for lunch. When I got back, Tina had progressed to cucumbers.

"I hadn't actually planned on making pickles today," I said.

"Oh, well . . ." She looked at the mound of cucumber slices. "I'll do them myself."

"You've never made cucumber pickles by yourself."

"Neither have you," she said. "Mom was always here. Like *Little Women*, you know? Marmie? Like *Little House on the Prairie*."

"Only both of us wanted to be Laura," I said.

We stared at each other.

"Dear Miss Manners," said Tina. "My sister and I both wanted to be Laura. Who gets to choose? Signed, Confused."

"Dear Confused," I said. "Laura was a child. You have both outgrown the role. Drop it, and get on with your life. Signed, Miss Manners."

"Do you really think she'd say that?"

"I have no idea."

"You've always gotten everything, you know," said Tina. "You just reached out your hand and took it. You never left anything for me."

"Is that right?" I said. "Are you serious?"

"I wanted what you got. Didn't you know that? Of course you did. I wanted Dad to take me out with him hunting, but he always took you. And who did Mom want to go shopping with? You. You all just stood there and rolled your eyes and gave each other looks when I wanted to go along. It was so much fun to be the tagalong. I enjoyed it so much, always."

"Are you kidding me? You were Princess Pet, Tina, the apple of everyone's eye. How could your memory be that bad?"

"In pretend I was Princess Pet. In games. In real life it was you. You had it all, and you kept it all, too. You and Elizabeth. That twit."

"Is this some kind of therapy thing? What are you talking about?" I began to gather the cucumber slices into a pan. "You were the pretty one, Tina, Miss McAdamsville, the Miss South Carolina finalist."

Tina picked up her knife. "So what? You thought it was a joke. Didn't you?"

"Well . . .," I said.

"You're just so almighty superior," she said, slicing. "And now so is Jimmy. So forgiving. I can't stand forgiveness. It's so mealy-mouthed. I refuse to be a missionary's wife."

"Can I just mention something to you in passing? Between here and Nicaragua or graduate school or wherever you decide to go, or whatever you decide to do with your life?"

"What?"

"Don't go as Jimmy's wife. Go as yourself. This attachment thing doesn't work. Not really."

"You're a fine one to talk."

"Grow up, Tina. Do it now. Don't wait."

"So that I too can move out to some trailer by a farm pond and discover nature?"

"So that you can begin to live your own life," I said, "instead of mine."

Tina stared at me. "Ouch," she said. "That one hurt. Grow up yourself."

"I'm trying," I said, "but it's a long haul for me. I'm not sure I'm cut out for adulthood."

"Yeah," she said. "I know what you mean."

We looked around at the piles of vegetables on the counter, on the stove.

"I'll get some more jars," said Tina.

While the first batch of pickles was processing, we put the flea collar on Fluffy. I poured a bowl of milk and set it on the floor, called the cat. A white streak flashed across the kitchen floor and materialized at the bowl, drinking. Tina reached down and stroked her.

"Sweet little Fluffy," said Tina. "Nice baby cat."

Fluffy paused to slap Tina's hand away.

"That animal must weigh twelve pounds," I said.

"Be quiet, you're making her nervous. She's precious," said Tina, bending over. "Our baby precious. Is she lonely without her mommy? Poor baby."

Tina picked her up. The cat grabbed Tina's thumb between her front paws and began gnawing it, scratching and purring.

"Ouch! Shit!"

"Don't let go," I said, ripping the flea collar from its package. "This won't hurt a bit, Fluffy."

"Speak for yourself," said Tina, sucking her thumb.

Finally, I held Fluffy while Tina put the collar on. Fluffy lay in my lap panting, like cats used to do when I twirled them in umbrellas, resigned to death but ever watchful for a chance to beat it. When Tina got the collar secure and the ends cut off, I let go, and Fluffy raced out, scratching a long furrow in my leg as she peeled off.

I put on some antiseptic and started the water for the squash. Then Mr. Amos came. He was wearing bermuda shorts. Seeing Mr. Amos in bermudas is like seeing God in bermudas. I offered him a cold drink.

"So you doin' some canning, are you?" he said, in the kitchen. "I saw your mama the other day. The wife and I went by and took her a chicken." He glanced up at us, a sharp, studying glance. "Terrible, to see your daddy like that."

298

"Isn't it?" I said.

"He's improving, though," said Tina.

Mr. Amos picked up a tomato, hefted it in his hand. "I was wondering how your mama would manage here at home. She's not a big woman. Getting a man the size of your daddy up and down is a big job. Thought—" he sketched with his fingers—"some rails, like. Maybe a pulley. But your mama says, no pulley. She says your daddy's gonna be able to get himself around without a pulley." He set the tomato down.

"I truly hope so," I said.

I hadn't thought about a pulley, or anything at all connected with Daddy's care once we got him home. I remembered the Hoopers' dining room with its metal bed.

"My brother-in-law's father got down like that," said Mr. Amos. "His wife couldn't manage alone. Had to get her youngest to come back and stay for awhile. Takes two to get him up mornings, two to get him down at night. Like a baby. He's all right once he's vertical, like. But . . ." He shook his head. "Your mama's a little-bitty woman."

We led Mr. Amos to our parents' bathroom, where he was to see what he could do. We watched silently for a minute as he measured, probed, calculated, scribbled.

"Like I told my wife," he said. "'Buddy,' she said, 'Edna's gonna have to put Bob in a home, isn't she?' and I said, no, she never would, not as long as she has breath in her body, she never will. Your mama is a saint from heaven, yes she is."

Tina and I went back to the kitchen. I turned on the faucet and dumped some beans into a colander, washing them, turning them this way and that under the spray, picking out bits of trash and flicking them away.

"Well, that was certainly a cheery conversation," said Tina.

I began to blanch the beans, dumping them by the handful into a pot.

299

"Why are we doing this?" I said later. "Dad won't be able to eat any of this. Why are we bothering?"

"Dad can eat," said Tina. "He eats regular food."

"It's not the same," I said. "Nothing is the same."

The tomatoes and cucumbers and beans were ripe and silent beside the sink.

Mr. Amos came back into the kitchen.

"I can start on those bars for you tomorrow, if one of you girls'll be here to let me in," said Mr. Amos.

Bars in the bathroom, bars by the closet. A special tub.

Tina and I stared at each other across the stove.

"I'll be here," she said.

Later, when we were cleaning up, she said, "Guess what? Nick Stephanopolis has a girlfriend. We saw them the other night. Her name is Anna, and she has long black hair and she's gorgeous. Helen says she thinks Anna's the one."

"Good for him!" I said.

"Yeah. He needs somebody, you know? Don't you think so?"

"Why are you asking me?"

"Don't you care? I thought you guys had the hots for each other."

"Give me a break, Tina."

"Why should I? You never gave me one." She bent over, cleaning the front of the stove, stood up, refolding the washcloth. "Actually you did give me one. I'm sorry I was such a jerk about Hamp." She walked to the sink, rinsed out the cloth, her back to me.

"It's done."

"If I could take it back, I would."

"You can't."

"I know."

"Well," I said, "let's get this stuff cleaned up, okay?"

We wiped off the jar tops with a damp cloth. We froze six bags of squash and beans, canned twelve quarts of tomatoes and fourteen pints of pickles. We left the jars on the counter to cool.

■ —— ■

A week later Dad came home. We had the house clean, and Hamp and I got a hospital bed installed in my parents' bedroom—Granny Glendinning's, from the Hoopers' house. I hated it, hated that it had belonged to a woman now dead.

"Don't be ridiculous," said Mom. "It was nice of them to offer."

The bed looked mechanical and incongruous in the middle of the calm beige carpet, like a robot had wandered into an oriental garden. Hamp cut the grass, and I sprayed the roses, knowing Dad would be unhappy with the shape they were in.

Curtis and I were waiting on the back steps the day Dad came home. Mom got out first and stood by the car door. Tina got out of her car and stood beside Mom. Tina had driven Hamp to Columbia and then followed them home. I had set that up myself; I no longer felt like cutting them any slack. Anyway, they hung there by the car, gesturing and flickering at the form in the back seat, until Curtis crept out to meet them. He stopped eight feet from the car, as though there was a wall there, and leaned over to have a look.

Finally a foot appeared, and a leg, and the tips of metal crutches. Hamp came around the car and everyone scattered before Dad like birds, then settled behind him.

"Steady now," said Hamp. "That's it."

"Watch the grass. Hamp, watch that clump of grass there," said Mom.

They inched toward me, their hands floating out toward Dad as though to catch him. Curtis circled, whirling.

"Come on in, Granddaddy! I can swim now. I made a picture. And there's ice cream!"

Dad was white faced by the time he made the back steps. I held open the door, touched his arm as he passed. He smelled dry and antiseptic, like the hospital, but his arm was solid, hands muscled and thick. On the porch, Hamp took one of the crutches and held Dad's arm. They proceeded into the den. We all followed, weaving in and out behind them. In the den, Dad grabbed his armchair and sank down heavily, the crutch clattering to the floor. He closed his eyes, his face slack and gray. But in a minute he opened them again, looked around at us and smiled. His smile was a little lopsided.

"Tang God," he said.

He patted the armchair, leaned his head back and rolled it back and forth against the back of the chair. Mom touched his cheek, lightly.

We spent the rest of the day setting up the exercise machine in the living room. All the furniture in there was shoved to one side to make space. There was a lot to do, but every few minutes one of us would drift to the door of the den and peer in. We watched Dad eat a light lunch. He did feed himself. Mom sat beside him with a napkin and wiped crumbs off his lips. When he dozed, we all went back to the kitchen and ate tomato sandwiches.

"It's good to be home," said Mom.

*E*ighteen

18

HAMP AND I RARELY SAW EACH OTHER. At work he was in and out, always polite and businesslike. At home—well, he was never at home. Curtis and I spent more and more time at the lake, fishing or catching minnows.

One day I was ironing, a rare enough occupation for me. I got to one of Hamp's shirts, spread it out on the ironing board and looked at it, smoothed out the collar, the shoulders, the back. Then I picked it up, refolded it, put it back in the basket unironed.

Dad was going to Demaro every day for therapy. I drove him; I insisted. It got me away from my life.

"Take a break, Mom, give it a rest. Live it up! Go into the office and save us all from bankruptcy."

"Gee thanks," she said.

■ —— ■

At first I talked to Dad on the way to Demaro. "Guess what, Dad!" Bright, uneasy chatter, while he looked at me or out the window, swiveling his neck slowly, like a tank turret, at the view. Gradually I quit talking. We listened to the radio.

Occasionally he would touch my shoulder, point to a hawk or a change in some field. We had our favorite fields.

■ —— ■

At the hospital, Dad insisted on walking. He dragged himself laboriously out of the car, up the ramp, through the several doors. Usually I went shopping during the hours it took for Dad to get through his workout, but occasionally I sat with a book and waited on one of the plastic sofas outside the therapy rooms. Once Nick came into the waiting room and sat down beside me. He had on his doctor clothes, his stethoscope and his white coat.

"So how've you been?" he said.

"Fine." I smiled. "How've you been?"

It changed things, knowing that Nick had a girl. I could relax.

"Okay." He looked around, glanced at his watch. "I'm on break now. Want to get a cup of coffee?"

"Sure."

We went through the cafeteria line, found a seat by a window overlooking the muddy construction site for the new hospital wing.

"Jimmy told me you were bringing your father. How's he doing?"

"Fine. Fine. The therapist says he's making great progress."

We talked about Dad for awhile.

"I hear Helen's doing great," I said. "Have you seen her?"

"She's furious at me," he laughed. "She's got a new boyfriend, looks great, lost a lot of weight using that Slim Trim."

"So why is she furious?"

"I told her Slim Trim was a pile of crap, and that she should spend her money on a good nutritionist where she will learn how to eat right."

"Gosh, I can't understand why she would be upset!"

"Me either." He looked perplexed.

"Speaking of friends," I said, "Tina tells me you are actually dating somebody, and she's perfect for you."

I smiled to show how happy that made me. Nick looked at his coffee, then out the window. I looked, too.

"They'll never finish this place," I said. "They've been building it since I can remember. Somewhere around this hospital, there's always an ugly hole, a torn-up parking lot, a blocked off street."

Nick was silent.

"Is Anna a local girl? Will you be staying or leaving here when your residency's over?"

"I don't know."

"It's a pleasant place to live in spite of that," I gestured outside.

"Am I to get the travelogue now?" he said. "You really get into this how-are-you-I'm-fine-we-are-all-nice-and-everything's-grand stuff, don't you?"

"I'm pretty good," I said. "Trained by the best."

"You are." He nodded, shifted in his chair, leaned forward. "So how's Hamp?"

There was a long silence. I listened to my heart beating. It seemed to be beating very fast.

"Hamp's not good," I said finally.

"Oh? What's wrong with him?"

"I don't know."

"A lie."

I felt my face grow hot.

"He's stressed out," I said.

"That's not what I heard," said Nick. He stirred his coffee, glanced up at me. "I heard he's in love again."

My head was pounding, and I put my hand up to it.

"That's what he tells me," I said. "Do you have any aspirin? I have a miserable headache."

Nick left, returned in a minute with another cup of coffee and a package of aspirin. I took three tablets.

"The coffee's too black," I said.

Nick brought me a packet of cream, sat down.

"We were talking about Hamp," he said.

"*You* were talking about Hamp," I said.

I couldn't get the cream open. Nick took it from me, opened it, poured it into my coffee.

"You have a terrific bedside manner," I said. "You ought to become a doctor or something."

"And you have a hundred ways to change the subject," he said.

"I really don't. I just don't have anything to say. What can I say? My husband is a jerk. I married a jerk. He's Curtis's father, and he's a good father, but . . ."

"But what?"

"I don't know," I said.

Nick took my pulse. "You ought to see somebody about your headaches. How often do you get them?"

"Whenever I'm bullied."

"I didn't mean to bully you."

"You can't help yourself. You're a doctor."

"You do need to resolve your situation."

"And I will."

"There's talk, Judy, about Hamp and the girl. What's-her-name."

"Heather."

"Do you need to know what the talk is?"

I sighed. "No. I can handle it."

"I care about you, Judy. A lot of people do. You have a lot of friends. Are you listening?"

I nodded, to that and to some other things he said. But I was not listening. He left to go back to saving lives, and I went into the rest room and threw up, rinsed off my face, got a cup of ice, sat on the plastic couch again with my eyes closed, waiting for my father to go home.

■ —— ■

Later that afternoon I walked into the yard office and stood in front of Hamp's table.

"We need to talk."

"I'm busy," Hamp said, scattering purchase orders. "Where is the paper on that PVC pipe we got in last week?"

But his eyes gave him away.

"Why didn't you tell me you were screwing the baby-sitter?" I said.

He put down the papers and looked at me.

"Watch your language, Judy."

"You *are* screwing her!" I yelled. "Hamp, I can't believe it. It's one thing to have the hots for her, but I thought you had more sense than . . . she's a kid, Hamp!"

"For some reason you're just nuts on the subject of sex," Hamp said. "No. I am not screwing anybody. Least of all my wife. You ought to know all about that, since you are the one who used to be my wife occasionally, when you could spare the time. Now if you'll excuse me . . ."

He stood up, grabbing his ruler and level. I followed him outside.

"No," I said. "You stop and talk to me."

He turned at his truck. "I'm tired of talking to you, Judy. I'm tired and I'm busy. I'm trying to hold the company together until we can figure out what to do next. That's all."

"And you're not courting your son's baby-sitter? You're not in love with her, romancing her, spending all your free time with her, telling her how misunderstood and overworked you are?"

"I don't have any free time," he said. "If I did, I'd spend it with Curtis. And you of course. But you are never there. You are driving your daddy, and exercising your daddy, and fixing your daddy's garden, and sitting up at the hospital with Dr. Nicky, sitting up at the country club with all your old boyfriends. If I had any free time, which I don't, I'd have to get a ticket and stand in line. Because Miss Judy has a lot of friends."

"And Hamp has only one."

"You got it," he said.

"You know," I said, "it used to bother me when you lied."

"I do not lie."

"It used to bother me. But I just figured something out. It's yourself you're lying to. That's how you're able to stand here straight-faced and full of righteous indignation; you actually think you're doing me a favor, living with me, sticking it out, helping old Dad with the business. Hamilton the Brave. You figure whatever you get on the side is just your little reward for putting up with the rest of it, don't you?"

He was furious. He looked pointedly at his watch.

"I don't have time to go into this now," he said.

"If you're in that much of a hurry, darling, please go on."

I stepped aside and bowed. Hamp got into the truck and slammed the door.

"I'll see you tonight," he said.

Don't count on it, I thought. I went back into the office and sat down. There was a roaring in my ears, so that I couldn't hear anything. I put my hands over them.

"Judy?"

I looked up and Tina was standing over me.

"Judy, are you all right?" she said.

"Yeah," I said. "I'm fine."

"I heard you and Hamp fighting," she said. "Judy?" She pulled up

308

a chair and sat down beside me. "Judy, what's going on? What's the problem?"

Her voice sounded far away. Finally I heard her, as though coming to the surface of a pool, with a rushing roar.

"—talk about it?" she said. "—talk to him, and . . . I can—"

"I can't hear you," I said. "Wait a minute."

She leaned closer. "—want you to—"

"Like Mrs. Martin," I said.

"What?"

"Mrs. Martin. French. 'Comment sa va?'"

"What are you talking about?"

"Mrs. Martin used to say that. 'Asseyez-vous?' And she'd look at me. And I'd look at her. 'Comment allez vous?' she'd say. And I did not understand a word that the lady said." I looked at Tina. The roaring had subsided now but lived at the back of my skull, threatening to surge out again.

"I think you've lost it," Tina said. "Will you let me get Mom?"

"No. Do you have any Tylenol? And then after class she'd come and sit down with me. Right beside me, as you are doing now. She'd point to something on a paper. '. . . explain to you,' she'd say. 'Do you understand?' and she'd talk some more. My ears would roar just like they are now. I called it the hum. Other people have it, too. The hum. Charley and I both used to get it."

"Let me get you a coke," said Tina.

"I think it happens to Dad," I said.

I'd made a great discovery, I felt. I had the solution.

When Tina went away, I felt better. I stood up so that she would not get too close again, and walked toward the door.

"Got to take Curtis swimming," I said. I took the coke and the Tylenol out of her hand, grabbed my bag, and left.

"But are you—"

I waved and smiled. "I'm late now. See you later!"

■ —— ■

Curtis was at Wonderful Wednesday at the church. I picked him up and took him to the club for his swim.

What am I going to tell you? I looked over at him, with his little lunchbox and his Jesus picture. *How am I going to make this right for you?*

But I couldn't figure it. The roaring white-out surged forward again, swamped my thoughts.

At the club I put on my suit too, but took a chair in the shade, away from the other mothers. After awhile Charley came out and sat down beside me, all edges and angles, his wrists like bones. He had on a long-sleeve white shirt and was carrying a sandwich, gave me bites of it, sips of his coke.

"Charley," I said, chewing. I felt much better. "I've got it now. Remember Mrs. Martin? Asseyez-vous? It's not the words you listen to, Charley; it's the spaces between the words."

"Really?"

"Because they're more important. The silence, Charley, is more important than the words. It conveys. It matters."

"Are you on something?" Charley said.

"I've been confused," I said. "But now I'm fine."

I stood up, brushed sandwich crumbs off my suit, and walked over to the edge of the pool where Curtis was practicing his kicks. "I think I'll swim for a few minutes before we leave, buddy," I said. "Stay in the shallow end. Okay?" I swam and then Curtis showed me his strokes. He is quite good, for a fellow who sank like a stone six weeks ago. He pushes off from my leg and paddles furiously for the side, ten feet away. Then he turns around and swims back, grabbing me and climbing as though I were a tree and he, a monkey. He clings to my neck and kisses with a loud smack.

"My mommy!" he says. Then he pushes off again. I am his own personal island.

■ —— ■

Charley met us coming out of the dressing room.

"Listen," he said. "You sit here a minute while I get somebody to fill in for me, and I'll drive you home."

"Why? I can drive myself home."

"You're not right." He looked immaculate standing there, and my hair was dripping onto the floor.

"Au contraire," I said. I put my hand on his arm. "I've never been better. Forget it, okay? I just had a brainstorm. I'm fine." I grabbed his hand, did a little shag in the hall.

■ —— ■

When we got home, I turned the air conditioner up as high as it would go. The trailer felt like a little cage. Curtis watched cartoons. I went and looked at myself in the mirror. I looked all right to me, except my hair had dried frizzy and was too long. I picked up the scissors and began to cut.

Five minutes later, I had short hair.

I stepped out of my work clothes and found a halter top and some cut-offs. I went into the living room.

"Come on, Curtis," I said. "Let's go over to Granddad's and get some stuff we need."

"Where's your hair?" he said.

"I cut it off," I said. "Come on."

He stole looks at me all the way over to Mom's.

"Don't you like it?" I said, looking in the car mirror. It did look sort of raggedy. "I used to have short hair when I was a kid. And I thought maybe we'd go camping. Would you like that?"

"Oh boy! Yes! When?"

"Today. So I cut my hair, so it wouldn't be any trouble."

He looked dubious, but willing.

311

■ —— ■

I pulled up into my parents' yard and sent Curtis to the swing set. I had been a girl scout and had a vague recollection of how to set up a tent. I had been camping with Dad once or twice, too—fishing trips and so on. Anyway, I figured there would be some equipment still in the shed. There was a nylon tent, the Coleman lantern, and some of Dad's army-looking duffel bags from Korea. I put the tent and bags into the car and carried the lantern into the house. Dad would tell me how to use it, I thought. He was sitting in his chair in the den, watching an afternoon ball game. The Braves were ahead.

"How you doing, Dad?"

He grimaced, still looking at the TV.

"I'm going camping down by the pond," I said. "How do you turn on this lantern?"

"You rarip," he said. "Tay bessel . . . ah man it." He swallowed, rubbed his face with his hand.

"Hey," I said. "I'll read the directions. When in doubt, read the directions." I sat on the couch, set the box down on the coffee table and wiped it off with a Kleenex. Incredibly, the directions were still in the box. Not so incredibly. My father is a very careful man.

The lantern came out of its box still a shiny red, its globe clean, sloshing with kerosene. There were extra wicks. It smelled wonderful.

Dad leaned over, touched the lantern, touched my hair.

"Wa you do dat for?" he said.

"It's my summer cut," I said. "Like it?"

Fred McGriff hit a home run. I repacked the lantern. In the kitchen I picked up some likely looking tomatoes and cucumbers from the basket on the counter, put them into a sack. Mom wouldn't mind.

I was euphoric driving back to the trailer. Curtis sat beside me munching a cucumber.

I had this scene in my head. It had come to me while I was in the den with Dad. It was a scene of me and Dad camping, Dad leaning over to poke at the fire with a stick, just like he used to when I was a little girl. I could feel again the glow of it, the itching heat, the way the air quivered and shook.

"Come on," I said to Curtis, when we got back to the house. "Let's go get some stuff from the shed."

I was afraid of lighter fluid. On the other hand, I really wanted a fire.

We found a can of fluid, also a half-bag of charcoal. Charcoal! And the top of the grill. We took it all. I stuffed the duffels with things from the shed, and we walked down to the lake. Reddie was going crazy, so I let her join us. We made three or four trips, and I set up the tent by myself, in the clearing by the slab. I found my old sleeping bag in the back of a closet and Curtis's sleeping bag still in the back of the car. We got the cooler, too, and some ice and cold drinks and frozen hot dogs. It was a job hauling it all, but I was afraid to use the car, the road is so rutted now. By the time I got down that hill with the cooler, I was so hot and tired that I lay down on the ground and let Reddie shake lake water all over me.

"Can we roast hot dogs now?" said Curtis. "Where's the fire? Can I build the fire?"

"Sure thing," I said. "First find some rocks. Clear a space. Make a circle. I'll do the rest."

"You do those parts," said Curtis. "I'll light the match."

"Oh shit," I said. "I forgot the matches."

Eventually we had a fire. So what if it was made out of charcoal? I put wood on top of it, and it looked great. We had hot dogs, too, cooked on sticks cut and sharpened by me. Was the wood poisonous, I wondered? Was it only indoors that charcoal killed you? What if fumes blew into the tent? Did neanderthal mothers worry like this about snake bites?

I had found the old snake-bite kit in Dad's things. I read the directions printed on the back of the tube as I had read them a thousand times as a child, fascinated by the horrible sequence of pictures calmly numbered 1,2,3. "Tie a tourniquet above the bite. Cut an X in the flesh directly over the puncture wound, until it bleeds freely. Placing your mouth on the cut, draw out the venom, and spit it out. Remove or loosen tourniquet every two minutes." There was no way I was going to do any of that stuff, of course, not with a hospital emergency room twelve or fifteen minutes away. Besides, I had read somewhere that wasn't what you were supposed to do any longer for snake bites. It would be just my luck to cut a huge hole in my leg, or Curtis's leg, suck out all of some snake's venom, and then have some nerd in the emergency room tell me that I had practically killed myself or my son for nothing. Plus, I remembered Daddy telling me about people using their mouths to suck out poison and then spitting it out, but having a cavity that the poison went into, and poisoning themselves that way after all. And how could a person know if she had a cavity or not. A person can get a cavity practically overnight.

"Curtis," I said. "Did you pack your toothbrush?"

He had not. I made him use mine.

Anyway, I did not have the snake-bite kit along because I intended to use it. I had it along for sentimental reasons.

■ —— ■

Hamp came up about dark. I guess he saw the glow of the fire.

"What the hell are you doing?" he said.

"Camping out," I said. "Have a marshmallow." I offered him mine, which was perfectly golden brown, with not a speck of soot on it.

"Come home," he said.

"I promised Curtis," I said. I ate that marshmallow myself, and put on another.

"Are you crazy?" he said. "I found all your hair in the bathroom. Judy, you cut off all your hair."

314

"It feels better, too," I said, shaking my head. "I don't have the time anymore to fix it. Curtis, if you drop your marshmallow in the fire one more time, I'm confiscating your stick."

"What's confiscating?"

"Taking. Help him, Hamp."

Hamp sat down beside Curtis and threaded his stick with marshmallows.

"Look," he said. "This is crazy. Are you mad? What is this about?"

As if you didn't know.

"Space. Silence."

"What is it really about?" he said. "Heather?" He wanted me to fight with him so he could win again. He always wins, in his mind.

"It's about me having enough," I said. "I have just had it. I have had enough. I just can't live in the same walls with you anymore. You keep me off balance. I need balance. And you need . . ." I shrugged. "So I've got the perfect solution. I'll live out here in the silence, and you can do as you please. And we don't have to put up with each other anymore."

He looked at me. I was a little hurt by the relief in his eyes.

"So what about the business?" he said after awhile. "What about Curtis?"

"What about them?"

"You can't just drop out like this," he said. "There are things to do, decisions to be made. You can't just quit."

"Oh yes I can. I can, and I have. Goodnight, Hamp."

"Talk to me, Judy, dammit." He snapped.

"About what?" I snapped back. "How can I talk to you? You just say any damn thing that pops into your head. If it upsets Judy, let's not tell her. Let's not have any friction, for Chrissake. Let's just do what we like, and then lie about it. I can't deal with that, Hamp. It's like silt. No bottom."

"Ahhhh!" Curtis yelled and dropped his stick. His marshmallows

315

were on fire. He began to cry.

"It's all right, buddy. Look!" said Hamp, picking up the stick. He blew out the marshmallows. "Look. We take them off, like so, drop them on this napkin, get us some new marshmallows. Now. Come sit in my lap."

Curtis settled himself between his daddy's knees and took the stick, wiping his face unobtrusively on his sleeve.

"The trick to these things is, to find a good spot. Not too hot. And to balance the stick on somebody's knee. Like so. See? You want some heat, but you got to watch 'em. When they smoke like that, twist the stick, and let 'em brown on the other side. Twist the stick, boy. Turn those boogers over. Now! We got some marshmallows! I tell you what! Look at that! Now bring the stick back. Now. Open wide."

"Mfffpp," said Curtis.

"I believe we got us an expert marshmallow man, Judy. Yessir." He handed Curtis the stick with the last toasted marshmallow on it. "And your mama's an expert fire builder." He looked at the fire. "Yessir." He rubbed Curtis's shoulders absentmindedly, staring into the fire.

"So!" he said finally, looking at me. "I'm a liar, and you guys are going camping this week. Tina's been buzzing at me all afternoon about what an asshole I am. Jesus, that girl can bitch."

"It runs in the family," I said.

"I had noticed. Well, she says to me, I got to take everybody on vacation, and I got to build everybody a house, and I got to get her and Jimmy some more money, 'cause Jimmy's getting ready to go to seminary and save the world. And I got to do this, and that, and I forget what all." He looked down at Curtis, nudging him. Then he looked up at me.

"I got a lot to do," he said.

"Sounds like it," I said.

"I got to talk to Jimmy some," said Hamp, and set Curtis aside, and stood. "Tomorrow." He brushed off his pants.

316

"Well, what? You settling in out here for a regular wilderness experience, or you coming in to work tomorrow?" The anger had gone out of him. I looked at his face in the firelight. There were two little lines bisecting the angles of his face above his mouth that had not been there at the beginning of the summer.

"I'll be in," I said. I stood up too, gestured to the darkening woods. "I brought a clock."

"Are you going to be all right out here by yourself, you think?" he said.

"Oh, sure," I said. "I was a girl scout. I know all about this woods stuff. This is great. Right, Curtis?"

He was playing in the fire with his stick and smiled briefly, blowing ashes off the tip before sticking it back into the fire.

"Well," Hamp said. "I'll leave Reddie down here to keep you company."

Reddie, dozing away from the fire, rattled her tags to show she was listening and put her head back down.

"Okay then." Hamp shrugged. "Goodnight, bud." He picked Curtis up and gave him a kiss, dangling him in the air. "Don't give your mama a hard time, sport, okay?"

"I can pee in the woods," said Curtis. "Standing up."

"Can you now," said Hamp. "Go do it then."

Reddie got up and accompanied Curtis eight feet to a pine tree, looking very dutiful.

Hamp took a step toward me. I backed up.

"Sure you're okay?" Hamp said.

I nodded. The hum had started again.

"It'll be all right," I said. "Good night."

Reddie stood at the bottom of the road and watched Hamp disappear. Then she followed Curtis and me down to the edge of the lake to rinse off, made a big show of circling the perimeter of the clearing to let any deer and rabbits that might be lurking know that she was on the job.

317

Curtis went right to sleep, his blanket and his stuffed monkey balled up beside him. I sat up for a long time with Reddie, poking the fire and staring out across the lake into the darkness beyond.

Nineteen

19

THE NEXT WEEKEND ELIZABETH AND PETER brought their baby home to be christened. I was godmother. On Sunday right after the eleven o'clock service, we, the family, all assembled in the sanctuary of the Methodist church down by the baptismal font. Lee had flown in from New York, and of course Bessie and Uncle Fred and Elizabeth's brothers and their wives were there, along with Mom, Tina and Jimmy, Curtis and me. Not Dad, who stayed home. Not Hamp. Baby Patrick fretted his way through the ceremony with a series of mews and scrinched-up grimaces, wriggled under his trailing gown as he was passed from parent to preacher, suffered the water to be dribbled on his head from the silver dipper, suffered the prayers and the promises, and was pronounced a Christian.

Elizabeth squeezed my elbow on the way out.

"Hear you've been a busy girl," she said. "Have you really left him?"

"Well," I said, "I've moved out into the yard anyway."

Mom invited everyone over to eat and see Dad.

"We are just going to have a quiet family afternoon," Mom said on the way home. "We live quietly now."

"Right," I said.

At my parents' house, I went into the den where Dad was sitting in his wheelchair watching a Sunday news show.

"Mom sent me in here to straighten up," I said, plumping pillows, folding the Sunday paper.

Dad cut off the television. I noticed he was wearing his watch again.

"Oo sti live i da ten?" he said.

"For the moment," I said.

He closed his eyes.

"It's only temporary," I said. "Dad, it's not like I'm homeless or anything. People go camping all the time."

"Moob ba i here," he said. "Moob ba here."

"Maybe I will," I said.

"Wha oo waitin' fo?" he said.

"I don't know. It's not bad out there, Dad, you know? Peaceful. I can think out there, sit at night and listen to the crickets. It's all right. I was thinking of building a house out there, maybe. A real house."

Dad jabbed his finger into the wheelchair arm.

"First moob here. Den buil."

"Will you help me with the house?" I said. "I have this vision of how it should look, but . . ."

He nodded. "Bu wha?"

"But I can't figure how to get what I want," I said.

"Wha do oo wan?"

"A tree house on the ground."

He rolled his eyes.

"Seriously. Big screened porch, living room with a kitchen in the corner, two rooms in the back. I was thinking of making the furniture built-in."

He raised his eyebrows.

"Built-in bunks for Curtis. Cantilever the top bunk to get rid of the post. A wall of low shelving with windows above. Fireplace in the living room. Maybe a built-in desk."

I grabbed a piece of paper and started drawing. Dad jabbed the paper with his thumb.

"Oo nee mo spaa dere."

"Space. Right. And what about here?"

"Mo Spaa."

We worked a few minutes until cars began pulling up in the driveway. Lee came into the den wearing a white suit and fanning herself.

"I'm barely ahead of the pack," she said. "God, it's ninety-five degrees out there. I don't see how you people live in this heat."

"New York being so temperate and all."

"Dry, anyway. This place is like a steam bath." She stroked Dad's shoulder. "But we used to think it was nothing, didn't we, Bob? Remember the convertible somebody had up at Clemson? How we used to ride in that thing with the top down? We thought we were something. Didn't we?"

Dad nodded. He has developed a vast array of nods to suit any occasion. For this one he used his reminiscent nod—head tossed slightly back and to one side, one-way smile. It's one of his social nods, meaningless and self-protective.

People started filing in.

"No need to flutter," said Mom, fluttering. "Now Bob, don't tire yourself out. Lee, if you would just—Bessie, could you—"

Elizabeth had streaked her hair and cut it so it stuck out in a sort of executive frizz, which suited her, and she had on a blue silk dress that make her skin look milky.

Peter had young Patrick, still in his fancy dress, and a bag full of cameras. I took Patrick and balanced him in Dad's lap, and Dad played with his fingers while Peter took some pictures and videos. Then Elizabeth and I carried the baby off to change clothes. We took him into Tina's old room, now stacked with leftover furniture from the living room. We laid him on the bed, undressed him, changed him, buried our faces in his baby belly and kissed him repeatedly in motherly places like the tips of his ears and the crease of his neck, absorbing the sweet smell of him, the way his nose crinkled when he smiled. When he was finally dressed again, Elizabeth propped herself up on the bed and fed him.

"Nothing's better than a baby," I said.

"You're right. But they're so exhausting, so—"

"Time-consuming, all-consuming."

"Exactly. They really do change your life. Hamp said that Easter. Isn't that funny, I can still see him. Doesn't it make you feel weird? It does me. But of course, I didn't believe that stuff about babies. Nobody ever does, I guess. Do you hate Hamp now?"

"Sort of. You have to keep making yourself hate, screwing yourself up to it," I said. "You choose it. You reach a certain point of unhappiness and you decide: I have to get out of this. It's killing me. So you start walling yourself off from it. It's a deliberate process, a deliberate choice. Start getting mushy again, and you're doomed. But to answer your question, no. I don't hate Hamp. I don't hate him at all. Fondness and mere irritation lurk at the edges of my feelings all the time. I stomp them down."

"Well, keep stomping," Elizabeth said. "I don't want this to end badly for you. And I don't want you to feel alone in this, or feel you're making the wrong choice. I am furious with Hamp, and he doesn't deserve you. I want you to cut him loose and come down to Atlanta and meet some decent men. Promise."

So I promised.

I could not tell her that I was incapable of making the trip. Atlanta stretched so far beyond my ability to get there, it was like India or the nineteenth century. Maybe, I thought, her invitation could stretch a thread between us that would bridge the gap, and I could slide along it down the highway into Georgia. But I didn't believe it. I didn't believe in anything except the lake, Curtis, and the ground on which I lay every night, listening to the wind.

■ —— ■

We ate lunch—sandwiches and tea. Jimmy and Tina came into the den with a large box that turned out to be Dad's new home computer. Jimmy set it up while the rest of us kibitzed.

"Plug this here. No, it says . . . the one in the office—"

"I can do this," said Tina. "Just give me a chance, will you?"

Finally it was ready. Dad pulled himself up and over into the desk chair. His hands hesitated over the keys. Then he began to type.

"xipeh," he typed. "elizabeth cute kid you got whres EDNa/ judy get your mom" He looked around, grinning.

Mama came in and stood behind him while he typed some more. "the quick brown fox look at this edna i love you. I love you."

Mom squeezed his shoulder and wiped her eyes. Elizabeth, Tina, and I jumped up and down like fools.

■ —— ■

Later in the kitchen Aunt Bessie mentioned several times that my hair looked terrible, and she ran her fingers through it and suggested a real good man she's been to in Demaro.

"Oh, no," said Tina Lee. "Judy is going to Antoine's in Columbia. I know a woman there who's marvelous with short hair."

"How would you know?" I said. "You've never had short hair."

"I have friends who do, and they swear by her."

"Actually, I think Judy needs a weekend in New York. Don't you, darling?"

By which I knew that my private life was now the topic of general family conversation.

"I'll get it fixed in Atlanta," I said. "When I go to see Elizabeth."

"Judy's hair looks okay for now," said Mom. She walked around behind me and hugged my shoulders. "Y'all stop picking on her." Of course, that was not the tune she sang in private, but I appreciated it nonetheless.

Some of us watched the Braves game with Dad. Peter gave us the Atlanta perspective on their chances of winning the series again.

In the kitchen Mom talked with Aunt Bessie about sex, just like they used to when we were children, lowering their voices and leaning toward each other, speaking from behind their hands.

"That blood pressure medicine they keep them on is enough to take the starch out of an iron rod, Edna. Flora said her Jack was two years getting his functions back." Aunt Bessie shook out a dish towel.

"Functions?" I said.

Elizabeth and I were fixing cokes.

"Plus there's the blood thinners, and the metabolic stuff. But Jack did. Eventually."

Mom shook her head. "I don't know, Bessie." She cut her eyes at me. Obviously, I still qualified as a child.

"People don't say 'functions' any more," I said. "Get with it, Bessie."

"You and Elizabeth," said Bessie, nodding at her daughter. "Your generation thinks you invented sex."

"You mean we didn't?" said Elizabeth.

"You mean our parents *do* it?" I said. "It can't be so."

"They don't do it much," said Bessie, blushing furiously, "with nosy children in the house."

"Listen, Judy," said Elizabeth. "Now they're blaming us."

"You'll find out soon enough what children do," said Bessie darkly.

"I already have," said Elizabeth.

"Wait till they can open doors," I said.

"Wait till they know what you're doing," said Mom.

"Wait till they leave home," said Bessie, "and you realize you hardly remember how."

"That's the most depressing thing I've ever heard," said Elizabeth.

■ —— ■

After Elizabeth's family left, Lee cornered me in the den with Dad and lectured me for awhile.

"Listen, Judy," she said. "Are you serious about this business with Hamp, or are you just teaching him a lesson?"

"I'm seriously teaching him a lesson," I said. I hunkered down in front of them, watching the end of the Braves game.

"Oo behtah be caaa-ful," said Dad.

"I know it, Dad."

"No." His hand was suddenly gripping my shoulder. He has a surprisingly strong grip. "Ook at me."

I turned to face him. His other hand touched my hair.

"Cuh yah hair," he said. "Liff in a tennn. Whah you doing?"

"I'm okay, Dad. I really am. I go to work every day. I cut my hair because I wanted to. That's all."

"Shhhh." He dropped his hands, turned away from me, rolling his eyes in frustration. I took his fingers.

"Dad," I said. "I'm okay. Really. The business is fine. Nothing is wrong."

"I don't mean to pry, Judy," said Lee.

"Then don't," I said. "Don't pry."

"That is what bothers us," said Lee. "We are concerned because you are acting like an adolescent. And you're running a million-dollar business with a man you're apparently getting ready to leave, or you've already left him, or at any rate, you're not staying in the same house with him."

"Trailer."

325

"What?"

"Not staying in the same trailer with him," I corrected.

"And you keep changing the subject every time anybody tries to talk to you," she said. "But I'm going to say this once, and you're going to listen. For your father's sake." She took his hand. "Your father is one of the dearest people I have ever known."

I hated the look that passed between them. She turned back to me.

"You're cutting yourself off," she said. "You're alienating yourself. I don't know why, and I don't care. But it hurts your father. It grieves him deeply. And it hurts me, too."

And so on.

■ —— ■

Outside the sun was hot, but the garden already looked like September. The tomatoes were getting small and peculiar, the peppers were shriveling, and the leaves were sagging, tingeing with yellow and brown. There were a few roses open, which I picked for Dad. After awhile I felt better. I always feel better outdoors. I sat down in a lawn chair and closed my eyes.

I was free, except for the nattering. I felt that I could live with that for awhile. Essentially, I was free.

When I was little, I used to be afraid of the dark. I would lie in bed at night with my whole head under the covers, my nose pressed up against the edge of the blanket to breathe. If I stuck my head out, monsters would get me. But after awhile it would get so hot under there I'd yank down the blanket, thinking, Let them get me. I don't care. I'll take my chances with the monsters before I'll suffocate. And I would breathe the cool fresh air. Ah! It smelled so good. Nothing has ever smelled better.

That's what it was like out there beside the pond with Curtis.

■ —— ■

Hamp's truck pulled up behind the house, and I thought, Why did he have to come up here? I picked up the roses I'd dropped beside the chair, glancing at the truck. The door didn't open. As I walked toward it to get to the house, I peered into the cab and saw Hamp, resting his head back against the seat as though he was asleep. There was something wrong with his face.

I opened the cab door. He turned his head and looked at me. One eye was swollen shut, and he touched that side of his face gently, as though to make sure it was still there.

"Your nose is broken," I said unnecessarily.

He nodded.

"Looks like maybe your jaw, too."

He touched it, tentatively.

"How did you drive?" I said. "Oh never mind. Let me get my purse."

I went into the house, into the bathroom, wet some hand towels with warm water. Jimmy and Dad were alone in the den.

"Could you help me, please?" I said. "Hamp is outside in his truck. He is all beat up, and he needs to go to the emergency room. Dad, could you keep Curtis here maybe overnight?"

"Wha appen?" said Dad. "A wek?"

"A beating. A fight."

"Who?"

"Heather's daddy, I imagine," I said. "He's mad enough."

Jimmy went with us to the little hospital in McAdamsville, Jimmy driving, me holding Hamp up. Jimmy stayed with me while they stitched Hamp up, and later he drove us home.

"Will you be all right?" he said, after we'd gotten Hamp to bed.

"No problem," I said.

Twenty

20

I STUDIED HAMP'S FACE ALL THAT NIGHT and the next day, watched the skin swell and puff, hiding the stitches like raisins in a bun, and then gradually deflate again, leaving hard knots here and there and streaks of purple turning green. He didn't sleep much. Neither did I. He'd doze off after each pill, swept under by the morphine undertow for an hour or so until his brain kicked in again. Flutterkicked. I'd watch him sleep. He'd wake and watch me too, endless minutes.

He ate soup.

After awhile I let Curtis visit. Curtis was scared at first, shy, as though his sewn-up father were not his true father at all. Gradually he forgot, watching cartoons in the bed with Hamp, and before he left touched Hamp's face tentatively with one finger, poking.

"Does it hurt?"

I asked Curtis if he wanted to spend the night. No, he said, his granddaddy had promised they'd make ice cream.

"You know I always loved you," Hamp said one day, I forget which one, they all blended in together so.

"This isn't love," I said. "I remember love, and this isn't it."

■ —— ■

When it was safe to leave Hamp alone, I went back to work. Then I moved back into my tent. Curtis came too, for the weekend. Mom had seven fits, like camping is some kind of illicit activity.

"What are you pulling?" she said. "What is this? You're a grown woman with a child, Judy. You've got to start acting like you've got some sense."

I honestly could not see what everybody's problem was. Tina was no longer even speaking to me. Jimmy prayed for me.

"I'm thinking about you," he said, but he meant praying. I could see his lips moving.

If I had taken my tent to the Rockies or somewhere, they would've thought it was great. Judy gets away. Judy's on vacation. But when I moved back into my own back yard, so I could still go to work and maybe swing making our payroll on time, the whole family went apoplectic.

Suddenly, the lake was Grand Central Station.

Mr. Carruthers, our minister, came to visit. He sauntered up the hill, sat down by the lake, asked about the fishing.

"My mom asked you to come," I said.

"She's worried about you, Judy."

"I'm fine," I said.

"Sometimes," he picked up a stick, poked holes in the dirt with it. "Sometimes it's good to do this, to get away for awhile. This is really a beautiful place." He laid the stick down. "The fishing any good?"

"So-so. The bream are all tiny, but they make good eating. Fried, you know. In cornmeal. Or like Curtis and I do them, in foil on the grill."

He looked at me. "So what are you going to do next?"

"I don't know," I said.

I didn't. I was floating free. We sat for a long time. Finally he spoke.

"Is there a problem? How about counseling?" He leaned forward, looked at me. "Are you depressed or anything?"

"I feel great," I said. "I like this."

"For now."

"Yes. For now."

"The thing is," he said. He looked out over the lake, his eyes flat and bland. "The thing is, you may start feeling bad."

"Pessimist."

"Possibly so," he said. "Possibly I am." He seemed to forget where he was and to daydream a little. I forgave him, being like that myself. Finally he looked back at me.

"Mind if I come back in a day or two and fish?" he said.

"Of course not," I said. I knew he was just keeping an eye on me. But what could I say? I didn't want to sound ungracious.

He stood up, stretched.

"In the meantime, I have a thought for you to mull over."

I was afraid he was going to pray over me, or tell me God loved me.

"What do you think is going to happen?" he said.

"I don't know," I said.

"I know you don't," he said. "That's why I want you to mull it over. See you tomorrow."

"Thanks for coming."

"Tomorrow," he said, "I'll bring a pole."

■ —— ■

Helen and Nick came.

"Guess what," Helen said. "I'm in love."

330

"Congratulations!" I said. "I'm not."

"I know you are hurt."

"Don't be silly."

Nick talked to Curtis. I caught him looking at me. He examined my tent, took Curtis to the lake. They had a race; Curtis won. Then Nick twirled him around and around, put him down, and they set off around the lake.

"Pull up a chair, Helen," I said. "May I fix you a soda? Some coffee, perhaps?" I have excellent manners when I remember them, and my mother had brought me two deck chairs for entertaining.

"Nothing, thanks." She nevertheless took a chair, and I resigned myself to a chat.

"You look great, Helen," I said.

She did, too. She had on a skimpy shirt and a little halter top, and she looked as good as it is humanly possible for her to look. Apparently love and Slim-Trim can do a lot. She has breasts now instead of a wide shelf across her chest, and hips and everything. And she is more graceful. She wears jewelry, long, clinky earrings. I find her fascinating, a sort of lamia, like a snake I saw once in the Atlanta zoo. He was bright emerald green, and he sat up and looked around so alertly, and his little tongue flicked in and out like a hand. The card above his glass said he was terribly poisonous.

"We have been so concerned about you," she said. She put her hand on my arm. "If you could join my support group, I'm sure we could help."

I looked at her hand until she removed it.

"Thank you so much," I said finally. "When I have the time, perhaps."

"We have a new program," she said, wagging her finger. "You'll just love it."

"I am certain that I will. But I am terribly busy right now," I said. "I'm sure you'll understand." I stood back up.

"You must come!" she said several times as I walked her and Nick to their car.

I do like Helen. I really do. Now she's more my friend than Tina's, I guess. It's just that she drives me crazy.

"Is this fun for you?" said Nick at the car.

"So far," I said.

"It's a game. You're playing house."

"Living outdoors is a very time-consuming operation," I said, "especially after working all day in an office. There's ice to be got, food to prepare, a fire to keep going, not to mention the hours devoted to catching crickets and helping Curtis fish."

"You're breaking my heart," he said.

■ —— ■

Charley came to see me. He brought pizza and Cheerwine, our old favorite, and a new sort of tackle box for Curtis. I gave him a tour, and he admired the improvements I had made on the camp—besides Mom's chairs, three crates to sit on by the fire and a couple of quilts for lying around. Then we ate.

"So how is Walden Pond, nights?" he said, draping a long string of pizza cheese into his mouth.

"Buggy," I said. "How did Thoreau cope without spray, do you think?"

"Better ask, how did Thoreau cope in cold weather. Or had you planned on staying that long?" He glanced nonchalantly around, as though the question had just occurred to him.

"I don't know. Guess not. It's pretty miserable in the rain. The tent doesn't leak, but everything gets dampish, and I have to cart it all to the trailer and put it through the dryer."

"And you can't very well keep a child here all fall and winter."

"I suppose not. Maybe I could get another trailer. Temporarily. Until I get my house built."

"Why don't you just move back into the one you have?"

"Because Hamilton is still living in it," I said patiently. "And we no longer occupy the same shell. Like hermit crabs."

"Then why don't you wait until he moves out," Charley said even more patiently. "And then you can move in."

"He isn't moving out."

"Yes he is. He hasn't told you." It was a statement not a question. I didn't answer.

"Would you like to move in with me?" Charley said. "Then Curtis could go to school in town." He was silent for moment. "How desperate are you, exactly?" he said.

"I am not desperate. I just didn't know about Hamp leaving. I hadn't thought, is all. I know I have to do something, and I will. Really. I just want it to be the right thing. Before, I have made . . . mistakes. Mistakes that messed up my whole life. I'm trying to be careful this time."

"Well think about this: think how it will look at a custody hearing to give your address as a tent by the pond," he said.

"I see what you mean," I said, poking the fire. "Goodness. That sets my heart all aflutter."

"Good. Maybe it will push your brain into gear as well. Because while you meditate, your ex-husband may be organizing a case against you."

"He wouldn't."

"Are you sure?"

"No," I said.

■ —— ■

But it was all without meaning. Some words have meaning. You hear them, and you can hold onto them. They are like small life preservers, floating in the sea of your mind. Other words are like a roaring sound, or a fog. They are the hum. They make noise, but there is

333

nothing in them for you. You can walk straight through them. They are ghost-words. Out there by the pond, I heard a lot of them. But I kept listening.

■ —— ■

Hamp came by and told me he was leaving. His face looked better; I hadn't seen him in several days. He hadn't been back to work. He brought some fried chicken, which we ate for supper. After supper he stayed a long time, wading with Curtis with his pants legs rolled up like a little boy, feeding the fire, watching the sun go down. He put Curtis to bed in the tent and rejoined me at the fire.

"Heather told me you fired her," he said.

"Yep," I said.

He was silent, stared out over the lake for a long time.

"Well," he said, "I should go now, I guess."

We stood up, and he brushed off his pants.

"I need a divorce," he said in the dark.

"Okay. Fine."

"I guess I'll file in Columbia. Or would you rather?"

"I don't care."

"Well, think about it. Okay?"

"I will," I said. "I truly will. I will give it serious thought, Hamp."

We stood there for a long minute in the dark. Then he backed away, touched my face with the back of his hand.

"You all right?"

"No, I'm really not," I said. "I feel terrible. I trusted you. Not that I still loved you, but that I expected the truth."

"I never lied to you. I'm not a liar."

"Your whole life is a lie."

"I am doing the best I can to straighten out my life," he said. "What are you doing about yours?"

"What about mine?"

334

"How long are you going to sit out here and sulk?"

"I'm not sulking."

"Don't know what else you'd call it. It's dangerous. You're making a point about how noble you are, which God knows we all know already. What about our son? It's dangerous out here, Judy."

"He's perfectly fine."

Hamp shrugged. "Okay. I'll see you in the morning."

We were going to town to sign some papers at the bank.

After he left, I sat by the fire until it went out, then slipped into the tent and lay down. The cicadas were going crazy, rasping a crescendo and then falling silent for a few seconds the way they do. Tomorrow, I thought, I'll move back in with Mom.

■ —— ■

I woke up with the sun shining in my face. Curtis was gone. He had unzipped the flap and walked out. I jumped up, still half asleep, afraid he might be trying to light the fire by himself. But he wasn't by the fire, or walking around the lake, or in the rowboat. He wasn't up on the slab.

"Curtis!"

Circling the pond, I thought, he's in the water. Like Hamp said he would, he's fallen in and drowned.

I ran up the road to the trailer, but he wasn't there either. Hamp's truck was gone. I let Reddie out of her pen, and she raced me back down the hill, jumped into the pond. I stared at the water, calling.

"Curtis! Curtis!"

My voice echoed across the water. The pines around the lake were still, silent, their shadows stretching along the ground into the pond. The surface of the water was blank, opaque except where Reddie swam, leaving ripples. Shadows lay across the water like it was a solid thing. But it was not.

I could imagine Curtis down in there, caught in a submerged tree

335

branch, nibbled by fish. The pond fascinated him. I had promised I would let him swim in it when he passed his test, but I never had. I had been afraid. I had caught him sneaking out, wading up to his waist just yesterday. This morning must have presented an irresistible opportunity. I stared at the glassy surface, then kicked off my shoes and waded in.

It was breathtakingly cold. I gasped, splashed out to where he had been playing the day before, and dived, touched bottom and kicked to the surface. The bottom was slimy. I dived again, again and again, swam in circles through the murk at five and six feet, grasping the mud to hold myself on the bottom. There was nothing there, though I couldn't see a foot in front of me in the water. Perhaps he had been grabbing at minnows and fallen in. I waded back toward the shore, felt my way through the reeds and black logs embedded along the east bank. The reed stubble and some branches did my feet in pretty badly. I felt something, lifted up a foot, and watched the thin lines of red trace themselves along the ridges of the sole. I waded out, stuffed on my shoes, and waded back in. Thinking snake, snake. Thinking, how long can a child stay drowned? Isn't it hours? Can't they come back after hours? That's in cold water. This water, though I was blue from it, was not that cold, even at the dam.

There was nothing among the reeds except a lot of slick stuff I never wanted to touch again.

I sloshed up onto the bank and ran around to the dam, grabbing an abandoned cane pole as I rounded the bend.

"Curtis!"

I rammed the pole into the water at the top of the dam and ran along, poking for a child, hoping for resistance. The pole bent help-lessly in my hand. It was maybe eight feet long and didn't touch the bottom. Curtis was afraid of the dam, as I was, afraid of the little pipe that stuck out of the water and had a drain over it, the little sucking pipe. That pipe used to give me nightmares. Curtis would never have gone willingly into the dam end, but he might have slipped. Or drifted. I dropped the pole, kicked off my shoes again, and jumped off the dam.

The water was thick and cold, black and empty except for the bottom, which was very soft. On the fifth or sixth try, I brought up something solid—a branch. Reddie swam circles around me, and I held on to her for balance sometimes between dives. Finally I knew I couldn't do it any more. I had gotten too cold. If I didn't get help, I would drown too.

I pulled myself up on the dam and stumbled on around past the tent, up the hill to the trailer, followed by a dripping Reddie. The door was locked, and my keys were in my purse back at the tent. I beat on the door, looking around for a rock. Then I heard the truck coming. I stood by the door, waiting.

Hamp was driving, singing, his mouth wide open. I could hear him over the radio. In the cab beside him sat a little boy, also singing, off-key. Curtis. I sat down on the step and cried. It wasn't until Hamp pointed them out to me that I noticed my feet were still bleeding.

"I am so sorry," he said over and over. "I am so sorry. I never thought . . ."

He opened the trailer door, and I hobbled back to the bathroom, turned on the shower, and stepped in with all my clothes on. Hamp followed me, peeled off my clothes, and held my head under the nozzle to get out the mud, while Curtis stood in the doorway and sucked his thumb. In a minute I was wrapped in a blanket on the bed, shivering. Curtis had burrowed in beside me, and Hamp left and came back with a Styrofoam cup of coffee and two towels in which he wrapped my feet.

"Warm up and rest for awhile," he said. "Then you're going in for a few stitches."

I drank my coffee and went to sleep with Curtis curled up beside me in a ball. When I woke up, I just lay there and watched shadows climb across the wall. My feet felt like there was a piece of glowing charcoal wedged in between the bones and the skin. But the bed, oh God, the bed felt good. I reveled in the bed.

Twenty-one

21

"I DON'T KNOW WHAT'S GOING TO HAPPEN TO YOU," says Mom, shaking her head. "I don't know what's going to happen to Curtis."

She says this wonderingly. Mom and Dad watch the news and talk to the television, shrugging in flat satisfaction. "I don't know what the world's coming to. I don't know what they'll think of next." But they really do know, or they think they know, what the world is coming to, disaster maybe, maybe a hurricane, nuclear accident, another stroke. Two things you can be sure of, they say: death and taxes. Both are respectable foes. For death and taxes, they have a game plan, Dad at his computer, Mom at her desk, figuring. They can use one to stave off the other, exercise, take deductions, eat right, apply for disability.

About me and Curtis, their indecision is real. They really don't know what's going to happen to us, but underneath their head-shaking, I sense hope. We will be all right, they sense, because we must. Because the Bible tells us so. Because great-granddaddy came over on the boat from Scotland, because McAdamses have hung on here and survived ever since the Civil War, because that's the way life is, that's all, and that's all there is to it.

So Mom and I sit in the back of the lumberyard office at our machines, computer phone fax intercom xerox, like spiders sharing a web, black and amazed, but not unhappy. Expectant. Change, like disaster, has a calming effect. Well, we think, checking to see if we still have all our arms and legs, we survived that. Let's see what's next. I try not to worry the family.

"Mom," I say, "It's all right. I know what I'm doing."

Of course I haven't the vaguest idea what I'm doing, but like the spider, I can have babies and get my own breakfast. I can run the company. For that, we discover, I have a flair. My lawyer tells me so. "I must inform you," he says. "Selling that housing development of Hamp's when you did was really smart." I went to school with the lawyer, Johnny. Why do lawyers look older than other people? Johnny is twenty-seven, and he rubs back his hair, folds his chubby fingers on the blotter like an old man.

He is arranging the divorce for us. I decided I didn't trust Hamp to do it.

"I must inform you, Hamp," says Johnny, "that I am acting in this case on Judy's behalf, and that I do not represent you, and may not be considered to be acting for you now."

"I understand," says Hamp.

"Do you have your own lawyer?"

"No."

Johnny gives Hamp a long, unblinking stare to inform him that he is being an idiot. They are, after all, friends. The Johnny who used to drink beer with us at the club on Saturday nights, who played in

Hamp's foursome for the golf tournament every year and has a daughter in Curtis's kindergarten class, that Johnny is not the Johnny who draws up settlements and divorce decrees. Nothing personal.

But Hamp leans forward in his chair, trapped in Johnny's office, Johnny's mode, longing to be free.

"I have no problem with the agreement, Johnny. Judy and I have discussed it. This is what we want."

Johnny sighs, drumming the fingers on his desk.

"Okay, folks," he says.

As we leave, Johnny gives the small of my back a tiny, lawyerly squeeze of success: We did it! Hamp is out of the company. His only rights now are fatherly. Those I am happy to concede.

■ —— ■

After Curtis's nondrowning, we moved in with Mom and Dad. We had no choice. My feet had to be stitched up, and for awhile I couldn't walk. Tina went to work at the lumberyard. I stayed home with Dad.

At first I slept a lot. I think I slept for most of two days. When I began to wake up, it felt wonderful just to lie still and drift. Curtis wandered in and out, bringing books and plastic figures. He played war in the bed, setting his people all up in the wrinkles of the covers and then mowing them down again, using his finger for a gun, Ra-ta-ta-ta-ta. I was the mountain. Plastic men fell off me to their deaths and rose to die again.

Once Dad and Curtis brought me some lunch. They came tottering in with it on a tray, tomato soup and sandwiches, and sat and watched me eat.

"This is really good," I kept saying. "Gosh, Curtis, what a good helper you are."

After I had eaten, used the napkin Curtis handed me, drunk the cola from my childhood bunny cup, Curtis ran off, satisfied. Dad remained seated on the foot of my bed.

I could hear him breathing. His head swiveled, taking in the details of my room. Absently, he patted a corner of my sheet, smoothing it down. He spoke slowly.

"Wha ie Hamp?"

"In Columbia. He's getting a job down there."

"He na comin baa?"

"No. He's not coming back. He's in love with another girl, Dad. He wants a divorce, and he's in a big hurry about it."

"Why?"

"Because his girlfriend's pregnant. Heather. The little girl that worked for us this summer? They want to get married."

"Bu she's a chile."

"Eighteen now. She had a birthday."

"Her da—"

"—Was not happy."

Dad shook his head. "Por Hamp," he said.

"What do you mean poor Hamp? He's not the one who got dumped on," I said. "He's not the one who has to walk around this town and have people talking about him. He's gone. He's not the one with the son to raise and explain things to."

"I don fee sorry fo you," he said. "You fee sorry enough fo yo-sef."

"You always liked him best anyway."

"No," he said. "I di not. You chose him. I di not."

He stared into space for awhile, rocking, then collected himself and carried out my soup bowl.

Dad was right. I did feel sorry for myself. The relief Hamp obviously felt when he got rid of me, the easy way he was settling in with a new girlfriend, a new family, really bothered me. His old family was still reeling from the shock. His son was still waking up in the night saying, "Daddy!" and then remembering his daddy didn't live there anymore.

I tell Curtis now, as I told him then, it doesn't mean Daddy loves him any less. Now Curtis is quieter, sometimes pensive, has long moments of silence. You would have thought I'd be happy about that, wouldn't you?

Sometimes I imagine Hamp with Heather and the new baby-to-be, think of him finally settling down, growing up. Liking his wife. Then I think, no way. He'll never change. Soon he'll be lying to Heather just like he lied to me.

I believe that's the thing that has hurt the longest; that's what I think about in the middle of the night—the easy way he lied. Hamp is an excellent liar, I think because he half-believes his lies himself. All those times he said to me, I love you, Judy, I can't live without you, Judy, We'll start over, Judy—he sincerely meant it. Sort of. For the moment. You know the worst thing about living with lies? They numb you. They're like the Novocain you get when you go to the dentist. You know you're being hurt somehow, that there's pain there somewhere, but you can't feel it. Later, you'll feel it.

■ —— ■

When Nick came to see me, I had been lying around the house for three or four days and was itchy and irritated. Nick stood in the doorway, Daddy behind him. He looked freshly scrubbed, his black curls tight and damp.

"I came before," he said, "but you were asleep."

"I heard."

He glanced back at my dad.

"Want some fresh air? Let's go for a ride."

I shuffled out to the car on Nick's arm, whining.

"My hair looks terrible. I can't wear decent shoes. Haven't shaved my legs. Why didn't you call?"

"I wasn't sure I could get off. You look fine. Get in the car."

We drove aimlessly up and down the logging roads that crisscross the national forest around our house.

"So how're you feeling?" he said. "Where's Hamp? What will you do now?"

I answered him as well as I could.

"You still seem tired," he said. "Are you taking antibiotics? Is there any infection?"

"I'm just tired of talking about my feet," I said. "And tired of explaining about Hamp, and of people wondering what I'm going to do. I'm tired of this invalid shit. There's nothing wrong with me. It's just a huge hassle not being able to get around, and I'm a bitch. I'm sorry. Do you know what the people in Dad's therapy class call people who can walk? Tabs. Temporarily able-bodied. Isn't that a stitch?"

"How long did the doctor say you had to be off your feet?"

"I can do the crutch-and-hobble thing any time now."

Nick looked carefully at the road, not at me. "I was hoping I could take you to my house for a visit this afternoon."

"Turn down here," I said. "I want to show you something first."

We drove to a dead end, a grassy meadow beside the river. A half-dozen people were fishing from the bank. There were a few picnic tables scattered in the clearing, and Nick half-carried me to the one nearest the car. My skin tingled where his arms touched me, and when he sat down next to me on top of the table, I put my hand on his arm. He jumped.

"Sorry," I said.

He took my hand and held it to his face, began to kiss my fingers.

"Do you like the river?" I said.

"It's great," said Nick.

He kissed me.

"You're shaking," I said.

"So are you."

"I'm nervous," I said.

"So am I."

"Why?" My face was against his chest. I could feel his heart pounding.

"I want to get this right," he said.

We kissed until it got embarrassing; we started loosening each other's clothes.

"Let's go," I said, and he carried me to the car. We kissed some more in the car, until we heard somebody coming. Nick slid back to the driver's side.

"Guess I ought to take you home now," he said.

"But I'm starving. You can't just dump me off without supper."

"Where do you want to go?"

"Your house."

We drove to Demaro, picked up some hamburgers and took them to Nick's apartment. We sat on the floor and ate, and I began to feel sort of creepy and bad.

"Don't you have a girlfriend or something?"

"No," he said. "I'll take care of it. Shut up. Don't spoil it."

"I feel weird and sordid, like the Other Woman or something."

Nick laid down his hamburger, drew me into his arms. "I love you," he said, nuzzling. "Don't you trust me, Judy?"

"Not really."

"But you want me."

I swallowed and put my hand on the bulge under his zipper. He pushed me to the floor with a groan. We rolled around on the rug for awhile, grabbing at each other, sloughed off each other's clothes until we got all the essential parts uncovered, and did it right there in the middle of the french fries. Then we licked the ketchup and salt off each other, and Nick took me home.

The next night Nick came for me again, and as often as he could after that. After I got the stitches out of my foot, I began driving to Demaro myself.

"I hear Nick broke up with his girlfriend," said Tina.

"Guess they just weren't right for each other," I said.

■ —— ■

The other day Mom and I were sitting out in the yard watching Dad and Curtis mulch the roses. Dad always mulches the roses the beginning of November. Mom pretends she needs the sun; actually she is afraid to leave Dad outside alone. He is perfectly safe. Mr. Amos rigged up some fenceposts Dad uses for support.

"What's the deal about Tina and Jimmy?" Mom says. "Are they getting back together, do you think?"

Like I ought to know. Actually, I do know. Supposedly they are apart, having split, finally, over the missionary bit. Tina figured Jimmy'd come round to being a lawyer by September, but he didn't, and he figured she'd reconcile to being a seminarian's wife, but she didn't. So Tina lives with a friend, takes a couple of courses, studies to take the graduate school exam. Jimmy lives in the trailer. The other Saturday I was down in Columbia delivering Curtis to his dad for the week-end, and Sally and I stopped by the trailer on the off chance Jimmy'd be there, and Sally could say hello. He was there, and so was Tina, looking sheepish in their pajamas. So you never know.

"Nothing would do her," says Mom, "but to marry that boy. Not that I have anything against him. But another preacher's wife. Honestly! I guess it must run in the family."

She stares off into the distance for a minute, beyond Dad, beyond the garden and the line of woods.

"I always thought I'd travel," she says. "I always thought there'd be more time."

"Nonsense," I say. "You will travel. You're going to Disney World with us Thanksgiving, aren't you? I've bought the tickets. And they say with Dad along in a wheelchair, we can break into every line."

Mom is fretful about it, but I know she'll go.

Mr. Amos is fretful. We meet at the pond where he is helping me frame my house, and he carries on about this and that. It's ridiculous, he says, to build a house so slowly. Why don't I hire someone else and get the thing done? Because, I say, I don't trust anybody but him to help me with it. That shuts him up for about a minute.

Everybody's fretful. Such a bunch of babies.

Curtis whines about kindergarten. His teacher is mean, he says; she makes him sit with a girl. He keeps a big picture of his daddy by his bed. Sally keeps a picture of her parents in Nicaragua by her bed. There's a concrete-block church in the background. By my bed I keep nothing, because everything hurts too much. The past hurts, and so does the future. The present feels okay; I'm staying there for now.

Hamp taught me this: just because you love someone, everything will not turn out all right. We do not live happily ever after. My son wakes and cries. I lived in a tent. I created, from my own desire, a person who did not exist, imbued him with qualities he did not have, and I could not bear, could not hear, could not understand his grief and pain any more than he could mine. He will, or will not, fare better with his new wife. He loves awhile, shakes his head, and grows numb.

Poor Hamp, Daddy's right, searching for surcease of sorrow; he'll never find it, outside himself.

We live how we can, float, paddle—aim for shore, expecting every moment to be swept away. Often we are. Sometimes, miraculously, we are not, are saved, laid gently on the shore to clutch the sand and sink our cheeks into the grit and smell of survival.

It smells good.

Once when I was a kid, Dad came out to take my picture, and I said why, and he said, "For posterity." I looked into the camera and said, Hello posterity, Hello out there. Here I am, bony knees, Buster Brown haircut and all. I am happy here, in the hot sunshine of eight. I am feeling great, standing here by this tree root holding this doll. Greetings from me to you. Hope you're doing fine out there in the future. I send you all my love. I send you all myself.

Now I take a picture of Curtis, willing the same: Be happy. Look at this picture in twenty years and smile. Survive.

■ —— ■

Christmas, Sally and I are both going to be bridesmaids in Diane and Charley's wedding. Another bridesmaid's dress. Just what I need.